RUSS LITTLE. ... .rn at the end of the .... os a ... . e subsequent decades in a variety of jobs before becoming a full-time writer at the turn of the century. After writing drama for television, radio and film, his first novel, *Scream If You Want to Go Faster*, was published in January 2011. He lives with his family in Kingston Upon Hull.

SWEAR DOWN

RUSS LITTEN

Tindal
Street
Press

A complete catalogue record for this book can
be obtained from the British Library on request

The right of Russ Litten to be identified as the author of this work has
been asserted by him in accordance with the Copyright, Designs and
Patents Act 1988

First published in 2013 by Tindal Street Press,
an imprint of Profile Books Ltd
3A Exmouth House
Pine Street
London EC1R 0JH
website: www.serpentstail.com

ISBN 978 1 90699 441 9
eISBN 978 1 90699 498 3

Designed and typeset by sue@lambledesign.demon.co.uk

Printed by Clays, Bungay, Suffolk

This one is for Geordie Mark

... Yeah, yeah, yeah, I got ya guv, I understand all that, yeah, yeah, sweet ... OK ... Carlton Nesta McKenzie ... fifteenth of the tenth, nineteen ninety-one ... Flat 56a, Hyacinth House ... Crown Heights estate ... Hackney ... E8, innit. So we rolling, yeah? All right, here's the thing ... it was me who killed the man on the news. The man who got stabbed, yeah? I ain't even gonna lie guv, it was all down to me. I stabbed him in the chest, boom, right through the heart. You got the man you looking for. Don't listen to Jack, he's all mixed up in his head, ya get me? He all emotional about stuff. He don't know what he's saying right now. I know he gonna be sat in that other room saying he did this an that, but he just chatting shit, believe me. He feeling all guilty an that, but he never stabbed up no one. The old man is not to blame, trust me ...

Ndekwe first learns of the Stewart job while flicking through a discarded English newspaper in a Portuguese bar. A page six headline: YOUTH STABBED TO DEATH IN LONDON STREET.

It is a depressingly familiar story; eighteen-year-old Aaron Stewart died as the result of a fatal knife wound outside a row of shops on the Crown Heights estate, Hackney. Stewart is described as being known to the police, a prominent gang member with a history of drugs and violence. There is a photograph; a sullen-eyed, police-issue mug shot. He looks older than eighteen. Knifed through the heart in broad daylight, it says.

A quote from a Metropolitan Police spokesman emphasizes the need to retain an open mind regarding the circumstances surrounding the death and any possible motive at this very early stage of the investigation. A dedicated team of officers is questioning people on the estate and combing the surrounding area for clues, it says. In the meantime, residents are assured that any information made available to the police will be received in total confidence. Ndekwe can almost hear Gorman's telephone voice dispensing those carefully chosen words to some drama-hungry hack.

He reads the report out to Sonia, but she feigns disinterest. Just shrugs, spins the ice around her glass and looks beyond her husband to the white and blue boats rested up in the harbour outside. It has been a much-needed break for the pair of them; glorious weather, fantastic food, welcoming locals. Nothing to do except laze around on the beach and take evening strolls along the waterfront. It has been good to get away. But it is coming to an end.

The sardines and salads arrive. Sonia tells him to put down the newspaper.

– We're on our holidays, Peter, she says. – You promised. Remember?

She is right. He had promised. The holiday had been a last-minute deal; two weeks in the Algarve for just under a grand. They had both agreed that it was exactly what they needed; time spent far away from the stresses of the job and the relentless grind of the city. Early nights and long lie-ins, the chirping of crickets after dark and the lapping waves beneath their window. No streets with raised voices or sirens screaming past, no staring at screens. No dwelling on recent disappointments. No drama. They had both agreed.

They pick at their food and Sonia talks about various things; the sunshine, the boats, the people at the hotel, those funky yellow wedge sandals she's seen in a boutique window; that cosy little bistro just off the square where they could maybe have their final night's meal and what does he think they should get her mum for a present? Ndekwe eats and smiles and nods, but her words are just a vague background noise. In his head, he is already back at work.

Detective Sergeant Ndekwe. He is still getting accustomed to his new title. And he is still getting to know all the other notable names on his new manor. The dead youth staring up from the newspaper at his elbow was certainly one of them. Ndekwe had heard of Aaron Stewart and his alleged activities on the Crown Heights estate almost as soon as he'd landed at Hackney nick. Aaron Stewart; street name Knowledge, thought to be the head of a small but tightly knit group of young men specializing in drug dealing, robbery, violence and intimidation. Ndekwe runs a mental checklist of the other prominent names in Stewart's orbit, but he can't come up with any clear motive to murder. Drugs, he thinks. Either drugs or a postcode dispute; some petty slight or perceived disrespect amplified beyond all reason. The usual excuses.

They land at Heathrow airport two days later and he checks his phone as they stand among slow-moving lines of luggage. The signal is weak and he has to walk around to find a sweet spot. He gets through to Tom Halliwell at the third attempt. Halliwell tells Ndekwe that they are holding two men on suspicion of murder: a kid in his late teens off the Crown Heights and an older guy.

Sonia tells him to turn his goddamn phone off.

– C'mon, Fast Track, she says. – Fourteen days, yeah? Fourteen full days. Remember?

That's what she's started calling him since he got the promotion: Fast Track. It had been affectionate at first, a teasing term of endearment; but now it carries a definite undertone. Everything has happened quickly for them, ever since they met four years ago when her temping agency sent her for a six-week stint filing data at Lewisham police station and they'd progressed from lunch dates to evening dinner to the headlong tumble into love, a short engagement and then the wedding, followed by two house moves back and forth across the river; a new job for her, and promotion for him.

He pockets his phone and they wheel their suitcases across the car park under a bright blue cloudless sky. It is nearly as hot as the Algarve; the same relentless sun, the same clinging humidity. They drive back to their house in Woolwich and unpack. They shake the sand from their clothes and open two-week-old post. They go to bed early and rise late. At Sonia's insistence they keep their phones turned off and their dressing gowns on until at least midday. They eat takeaway food and drink cold white wine and lemonade in the back garden. On the Sunday they go to church with Sonia's parents and share souvenirs and photographs over a roast beef dinner in the afternoon. They return home and watch TV while he irons five freshly washed work shirts in preparation for the coming week. The Stewart job is mentioned on the local news round-up. Police are holding two men in connection with the murder. No further comment is offered.

They go to bed and Sonia curls herself tightly around him. She strokes his shoulders and arms and kisses his neck, timidly at first and then with an increasing intent until he puts his fingers to her mouth and tells her he has to rest; big day tomorrow. And then he turns over, away from her, and his breathing deepens and steadies until he is asleep.

She lies behind him in the dark, the sheets balled up in her fists, the noise of the traffic outside and the ache in her chest that keeps her from sleep.

••••••

The next morning Ndekwe is at his desk before seven, wading through the debris that has gathered in his absence; an endless column of unread emails, angry, blinking voicemail lights and a mountain of memos and paperwork, all demanding his immediate attention on the vital issues of modern police work: health and safety, diversity awareness, prejudicial behaviour and coordinated community planning. He works slowly and methodically as the station around him fills with the bustle of the incoming day shift.

After nearly two hours shining the seat of his pants, he can't stand it any longer. He rises from his desk and heads for the clamour he can hear coming from the other end of the corridor.

The incident room is buzzing, but not with the tight-lipped urgency that characterizes most murder investigations. The atmosphere here is more akin to a Saturday afternoon down the local pub; officers lolling back on chairs and sitting on desks, banter swapped over computer screens and coffee cups. Laughter and backslaps and good-natured insults. Ndekwe knows this mood: liberation. The intoxicating release of tension that comes with a result. He quietly curses his decision to take a holiday.

He weaves his way between the bodies. A few of the civilian support staff offer a quick smile of greeting, but most of the other CID barely glance his way. Ndekwe is well aware that his arrival three months ago has put a few noses out of joint. There are people on the team who have been sat waiting patiently for years for that DS job to come up and here he is, Mr Fast Track, parachuted in from

Lewisham Super Nick on the high potential development scheme. Not that he is overly concerned. Ndekwe isn't there to make friends. He is there to do a job. And this is the first big one since he landed.

Gorman is seated at the far end of the room at a desk beneath the whiteboard. He is on the phone. Detective Constable Tom Halliwell sits at an adjacent table, organizing a stack of paperwork into neat and stapled piles. Gorman raises a hand in acknowledgement as Ndekwe approaches. Halliwell glances up, nods a greeting and returns to his filing.

Aaron Stewart glares down from the centre of the whiteboard, the same mug shot that was featured in last week's newspaper. He's surrounded by a trail of red and black arrows and asterisks. The names SHEPHERDSON and McKENZIE are underlined to his left.

Ndekwe indicates the board.

– We got a result?

– Hopefully, says Halliwell.

– Two of them, yeah?

– Yeah. The boy's the collar, though.

Gorman finishes his call, puts down the phone. He leans back in his chair and links his hands across his belly like a Metropolitan Buddha, bestows a courteous nod upon Ndekwe.

– Detective Sergeant, he says. – Good time?

– Very good, sir, thanks.

– Nice place?

– Yeah, quiet ... well, bit boring, really. Glad to be back.

The detective inspector grins. – Oh we've had a right jolly-up here. Haven't we, Tom?

Halliwell grunts in the positive, head down in his paperwork.

Ndekwe looks at the names on the board. – So where did we find these two then?

Gorman heaves himself to his feet.

– Come on, he says. – I'll fill you in.

■ ■ ■ ■ ■

The usual bedlam down in the custody suite; a constant flow of human traffic; stony-faced solicitors, civilian processors and a queue of officers waiting to book in their handcuffed charges. A squabble of raised voices and the booming slam of distant doors. As soon as one body is processed another jostles forward to take its place; as one telephone is picked up and silenced another immediately begins to ring.

Gorman and Ndekwe push their way through the throng of bodies in the admissions office, and head down to the cells. It is cooler here, but despite the hum of the air conditioning there is the constant stink of vomit and stale bodies. A dull banging from somewhere further down, a voice raised in cracked fury:

– *I WANT MY SLISSITOR! I WANT MY FACKING SLISSITOR! CAM TO THE DOOR, YOU FACKING CANTS!*

The two officers walk past doors of heavy blue steel. Ndekwe adjusts his pace to accommodate that of the older man.

– Shepherdson's the old guy, Gorman tells him. – They're both trying to put their hands up, but McKenzie's the collar, I reckon. Looks like he's one of Stewart's boys.

– Yeah? Where does Shepherdson fit in then?

– He was with McKenzie when he got lifted. In Hull, of all places. We brought the pair of them back yesterday.

– Hull?

– Shepherdson's from up that way, originally. Looks like he's been trying to help get the lad away.

– Why would he do that?

– Frightened, probably. My guess is McKenzie put the arm on him. Seems like the old boy owed him a few quid.

– Drugs?

– Gambling.

– Yeah?

– Yeah. Horses.

Ndekwe considers this for a beat.

– Are they known to us? he asks.

– McKenzie's got a bit of form as a juvie: possession, riotous assembly, suspicion of handling stolen goods. Not a serious player; not in the Crown Heights crew anyway. Never heard of the old man before. Nothing on him at all.

Ndekwe nods, sets his face to a serious frown and bites his bottom lip to keep the grimace from forming. He feels slightly uneasy when Gorman throws words like 'crew' and 'player' around. He can't be totally sure, but Ndekwe gets the distinct impression that Gorman makes a point of using these phrases when he is in the presence or earshot of black officers. On his first day at the nick Ndekwe had overheard Gorman in the staff canteen loudly informing a CO19 sergeant that it was 'time to end this beef' and that they should 'get the straps out'.

Gorman stops at a door: J. H. SHEPHERDSON.

Ndekwe tilts open the suicide hatch and peers inside. A prone figure on the bed wrapped in a dark blue blanket; a shock of greasy, sandy-grey curls at one end and two grubby grey socks at the other. A laceless pair of battered shoes set carefully to face the far wall, side by side. The blanket rises and falls; a laboured wheeze that builds to a serious of ragged exhalations, suddenly erupting into retching coughs.

– Ahjesusfugginchrist …

The figure rolls over to face the wall, pulling the blanket more tightly around him.

Ndekwe shuts the hatch and looks at Gorman.

– He don't sound too clever.

– Doctor gave him the all-clear before we questioned him. He won't be running the marathon this year, but yeah, he's well enough. Needs to pack the fags in, though.

Gorman gestures for them to move on. They pass another three blue doors until they reach: C. N. McKENZIE.

They stand either side of the name. Ndekwe looks at Gorman.

– Your money's on this one, yeah?

– Yeah. His story holds together. The other guy's a fantasy merchant.

Ndekwe tilts the hatch. The boy is sat bolt upright on the edge of the bed, upper body rocking gently back and forth, hands drumming against the tops of his thighs. Ndekwe guesses late teens, early twenties. His eyes flicker towards the door at the noise of the sliding metal, then fix themselves back steady on the wall as the body beneath them shudders.

Ndekwe tries to equate the snoring bag of rags in the room three doors away with this agitated young kid.

– What was it over? he asks.

– Money, basically. Gorman scratches the back of his head and feels wet skin. He is beginning to perspire. It is warm down here under the station, the air trapped and heavy. He plasters a few stray strands of pale ginger hair down across his forehead. – And McKenzie's alleged that Stewart and the rest of the crew raped his sister.

Ndekwe looks sharply. – And did they?

Gorman pulls a sour-faced sneer, shakes his head in the negative.

– Halliwell and Frampton visited the family last night. The sister flatly denies it. Our guess is he's trying to go for mitigating circumstances.

– Who's the brief?

– Said he didn't want one. We put the duty in with him, but he hardly said two words to her.

– And we've not charged him yet?

– Not yet, no. Still interviewing. We've got till Wednesday though.

Gorman is talking, but Ndekwe is only half listening. A muffled bell is chiming somewhere. Something about the kid's face in profile seems vaguely familiar. He looks again through the hatch, tries to reframe the boy into some firmer context; a witness box, an interview room, a street corner, the back of a police car. But no solid connection is made. Ndekwe wills the young man in the cell to turn his head so he can get a better look at him. He feels a sudden urge to bang on the door, to startle McKenzie into movement, force him to look fully in his direction. But McKenzie just sits there, quietly vibrating, his hands beating an endless tattoo on his knees, rocking back and forth, back and forth, staring sightlessly ahead.

Where do I know you from?

Gorman is asking Ndekwe a direct question. Something about Halliwell.

– Sorry, sir?

– I said are you OK with Halliwell?

– Oh, yeah, says Ndekwe. – Yeah, absolutely.

– Good, says Gorman. – Take him, and whoever else you need. Frampton's a safe pair of hands.

It takes Ndekwe half a second to realize the full import of these words. Gorman is putting him in charge of the case. His first job as a DS. He snaps the hatch shut on McKenzie, on the inklings of recognition, and focuses his mind back into the present.

– Yes, he says, yes, no problem.

– Good man, says Gorman. – Right, let's get you up to speed. He fishes around in his pocket, pulls out a handkerchief, wipes the back of his thick pink neck. It's too cosy for Gorman down here. He can feel damp patches forming on his shirt.

Detective Inspector Graham Gorman turns on his heel and strides away up the corridor. Ndekwe follows, quickening his pace until he falls back into step with his senior officer.

■ ■ ■ ■ ■

Ndekwe goes through the case notes in Gorman's office as Halliwell inscribes a CD with permanent black marker, tongue fastened between his teeth in concentration. He pauses to examine his handiwork, frowns.

– Shepherdson, he says, is that with or without an 'H'?

– With, says Ndekwe.

Halliwell looks up, exchanges a glance with Gorman and then taps his teeth thoughtfully before making the amendment.

Bollocks, thinks Ndekwe, he wasn't asking me. He is acutely aware that he's already irked the Detective Constable by asking him to transfer the interview tapes onto CD. It had taken Halliwell almost an hour to find the necessary equipment and although he hasn't said as much, his annoyance is tangible.

Ndekwe concentrates his attention back on the notes. It doesn't take him long to soak up the bare bones. From the information on his knee he learns that both of the suspects insist they had acted alone when putting the knife into Aaron Stewart. Two different motives are offered: Shepherdson claims that he had confronted Stewart over a debt. McKenzie maintains he stabbed Stewart in revenge for an alleged sexual assault on his sister. The body of Aaron Stewart had been discovered on the pavement by a young woman taking her daughter to buy an ice cream from their local newsagent. Stewart was already dead by the time the ambulance arrived. Although there were no bullets in Aaron Stewart, there were eight marks that forensics had identified as ricocheted bullet shots; three in the pavement and five holes in the wall of the chemist's at the end of the block. Beyond that, there wasn't much to go on; no other bodies, no murder weapon, no CCTV footage; two cameras, both of them long smashed, defunct; no eyewitnesses, no firm leads or local knowledge. It seemed that the usual collective sensory deprivation had descended upon the residents of the Crown Heights estate. Nobody had seen anything. Nobody had heard anything. Nobody was there. Ndekwe is not surprised. In his experience, nobody ever is. He flicks through the notes once more.

– And the guy in the newsagent's? Mr ... Mr Akhtar?

– Nothing, said Halliwell. – He's pleading total ignorance, despite it all taking place less than ten feet away from his door. Says he heard the shots and shit himself, understandably. Hid in the back.

Ndekwe frowns, returns to the file. He reads it through again, twice.

Pregnant silence descends upon the room. Halliwell finishes his inscribing and puts down his marker. He leans back and folds his arms behind his chair, looks at his new Detective Sergeant with polite detachment. Gorman maintains a calm and easy posture, elbows propped on his desk, fingers templed, a study in professional patience. But Ndekwe can hear his foot begin to tap a tetchy rhythm beneath the desk.

Ndekwe shuffles the papers back into the file and lays it down on the floor at the leg of his chair. Gorman unlocks his fingers, leans forward. Halliwell unfolds himself from his slouch and sits up straight in his chair.

– Thoughts? snaps Gorman. – First impressions?

Jesus, thinks Ndekwe; I thought I'd already got the job. He clears his throat before he speaks.

– Well, one of them is obviously covering for the other. Question is, why?

– No, says, Gorman pointedly, the question is *who*.

– Amounts to the same thing, surely?

– McKenzie's the collar, says Halliwell. He says this in the same way he might have said 'rain is wet' or 'the capital of England is London'.

Ndekwe looks askance at his colleague.

– Yeah? What settles it for you?

That flicker of a glance between Halliwell and Gorman again.

– Come on, Pete, says Halliwell. – Can you really see an old age pensioner doing a bloke like Stewart? Yeah, maybe they were both there, but the smart money's on McKenzie. Got to be.

Ndekwe doesn't answer. He searches Gorman's expression, but the DI's face is set to neutral. He looks evenly across his desk, blank, detached, mildly expectant. Ndekwe picks up the file again and quickly scans the main points.

– Shepherdson says he put the knife down a drain, he observes.

Gorman nods patiently.

– We're sending the search team down there this afternoon.

The search team? Ndekwe looks beyond Gorman and out of the window; a holiday brochure sky, boundless blue, not a scrap of cloud in sight. Sonia's mum had said it had been roasting all last week, and every day the week before that. Like being back home, she'd said, that same clinging humidity, that same inexorable sun hanging uncovered long into evening. There had not been a drop of rain for days, certainly not since last Thursday.

– Why are we sending divers down? he asks.

Gorman frowns. – Who do you suggest we send down there, Detective Sergeant? The dog section?

– Well, if the fingertip didn't turn it up …

Gorman bristles.

– I don't know how they do things down in Lewisham, he says, but in this operation we don't leave stones unturned. Belt and braces, Detective Sergeant; belt and braces.

Ndekwe has heard about Gorman, how he could turn nasty if his balloon of pomposity was pricked. The word among the rest of CID was that, despite his carefully cultivated laidback demeanour, the Detective Inspector could and would be a vindictive bastard if pushed. Ndekwe decides it best not to persevere. Instead, he turns to Halliwell.

– So, you interviewed McKenzie, yeah?

– Yeah.

– What do you make of him?

The DC shrugs. – Slightly better manners than our usual class of customer.

– What about this rape thing?

– Bullshit, in my opinion. I went to see the sister and the mother last night. The sister's having none of it. Got quite uppity, in fact.

– Why would McKenzie say that, though?

Halliwell sighs, exasperated, as though explaining something to a child for the seventh time. – He's going for mitigation.

– Hoping for some leniency, adds Gorman.

Ndekwe considers this. He is aware that impatience is building in the room, and he is equally aware that it is directed at him. He decides to ignore it for the time being. He also decides to ignore the attitude coming off Halliwell. Probably still smarting from his sudden demotion to second fiddle, Ndekwe reasons. Bound to be a bit defensive at first. And Gorman, he just wants to wrap the job up as soon as possible; that much is obvious.

The Detective Inspector looks pointedly at his watch and then at his computer screen, shakes the mouse on his desk, clicks several times, then starts typing.

– But he's mentioning drugs, yeah? says Ndekwe. He slaps the sheaf of papers on his knee. – It says here that McKenzie claims Stewart had given him drugs to sell.

– He reckons Stewart gave him a kilo of weed to shift, says Halliwell. – He's either spent the money or didn't want to pay him, I reckon. One of the two. There seems to have been some bad blood between them. Power struggle, maybe.

– They had beef, definitely, states Gorman, not taking his eyes from his computer screen.

Ndekwe flips opens the file marked McKENZIE.

– But McKenzie's been off the radar for what ... nearly three years?

– Don't mean he ain't been bang at it, says Halliwell.

Gorman closes down his computer screen and tugs a finger beneath his shirt collar. He's becoming tired of this. The sun is pressing on his back and the heavy lingering odour of Halliwell's permanent marker is making his head swim.

– Look, he tells Ndekwe. – McKenzie has got gang connections. *Proven* gang connections.

Ndekwe knows he is being steered none too gently towards a ready-made conclusion. There are two minds already made up here, he thinks. He looks at the notes again and then at Gorman and Halliwell.

– You think they plotted all this up between them?

Gorman shrugs.

– Why would they do that? snorts Halliwell.

Ndekwe ignores him, asks the question again of Gorman. Gorman shakes his head.

– I very much doubt it. They're not exactly the brightest. McKenzie certainly isn't.

– So, you want me to prove that one of them is lying. Right?

– Right. That's why we need to find this charmer. Gorman hands Ndekwe a file with a photo clipped to the front; a black youth with eyes so spectacularly crossed that he appears to be staring in two different directions at once. He looks like a cartoon character struck from the sky by a falling anvil. Ndekwe imagines a flock of tweeting birds encircling the boy's head. He would look almost comical if he didn't wear such a dementedly fierce scowl.

– Who's this?

– Samuel Isaacs, says Halliwell. – Stewart's second-in-command. Known to his friends and enemies as Bam Bam. A real piece of shit, this one.

– You know him?

– Been nicking him since he was twelve.

– Where does he fit in?

– He was there when it happened, according to McKenzie. He'll tell us who was or wasn't there.

Ndekwe hands back the photo.

– Why would he tell us anything?

– Because, says Halliwell, McKenzie killed his mate.

– Or so he claims, says Ndekwe.

The other two men look at him and say nothing.

Ndekwe can feel which way the wind is blowing. He looks outside at the brilliant sunshine bouncing between the glass-fronted buildings. Far too nice a day to be stuck inside, he thinks. He lays the file on Gorman's desk, turns it round to face him.

– If McKenzie's killed Aaron Stewart, says Ndekwe, I'll charge him.

Gorman nods in firm approval.

– Good man, he says.

The three police officers rise to their feet.

It is Detective Sergeant Ndekwe's first job in Hackney and he feels as though he has been given a birthday present that has already been unwrapped.

■ ■ ■ ■ ■

Ndekwe slides the disc marked SHEPHERDSON into the car's CD player. He starts the engine, manoeuvres out of the station car park and onto the streets of East London. The vehicle has been sat in the full glare of the sun since early that morning and is already a mobile sauna, the trapped air cloying, the steering wheel and gearstick red hot beneath his hands.

The recording begins with a bump and whine of feedback before Detective Constable Tom Halliwell identifies himself and those present, followed by the time, date and location of the interview. The next voice is that of an older man. It is a voice stained with a lifetime of nicotine, late nights and liquor. He sounds like he's been gargling broken glass.

... no problemo ... start now? ... okey dokey ...

Name: John Henry Shepherdson ... Date of Birth: twenty-fourth of April, nineteen forty-one ... Address: 34b Conway Court, Bethnal Green, London E2 8UJ.

Halliwell winds his window down and flaps his hands up and down in front of his face.

– Jesus. Sweating like a fucking rapist.

He tugs his polo shirt away from his body, looks at Ndekwe, his buttoned up jacket and tightly knotted tie.

– Don't know how you can wear a suit in weather like this.

Ndekwe doesn't respond, just lowers the driver's window a couple of inches, turns up the volume on the CD and punches the air-con button, waits for the icy rush.

*... OK ... well, for a kick-off, don't believe anything the lad tells yer.
It'll all be a load of baloney. He's a good lad, don't get me wrong, but
his head's all over the shop right now. He hasn't got a clue what he's
saying. I've been trying to talk some sense into him, but he won't
listen to a word I say ...*

Halliwell is talking about Portugal, how he went there once and
thought the sea was too cold. How the beaches in Spain were better.
He asks Ndekwe about the hotel and the food, what the clubs were
like, but Ndekwe isn't listening. He bumps the volume up another
couple of notches and Halliwell eventually gets the message. The DC
slips his sunglasses down from his forehead onto his nose, falls into
a silent survey of the shop-fronts and pedestrians moving past.

*The lad's very upset. So owt he tells yer, it'll all be a load of
Jackanory. OK? You might as well let him go now and not have him
waste any more of yer time. I'm the fella yer want – me. And I'll give
yer the full shebang, don't you fucking worry about that ...*

Ndekwe divides his attention between the slow-moving traffic in
front of him and the old man's voice in the speaker at his knee. He
has to concentrate closely to decipher his words. Ndekwe knows
that Hull is up north, somewhere in Yorkshire, but this accent lacks
the rolling smoothness he associates with that part of the country.
The vowels are flat and elongated, almost Scandinavian sounding.
And there are wheezing gasps for breath between every fourth or
fifth sentence, followed by bouts of deep, liquid coughing. Ndekwe
finds himself clearing his throat in sympathy. He reaches down for
the bottle of water rolling around in the footwell, clamps it between
his thighs and unscrews the top, takes a slug. It tastes like warm
metal in his mouth.

*... Right, here's the script – I'm confessing to the killing last week on
the Crown Heights. That lad who got stabbed outside the shops. I'll*

sign a statement, owt yer like, no bother. You can close the book on
that one, pal, cos it was me that did it ...

– OK, yeah, we'll come to that in a minute, Jack. But first I want
you to tell me how you and Carlton ended up in Hull.

– Yeah, right ... well, as you've probably guessed I'm not from
London originally, Christ no ... been down here for a good while
now though ... about ... oh, donkey's years now. Left Hull in ... what,
early seventies? Hang on, bear with me ... Nineteen seventy-two,
seventy-three, I think it was. Just after they started work on that
bridge, whenever that was. Hardly ever go back these days. Once or
twice, like. First time I went back was when Hull won the Challenge
Cup in that replay at Leeds. Nineteen eighty-one, was it? The rugby,
like. Met up with a few old faces and ended up going back on one of
their coaches, pissed up, like. Darted in and out a couple of times
more since then, to see family, mainly, but ... no ... not been back for
a good while now ... tell you what, though; it's altered a bit up there.
By hell it has. I was shocked when I saw how it had all changed.
Inevitable really, I suppose. March of progress and all that. Shame,
if you ask me, it used to have a bit of character, that city. Used to be
a proper port. Looks like everywhere fucking else now. Same shops
and all that carry on. I didn't hardly recognize the city centre, the
train station and all round there. Knocked the ABC down, the picture
house ... cinema, like. Got this big glass and metal shack thrown up
now. And then there's that daft bloody pointy affair sticking out from
the pier. What's that meant to be? They've tried to make it look like
a ship, the bow of a ship, like. Strangest bloody ship I've ever clapped
eyes on. A submarium, that's what they call it. They just make these
names up don't they? A bloody submarium. What the hell's that
when it's at home? Sounds like summat out of Captain Nemo ... but
aye, anyroad ... I left Hull years ago.

Marriage went tits up; that was me main impetus. Pressure of
being away all the time, I suppose. Most of the other women just got
on with it, their men being away at sea, but my Dorrie was never any
good at coping, God rest her soul. Very highly strung woman. Lived

off her nerves, she did. First few years were all right, but then we moved out to that new estate ... this was after they condemned half of Hessle Road; slum clearance, they called it. Unfit for habitation, they said. Cheeky bastards. Had a little palace down there we did. Mind you, I suppose it did need doing. I drove past to show me laddo where our old house was. It's a bastard supermarket now. One of them super-duper king size jobs. Half the shops down Hessle Road are boarded up. It was sad to see, that, I must admit. Was always thriving down there. Progress, though, innit? Anyway ... after the council turfed everyone out we moved out there, onto North Bransholme. I didn't mind it, meself. I thought it was more than adequate. Plenty of space, plenty of green fields. Nice new house as well. Decent neighbours. I thought it was all right, me. Dorrie, she bloody hated it though. You'd think she'd been left stranded on the bloody moon the way she carried on. Too far away from her mam and all her sisters, that's what it was ... too far away from her coven of bloody witches. That's when all the rows and the upset started, after we moved on there. We'd be at it the minute I dropped me bag in the hallway. Then you'd get her sister round and her mother and all the rest of it, the full fucking shebang. I just used to go straight back out to the alehouse and stay there until it was time to sail again. Bollocks to the lot of em ... went on like that for months, it did. A good two years or so, anyroad. Then I come home from one trip and she'd just cleared off, handed the rent book back to the council and flogged all the furniture, the chairs, the tables, oven, fridge, the lot; lock stock and frigging barrel. Took the bain and moved back in with her mother. So that was that, twelve years of marriage; over, kaput, do not pass go do not collect two hundred pounds. I thought, balls to it, I aren't coming back to an empty house every month. So I come off the trawlers and I left the city, left for good ... Y'see, I'd been fishing since I left school, since I was fifteen and I just fancied a change, I suppose. There's only so many times you can stare at a bloody iceberg before the novelty wears off. I wanted to widen me horizons, see what else the world had to offer ...

– And that's when you came down to London?

– Aye ... Well no, not at first, like. First off, I pitched up with
some pals in Great Yarmouth and joined the Merchant Navy.
Marvellous life. Went all over the shop – Spain, Portugal, France,
Africa, Far East, Caribbean. Everywhere. Loved it, me. Had a
marvellous time. Fit as a butcher's dog. Earning a fortune, I was.
Mind you, I spent a bastard an'all. But that was how it was, you
know? C'est la fucking vie, brother. Whatever will be will be. Can't
buy freedom, can yer? Anyway, bear with me, this is all leading
up to ... this is part of the entire script, this is ... how I came to be
down here ... Hang on, let me think ... aye, that was it ... came ashore
for good just after I turned forty. Had a chance of a pub in South
London and me and me partner at the time just decided to go for
it. Made a good fist of it an'all, to be fair. Happy times over there,
south of the river. Greenwich, it was. Lovely place. Good time to be in
London, an'all. Plenty of money sloshing about back then. The Queen
Mary. Good little boozer that was. Had it running like clockwork, we
did ... but anyway, yeah, to answer yer question ... that's how I ended
up here in London. Been down here for nigh on thirty year now.
Never lost me accent, though. Never found a better one, I suppose ...

– And you've known Carlton for how long?

– All right, here's how it panned out. I'd been getting some
decent tips off this owner, this Irish fella who had two or three nags.
I'd done a few bits of graft for him here and there and we both shared
an interest in the gee-gees so he started giving me the nod when
there was summat going off. Nowt massive at first; just the odd little
each way, mebbe a decent long shot every now and again. Enough to
keep yer interested, like ... so ... anyway ... I used to use this bookies
down Bethnal Green Road and I got talking to this other fella in
there, this fella called Paulo. Italian lad. He was always putting these
big bets on, and not doing very well it has to be said. Show better,
yer know? Always flashing his wad about. Used to back some right
lemons he did. He'd slap a fortune down on some barmy long shot
and then stand there moaning and groaning as it staggered in last.

In my book there's only one way to bet and that's to back the winner. Wanna know how to double yer money in a bookies? Fold it in half and put the bastard back in yer pocket ... Anyroad, I'd seen him in there but I'd never let on to him or owt like that. I usually mind me own business when I'm having a bet. I don't like to get too pally with anyone cos it generally leads to a load of heartache. But he seemed a nice enough bloke this Paulo, a decent fella like ... so I was in there one afternoon, filling me slip in and he's stood right next door to me. He's running his finger down the list for Newmarket and he catches me eye, asks me what I fancy. I was having a couple of bob on this two-year-old I'd been following. It was about four to one, five to one, summat like that. I wasn't having a proper bet on it, just a few shekels each way like, but this Paulo was all like, right, here we go, this is it, I'm getting on it. I told him it wasn't any inside info or owt like that, just one I'd had me eye on for a bit. But he decides to put his shirt on the bugger. Like I said, he was that type of punter. Impetuous. I'm more of the cautious type, me. I like to sit back and weigh it all up, properly study the form ... I stick me daft little bet on and he ships out this big roll of notes and peels a slack handful off, sticks about a hundred quid on this two-year-old. I'm thinking, oh aye, fucking Rockefeller here. Seen loads of punters like that down the years, me. Flash Harrys with more money than brains. They might have one or two results but it always ends in tears. One week they're slinging their money about, buying drinks for every bastard in the pub, the next week they're looking for tab ends in the street. Gambling's an illness with characters like that. Me, I like to cover all me options. Bet to win money. That's the only way to approach the job. No sense in doing owt else, is there? I don't mind piling it on if I've done me homework and the odds are right. But I don't go for any of that gut instinct baloney ... Well, bugger me, it romps home! Pissed it by about five lengths! I'm twenty quid to the good and he's hauled in about five hundred quid, summat like that. Well, I would have been grateful for that, anyone would, but this Paulo ... Christ, you'd think I'd given him the secret to eternal life. He's slapping me on the back and giving me these big bear hugs and telling me I'm his pal for life and all this carry-on. You know what them Eyeties are like, how carried away they get ... well, I got to bumping into him regular after that. He'd come in the bookies and greet me with open arms, like I was his long-lost brother. Giving it all the old pals act. My friend, Jack, he used to say, my friend, my friend! I knew his game; he was after some more winners. Thought I had the Midas touch he did. The truth of the matter was I didn't have two farthings to scratch me arse with. That was the bloody joke of it ...

... One day, though, I did have a tip, a proper one, off the Irishman. He had this horse. I think it was called Singing the Blues. Summat like that. Anyway, it had done nowt all season, but they'd been holding it back and holding it back, waiting for the right meet and this one afternoon the Irishman reckoned it was gonna be trying. So I puts Paulo onto it and it comes sailing in and he's all chuffed to jolly bits again. Course, he'd put his usual king's ransom on while I was pissing about with spare change. That's when we got properly chatting and he asked me what I did and I told him I was looking for work. I'd been nightwatchman on this site up near Stratford, this big development for the Olympics. Anyway, there was a bit of bother and I got laid off. Nowt to do with me; some of the lads were thieving and the charge hand decided to make a clean sweep and get rid of all the suspects. Opportunity to get a load of his chinas on the job, no doubt. More fiddles down there than the London Philharmonic, I'm telling yer ...

A fresh bout of hacking and coughing. Ndekwe pauses the CD.

– Doesn't exactly cut to the chase, does he?

– I had a full afternoon of him yesterday. Halliwell grimaces. – He nearly sent me to fucking sleep.

– Sounds like he's coming apart at the seams.

– Full of shit, I'm telling ya. Look, Sarge, do I have to sit through all this again? Halliwell stifles a yawn and stretches, pushes the full length of himself against the confines of the car. He collapses back into his seat, watches the passing streets. – Anything you want to know just ask, he says. – I'll fill you in.

– I'll just keep it on low, says Ndekwe. He catches the incredulous look on Halliwell's face in the passenger-side wing mirror.

– I just need to hear it for myself, all right?

■ ■ ■ ■ ■

Gorman hangs the INTERVIEW IN PROGRESS sign on the other side of his office door and settles down at his desk with a fresh mug of PG Tips and a packet of Rich Tea biscuits. Not as bad as HobNobs, he reasons, or his personal favourites, Gypsy Crèmes. At least a Rich Tea isn't covered in chocolate, Gorman thinks. He allows himself three in quick succession and then reseals the packet, pushes it out of reach.

The doctor has told him to cut down on the sweet stuff after his last check-up, but Gorman has got up late this morning and skipped breakfast. He is in dire need of sustenance; he can feel his blood sugar levels plummeting. In stark contrast to his stress levels, which are rising more rapidly than Her Majesty's prison population.

He takes another biscuit, dunks, dips, and considers Ndekwe.

Gorman has been careful not to broadcast the fact, but Ndekwe had not been his choice for the DS role. Gorman would have preferred Halliwell or possibly Frampton; both decent, hungry young coppers who know the manor like the back of their hand. But the final decision had come from above and Peter Ndekwe had been chosen. Ndekwe had come highly recommended and with a host of glowing commendations from his previous senior management team in Lewisham. And, from what Gorman has seen these last three months, Ndekwe seems to be a trustworthy and capable police officer. No denying that. More than capable, in fact; his track record south of the river was undeniably impressive. He'd been involved in some pretty decent results, it seemed. Hurrah for him, thinks Gorman. But there is something in Ndekwe's demeanour that doesn't quite sit right with him. Gorman isn't sure what, exactly. Ndekwe isn't insolent. He's not a boat rocker or a back stabber or a shit stirrer or any of the other loathsome movers and shakers that Gorman has seen gradually infesting the job over the last twenty or so years. He doesn't seem to have that naked ambition that a lot of young lads who fancy themselves seem to have. Ndekwe isn't even particularly aggressive. Not that that would ever be a problem; Gorman is not averse to a healthy streak of aggression in the people beneath him; encourages it, even. Gorman is of the firm opinion that there's no way an officer can function in the modern policing environment without a sizeable pair of hairy, swinging bollocks. Especially not in this part of London.

Gorman takes another biscuit, but declines to dunk. Instead, he snaps it thoughtfully in two. He can't pin it down, what it is about his new Detective Sergeant that irks him so. But, he has to admit, Ndekwe gets right under his skin.

Gorman crunches up one half of the thin golden disc, slides the other half back into the packet and bundles the lot away into his drawer. He rises from his desk, takes his tea and looks down onto the street from his window. People, he thinks, all look the same when they're beneath you.

Gorman likes to pride himself on being relaxed and open in his dealings with the officers under his command. He invites discussion and debate in their day-to-day operations; welcomes it, in fact. Unlike some other senior officers he could mention, Detective Inspector Gorman does not mind being challenged. As all the training courses and awareness seminars constantly stress, an atmosphere of open and frank discourse is conducive to good working practices and relations in the modern policing environment. Gorman agrees with that sentiment, agrees with it wholeheartedly.

But from what he has seen so far, Ndekwe always seems a bit too quick with his assertions. A bit too keen to stick his two bob's worth in. Like that remark about the Search Team. Speaks before he bloody well thinks, that fella.

Gorman watches a group of school kids cross at a zebra crossing below. They shout and laugh and jostle, take too long in crossing and provoke a volley of honking from the waiting traffic, which elicits jeers in reply.

Self-confidence, thinks Gorman. All well and good in small doses, but Detective Sergeant Peter Ndekwe seems to be a little bit too convinced by his own hype. If he were a bar of chocolate he'd eat himself. Gorman allows himself a small chuckle at this observation, but reminds himself to never repeat it aloud. He is painfully aware that you can't make a remark like that these days – however innocently it's meant. Remarks like that can land you in a lot of bother. Certain types of people delight in taking things the wrong bloody way, quick to take offence where there's none intended. Bloody bleeding heart liberals, thinks Gorman; add them to the long list of people who are slowly but surely fucking up the job.

At the end of the day, Gorman considers himself one of the old school. He is fifty-eight years old and has locked up more criminals than he cares to remember. His copybook is spotless and his retirement is on the near horizon. In Gorman's book, that demands a certain amount of deference. He does not make a habit of pulling the chain of command, but when he does he expects his men to fall into line, to acknowledge the greater insight and experience of their commanding officer. You do not, repeat *not*, argue the toss with your elders and betters – no matter how much smoke you happen to have had blown up your arse by the top brass. The high potential development scheme is all well and good when it rewards genuine talent. What it should never be used for, thinks Gorman, is a weapon of positive discrimination, a way of boosting the representation of a particular sub-section of the force. Gorman holds very strong views in this respect. Ability and expertise are developed from the inside, not the outside. All the fast track progression in the world will not alter that fact.

But there it is, he thinks. Despite his own personal views, he has to work with the bloke, and that is the end of the matter. And

Ndekwe cannot bollocks this one up, reasons Gorman, surely to Christ. Talk about an open goal. The statistics speak for themselves: the vast majority of young black men in London are killed by other young black men. And that's not opinion, that's fact. Gorman can access all the data he needs to back this up. And anyway, the McKenzie lad has coughed, loud and clear. All Ndekwe has to do is tidy up a few loose ends and, bingo, job done. And if that other barmy old bleeder wants to go down with him, well, Gorman is certain Her Majesty can always squeeze one more in.

Gorman looks down at the streets below; a constant flow of human sewage, he thinks.

Carlton McKenzie. Gorman tries to remember his body language and bearing from the interview room. Gorman prides himself on his ability to sniff out a liar. He can always tell when someone is spinning him a line. He encounters falsehood every day, on both sides of the law. Almost thirty-five years' experience; Gorman can spot a lying bastard at a hundred paces, can smell them even, the salty stink of bullshit as it seeps out of their skin.

He turn away from the window, walks back to his desk, sits down, loads the CD into his computer, presses PLAY, adjusts the speaker volume and, for the second time in two days, he listens to the words of Carlton McKenzie:

... OK ... so ... start at the beginning, yeah? ... first time I saw Jack was in the bar with Paulo. Paulo's the boss of the Café Bar Russo, which is the place where I was working as barman. Back of Liverpool Street, innit. Head barman an cocktail maker. That was me. That was the first place me an him crossed paths. Him an Paulo both sitting there at one of the tables having a good old drink up. Man caught my eye, cos he didn't look like one of Paulo's usual crew. For the first thing, man's a proper old timer, yeah? Guess how old he is? Seventy years old, yeah? You believe that? I could tell he was old, yeah, but I didn't think he was that old. I couldn't work out what he was doing hooked up with Paulo, that was the thing. I could tell he

weren't no uncle or older relative cos he was so scruffy looking an that; most of Paulo's boys are all that flash way a lot of them Italians are, with all the hair gel an the leather jacket an all that, yeah? This man, though, he dressed like a tramp almost; tatty old jacket, busted shoes, all unshaven an everything. If you think he look a state now you should have seen him then, trust me. Man was proper scruffy. His hands as well guv, you seen his hands? All full of them big sovereign rings an old-style tattoos, all dots an letters across his fingers an ting, like some old jail bird, ya get me? If he hadn't have been with Paulo I would have thought the man was just some trash that had drifted in from the street. Like I say, I'd never seen the man before, but him an the boss seemed real tight that day, knocking back the beers an giving each other high fives across the table. Proper celebration, innit. I was ghosting about clearing the glasses from the tables an I overheard em chatting about some stable an some owner or some such an I figure out that they had a big win on the horses. Paulo loved them horses, man. Always a big beef with him an his brother Antony about the amount of paper Paulo be throwing at the bookies. Two of them trying to run a business an Paulo be giving all his money to sick animals – by which I mean he lose more time than he win, ya get me. But it looked like this day the man got himself a winner. Him an the old boy were still there laughing an drinking by the time I got off the clock and headed back home.

– So why, in your opinion, is Jack claiming he murdered Aaron?

– First thing you gotta know about the man Jack is that he don't let the truth get in the way of a good story, ya get me? He can tell a good story, though; I gotta give the man that. He can entertain a man. He ain't no killer, though, believe me … the man is chatting shit, trust me guv, trust me … I got to learn that much. But I never took no notice after I first saw him, cos I had more immediate concerns on my horizon; namely the paper situation, or should I say the lack of. Even though I was putting in bare hours at the bar I was not making any headway whatsoever with the Montego Bay thing. That was my plan yeah, to get to my dad's place in Montego Bay. That was my escape hatch, yeah?

– You wanted to go where? Montego Bay?

– Yeah, listen, right, the target figure was five hundred and eighty-four pounds including tax ... an that was just the plane ticket, the bare minimum required without even any spends on top, ya get me? I had at the time four hundred and fifty-eight pounds an seventeen pence in the account. I know the exact number cos it was all I thought about from dawn till dusk. I was totally focused, total tunnel vision. That running total was lit up permanent in my mind, like a neon sign, yeah? Four hundred and fifty-eight pounds an seventeen flippin pence. It seemed like I was stuck on that figure for time, man, all the summer long. I was working the hours an the money was trickling in, true, but it was bare flooding out again the other end, ya get me? All I wanted to do was to get above that five hundred figure and feel like I was at least making some headway with my plans, but there was bare taxation left right and centre. Like it was my mum's birthday at the end of June. It was the big one – the big four-o. She weren't happy about it being her fortieth y'know, not happy at all. She kept trying to say it was like just another birthday, no big ting an all that, but me an my auntie Sharon would take the bare mick, saying she be needing some Tena lady an all that, saying we gonna pack her off to a care home, innit. She would go sick on us, proper lose her rag an that. Anyway, we were having a party an everyone was invited; all my mum's sisters and my cousins and everyone from round our way, all the neighbours, all my friends, Melissa's friends, everyone, man. Everybody knew about it except my mum. She was the only one who was not in the loop. Surprise an all that, yeah? So there was the food and drink to get organized as well as getting her a special present for her most special birthday, ya get me?

– Melissa is your sister, yeah?

– Yeah, but listen, before I start, yeah, the thing that you should know about me is that I come from a good family, yeah? Good strong *family. I ain't just some nasty stray dog running round, some wild ghetto child, ya get me? I ain't from a crime family is what I'm saying, despite what I'm about to tell you, OK? Apart from me, now, it is not a crime family, yeah? There's me and my mum and my sister. We're a normal family, yeah? Loving family. Let that be on the record, yeah? We have our ups and downs, innit, course we do. My sister is fourteen, which is why she acted like a dick. But that's just part of growing up, innit. I acted like a dick when I was fourteen. Melissa argues fierce with my mum, but that's just normal. My mum can start a bare argument herself when she's in the mood, trust me. Strong woman, guv. She's had to be, to put up with the life she got dealt.*

– Hard life, eh?

– No, I ain't saying that ... what was I saying ... yeah, right, OK, yeah, it was all about this party, and it was all down to me, naturally, cos Melissa ain't got no money since she got sacked from that Saturday job at the hairdresser's. She got canned for mouthing off to the boss. She reckons she walked, but she got canned, man, I know it. Girl thinks I go about with my eyes and ears closed, innit. Fourteen years old, man, an she got a proper mouth on her. Thinks she's all that, acting like some big ting like all them youngers do. But she didn't deserve what happened to her guv. She did not deserve that.

– What do you mean, Carlton? What happened to her?

– I'm coming to that bit ... but yeah ... I went round to see her dad an asked him if he'd consider throwing something in the pot. For this party, ya get me? But he was pleading bare poverty as usual, the flippin prick. My auntie Sharon kicked in with a bit of dough from the insurance money she got for her car accident, but the funding was mostly down to me. I put some paper aside for some slabs of beer an a few bottles of brandy from the Cash n Carry an then I picked my mum out some sick gold earrings from a shop in town. So that last month of June all my wages from the bar was clean wiped out. Running to stand still type situation. It was vexing, true, but I didn't really mind, though, cos at the end of the day it was my mum, innit. She deserved a proper party for the big occasion, although like

I say she totally hated the thought of being forty. When I got home that evening Mum was on the settee watching the box. Melissa was in her room with her mate from across the way. She was getting new hair extensions put in, so the pair of them had probably been in there all day long. They were playing some new mix tape. I could hear it thumping through the wall, some living fool shouting about how many people he smoked an how many bitches he fucked an rah rah rah. Not my thing, bruv. I used to listen to that gangsta shit when I was little, but what I really like is my Jamaican tunes, the old skool stuff, ya get me? Righteous tunes. I don't really go for any of that grime or gangsta shit any more. Heard it done to death, man. One thing my dad did leave was all his CDs, the History of Trojan Records box set being my personal favourite among them. You know them tunes? The Upsetters, the Mighty Diamonds, Jimmy Cliff, Delroy Wilson?

– Never heard of them, no.

– All the greats, guv. Proper original rude bwoi, ya get me? So I put some tunes on while I was getting changed out my work clothes. I turned it up, but I could still hear Melissa and her mate yapping away, having some debate on the other side of the wall. I got black blood in me, though, Melissa was saying. You can't say I ain't black, Ella, cos I got black blood in me, though. Melissa gets all heated on account of her being so light skinned. Peeps who don't know us often won't have it that me and her are the same blood, despite us living in the same place an calling the same woman mother. Her old man is mixed race an he passed on his light-skin part to her, true, but I don't see why she get so heated about it. I think that was why she was always messing about with her hair, getting cornrows or else them extensions and all that. Trying to look like a pop star, ya get me? But that was Melissa. Not happy less she was looking in the mirror or vexing about something.

– She's your half-sister?

– Yeah, that's it. Still, at least she still got to see her father, least he still on the manor. He might be a bit of a prick an that, but at least

he still be visible. Up until the other night, right, I ain't seen my dad since I was about five, six years old, ya get me? You should be clear on that from the start guv, yeah? He ain't in my life any more. He ain't nothing to do with me now. I ain't seen the man for time.

    – Until the other night?

    – Yeah.

    – And you saw him ... where? In Hull?

    – Yeah.

    – All right, carry on ...

    – So yeah, anyway, after a bit I got sick of hearing Melissa an her mate chatting shit through the wall so I went through to the front room an watched the telly with my mum. I don't go outside on a night any more. I just stay in the flat.

    – Every night?

    – Serious. I ain't been out on the streets since my boy got took. My boy, Joseph, RIP ...

    – Joseph?

    – He was my boy. Yeah, me an Joseph were gonna go together. Go to Jamaica an stay with my pops. Roger Barrington McKenzie. I don't remember much about him, but I do remember when he left. I can recall that clear as the day. We didn't live in Hackney back then, we were in South London, Brixton to be exact. Not sure where, but I remember the flat an the colour of the carpet; it was an orange carpet with these little dark brown swirls an I was sat on the floor watching Batman on the telly and he came between me an the screen, kneeling down to put his face close to mine, his hands on my shoulders. He had real heavy hands. He was telling me something but I wasn't listening. I wanted to watch Batman an he was in my way. I kept trying to look round him to see the telly an he kept holding my face in his big hand, making me turn to look at him while he was chatting. I don't remember much of what he said except how he had to go away to work for a bit an how I had to be the man of the house now. He said some other stuff, but that's the only bit I really remember. I remember his gold teeth, flashing and winking in

his mouth. I thought it was sick. I always wanted gold teeth like that. He finished what he was saying, said goodbye an picked up his bag, walked out of the door. I knew it was important for some reason. But I just wanted to watch Batman mash up all the baddies. Me an my mum moved out of Brixton soon after he left an we came to live in Hackney, to be near Mum's sisters on the Crown Heights. Then she met Melissa's dad an Lissa was born after that. He lasted a couple of years till my mum threw him out on account of him being a bare prick. I never heard from my own dad again till I was sixteen years old an I got the postcard with the picture of his bar on the front.

– He had a bar?

– Yeah. The Jolly Roger, Montego Bay, Jamaica, an his writing on the back: Dear Carlton, this is where I live now, an this is my bar you see on the front – the Jolly Roger, just like me ha ha!! Jamaica is a paradise on earth an I want you to come an see me as soon as you can – never forget I love you, look after your mum an be a good boy, your loving father.

– So you were intending to save up and go and visit your father in Jamaica? That was your plan?

– For real ... Listen, that postcard came at a crucial time for me. It helped me get a lot of stuff clear in my head, cos it was a mad time for me back then, believe. I'll be straight with you, yeah, I was involved with everything going on round the estate, had been since I was about eleven years old, all the running around on the stairwells an along the balconies. Check my record, it's all on there. This ain't the first time I been sat in a room like this, I ain't even gonna lie. But I've been off road for time, swear down. That was just when I was a younger, yeah, an I don't feel no way about it now. It was just something we all did, all of us. All except Joseph, though ... OK, so let me tell ya about Joseph, yeah?

– Go on then ...

– He was my best friend, man, my true cuz. He came to live on the estate when he was twelve an me an him were tight from day one. His parents had brought him over from Sierra Leone, yeah, an they were very religious an strict. Joseph was a very quiet boy, never no hype or drama. But he was for real, ya get me? Joseph did not run with no crew or nothing an he didn't care what people said about him. Aaron and all of them thought he was a pussy, but he didn't take no notice of them fools. He had something solid at the centre of him, ya get me? I don't know no other way to describe it than that. Yeah, that's it. He was pure solid, all the way through. I admired him, if the truth be told. He was his own man. I was doing things I didn't really want to do, but I could not see any way around it all. But it was all blowing up, I can see that now. Things were getting proper wild.

– Wild like how?

– OK, so I'm telling you everything now, yeah? This still recording, yeah?

– We're still recording, yes.

– All right, all right ... One time me an some other boys went out to some place in the country, some travel agent shop I think it was, in Bromley or Beckenham, some place like that. One of the boys said there was bare paper in there. This was like a step up for us at the time, ya get me? This wasn't like tiefing out of cars or serving up in the stairwell. This was like a proper big man's caper, ya get me? Proper money. I wasn't sure from the start about this, but I went along with it anyway. I was scared, true, but I didn't want to look like a pussy in front of the other boys. Peer pressure, innit. Didn't have the balls to stand tall an be my own man. I was supposed to stand outside while the rest of the crew steamed it, but a police car came tearing down the street almost as soon as they rolled in there. Rah! I was on my toes straight away guv, rapid, trust me. My arse totally went, I don't mind admitting it. Everyone else got away as well, but I got bare grief for running when we got back home. Aaron and Bam Bam an all the rest of the boys were calling me a pussy an a batty boy for running away. But I didn't even flippin care. I heard later that Aaron had bust some old lady's jaw in that travel shop. They were all screaming with laughter about it. But I wasn't *flippin laughing. That Bromley thing was the end of the road for me. I stopped going out every night. Most times I just went round to Joseph's to play on his Xbox and listen to tunes. I mean, yeah, I was still doing a little bit of graft an that, but really I was trying to put some distance between me an all that stupidity. Gradually is what I'm saying, yeah?*

– Oh yeah. You can't rush these things.

– This is what I'm saying. But it's hard, trust me. It's hard to do the right thing when you're surrounded by badness. But when that postcard from my dad dropped through the door it proved to me an Joseph that there was another place we could be other than the ends. We planned to get out there, me an him. Get real jobs an save up an go to Jamaica. Work in my dad's bar, the Jolly Roger, Montego Bay. That was our new mission, yeah? When things would get rough we'd look at each other and say: Montego Bay, cuz. An then Joseph got smoked by some boys from some other ends. Some say Tottenham, some say it was E5; either way, it don't matter to me. You can lay the blame anywhere you want guv, won't bring the man back.

– What happened?

– What happened? Joseph was walking across the park on the way home from school an two boys on a motorbike came by with the strap, blam blam blam, caught him one in the hip and one in the leg. The police officer said that the bullet in the hip would have been enough to at least put him in a wheelchair for the rest of his life. But Joseph weren't that lucky, man. The leg shot hit the main artery an that was it, game flippin over, ya get me? Joseph crawled as far as the houses on the other side of the park before he passed out. Some lady saw him from her window an call the police, but by the time they got him to the hospital he was stone cold dead, man. He was my best friend. Fifteen flippin years old, man.

– Why did they smoke him?

– Well, you know what, he got killed cos of his jacket. That's what I think, anyway. These boys had come on the manor looking for some other boy who wore the same jacket as Joseph an they see

him walking across the park an they just come after him an open fire. That's exactly the sort of lame flippin mistake where someone's life get taken. Don't have to be specific. You don't even have to be in the life. You just have to be near it, ya get me? Just have to be around it, yeah? An me an Joseph were surrounded, believe me.

– I believe you ...

– His funeral was just the flippin worst though. His dad all stony silent an his mum wailing in the church as the coffin went through the curtains. And my mum getting hold of me outside, an grabbing hold of me, desperate like, saying don't let me put you in a box, Carlton, don't let me be burying my boy. All the big heads round our ends were like rah, we gotta go up there to Tottenham an show these fuckin niggas some proper heat an all that stupid gang banging shit, but I was sick to death of all that flippin shit, man. Sick to the pit of my stomach. Joseph's death punched a big hole clean right through the middle of me an I had no heart for any of that bullshit any more.

– Apart from killing Aaron Stewart presumably?

– Listen, from that day on, I went home an stayed in my room an I didn't come out for time, just sat there plotting my escape, from the zones, from London, from this entire flippin island. If I was in the house an anyone knocked on the door for me my mum would say I was out or in bed or something. After a bit, they stopped knocking. An I was glad, yeah? I didn't want nothing to do with all that nonsense no more. Montego Bay, guv. Destination number one. I carried that postcard everywhere I went, kept it close to my heart, always.

– And you've got no idea who killed this mate of yours? This ... Joseph?

– Nah ... All right, listen, the truth of the matter is I think them mans who did it were looking for me, yeah?

– For you?

– Yeah ... I done some stuff here an there, an my face was known. An I was always wearing that jacket. It was my flippin jacket that got him killed. Ya get me, yeah? I think whoever done Joseph was *looking for me an they got the wrong man. Joseph be wearing my jacket, ya get me? ...*

Gorman wanders back to his desk with a fresh cup of tea and flicks through the morning paper as he continues to half-listen.

A photo of a bug-eyed Fabio Capello dominates the inside back pages. Gorman amuses himself by scribbling a Hitler-style moustache, a pair of thick black Groucho Marx eyebrows and a magician's goatee on the England manager's face. The headline is screaming for the Italian's resignation following the poor perform-ance of the England team in South Africa, a demand with which Gorman heartily concurs.

'I need to find the answers for why our team did not perform,' Capello is quoted as saying.

– *Our* team, Gorman mutters to himself. – Not *your* bloody team, mush.

He scans the rest of the sport pages and then sets the paper aside. He shouldn't read such trash, he tells himself, but it's useful for a quick update on the less vital matters of the day. Gorman prises another Rich Tea from the cylindrical stack at his elbow. He dunks once, twice and then swiftly withdraws, but too late to stop the lower half of the darkened biscuit folding off and falling, slipping back below the surface of the steaming hot liquid.

– Cunt fuck shite!

■ ■ ■ ■ ■

The Crown Heights estate is fringed by fields to the south and east that host two playgrounds and a parade of steel-shuttered shops, hidden by hedges from the main road. Strips of low-rise housing lie beyond the green and surround the four main tower blocks, uniform grey picked out in red, blue, yellow and green coloured concrete, their cantilevered balconies jutting over a series of courtyards and walkways that connect to form the centre of the estate.

By the time Ndekwe and Halliwell park their car, the morning commuters have all caught their buses to work and there are very few people around. The address they have for Isaac's grandmother is on the third floor of one of the blocks. Despite a prolonged bout of knocking, there is no answer from her door or the doors of her neighbours. The two police officers walk along the balconies and up and down the stairwells. They hear music and TV behind several doors, but there is nobody coming out and nobody asks them their business. They descend back to ground level, stand in the shadows of a courtyard and consider their options.

– What now? asks Halliwell.

– Newsagent's, says Ndekwe.

They get in the car and drive back towards the edges of the estate, pull up opposite the row of shops where Aaron Stewart was stabbed and bled to death four days previously. The council cleaning team are just finishing their second and final wash down of the scene, winding up the power hose and packing the jet-wash machine into the back of the van. The yellow and black incident tape has been taken down, the few tributes, soft toys and handwritten notes bearing such legends as REST IN PARADISE, SLEEPING WITH ANGELS and TRUE E8 SOLJA have been moved away and placed carefully along the bottom of the steel shutters that conceal the shop next to the launderette. The pavement is shiny black and slick with water, the last bubbles of foamy detergent popping in the gutter. By the time the sun reaches the middle of the sky everything will have dried up, all remaining traces vanished.

There are seven shops on this row; a hairdresser's at one end, then two fronts covered by heavy drawn metal, then a launderette, a newsagent's, a Chinese takeaway, and then another grey shutter. Ndekwe checks his watch and keeps his eyes on the newsagent's door. He counts three customers in the space of sixteen minutes. Halliwell fidgets in the seat beside him. It is hot and uncomfortable in the car. He places a hand on the passenger door handle and looks enquiringly at his DS.

– We going in?

Ndekwe shakes his head. – Not yet. I just want to listen to a bit more of this. He taps the display panel on the CD player.

Halliwell exhales hard, slumps back into his seat. This is all so much pissing about to him; listening to a testimony he heard first hand, talking to people he's already interviewed.

– Look, says Ndekwe. – You know where Isaac's usual spots are. I'll sit here and listen to this and you go and have a bit of a mooch around, yeah?

– Yeah, agrees Halliwell. – Yeah. Good idea.

– Meet back here in … what? An hour?

– Sweet. The word is barely out of his mouth before Halliwell is out of the car, throwing the door hard shut behind him, just the other side of a slam.

Ndekwe watches him stride off across the park and disappear through a gap between the houses on the other side of the green. Then he turns his mobile to mute, presses PLAY and tilts his seat back, settles down to listen.

… Anyway, Paulo insisted I went for a drink with him so we went round the corner and got into a session in this boozer. We had a few scoops in there and then he said to come and have a meal on him at his place, like. By way of thank you, he said. So I says aye, go on then … Well, it weren't really a restaurant, more like one of them modern café bar affairs, are you with me? Nicely done out and that, but it was just a big pub that did food, basically. It belonged to him and his younger brother, Antony, a right miserable twat. Face like a slapped arse he had. I'll come to him in a minute, that bastard. Anyway, Paulo ordered us up a load of grub and we stayed in there the rest of the afternoon and most of the night, filling our faces and having a few drinks, like. Had a right good night we did … and that's where I met me laddo. He was working in Paulo's pub. I'm not sure if he was there that time, on that night, but that's where our paths first crossed, like. I knew right away he was a decent enough lad, if a bit fucking daft like …

– Daft? How do you mean, daft?

– Well, y'know ... Gullible. Naive, like. Listen, though, Carlton wouldn't hurt anyone. No way. He's not that type of lad. He might carry on like he's some kind of tough guy gangster, but it's all a big act, believe me. He's no hard man, not by any stretch of the imagination. He couldn't smack his bloody lips, I'm telling yer ... I mean, you've only got to talk to him for five minutes to know he's incapable of killing anyone. He's just not got it in him. Not like some of them young lads round my way. I suppose it's the same everywhere now, but them little bastards round our end are totally out of control. They've got no fear whatsoever. Certainly not scared of your lot. When I was a lad you'd get a clip round the lughole off a copper if you so much as looked at em the wrong way. And it was no good going roaring to yer mam cos you'd just get another bastard. Fuck me, when I was a lad you wouldn't dare swear in the street in case yer mam or one of yer aunties heard yer. This lot, though, a police car rolls up and they're all queuing up to sling abuse. Seen it out me back window many a time; they all gather round the back of the flats. Asian lads they are. About thirty of them down there some nights, music banging out the cars and all that carry-on. Law and order? Forget it, brother. Not in this day and age ... Anyway, I make sure I'm off them streets on a night, me. Safely tucked up in me quarters. Too old for all that lark now. There was time I'd have stood up to em, y'know. Take me jacket off to anyone, me, once upon a time. Not now, though. Fuck that for a game of soldiers, gerra fucking machete round yer head. Trust me, I know. I saw one of em out me back window one day, brandishing this big fuck off blade, swinging it round like a golf club he was. This was at half past four in the bastard afternoon. Like I say, a law unto themselves. And they've all got that hardness in em, you can see it written all over their faces ... that lad you've got through there, though, he's not like that. He's a decent lad. He makes out like he's all street-wise and all that carry-on, but he's as daft as a brush, trust me. Lives in a world of his own half the time. Barmy little bugger thought he was off to live in Jamaica ...

– *Jamaica?*

– *Aye, that was his big plan. Go and see his dad in Montego Bay, the dizzy twat. Anyway, where was I? Oh aye, yes, the job ... So Paulo was giving it all the big one, saying you come and work for me, Jack, I will look after you, you are like a father to me, and all that baloney. You know how emotional and over the top them Italians can get, all that 'you are family now' business. Well, I weren't about to debate the issue, I just said aye, thank you very much and I started there a few days after that. I must admit, I did need the money. I'd copped for a bit of brass when I got paid off from the Olympics job, but you know how it goes, it don't last you five minutes. Flies out yer bloody pockets soon as you step out the door. So aye, it come at a good time. I didn't have a pot to piss in, to be perfectly straight about the deal. Totally pink lint I was ... Anyway, it was all right at first, Paulo's place. Yeah, it was good. Cushy number. Don't get me wrong, like, I've never been afraid of hard graft, worked hard all me life, oh hell aye. But I can't sling meself about like I used to. So this little turn suited me down to the ground. I suppose me official title was kitchen porter, like. I'd collect the glasses from the bar and clear all up, go and get the provisions for the kitchen and sort the deliveries out, all that caper. Bit like a galley lad, I suppose. Ironic, really, cos that's how I started out at sea. First job I ever had, galley lad on the* Ross Corsair. *Looks like it was me last job as well, eh? Turned full circle, I suppose ... anyroad, it was all fine and dandy when Paulo was there. Pleasure to do the job. But it was his brother who was the root of all the heartache, their Antony. He was the cause of all the bother.*

– *He worked there as well?*

– *Well, Antony was meant to be in charge of the day-to-day running of the place, but the silly twat couldn't run a bath. Didn't have the first idea about managing a pub, or a bar or whatever you want to call it. I know all about the licensing trade, me. First thing you got to do when you're running a pub proper is look after yer staff. A pub is no different to a ship sailing into battle. Battle cruiser equals boozer, see what I mean? Yer got to have it all shipshape. Can't* win a war without feeding yer crew, can yer? And if yer staff are all on-side then that's half the battle won. When we had our little place in Greenwich we had it running like clockwork, and that was largely down to the staff. They worked their bollocks off for us and do yer know why? It was cos we treated em right, that's why; we treated em with respect. A right tight little crew we had. They'd have followed us into a hurricane them lads and lasses, by hell they would ... This Antony, though, his idea of running a business was to march round barking orders and making everyone's life a total bloody misery. I know he used to upset the lasses behind the bar on a regular basis with his shouting and bawling and carrying on, me laddo as well. He tried it on with me a few times, but I soon put the bastard straight ...

– You had an argument?

– Well, there was a few instances ... for example, I had to ring the doctor's for an appointment one afternoon so I used the phone in his office and he come marching in and snatched the receiver out me hand and slammed it back down. You are not to use the company phone, he says, wagging his finger in me face like he was fucking Mussolini. I says, now hang on just one fucking minute, pal, don't you be raising your hands to me, I don't know the rules, do I, I've only just come on board. I thought aye, you carry on like that, mister, and I'll be putting you on your arse, no bloody bother ... He left me alone after that, for the most part. He knew better than to overstep the mark with me. I might not be twenty-one any more, but I can still look after meself, oh hell, aye, don't you worry about that, amigo. Eat gobshites like him for breakfast ... The rest of em were all right, though, the lasses behind the bar and Carlton, yeah he was a nice lad once you got to know him. Like I say, he acts all hard faced and that but he's actually a decent lad underneath it all. He told me all about his plans to get away, how he was saving up to go to Jamaica to see his dad. Course I've sailed all round that part many a time so I filled him in on a few details. Mind you, he seemed to know a fair bit about the place already. Knew all about Montego Bay and all round there. Most of these kids don't know any further than the

*end of their street, but Carlton had done his homework on Jamaica.
Well, they get it all off the internet, don't they? You can go round the
world without leaving your front room these days. Seen that thing
where you can beam in on a map, type in any location anywhere
on the planet and it shows you all the streets and the houses and
all that lark? You seen that? Amazing stuff. Could have done with
that when I was at sea. And they've got them all in their cars now,
haven't they, all them sat navs. Fantastic things they are. Just key in
your destination and off you pop. Like summat from a sci-fi movie.
Bastard things'll be driving themselves in ten years' time ...*

    – So, this bar, this is where you first met Carlton?

    *– Aye ... So anyway, yeah, I gave the lad a few tips every now
and then, cos he was trying his best to save up for his dream trip
to Jamaica. I don't mind helping them that are trying to help
themselves. The Irishman was coming up trumps and I'd had a few
decent winners out of him, so I put me laddo onto one or two of em,
he'd chip a few bob in, I'd go out and put the bet on and we'd split
the winnings. It was never nowt to write home about, like, just a few
quid here and there, but it kept us both in beer money. Mind you,
having said that, I don't think I ever saw me laddo take a drink while
we were both at that bar, not a proper drink, like. When I was his
age I was in the boozer every night of the week ... well, every night
I was at home, like. You couldn't sup at sea, strictly forbidden. Too
busy working, anyroad. Sixteen-hour shifts. Non-stop, it was. Brutal.
Maybe that was the reason why we all went barmy when we came
ashore ...*

■ ■ ■ ■ ■

The mug of tea is Gorman's fourth of the day. He feels the pressure
building in his lower abdomen, a balloon slowly inflating, but he
resists the urge to rise from his desk and head to the toilet. Recent
experience tells him that such a trip will have to be repeated several
times before his bladder is completely emptied. Best to hang on till the

last minute and then flush it all out in one go. Gorman has to get up to piss at least three or four times a night now. He nearly mentioned it on his last visit to the doctor when she'd stuck a needle in his arm, looking for signs of diabetes, prostate cancer, HIV and God knows what else. The nocturnal pissing is a minor irritant, though, nothing serious. Just a natural part of getting old, his missus reckons. But bollocks to that, thinks Gorman, fifty-eight isn't old. He's still got his own teeth and most of his hair, more than most men his age. He fingers the spreading bald patch at the crown of his head, tries to gauge its current parameters. He tries not to touch his cranium too often lest his probing encourages further thinning, but it's a nervous habit and in moments of stress he often finds his hand wandering to the back of his head. He flicks a few locks back into place and then picks up his pen, tries to concentrate on the job in hand.

The Café Bar Russo; Gorman doesn't think he's ever heard of the place, which is surprising because he used to drink all around Liverpool Street back in the day. He's fairly certain he would remember the name. But then again, it could have been called something different back then. Pubs these days, he reflects, they change their name more times than Salman Rushdie.

There's a respectful tap on the door.

Gorman lowers the volume on the CD.

– Yes?

Frampton pops his head round.

– Cuppa, sir?

Gorman drains the last dregs from his mug and offers it across the desk.

– Thanks, Alex. You're a lifesaver.

... So I go to work one morning an the old man is in the kitchen. Paulo give him the position. Chantelle, the girl who worked with me behind the bar, she confirmed what I was thinking, that the old man give Paulo the word on some horse or something and Paulo come up with bare dollar. So him and this old guy real tight now, big amigos, yeah?

His job be to collect the dirty glasses, load them in the machine an then put them back behind the bar, as well as keeping the kitchen an the back yard clean an emptying the bins an ting. Odd job man, ya get me? I could tell Antony was not impressed with this situation. I heard them two brothers going at it one afternoon, Antony saying that the old man was a drain on the resources an I must say I was in agreement with that. Most times the old man – who by now I learned is called Jack – he be stood outside the back way smoking a roll-up or else sat in the kitchen with his nose in the back pages of the paper. When he did rouse himself to collect some glasses or do some tidying he was never in no rush, even when we got bare busy an that. Another thing, he usually dropped one glass for every three he washed. He be forever sweeping broken glass up off the kitchen floor. So, in my opinion, he was not exactly an asset to the Café Bar Russo. I kept my mouth shut, though, innit. No business of mine. I figured he'd only be around for a couple of days or so, but after a few weeks it was obvious it was a permanent thing. Every so often he'd come in drunk though. I could smell it on him, real strong sometimes. One time Antony caught him asleep in the chair in his office an Antony went crazy, told the old guy to get the fuck out of there, man, and never come back. But then a few days later Paulo sweet-talks his brother back round to the one-more-chance way of thinking. So Jack come back. Return of the Jack, innit. After that, man kept his head down for a bit, didn't have a drink for a good few days, kept everything shipshape, ya get me?

– So you were work colleagues and then you became friends?

– I wouldn't say like, you know, friends or nothing ... but the first time I really spoke more than two words to the man was one day when I slipped into the office and jumped on Antony's laptop. I was trying to find the Jolly Roger on Google Earth, but it was hard to see the names on some of the buildings. Some of them were just like rooftops sticking up above the trees. I'd tried loads of times to figure out the exact location of my dad's bar, but I could never find it no matter which I way I searched. I used to go into those internet

cafés on the Kingsland Road an have a serious deep search, but I could never seem to make any progress before the dollar run out. Montego Bay was sick, though, no doubt about it. Hip Strip, rah, that the place for me. Man can kick back there, live a life worth living. Fresh fruit. Sunshine. Swimming every day. Those beaches ... yeah, all that golden sand an the sea like a mirror an the mountains in the distance. Dunn's River Falls, innit. Paradise, guv, bare paradise, just like the man say. Anyway, I'm sat there surfing the net an someone appeared in the doorway behind me. For one nasty second I thought it was Antony, but I look round an it was only Jack. He's peering over my shoulder at the screen. Montego Bay, he says, been there loads of times. Marvellous place. Shut up, I said, you ain't been to Jamaica. Reckoned he'd been all over the Caribbean, though, went to Jamaica, Cuba, St Kitts, everywhere he said. Merchant Navy, he says. Went out there about a dozen times or something like that. I was like, for real, yeah? You been to Jamaica? Been all round the world, son, he said.

– And that impressed you, did it?

– Nah. At first I reckoned he was just feeding me full of nonsense, ya get me, just the ramblings of an old fool. He rolled up his sleeve an showed me an armful of faded blue mess; snakes an scrolls an playing cards an women's faces. He pointed to a skull on his forearm, this grinning skeleton head over a pair of crossed swords. Got that after a good piss-up in Montego Bay, he said. Nineteen seventies. Serious wild place it was back then, he reckoned. What, you some sort of pirate man, I says to him and he laughed. His laugh sounded like you'd imagine a pirate to sound. That bare smoker's cackle. Aye, lad, he says, if you like. An then he tells me all this stuff about pirates protecting Jamaica back in the day, how the British paid for them to run everyone else out of the area, keeping the island's booty safe for the Commonwealth an that, innit. I already knew that shit, man, I knew Jamaica had been gangsta for time. I started testing him, asking him bare questions about Jamaica, cos there ain't no one know more about Jamaica than me.

I asked him about which parts he went to an what it was like, an he sits himself down an gets his tobacco pouch out, starts rolling a smoke an launching into his reminiscing. But then we heard Antony giving Chantelle grief in the bar so I slapped the laptop lid down double quick an we both jumped up an slipped out the office, went about our business. After that me an him started to have a bit of a chat an ting, a bit of banter flying back and forth, ya get me? How's things on deck, skipper? he'd say to me, as he shuffled round the bar collecting his glasses. All shipshape, captain, I'd say back, an he'd chuckle away to himself. He'd always stop an have a drink at the bar before he got off. Half the time I couldn't understand a lot of what the man was saying because he's got that bare northern accent, innit, which got even worse when he'd had a few rums an that.

– Boozer, is he?

– He likes a drink guv, trust me. First night I ever really stopped back an talked to him deep was when he was doing his magic tricks for Chantelle. Did I tell you he could do all them sick card tricks? Oh, man, he was proper good, I mean seriously good. Like Derren Brown or one them, innit. He did this one where the card you chose ended up stuck to a glass behind the bar. Do not ask me how the man did that. It was serious. I was like that, jaw hitting the ground, for real. Said he got learnt how to do tricks by this man in St Kitts, this proper voodoo magic man. Witch doctor, innit. I don't know if that part of it was true, but Jack got bare tricks, guv, trust me.

Some of the stories he told were outrageous, though, truly. Like when he told me an Chantelle about how he was chased by a French gunboat out this Bay of Biscay cos he was smuggling electrical goods out the Mediterranean. I was like yeah right, Jack, dream on, bruv. But he got all indignant an launched into this story about how he gave this big speech in court an the judge let him off cos he managed to convince them he was a secret agent working for the government or some such nonsense. Just bare lies, innit. Funny though, the way he told the story an that. Entertaining. Another time he told me he used to be a singer in some crazy rock n roll band who went all around Europe. Another tale he spun was about him an his mate going up the Amazon in a canoe, getting attacked by crocodiles and then getting a load of gum out of a tree. Another time he told how he won a petrol station in America in a game of dice with these Texans an how it all came on top an he had to pull a gun on a man to get out of the bar alive. These are the kind of things he came out with. Just chatting bare shit, innit. He was a lying old rascal, but he was well funny. I gotta say that about the man. I used to look forward to going to work just to hear some more of his mad tales. He had all these crazy theories about stuff as well. Like, for instance, get this, yeah; all retired school teachers are shoplifters. Trust me, guv, this is what he would say. Headmistresses, they're the worst. They go tiefing in all the big shops and they keep a bottle of tablets in their handbags in case they get caught. If the store detective puts a hand on their shoulder these old ladies take the tablets out and threaten to eat the lot. Suicide bid to avoid the jail, innit. Just nonsense. He had all sorts of theories about your lot as well. Like all policemen had special signs in their car windscreens so another policeman would know they were Five-O an let them go if they got stopped for drink driving. All policemen were part of a secret club where they rolled their trousers up and painted their legs blue. Swear down, I never heard so much nonsense in all my days. But it was funny to listen to the man. Some days me an Chantelle would be holding our ribs with laughing.

– A bit of a joker, yeah?

– He could be that way. Some days, though ... some days he would come in with a look of bare sadness on his face, wouldn't speak to nobody all day. Just went about his business, no chatting stories or jokes or nothing. I didn't like to see the old man like that. One day he'd been in an awful flippin mood, stomping about and growling like a dog. I was like, Jack, what's the problem? Too old for this bastard city, he said. I told him I was going to live in Jamaica. He didn't seem much interested until I mentioned my dad having a bar out there. Then he started asking bare questions. I tries to describe Hip Strip, *but then of course he's off telling me how much better it was when he was there in the flippin eighteenth century or whenever. When you actually going? he asks. When I get the dough together, I tell him. No doubt about it. So he asks me how much it is nowadays to get to Jamaica. I told him, five hundred an eighty-four pounds including tax. You know what he said, guv? He said, can you be a bit more specific? I don't know if he was trying to be funny. He didn't laugh or even smile. I told him I been saving up for time, which was a mistake cos then he asked to borrow a tenner off of me an I was like rah, Jack, I ain't got any money to lay out, man. In actual fact I did have a ten pound note on me, but I didn't really want to lend it to him. Nothing personal ya get me, but it was like my mum says, neither a borrower nor a lender be, innit. But Jack said it was for this horse, absolute dead cert he said. Them where his actual words – absolute dead cert. He said if I lent him the paperwork to bet on this horse he'd split his winnings with me, which he reckoned would be about forty quid each. Easy money, he says. I'd heard all that chat before; easy money, big payday, sweet as a nut, rah rah rah. Yeah, right. No such thing in my book. But the man kept pecking my head about how this trainer had given him the word on this horse an his word was gospel an all this nonsense. On an on an on, ya get me?*

– So you lent him the money?

– OK, so finally yeah I says to him, OK, Jack, I lend you this tenner an you give me twenty back tomorrow no matter what happen to this horse, whether he win by a mile or fall down flat on his face, whatever happen I want one hundred per cent interest on the investment, innit. I thought this would shut the old geezer up, but he agreed to the terms and conditions on the spot an he was out the back door double quick smart, soon as I handed him the dough. Rah, about an hour later he comes rolling back with a big grin on his face and a pocketful of cash, bare notes, straight up guv. Went to ten to one he says, an he peels off five ten pound notes and sticks them in my top pocket. I could not believe it, man. I didn't know what ten to one meant but I reckoned it must be all good. He might have been

full of shit about his adventures on the high seas an that, but when it came to the horses, Jack knew his stuff, trust me ...

■ ■ ■ ■ ■

The football slams against the passenger-side window so suddenly and with such force that for one heart-stopping second Ndekwe is convinced it's a gunshot. He throws his arms around his head and ducks down, bouncing his elbows off the steering wheel and sounding a blast on the horn.

Laughter from outside.

He unwraps his arms and lifts his head, scans the windows and mirrors. They are milling around the car, around half a dozen of them; kids, teenagers, younger, some of them. A mountain bike skids to a halt next to the driver's window and two pink-palmed hands press against the glass either side of a hooded black face.

– Five-O! Five-O!

The hands curl into fists and thump against the window, then the rider spins his bike away, bunny hopping off the kerb and circling the vehicle. More faces appear at the rear window and on the passenger side.

– Ha! See that? Man was *jumping*!

– Nearly *shit* himself, bruv!

– Ha ha ha!

Ndekwe kills the CD and steps out of the car. The boys fan out around him, some drifting away, others stopping to stand some ten yards away and lean against the wall of the shops, watching. The older ones stroll around the vehicle, peering in at the dashboard, bending down to check the wheels. The younger ones grapple and play fight over pushbikes and cigarettes. None of them makes eye contact with the police officer. They act as though he isn't there.

Dumph ... Dumph ... Dumph ...

A lanky youth in an Arsenal top is bouncing a football off the rear bumper of the car.

– Oi! Knock it off!

Ndekwe takes a step towards him. The boy doesn't move or look up, just keeps throwing the ball against the back of the car and catching it on the rebound.

Dumph ... Dumph ... Dumph ...

– Are you deaf? Keep that ball off my car.

Dumph ... Dumph ... Dumph ...

Ndekwe steps forward and snatches the spinning white sphere out of the air, midway between the rear bumper and the boy's waiting hands. Then he turns and lofts it, boots it on the volley as it drops, clean over the road and the railings that surround the green.

– Whooooooh!

– Wanker!

The boy races off, vaults the railings in pursuit of his ball. Ndekwe turns to face the rest of them. He addresses the youth stood nearest to him, a fat-faced boy with swirling concentric patterns shaved into the side of his head. His eyes are blanked by aviator shades. His T-shirt reads ONLY GOD CAN JUDGE ME.

– Do you live round here? Ndekwe asks him.

No answer.

– Do you know Bam Bam?

A voice from behind.

– Yeah, that's me.

Ndekwe swivels round. This boy is no more than ten years old.

– You? You're Bam Bam?

– Yes, mate.

– Yeah, me too, says the boy on the mountain bike.

– You as well, eh?

– Innit, though.

Ndekwe points to the car.

– Any of you lot so much as breathe on my car I'll lock you up and kick the living crap out of every single one of you. Yeah?

– Shit car anyway ...

Ndekwe stands and watches them drift away. The kid on the

bike is the last to leave. He circles the car a few times, stood up on his pedals, pulling little jumps and stunts, braking hard and swinging the back wheel around. Then he gets bored of the game and pedals off slowly. He takes a phone from his pocket and dials one-handed as he disappears round the corner.

Ndekwe looks for any remains of yellow chalk circles that mark the bullets' ricochet, but finds none on the pavement scrubbed clean by the council. There are three on the edge of the wall at the end of the block, one low down, around six inches above the pavement and the other two much higher up, further than a fully grown man can reach with his hand. Ndekwe takes a few steps backwards and places himself at the spot where Aaron Stewart fell four days ago, opposite the newsagent's, facing the corner. The window of the newsagent's is almost totally obscured by signs, stickers and posters; the National Lottery, the Euro Lottery, Oyster card top ups, mobile phone credit, Western Union money transfers. The door is open, but the counter is not visible from Ndekwe's position on the street.

It's cooler inside the shop. It smells of cardboard boxes and fried food. A young woman is at the counter, digging in her purse, paying for cigarettes and chocolate. Ndekwe stands before the racks of magazines and flicks through a copy of *PC Pro* until the woman has concluded her purchase. Ndekwe waits until she has left the shop before he approaches the middle-aged Asian man who stands by the till, eyeing him warily.

– Mr Akhtar?

But Mr Akhtar has already appraised the other man's dress and bearing and guessed who he is and why he is there, and Mr Akhtar is shaking his head.

– I have already spoken to the police, he says.

– I won't take up too much of your time, I promise. Ndekwe offers a tight, courteous smile that the newsagent chooses not to acknowledge. Instead, he starts to rearrange the newspapers on the counter.

– I did not see anything, he states. – I was in the back room.

– You didn't hear the gunshots?

– Of course, yes. Which is why I stayed in the back.

Ndekwe looks around the shop, peers over the newsagent's shoulder.

– No cameras?

– They took them out.

– Who? The council?

Mr Akhtar sighs softly, shakes his head no.

Ndekwe produces the photos of McKenzie and Isaacs from his inside pocket and places them side by side on the counter, directly in the man's line of vision.

– Seen either of these two before?

The newsagent doesn't reply. He turns and disappears into the back, returns with a gold and black sleeve of cigarettes. Splits it open and starts replenishing the shelves with fresh packets.

– Mr Akhtar?

– I don't know anybody. I don't see anything. Mr Akhtar does not turn around to speak. – These boys, he says, they are in and out of here all the time. I don't know them. I don't want to know them.

He tries to jam a packet of Benson & Hedges into a too-tight space on the shelving and it flips out of his hand, disturbing a box of plastic lighters, which drop and scatter onto the floor. Mr Akhtar mutters a silent curse and lowers himself to his haunches to collect them.

Ndekwe leans over the counter and addresses his back. – Listen, if you're worried about repercussions from anyone in the area, please, rest assured that anything we discuss will be in the strictest of confidence.

Mr Akhtar slots the last of the lighters into the box and stands up straight. He carefully fits the fallen cigarettes back on the shelf and then turns and leans on the counter, rubs his eyes with the heel of his hand. There are large purple rings beneath his eyes.

– Constable, he says.

– Detective Sergeant, says Ndekwe.

– Detective Sergeant. Do you have children?

The question throws Ndekwe.

– No ... not yet ... well, I mean ... no.

– I have daughters, says Mr Akhtar. – Three daughters. The youngest one is thirteen years old. She is thirteen. Do you understand?

Ndekwe opens his mouth to reply, but is distracted by a presence behind him. A man has entered the shop, a young guy in a baseball cap.

– Please, excuse me, says Mr Akhtar.

Ndekwe stands aside and the man asks for cigarettes, twenty Lambert & Butler. Mr Akhtar rings in the purchase and hands over the change and receipt. The man glances Ndekwe up and down before leaving. He stands and lights his smoke on the pavement outside before looking back through the doorway again and then walking away.

– Mr Akhtar, begins Ndekwe. – I ...

– Please, says Mr Akhtar. – I cannot help you.

Ndekwe persists for another few minutes, but every question is met with gentle rebuttal. Finally he thanks the newsagent and takes his leave.

There is a door between the launderette and the newsagent's, the door to a flat. Ndekwe leans on the buzzer; twice, three times, four times, five. There is no answer. He squats down and peers through the letterbox. No signs of life save a cluster of midges dancing madly in mid-air, caught in the dusty shaft of sunlight that slants down from the skylight. Heaps of free newspapers and fast-food flyers at the bottom of a staircase that disappears upwards into shadows. There is a faint whiff of milk, spilled and gone sour. Ndekwe drops the letterbox and stands up.

No one at home.

He walks to the shuttered shop at the end of the block. He turns and faces into the street, stands stock still for a second or two. Then he strides forward five paces and quickly turns, bolts for the corner, imaginary bullets whistling past his ears. He's around the corner and out of sight of the street in five seconds flat. He keeps running and spots a pair of concrete bollards marking a footpath curving away to his left. He sprints down the footpath and emerges ten seconds later into a main road full of traffic and pedestrians. He checks his speed, but is too late to stop himself catching a passing man by the shoulder, nearly spinning him off his feet. The man is launched into a running forward fall, hands nearly touching the floor before he regains his balance and rights himself. He stands and glares at Ndekwe, clutching the top of his arm, a skinny white guy with dreads in a vest.

– Fuck's sake, bruv!

– Sorry, says Ndekwe. He leans on his thighs, breathing hard.

– Watch where you're fucking going, yeah?

Ndekwe holds up a hand in acknowledgement. – Sorry, he says. – Sorry.

The man throws a few more choice remonstrations before walking away. People are looking. Ndekwe leans against a row of railings and waits for his breath to return.

Then he straightens up, walks back down the footpath and round the shops, back to the car. He turns on the CD and waits for Halliwell.

... I'd been badly for a while really, with me chest and that, but it was getting worse. Coughing and barking from the minute I got up. Keeping me awake half the night an'all. I was hardly getting any sleep. I knew I should have gone and seen the quack and got a quick MOT, but I'd been putting it off and putting it off till I got up one morning and brought up a right load of gunge and shit and there was a few spots of claret in there an'all. So I thought aye, well, I'd best go get meself checked out ... I went and saw Dr Lazarus at the clinic and she had a listen to me chest and said they needed to have a proper butcher's. She sent me down to Bart's, the chest hospital like, and they

run a few X-rays and reckoned they seen this shadow, across me lung, like, and they'd have to do a few more tests. So that was another bit of good news. Cheered me up no fucking end that did ... I was already a bit fed up anyway, to be honest, what with one thing and another. I'd just heard about an old pal of mine, who'd let go of the rope a couple of days previous. That was the about the third or fourth this year, old pals who'd fell off the perch. You get to my age and everyone you know starts biting the dust, like cheap extras in a Western. I felt like I was in the bastard departure lounge meself, to be entirely honest about the deal ... so I wasn't in the best of moods. And then, to top it all off, I lost me bloody job. Carlton as well. Both of us got the bullet on the same day. But that was all down to that Antony, that was. Like I said, the man was a complete bloody lunatic ...

    – You lost your job?

    – Here's the script: I was in the kitchen, stood having a yarn with me laddo when Antony comes marching through and he goes, HEY! YOU! OFFICE! NOW! Pointing at the lad, like. No please or thank you or kiss my arse, nowt. By hell, he was a bad-mannered bastard that Antony. Pig of a man, he was. So, anyway, the lad looks at me like what's going on here and he follows him into the office. The door slams shut and I can hear Antony shouting and bawling and it's all like half English half Eyetie ... but then I hear him going THIEF! THIEF! And me laddo starts raising his voice back at him and I'm thinking oh aye, there's gonna be tears before teatime here. So I puts me head round the door and I'm like, hey, come on fellas there's no need for all this carry-on, what's the bloody deal here, like? ... Anyway, Antony starts screaming at me to get out and Carlton's pointing at Antony saying he's accusing me of thieving and I can see the lad's about to get out of his pram so I try and intervene, peacemaker, like. I'm stood between them with me hands up like a bloody boxing referee while they're spitting and snarling at each other, and I'm saying come on, lads, this isn't the way to sort anything out. But then they start with the pushing and shoving so I'm like right, that's enough and I get a grip of the lad and spin him round, march him back through to the kitchen ...

– He was accusing Carlton of stealing?

– Aye, well, listen, now here's the proper script, right; someone
had been thieving, I knew that for a fact; but it wasn't Carlton. It
was one of the barmaids, the little blond lass, Carmel I think her
name was. Carmel, Caramel, summat like that. Saw her with me
own two eyes I did, one afternoon a week or so earlier, dipping into
the till when she thought no one was about. I never said owt at the
time. Didn't want to get involved. Once you start volunteering info
you generally get caught in the crossfire, one way or another. I just
kept shtum, me ... so I knew the lad was clean as a whistle. But he
was starting to get his right doe down, shouting no one calls me a
thief and all the rest of it. I gets him in the kitchen and says to him
look, stop in here for two minutes and just calm yerself down while
I go and talk to Rocky bloody Marciano through there, see what the
bloody score is ... but I didn't get chance, did I, cos Antony comes
storming into the kitchen and the bloody balloon's gone up again ...
They're shouting and pointing and trying to get at each other, and
there's muggins here in the bloody middle and it all just escalated
from there. How these things do, like ... Carlton starts kissing his
teeth at him, calls him some name, like pussyclart or summat,
one of them Jamaican names for knobhead, or whatever it is, and
Antony goes ballistic. He shoves me out the road and swings for
the lad, haymaker, like. Would have been lights out for me laddo
if it'd connected, but it misses him by a whisker and now it's game
on ... they're both grappling and slinging each other around like a
pair of rag dolls. They're bouncing off the walls and there's dishes
and glasses getting smashed all over the shop. I'm trying to rive
Antony off me laddo but he's a strong bastard is Antony, so I leaped
up on his back and fastened me teeth onto his lug'ole. Might sound
a bit extreme, but it had gone past the point of Queensberry rules
by this stage ... anyroad, it had the desired effect. Antony screamed
blue fucking murder and let go of the lad. He was spinning round
trying to dislodge me like, but I was hanging on to him for dear life,

literally. Like being on the back of one of them bucking broncos it was. If he was upset before he was fucking beside himself now. Well, yer can imagine, can't yer? ... I went flying off him and we ended up on the deck, him on top of me, his hands round me Gregory, trying to throttle me to fucking death he was. Trying to switch me lights off. He probably would have succeeded as well if Carlton hadn't kicked the bastard in the head. That soon shifted the cunt ... I grabbed hold of the side and managed to pull meself up but Antony's got hold of me by the legs, trying to drag himself up an'all, like. Or drag me back down, one of the two. Well, I knew if he got a grip of me again he'd finish me off, no two ways about it. I'd had all the wind took out me sails. So I just reached for the nearest thing to hand, like. I grabbed a full bottle of wine and I give him a bastard with that, right across the noggin. And then I give him another one an'all, just for good measure, but this time the bottle bounced off the side and exploded into a million pieces. Cut all me bastard hand as well ... Antony had stopped moving by that point. I stamped on his bollocks a couple of times and then Carlton was dragging me away, out the door. Good job he did an'all, otherwise you might have had two murders on your books ...

■ ■ ■ ■ ■

Gorman is getting increasingly restless, what with the ache in his guts and the slow, cooking heat of the office and the mumbling young man turned down low in the speakers on his desk. He keeps half an ear tuned in for anything that might leap out as he clicks back and forth between the sports sections of the Sky and BBC websites. Then he plays Bejeweled until the colours begin to hurt his eyes. He finds a Keep Ups football game, which he sets to with grim relish until his temper starts to fray and his clicking finger becomes numb.

He checks the time display in the top right-hand corner of his screen: 11:47. Lunchtime. He has a low-fat chicken salad from Tesco in the fridge downstairs, picked out especially by Mrs Gorman. He decides to save it for later. It's absolutely blinding outside. Far too glorious to be stuck at the coalface. Gorman leaves the station and visits a nearby pub and enjoys a leisurely sweat over Cajun chicken and chips with salad, garlic bread and two pints of London Pride. Then he strolls back to the station, installs himself back behind his desk and, emboldened by alcohol, decides to do some actual work. He puts a call in to downstairs. A civilian indexer answers on the fourth ring.

– Incident room.

A young, sleepy-voiced woman. She sounds flatter than cardboard, utterly bored. Not good enough, thinks Gorman. Not good enough by a long fucking chalk.

– Who's that? he snaps.

– Ursula.

– Ursula who?

– Ursula Obi.

– How many times can we let the phone ring before we have to answer it, Ursula Obi?

From the uncomfortable pause Gorman guesses that she's only just spotted the red light on the phone, only just realized where the call is coming from.

– Three, sir, she says eventually.

– Three, sir, he says. – Well done. Here's your next question: have the USCCT set up yet?

– Erm ... not ... sure.

Gorman smiles thinly, settles back into his chair.

– Do you know what the USCCT is, Miss Obi?

– Er ...

She places her hand over the receiver and Gorman catches a muffled exchange of words. Then:

– They're setting up now, sir.

– Where?

Hand over the receiver again. More words, lowered and urgent. Then:

– Corner of Hackney Road and Queensbridge, sir.

– Good. What does USCCT stand for?

– Not sure, sir.

– Never mind. Call Detective Sergeant Ndewakay, tell him I'll be down there if he needs me.

– Ndekwe, she says.

– I *beg* your pardon, snaps Gorman, then immediately corrects his tone. – Er ... I beg your pardon?

Nervous cough on the other end of the line.

– It's Ndekwe, sir.

Gorman picks up his pen and hovers the nib over a blank margin of the *Sun*'s showbiz column.

– Again?

She repeats the name.

– How do you actually spell it?

She enunciates the letters, slowly and deliberately. Gorman inscribes them above a photograph of Kerry Katona poking her tongue out. UN-DECK-WAY, underscoring each syllable with firm black lines.

– Right. Now get him on the phone and tell him the USCCT are setting up. Think you can manage that?

– No problem, sir.

– Good girl.

He puts the phone down, nudges his computer screen into life and clicks on PLAY.

... So, yeah ... if I think back to where it started to go properly wrong I would have to say it was on the day of the party. My mum's fortieth, yeah? That was the day it kicked off with Antony, the day it all started to turn to shit.

– *This is the day you lost your job?*

– *Yeah, that's it. Jack was drunk that day. Like I say, Jack's been drunk at work before, but this was like proper pissed up yeah, not just half-cut; Jack was loud drunk, singing an crashing about the* kitchen an that. It was like the third time that week that the man had come in drunk, but this day was the very worst. He weren't even trying to hide the fact. It was like he had some sort of death wish, ya get me? I mean, Antony was on the shift, but Jack didn't seem to give a fuck. He'd given Paulo a couple of winners the week before. Maybe he start to think he was bulletproof or something. I was behind the bar an I could hear the man from way back in the kitchen, hollering some real lame song, that rock n roll shit from the fifties, ya get me? Like Elvis Presley, innit, one of them types: OH YESSS AHM THE GREAT PREEETEND-AH, an then a load of dooby dooby doo nonsense. Tha man cannot sing, trust me. He sounded like a cat that got its tail trapped in the door or something. Like he in bare pain an that. Antony was sat at the end of the bar, his head in some paperwork. He was trying to ignore the racket, but I knew Antony an I could see he getting well wound up. His hand was tap tap tapping on the bar as he flicked through these papers, looked like some official looking shit, bills or contract or something. Whatever it was, it was not making for happy reading. An Antony's mood was not improved by the noise coming from the kitchen, yeah? Chantelle gave me a look and nodded towards the back, like you better get that old hound dog to shut the fuck up, man. I just shrugged. Me, I was staying right out of it guv. Man got a death wish coming in drunk like that when Antony there. Cos it was not like Antony got any love for him anyways, ya get me? Like I say, Antony never gave him the job or nothing, be Paulo who took the man on. But Paulo was not there that day an Antony was getting heated. Paulo always say give the old guy a chance, yeah? But Antony was not in the business of giving a man chances, especially not some old drunken sailor man who come and smash his kitchen to pieces. Antony would not piss on the man if he was on fire, ya get me? An right on cue there was the smash of glass an a load of cursing an Antony jump to his feet, swipe the papers clean off the bar, shouting, what the fuck, man, what the fuck. He stomps into the kitchen an all the drama start.

– What happened?

– Antony be shouting YOU CLUMSY CUNT and the old guy
be coming back at him, but I can't hear what he say, just sound
like rah rah rah. Both of them raising a right mad ruckus together.
Good thing there were no customers about to hear all that nonsense.
Chantelle was like, that man gonna get himself fired. She ducked
down on her knees an started fiddling with the bottles in the fridge
an that. I went round the other side of the bar an started picking
Antony's papers up off the floor. I didn't scan them or nothing, just
gathered them all up and stacked them on the bar. But I could see
that they were bills, some of them with angry red letters across the
top. Final demands, ya get me? There was a big shouting an crashing
from the kitchen an Chantelle say, Carlton, you better go an see what
happening, mate, Antony gonna kill the man. So I goes through there
an it's just flippin bare chaos, man; Antony got Jack by the scruff of
the neck, got him bent double over the sink, an he be trying to force
the old man's head under the taps shouting ARE YOU SURE? ARE
YOU FUCKING SURE THOUGH? Jack's thrashing about trying
to get his head up, water bouncing an spraying everywhere. I shout
for them to leave it, man, just flippin leave it, an I grab Antony by
the shoulders, but he spin round an smash me with his elbow, bangs
me full in the mouth, yeah? Jack take his chance to twist free an
he picks a pint glass up off the draining board an smashes it off the
side of Antony's head. Antony slip backwards, an me an him both
go crashing down, the pair of us thrashing about on the pissing
wet tiles. Antony totally flippin lost it by this point, ya get me, he
screaming CUNT CUNT CUNT an trying to get straight back
up on his feet an I'm trying to pull him back down, but he got the
strength of ten men, innit, like trying to wrestle with a flippin bear.
We both sorta get up together, me clinging onto him an him trying
to get to Jack who's holding onto the sink, coughing an retching an
spluttering. I get myself between the pair of them an hook my leg
round Antony's, try to flip him back down on the floor, but instead
we both go crashing round the kitchen, bouncing off the walls and
banging into shit left right and centre. A big stack of plates gets

knocked off the side and shatter all over the floor. Bare flippin chaos, mate. Then Antony gets me wedged in a corner between the wall and the big fridge freezer, his arm jammed up under my chin, spitting an snarling into my face, telling me I'm dead, I'm a fucking dead man an he's snatched a blade up off the side, big flippin carving knife, innit, an I grab hold of his wrist before he can stick me, point of the flippin blade waving about near the corner of my eye. I'm struggling like crazy to push the man off, but I can't flippin breathe properly, not with his big meaty arm crushing down on my windpipe. I'm getting all the fight squeezed out of me an I hear the blood banging in my ears an the room starts swimming round, but just as I feel my arm turning to water, Antony's gone flying sideways, nearly taking me with him. Man's rolling round on the floor moaning an groaning an Jack's stood swaying over him, a wine bottle in his hand, a full bottle of wine that he's waving about like a pirate with a flippin sword, innit. I'm gasping an coughing an I see that there's blood dripping down off Jack's hand. Flippin carnage guv. Jack looks at the blood running down his fingers an then looks at me. Fucking knife, he says, typical fucking Eyetie. Antony's trying to pull himself up by the freezer door an Jack steps forward an lifts the bottle again, ready to deal him another crack round the nut, but I seen enough of this now. I take hold of Jack's arm and wrestle the bottle out of his hand. Jack starts laying the boot in, kicks Antony twice in the bollocks before I drag him away.

– You pulled him off him?

– Yeah, I just got hold of him and I said come on, Jack, we gotta fuck off, bruv. I grab a tea towel an wrap it round his bleeding hand, take hold of the man by the shoulders an march him out the kitchen double quick, through the bar, past Chantelle who's looking horrified. As we get to the door, people are coming in, two women chatting away to each other. Office workers for their lunch, innit. I hold Jack up an we stand aside as they stroll past and then I have to practically drag him out onto the street to get him the fuck out of there, man. Jack, I said, Jack, we gotta move, bruv! But the man kept stopping *dead and trying to turn back round, trying to walk back in the bar, like he either so drunk he don't know which way he be facing or he just got a mad itch to go back an finish off Antony. I ain't even gonna lie, I did think in that instant that I should just leave him there and get the fuck out of it, but rah, I could not leave the old man to Antony, no flippin way. I reckoned very soon the man would be up on his feet and coming to finish this shit off, trust me. The traffic going up on our side of the road was backed up and jammed, just crawling along slow, an I steered Jack through the bumpers saying, come on, Jack, man, move, move, move, but then we got to the middle of the road an the traffic going the other direction be flying past at bare speed, so I had to stop, hold the old man steady an pick our moment to get through the vehicles, innit. Any second I expected Antony to come up behind us an send us flying under the wheels, but we got across quick through a gap, a car horn blasting as I tried to stop Jack walking straight in front of the traffic. There was a cab parked up in front of the station. I got the crazy old drunken fool in the back an jumped in beside him, told the cabbie to drive off double quick an we got the fuck out of Dodge City ...*

■ ■ ■ ■ ■

It is pleasantly cool inside the Café Bar Russo after the grubby heat of the street outside; the air stirred by three overhead fans, blades slowly turning above the heads of the half a dozen or so customers dotted around the tables at the far end. Ndekwe can smell food; tomato and garlic, warm bread and balsamic vinegar.

Ndekwe and Halliwell approach the bar and wait to be acknow-ledged. The girl is absorbed in sending a text, seemingly oblivious to her new customers. Then she looks up, puts down the phone and adopts a bright smile.

– Yes, gents, she says.

– Is the boss about?

Her smile fades as she glances between the two men, tries to assess the nature of their visit.

– Who shall I say is asking?

– Police, says Ndekwe, and the smile slides from her face.

– Just a sec, she says.

She opens the hatch, steps out from behind the bar and slips through a door into the back quarters, returning a few seconds later with a glowering bull of a man, shirt sleeves rolled up over thick forearms that are tattooed black with jagged Celtic designs. Aggression radiates from him like an open furnace.

– Yeah?

This is obviously Antony, decides Ndekwe. He tries to imagine him rolling around on the floor, trading punches with a seventy-year-old man.

– Antony Russo?

The man looks from Ndekwe to Halliwell and then back again. He wears an expression of impatience bordering on fury.

– Why?

Ndekwe holds up his ID.

– Detective Sergeant Peter Ndekwe. Can I have a word?

– About what?

– Just a couple of things, won't take a minute. Ndekwe motions to a table. – Can we ... ?

Antony Russo plants his fists on his hips, dark flowers of sweat spreading beneath the arms of his shirt.

– Make it quick, he says. – I'm busy.

– All right, says Ndekwe. – Carlton McKenzie.

– What about him?

– He worked here, yeah? Him and Jack Shepherdson.

– Yeah.

– When did you first realize McKenzie was stealing from you?

– Stealing? Russo looks genuinely surprised. – Is that what he said?

– That's why you fired him, yeah?

Russo shakes his head.

– I didn't fire him. I fired the old geezer.

– Why?

– Cos he was a waste of space, innit. Falling about the place drunk half the time.

– And that's why he left?

– Can't have it, mate. Trying to run a business.

– So why did McKenzie leave?

– I don't fucking know, do I? I told that old mingebag to sling his hook and the boy just followed him out the door.

– Why?

Muscle-bunched shoulders shrug.

– How the fuck should I know?

– Would you say that they were close, the pair of them?

Russo looks puzzled. He shakes his head.

– How do you mean?

– Did they get on? Were they friends?

– Pair of arseholes together, if you ask me. He stabbed that boy on the news, yeah?

– Who did?

– Carlton.

– Did he?

– S'what the papers said, innit. Eighteen-year-old man. That's him, yeah? Russo looks at the two police officers. – That's what this is all about, yeah?

– How well did you know Carlton? asks Halliwell.

Russo begins gathering foam-stained glasses off a nearby table, stands them on the end of the bar.

– Look, mate, he says, he just worked here, that's all. We had a row and the both of them took off, him and the other muppet. End of. Now, if you don't mind ... things to do, yeah?

He gives a curt nod in the direction of the door.

Ndekwe doesn't move. He watches Russo bang the dirty glasses down into rows. Then he looks at the girl behind the bar. She is busying herself with a cloth, wiping down the pumps.

– OK, says Ndekwe. – Thank you, Mr Russo.

They leave the bar and head back towards the car. They shield their eyes from the sun and don't speak until they turn a corner and enter a long rectangle of shade beneath a building.

– What a fucking cock, says Halliwell.

– No manners, agrees Ndekwe.

Liverpool Street is pulsating with people. It is as though a bright white flare has been shot into the sky and saturated everything below with a dazzling brilliance. Ndekwe and Halliwell thread their way through the human traffic, passing in and out of shadows cast by looming concrete and glass, office block edifices and shop-front canopies; temporary patches of respite from the beating ball of fire above them.

– Tell you what, though, says Halliwell, smelled all right in there, eh? What was it, tomatoes or something?

– Something like that.

They pass a newsagent's and Halliwell asks Ndekwe to hold up a second. He darts inside and emerges a minute or so later with a newspaper, a bottle of water and a cheese salad sandwich encased in triangular plastic.

– Fuckin Hank Marvin, he says.

Once back in the car, Halliwell unfolds the newspaper onto his lap and eats his sandwich, catching the falling debris on the open pages. He picks a curl of grated cheese off the face of Fabio Capello and flicks it out of the window.

– Look at this joker, he remarks between mouthfuls. – Fucking England manager, him? Couldn't manage a decent meal.

Ndekwe doesn't reply. He's reading the case notes again, frowning, lost in thought.

– Should never have appointed him anyway, says Halliwell. – Never gonna work, having a foreigner as England boss. They ain't got it in here ... He thumps the heart side of his chest with a clenched fist. – He'll be on his peddler anyway, after that balls-up. What do you reckon, Pete?

– Huh? Sorry? Ndekwe hasn't been listening. He fastens the
file back together and slings it onto the back seat. – What you say,
Tom?

– Who would you have for the job? Halliwell plucks a slither of
cucumber from the remnants of the first half of his sandwich, drops
it back into the empty container, licks his fingers. – Gotta be Harry,
innit. Only name in the frame.

– Harry? Ndekwe shakes his head, puzzled. – Who's Harry?

– Redknapp!

– Who's that?

– Spurs boss.

Halliwell looks askance at the Detective Sergeant. Is he taking
the piss? he thinks. Then he breaks into a beaming grin. – Aw, for
fuck's sake! Not a Gooner, are ya?

– A what? For second he thinks Halliwell has said 'Aguna'. Then
he realizes that he's talking about football.

– Ah, right, says Ndekwe. – Yeah ... he'd be good.

But Halliwell can tell Ndekwe hasn't the faintest idea what he's
talking about. He decides not to pursue the matter. He places the
empty plastic triangle in the footwell and flicks the newspaper over
to the TV pages, scans the evening listings. Ross Kemp on *Gangs*;
Sky One, ten p.m. It's the one in El Salvador; one of the best in the
series.

Ndekwe gets on his mobile and calls Frampton, tells him to get
a copy of the keys for 34b Conway Court off the council offices and
to meet himself and Halliwell outside the flats at three.

Halliwell looks up from his paper. – Shepherdson's flat, yeah?

– Yeah, says Ndekwe.

Halliwell folds up his newspaper, punches a pre-set on the
radio. Some transatlantic voice gurgles on about a party in a park
and how to get your free tickets and Jessie J's gonna be there along
with JLS, Ne-Yo, the Black Eyed Peas and the Wanted and many
many more big names yet to be announced. The presenter tells them
that it's shaping up to be the main event of the summer, so call the

ticket line now and make sure you guarantee your place and don't
you dare miss it.

    – What a pile of bollocks. Halliwell snorts. – Black Eyed Bleeding
Peas. Why don't they get some decent bands on?

    Halliwell starts yapping on about the time he saw Paul Weller
at some outdoor festival, but Ndekwe doesn't answer. Instead, he
switches off the radio, puts the CD back on, turns the key in the
ignition and watches his mirror for a break in the traffic.

*… I thought it best to stay away for a bit. I kept out of the bookies
as well for a few days. I didn't reckon there was much chance of
smoothing it all out with Paulo. I know they didn't always get on,
him and Antony, but it was his brother at the end of the day and
you know what they're like with all that family honour lark, them
Italians. Hardly gunna take my side against his own flesh and blood,
was he? … So that was me on the Nat King Cole again. Well, actually,
I didn't even bother signing on, to be perfectly honest about the
deal. I couldn't be arsed with it all; all them questions and the filling
out of forms and all that palaver. I had a few bob stuck away and I
weren't in any great hurry to get back to the grindstone. I reckoned
the Irishman'd come up with summat sooner or later, a bit of work
here or there. Him and his brothers ran sites all over London. Always
a crane on the horizon, int there? Summat was bound to turn up,
sooner or later. I was all right for the time being, though; as long as
the Housing paid the rent, balls to it, I could make do on what I had.
I was glad of the bloody rest to be perfectly frank … it was me laddo
I felt sorry for, really. Carlton, y'know? Personally, I couldn't give a
monkey's about losing the job, that was the least of me worries. If I
had a shilling for every place I'd had the heave-ho from I'd be sitting
in a mansion. But Carlton was genuinely upset, was the lad. That
was his one source of income, that barman job. Losing it meant his
Jamaica plan was up the Swanee…*

    – *And you felt in some way responsible, did you?*

    – *I did feel a bit responsible, I must admit. Well, when I say* responsible, I mean ... well, it weren't my fault, obviously, but I did feel as though I should mebbe try and help him get back on his feet a bit. Maybe if I hadn't have got involved, him and Antony could have sorted it all out. Because, like I said, it wasn't me laddo who had his hand in the till. What I should have done in hindsight was blow the whistle on that Carmel lass. But then again, she would have only denied it, wouldn't she? Hardly likely to hold her hands up, was she? And then it'd be her word against mine. So I reckon it was sort of inevitable, whichever way you looked at the deal. Him losing his job, I mean. That Antony, he'd already made his mind up, y'know? Judge, jury and executioner ... anyroad, there was nowt I could do, for him or for me, for that matter. So after that I just ... I just went on the lash for a bit. That's always been me response to any minor setback – turn it into a cause for celebration. As one door closes another one swings open. Usually the door to the boozer. Just the way I am, like. Irrepressible. Always have been. Knock me down, I come bouncing back. Like a rubber ball I come bouncing back to you. You won't remember that one, will yer? Too young ...

– I don't, no.

– Bobby Vee. Marvellous singer. Anyway, I honestly thought that would be the last I saw of me laddo. Then a couple of nights later a load of change dropped out me trouser pocket and I dug me hand down the back of the couch to retrieve it all, like, and I come up with his phone. His mobile, like. He'd left it in the flat after that day. He'd come back to mine for a cup of tea and that and it must have dropped out of his jacket. I didn't hear it ringing or owt like that so it must have ran out of juice, or be set to silent or whatever. I don't know, I don't bother with the bloody things. So I reckoned he'd be back to pick it up at some point. Can't live without their bastard phones can they, these young kids? Typing out messages to someone every five seconds. Never saw the point of that lark. They were all at it, all them in that bar, tapping away on their bloody phones, bleeping away every two minutes. I used to say to them, him and that Carmel and that other lass who was behind the bar, I said why

*don't you just ring em up if you've got owt to say? Just ring em up
and say your piece and then you don't have to be stood tapping all
day. Must cost em a bastard fortune ... age we live in though, innit?
The age of instant communication ... Where was I? Oh aye, yeah
... yeah, so I went and had a drink. I went up to Camden to a pub I
used to use a few years back, a place called the Beatrice. Good little
boozer, good set of lads in there. Irish lads. Old school, yer know?
They used to have a Monday Club ... y'know, where everyone would
turn up on a Monday morning when they couldn't face work after
a weekend on the pop. Declan, the landlord, he'd put sausages and
roast taties out on the bar, gratis like, and there'd be people coming
and going all day. Had some good sessions in there. Anyroad, I heads
back up to that stretch and reacquaints meself. Some of em had flown
the coop or let go the rope like, but there was still a few familiar faces
on the team. Frank the Boot was still in there, this plasterer. I'd done
some graft with him a few years back, was quite pally with him at one
point. He couldn't work so much now on account of his foot, he's gorra
club foot, like, so he was more or less a permanent fixture in there.
There was him and the Burns brothers, Jim and Martin and Terry
Donlan and his lad and a few others I knew from way back. Most of em
getting on now, but still good company. They know how to have a good
drink, them Irish lads. That's where I went to shift the weed.*

– Weed? What weed?

*– Hold fire, I'll come to that bit in a minute. I'm trying to tell you
it all in order, like. As it all unfolded. How one thing led to another.
That way you'll get the proper picture ... but aye, it was all right in
there. A proper old-fashioned boozer. I'd rather drink round there
than on my patch, if truth be told. It's changed has the East End.
Like I said, I've lived in London donkey's years and I've never had
a spot of bother, not serious bother anyroad. Not until them little
bastards jumped me after I'd been in the Beatrice that night. That's
when I started carrying the knife about.*

*– And this is the same knife you say you used to stab Aaron
Stewart?*

– Aye. That's why I had it on me, for protection, like ... cos it's
all altered, the East End ... Bethnal Green especially. I've seen it
over the years, seen it happen with me own two eyes. Y'see, when I
first moved up this end it was like the last of the old proper London
communities. Everyone would get on ... for the most part, anyroad.
People think it's a load of old romance, but it's true. People had
respect for each other. And you had everyone, all races, creeds
and colours ... Africans, Jamaicans, Irish, Greeks, white, black,
brown, fucking sky-blue yeller with pink fucking polka dots. No big
deal. It makes me laugh when the papers are all banging on about
this multiculturalism lark, like it's summat they've just suddenly
invented. We've had multicultures for donkey's years. Ever since
I've lived round here, anyroad. Difference was, back then, everyone
just got on with it. Now it's like big major news all of a sudden. I
heard someone in the pub the other night, back up the road, like
... I don't agree with all this multiculturalism, they were saying.
Made me fucking laugh that did. Don't agree with multiculturalism.
Yeah, right. You might as well say you don't agree with the bastard
weather ... I'll tell you what I will say, though; it's the Asians who
are causing most the bother round our end now. I've always had
plenty of time for em meself, the Asians. Hard-working people, you
know? Keep themselves to themselves. Like the Chinese. Never heard
a peep out of em. The older generation I'm talking about here, the
parents, I mean, not the kids; their mothers and fathers and their
grandparents. Good as gold they was, always have been ... the biggest
difference now though, as far as I'm concerned, is the kids. The
mentality of em, like. I mean, there's always been gangs of kids and
all that, that's nowt new. But these little bastards now ... like I said to
yer before, they're totally without fear, these young kids. No parental
control, that's the problem. No respect for their elders. There was a
time when the elders would keep em all in check, especially among
the Asians. All gone clean out the window now. These young Asian
kids who knock about in all these gangs now ... thorough-bred
bastards, no two ways about it. There was a time when you'd never

see the young Asians on street corners and what have yer. They'd
all be inside doing their homework or helping their mams and dads
in the shops. Oh you can laugh, boyo, but it's the truth. These Asian
kids now, they're no different to the white kids or the black kids. In fact,
I think they're fucking worse, to be perfectly truthful about the deal.
Especially round our end. They all congregate round near the flats, on
the courtyard and up near the shops on a night. Big bloody gangs of
them wandering about till all hours ... especially on these warm nights.
You lot should be getting a grip of these bastards. Int there some law
about congregating together in big gangs? Unlawful congregation?

– Unlawful assembly ...

– That's the fella. Plenty of that round our end. Anyway, I
always made sure I was inside before dark. I never used to be
bothered, but this pal of mine who lives near me, he got rolled one
night, walking back from the pub. Turned a corner, no more than
twenty yards from his front door and he walks slap bang into a
mob of these little cunts. They give him a proper good kicking, went
through all his pockets, took his watch, the lot. Made a right mess
of him, the poor bastard. Hospital job. He was lucky really, could
have been a lot worse. I think the ale cushioned him from most of the
blows. Anyroad, I took that as a signal and I watched me step after
that. The bloke in the local corner shop, he's been done a couple of
times as well. Held a blade to his throat while they cleaned his till out
and took all the tabs. On a dinnertime this was, in the middle of the
fucking day. Broad bastard daylight. He closed the shop for a couple
of weeks and when he opened up they came back and they did him
again. Fucking marvellous, eh? He slung his hook, he'd had enough.
Don't blame him. Steel shutters up now. And then the same thing
happened to me. This is why I started carrying that knife about with
me. Listen, if you want to know the truth of the matter, I've never
carried a blade before in me life, not ever. When I was sailing in the
Med all the Spaniards on our crew, they'd all carry knives, every
one of em. First sign of bother and they'd whip their blades out. Like
fucking Zorro they was. Not my style, though. I'm an Englishman,

me, I fight with me bloody fists, fair and square. But I got cause to reconsider me position on that one, oh fuckin hell aye, the night I got attacked, like ...

– You were attacked?

– Here's the script; I'm in the Beatrice with a few of the lads, some of the Monday Club, a few others. We're all having a good drink and the afternoon goes on, and gradually everyone drifts off and there's just me an Frankie the Boot left on the pool table. And we have a few drinks like and a few games and then before I know it, the landlord is asking for our glasses and it's got dark outside. I never realized it was so late. Now, what I should have done that night is stopped at Frankie's. I should have just got me head down there and none of this would have happened. I could have mebbe avoided all this caper, and mebbe I wouldn't be sat here in front of you two now, admitting to murder. But there we go and here we fucking are, as me mother used to say ... So yeah ... I got a bus back home. I won't go near the underground after them bombs. Fuck that for a game of soldiers. Now, what I should have done is got off at Liverpool Street and then waited for a number 8 and that would have dropped me off on me doorstep, near enough. But I'd had a few drams and I wasn't really concentrating on the job in hand. I must have bobbed off, cos next thing I remember we're swinging by that big roundabout at Old Street. So I dropped anchor there, got me bearings and set off back to the barrio. On foot, like. That was me downfall. Tried to steer by the stars and ended up in the gutter, so to speak ... so anyroad, I'm coming down Shoreditch High Street heading towards Bethnal Green Road and they're all gathered outside this beer-off, these Asian lads. About half a dozen of em there is, all milling about, some of em on pushbikes. I have to step off the pavement to get round the lot of em ... I don't know if one of them bumped into me by accident or pushed me or I just lost me footing off the kerb, but I nearly went arse over tit into the road, nearly got fucking mowed down. This car just missed me by bastard inches ... whoa there, Grandad, one of them says and he catches holds of me by the shoulder and straightens me up, stops me hitting the deck. They all start laughing. Man's pissed up, I hear one of them say ... I don't say owt or even look back, just straighten me sails and point meself homeward bound. I know they're following me, though. I know it without even bothering to look back. The old sixth sense was going off like a car alarm. But there's plenty of folk about still, so I just kept walking, tried to keep a steady pace, like. If I was drunk before, I sobered up pretty fucking sharpish then, I can tell yer. You know when there's bother in the offing, don't yer? Yer get that crackle in the air, like electricity. Like how the sky above yer turns heavy before a storm. I could feel these bastards virtually breathing down me neck as I made me way up the Bethnal Green Road ... Right, so picture this, there's this takeaway coming up on me left, so I think OK, I'll nip in there and order some tucker, see if they keep walking. And they do. I see em all stride past as I'm stood ordering me grub. At the time I thought this was a smart move, cos I knew I couldn't outrun the bastards, not at my age and certainly not in the state I was in. Like I said, I'd had a good drink ... I comes out of there with me tray of chips and it looks like the coast is clear, so I peel off the main drag and head down the side streets. As I turn off, I see this pushbike, in me peripherals, like, whizzing behind me then stopping and doing a sharp about-turn. I get a shift on and cut through the houses round the back of Shacklewell Street. I'm no more than three or four minutes away from me quarters here, you understand. All I've got to do is get across this courtyard, down the next street and I'm at me front door ... Well, these pushbikes have come either side of me and skidded to a halt, cutting off me progress, like. I try to go one way and then the next, but the little bastards have got me boxed in. Then they all come strolling across from the other side of the yard. It's the same lot from before, no two ways about it ...

   – You recognized them?

   – Oh, it was the same merry band of brothers, no doubt about that. And I'm fucking snookered here, backed up against this wall next to these bins. They all surround me and one of them just says *wallet, money, watch. I try and swing for the nearest bastard but I'm a bit slow with the ale and he sees it coming from a mile away. He laughs and pins me back to the wall while all the other little cunts are going through me pockets. Well, all I've got on me is a bit of loose change and me door key, which gets slung on the deck, and me billfold which is empty, like. That gets pelted as well. I hold me hands up and I tell em, I say look, lads, I've got fuck all, same as you, come on, play the game ... One of em, the biggest one, grabs me wrist and says, get them rings off. He's tugging at me sovereigns, but they're not shifting. He's nearly riving me fucking arm off and I tell him, I say they won't come off, them, they're fast on. So he reaches down into his pants and ships out this big bloody meat cleaver. He grabs me by the wrist and slams me arm down onto the top of this bin and says hold him, hold him still. I'm screaming blue fucking murder by this point, you understand. One of them gives me a dig in the guts and another one of them clamps his hand round me mouth. I'm trying to pull meself free, but there's about three of them got me by the arms and neck, slamming me right up against the wall with another one pinning me fucking arm down on top of these bins ... Then all of a sudden I hear these car doors slam and I'm blinded by this swirling blue light. These little bastards let go of me and they're off like a shot, just like that, vamoosed, off like a robber's dog. I've slid down this wall and I'm on me arse with a uniform stood over me asking if I'm all right ... Aye, I'm fucking champion, I tell him ... I tell yer, if your lot hadn't have turned up I'd have been auditioning for pantomime by now. Captain fucking Hook ... This officer helps me up and asks me if I knew em or if I'd recognize em again and all that deal. His mate, the one who had set off chasing them, he comes back and gets on his radio. Turns out these coppers had been trailing these little cunts all night and they'd spot-balled them all following me into the courtyard and tippled there was summat going off ... They ask me if I want a lift home and I say no, I'm all right, I only live round the corner ... I get back home and slam the door shut behind me and slide all the bolts across. Then I pour meself a dram, and sit meself down*

on the couch, try to compose meself. Jesus Christ, me heart was
banging like a shithouse door in a gale ...
   – Shake you up, did it?
   – Ey, listen, I'm no dolly mixture, pal, you know what I mean?
I been round the world more times than Christopher fucking
Columbus, me. I've had more tear-ups than I care to remember
and most of em I walked away from without a mark, I kid you not.
I've never been in the habit of starting fights, but I've finished a
few bastards. Oh, I can look after meself, don't you worry about
that, amigo. But I don't mind admitting, my arse went that night.
Properly went ... cos he would have chopped me fucking hand off, no
doubt about it, chopped the bastard clean off. Like cutting up a leg of
lamb. These kids nowadays, they're ... well, I was gonna say they're
crackers. But that dunt really cover it. A mad dog'll bite yer hand if
you try and pat it, but if you give it a wide berth it won't bother yer,
nine times out of ten. These bastards, though, they'll hunt you down
in packs and chop you up into tiny bits. Kill yer soon as look at yer.
They're evil, simple as that. Pure fucking evil, in my book. Anyway,
that night, I slept on the couch with a bread knife by me side. And I
never left the house without it again. Kept it in me inside pocket, like,
tucked away in me jacket ...

■ ■ ■ ■ ■

Gorman takes the McKenzie interview down to the motor and
continues to listens as he drives down the Hackney Road.
   Un-deck-way, he says to himself. *Un-deck-way, un-deck-way,*
un-deck-way.
   Un-deck-way, with his thoughtful pauses and his silly
questions.
   Un-deck-way, with his shiny-arsed suits and his stupid little
shiny glasses.
   Un-fucking-deck-way, with his big serious shiny face that never
cracks a fucking smile.

Un-deck-way.

Gorman turns the volume up full and wills the cars in front of him to get a bloody move on.

... Jack lived on the fifth floor of a tower block round the back of Bethnal Green Road. I helped him up the stairwell an into his crib. I was expecting some proper grotty dive, man, a sink full of dirty pots an trash an empty beer bottles everywhere, but it weren't even half as bad as I expected, y'know? There was a stink of stale tobacco in the front room, true, but the gaff itself was spotless; clean clothes ironed and folded into a neat stack on the settee, a pair of slippers by the gas fire, socks and shirts hung over the radiators to dry. All the furniture was old and battered, but the place was clean and tidy. I was surprised at that. I got the man sat down in an armchair and unwrapped the tea towel from his hand. It had stopped bleeding but you could see the cut, this flap of skin between the finger and thumb, stuck down with dried blood. Jack held up his hand and looked at it, all surprised, like he just noticed it for the first time. He was still real drunk. I could smell it on him. You better put something on that, bruv, I told him. I asked him if he had any plasters. He just sorta shrugged and nodded into the kitchen. Might be one in there, he said. I looked everywhere, through all the kitchen drawers and cupboards, but I couldn't find no plasters. I couldn't find much of anything else either. Man didn't have no proper food in the place or nothing, just a few tins of beans, a half-bottle of rum an a box of teabags. Yorkshire Tea. I opened the fridge door an that was sad an empty too, just a carton of milk an a lump of yellow cheese that looked like it had been there for time. I went through to the bathroom but them cupboards was bare as well, a squeezed out tube of toothpaste an a tired-looking brush, some tubes of ointment, a few rusting razors an a can of shaving cream. It was all clean though, spotless, same as the kitchen. I pulled off a few handfuls of paper, came back through to the living room an wrapped it all round Jack's hand. Yo, Jack, I said, you got a cleaning lady come round here? He didn't say nothing, but

pointed to a cupboard over the other side of the room. Get us that tin out that sideboard, he said. I open up the doors an sure enough there was this old biscuit tin sat there, one of them big round ones like you get at Christmas. I brings it over to the settee and Jack gets the lid off an straight away I smell it; weed, strong weed. Skunk, it smelled like. Jack started rolling a joint. I ain't gonna lie, I was surprised. Old guy like that. He told me to make a cup of tea, so I filled the kettle an flicked it on then went back through. While Jack rolled his smoke I went over to look at the pictures he had hanging on his wall. There was a few framed photos of ships an what looked like maps, like old-fashioned maps of foreign countries an that. There was a photo of a boy about four or five years old, stood in a back garden with a football under his arm. Who's that? I asked him. That's my lad, he said. I tried to see some family resemblance but it was hard to match up the sweet-faced boy in this photo with the drunken old dog on the sofa. I reckoned the photo must have been taken way back in the day. It looked old, all faded an that. He grown up now, yeah? I say, but Jack never heard me or never answered at any rate, concentrating on building his smoke. There was another photo; some guy in a black an white shirt holding up a big trophy. It said at the bottom: HULL FC, CHALLENGE CUP WINNERS 1981. I remember him saying he was from a place called Hull. I never even heard of it, I never knew about it or met anyone from round there. That your team, yeah? I asked. Oh aye, yeah, he said, black and white through and through, me. I thought Hull FC was a football team but he said it was rugby league. Man's game, he said. There was another picture next to it, some sharp looking dude in a suit leaning in a doorway, his hands in his pockets. Above his head was a sign that said DIVORCE YOUR LOVED ONE WITH DIGNITY. I asked him who it was and he was all shocked that I didn't know. Frank Sinatra, he said, greatest singer who ever lived. I thought he was some actor or something. I asked if he was dead and Jack says I hope so, they fucking buried him. An he starts chuckling away to himself as he licks his smoke together, jams it in his mouth an blazes up. It got me heated, the way he just started laughing like that, giggling like a stupid little girl. Yeah, well, glad you think it's funny, man, I told him. I just lost my flippin job back there. Fuck it, he said, just get another one. Jack took a few big tokes and offered the smoke over, but I told him I don't smoke that shit, mate. What, he says, a black man who don't smoke weed? You'll be fucked in Jamaica then, they all smoke it out there. I proper lost it for real then, started yelling at him, telling him what a stupid old fuck-up he was an how he'd ruined everything for me. He climbed out of the armchair and up on his feet, held his fists up like a boxer. Come on then, bastard, he says, an the crazy old fool come shuffling forward, his head bobbing up and down, throwing his jab like he Muhammad Ali. I just burst out laughing. Sit down, Jack, I said. And he did. He fell back down into his armchair and carried on sucking on his spliff. I sat down on the sofa opposite him and tried to figure out what I was gonna do. It was a bleak-looking sketch, though. The job was gone, no doubt about that. No amount of pleading to Paulo was gonna get me off the hook with this one.

– You didn't try and get your job back then?

– I belled the bar up on my phone, figuring if Antony answered I'd just kill the call, but Chantelle picked up an she tell me the man gone crazy, smashed up the kitchen then bounced straight out of there baying for blood. She said to leave it for a good few days cos the man was off the hook. After I hung up I felt lower than I ever felt before in my life. I went over to the window an stared down at all the rooftops and back yards an streets stretching out for miles and miles an I thought rah, I ain't never getting out of here, man. I ain't never gonna get to Montego Bay. This is all your flippin fault, I said to Jack. But the man was sparked out in the armchair, the smoke dangling from his fingers, ash dropping onto the carpet. I took it from him and put it out in the ashtray and then I got out of there. There was some Bangladeshi boys round the front doorway; just baby soldiers, but they stared at me hard. Bethnal Green, innit. Brick Lane. They run tings round there. It weren't healthy for me to be too visible round them ends, so I got off double quick. It was only when I

got to the edge of the Crown that I realized I'd left my flippin phone
at Jack's place. But I couldn't trek all that way back for it just then. I
reckoned I'd go back for it the next day. I had a party to go to, innit ...

   – This is your mum's birthday party? Her fortieth?

   – Yeah, the big four-o. The original plot was to have the party
in the flat, just a few close family an friends, but I should have
known it weren't ever gonna stay a low-key thing once Melissa got
on it. Before too long I had bare peeps coming up to me an saying
yo, Kez, where my invite to Janine's party? So I had to rethink the
original plan. No way was everyone gonna fit in our flat. So I went
to see Harry at the Centre an asked if we could have the back room
for the night an he said yeah it was cool. So I sent the word round
an that's what we did. Me an my auntie Sharon an Melissa made a
big banner saying HAPPY 40th JANINE! an we hung it up in the
back room. Then we had to get Mum out of the flat. At first she said
she just wanted to stay in and chill in front of the box, but Sharon
dragged her out an led her down to the Centre where everyone was
waiting. You should have seen her face when she saw that banner an
everyone stood there cheering guv; she nearly had about ten heart
attacks. It was a sick party, though, no doubt about that. Mum was
well happy to see everyone there. Harry brought his system down an
we had a massive night, all the old eighties tunes for my mum an her
mates an then all the youngers taking turns on getting on the mic an
spitting their bars. It was a happy time, but like most happy times
it wasn't too long before some prick had to go an cause a disruption.
Knowledge, I'm talking about. Aaron Stewart, yeah? The man with
the knife in his heart. Called himself Knowledge, but the man was
Aaron to me. Knew the man for time, from the school, innit. Three
years ago me an him were soldiers together.

   – Doing what?

   – All the usual nonsense ... But like I said, yeah, after Joseph
I got off from that life permanent. But Aaron or Knowledge or
whatever he call himself, he was the big name now, number one man
in the zones, innit. Sat licking stone all day in them empty houses

across the way, sending all the youngers out to do his shit for him.
Big gangsta man, yeah? I heard from people how he supposed to
have done this an that. Yeah, big fuckin man, Knowledge. You know
him, anyway. You know what he done. Him an his followers spread
themselves out in the corner with their matching hats an kicks, all
their bling an that. Living fools, seriously. I remember thinking, rah,
I could take one of them chains clean off their neck an fly to Jamaica
ten times over.

– You already had beef with him?

– He had beef with everyone. He had beef with the world.
Melissa, though, her an her dumb mates were all over these fools.
I told her every time, man, they is just flippin idiots. Bare living
idiots. I got on with my evening an tried to blank them out, but sure
enough one of em comes bouncing over an starts chatting shit. It was
Bam Bam, little man from across the way. Known him for time. He
was like yo, Kez, what's happening? Me an him start yapping about
this an that an eventually a few of these other boys come drifting
over. I knew one or two of them from road, some of them from back
at the school an I nodded at them but they just look at me cold. I
just blanked them all and talked to Bam Bam, telling him about the
madness of the day an how I lost my job an that. Then the main
man comes over with a few more of his boys and they're all stood
around me. I'm surrounded before I know it, ya get me guv? What's
happening, Kez, he says. Mum's party, innit, I tell him. Which one's
your mum? says this other prick. There, I say, pointing over to the
dance floor where my mum an auntie Sharon are dancing with the
youngers. Your mum ain't bad for an old gyal, he says. I look at him
stern, but he just smiles at me an raises his eyebrows, like you got
something to say, bruv? She a MILF for real, says Knowledge an all
his crew fall about sniggering. I was in a mind to step to this prick.
I knew all about his hype an that but I didn't care, to me he was the
same skinny little prick from back in the day. I didn't give a fuck
about who he was or who he thought he was or nothing. But just
as I open my mouth old Harry come over and put his hand on the

boy's shoulder. *Aaron*, he says to him, *this be a private gathering. Take your friends and leave now.* Aaron push Harry's hand away an his crew all bristle up an assume battle position, but Harry just smile in that slow gentle way of his an stand his ground. Harry is a churchgoing man, true, but wasn't always so. Man was serious back in his time, come from a big family, proper Yardie, ya get me? Mr Knowledge stroke Aaron knew this. For all his flexing, I knew he had enough knowledge not to step to the H-bomb. Aaron an his little crew throw some shapes an growl some threats, but Harry just keep saying *leave now, you leave now*, walking them slowly towards the door an sure enough they all start to slope off. Bam Bam catches my eye an shrugs. He was like, *in a bit, Kez, yeah?* I'm like, *yeah, whatever.* Melissa grabs my arm as I'm turning away. *Why you do that*, she says, *why the fuck you do that? Those are my friends*, she's saying. *Dickhead! You hyping yourself up to my friends! What the fuck?* I laugh at her an she gets off after Aaron an his crew. Her mate Ella shoots me dead eyes an then she gets off as well. Good riddance, I think. If they wanna roll with those dicks then that's their flippin lookout.

– And this is where it started, your fallout with Aaron Stewart?

– Nah, it had been bubbling under for time. I nearly went after her, though, Melissa. I should have done, should have made her stay put with me, but then I had Harry coming across and he was in my ear. *Carlton*, he said, *I don't want those boys in here, seen? I know H*, I say, *I know. Thank you.* I look across at my mum an all her mates and some of their kids, dancing round with their bottles of beer to their Beyoncé an Madonna an whatever. My mum was always happiest when the family was together and having a good time. I was glad she was happy. I was glad, too, that Aaron had got off without any drama. I didn't like the prick an he didn't like me, true. But I was not planning on killing him then. That part came later. An believe me guv if I could kill the fucker twice I would totally do it, trust me …

■ ■ ■ ■ ■

Gorman arrives at the junction of Queensbridge Road and Hackney Road and parks up near the Costcutter. He kills the engine and silences the voice of Carlton McKenzie.

The Search Team has already cordoned off the pavement on the other side of the road and the divers are getting kitted up. That's one job Gorman could not do for love nor money, swimming about in that lot all day. Bad enough, he thinks, dealing with all the human shit on ground level.

He dials Ndekwe on his mobile. It rings and rings and rings. Ndekwe answers just as Gorman is about to hang up.

– Sir?

– Where are you? Gorman can hear a car engine and muted music in the background.

– Just coming off Old Street. What's up?

– How you getting on? Any sign of the cock-eyed cavalier?

– No, he wasn't at the address. But I spoke to the newsagent and we've just been to see Russo.

– Russo? Gorman struggles to place the name.

– Antony Russo. I think Shepherdson was lying about that part.

– What part?

– The fight in the bar. He said on the CD ...

– The CD? Gorman grimaces. – You still listening to that? Get back onto the Crown Heights and find Isaacs!

– Yeah, we will, just checking a few things out ...

– What do you mean? Checking what out? Hasn't Halliwell brought you up to speed?

– Yeah, but I need to make sure ...

– Need to make sure about what? We need to charge McKenzie asap. Tick tock, tick tock. Gorman realizes he is wagging his finger from side to side like a metronome and stops, faintly embarrassed.

– I just need the full picture, sir, says Ndekwe. – I can listen to this as we're buzzing around, yeah? It's not a problem, trust me.

Not a problem? Trust him? Who the fuck did this joker think he was talking to? Did he think he was selling fucking life insurance in a call centre? This was a murder investigation, not lunchtime at Nando's. Gorman swallows down the hard lump of anger that is rising in his throat. He decides that his new fast-tracked superstar DS is in need of a swift reminder of the pecking order here at his new-found home across the river.

– Detective Sergeant, he says, I don't think you appreciate the full ...

A sudden high-pitched whine. Gorman winces, pulls the phone away from his ear then shouts into the mouthpiece.

– Hello? Hello? Hello?

Ndekwe's voice tiny under an avalanche of static:

– Can't hear you, sir. Talk when I get back, yeah?

– DETECTIVE SERGEANT UNDECKAWAY!

The line goes dead.

Gorman jabs at the recall button, brings the phone back up to his ear.

– Answer your phone! ANSWER YOUR FUCKING PHONE!

An automated voice invites Gorman to please leave a message after the tone. Gorman flings the mobile down onto the passenger seat.

– ARROGANT FUCKING COON!

He grips the wheel and breathes through gritted teeth. Then he picks the phone up and studies the display before placing it back to his ear. Dead. He presses the END CALL switch once, twice, then slides the phone back into his pocket before smoothing down the hair across the back of his head, straightening his tie in the rear-view mirror and getting out of the car.

■ ■ ■ ■ ■

Ndekwe can tell that Halliwell isn't too impressed with the stunt he pulled with the mobile. The Detective Constable doesn't say anything, but sits resolute, arms folded, body angled away, pointedly gazing out of the window. Just like Sonia when they were driving back from the airport; a silence that screams.

Ndekwe is tempted to pull his Detective Constable up, tell him to get the fuck over himself. But he decides against it. He can't be having any distractions or petty dramas while he's getting up to speed. And besides, it isn't the thumbnail scraped across the mobile mouthpiece that has given Halliwell the hump. Ndekwe knows the score; Halliwell feels slighted because Ndekwe is listening back to the Shepherdson interview. He knows how it must look; that he doesn't trust the judgement of his colleague, that he's looking for something that Halliwell has somehow missed. But it isn't about that. Ndekwe just likes to get everything first hand, straight from the proverbial. And once he's heard both Shepherdson and McKenzie's words for himself, Ndekwe can start to decide how he feels about things. It's nothing personal. This is how he operates. And if Halliwell is going to work with him, then he might as well get used to it from day one. Anyway, reasons Ndekwe, they have until Wednesday. Obviously Gorman wants to get it all boxed as soon as possible; slap a charge on McKenzie and then take everyone down the boozer for a jolly-up. Ndekwe thinks that McKenzie probably did murder Aaron Stewart. If a young man dies on a London council estate then it's odds-on that another young man has killed him. Short odds are fine if you're a gambler. But Ndekwe has no gut instinct, he has never had a hunch and he doesn't trust second-hand information.

He has to hear everything for himself.

... So yeah, me laddo turns up a few days after, and as it happened his timing was spot on. Or so I thought at the time. Turned out to be a right balls-up in the end. Well, it was a bloody disaster, if truth be told. But let's have it right, it weren't entirely my fault. Eighteen years old and he can't fill in a bloody betting slip? I didn't think for

one second he was that bloody clueless. Well you wouldn't, would yer? I just naturally assumed he knew what he was doing. I should have checked, though. Should have filled it out for him, the stupid little twat ...

– What happened?

– What happened was the Irishman had tipped me the wink about this horse. Absolutely nailed on, he said. I had a look in the paper and it looked all right, course and distance and what have yer. Top weight. Looked proper, no doubt about it. Nowt else on the track to touch it either, not in that meet anyroad. Aye, it looked kosher ... Golden Coast, it was called. Me laddo got all excited, saying yeah, Golden Coast, like Montego Bay. Once he got that in his head there was no stopping him. I told him not to go mad on it, but he was straight down to the hole in the wall and pulled out the maximum he could. I think it was a few hundred quid. I did remind him; I said they're only dumb animals, yer know. Owt could happen, I said. They can get in each other's road and cockle over, like. They can get up that morning and just not be in the mood. No such thing as a dead cert, I told him. And I speak from bitter bloody experience, oh aye. But he wasn't listening, me laddo, he was all excited and pumped up, convinced himself he was about to make his fortune. Optimism, it's a wonderful thing ... So anyroad, we gets in the bookies and we're a couple of races off ours so I runs him through the ropes. It was obvious he'd never had a bet before, didn't have a clue how the odds worked or owt like that. I don't think he'd even stepped foot in a betting shop before ... He certainly never even knew how to put a bastard bet on ... but lo and behold, he goes and picks the winner out in the race before ours and so now he's thinking he's got the gift of second sight. Thinks it's as easy as that, thinks all you have to do is just pick one with a shirt you like or a fancy name and off you pop. I told him to back ours each way, told him twice in fact. But he couldn't get the slip filled out quick enough and before I could check what he'd written he'd handed it over to the lass behind the counter, along with his money. All his bloody bankroll. I think he put about three hundred quid on it. Fuckin madness, brother. I should have stopped him. I should have looked what he'd put on the slip. But he's bouncing about like a jack in a box and the entire betting shop's taking an interest now ... It gets straight up, this horse, this Golden Coast. I thought it had gone too soon. It didn't look like it had enough in the tank, but I'm thinking, come on, just hang on in there, boyo, and the bastard creeps up steady and then keeps right on the shoulder of the favourite all the way round. The jockey's giving it plenty of whip and I'm thinking go on, yer bastard, go on, just hang on in there and that's how they come in, Golden Coast gets second ... I'm dancing about like a fucking loon but then I sees me laddo's face and I know summat's up. He looked devastated, like he was gonna spew ... What the fuck's up with you, soppy bollocks, I say. I have a look at his slip and I can't believe it. He's got it to win. Golden Coast – winner, it says. Fucking unbelievable. I told him, I swear on my grandbain's life, I told him at least three times – back it each way, I said. Fourteen to one! Each way! I did tell the silly little twat, but he'd been like yeah yeah yeah, the exact way he goes when he's not bastard listening ... So that was it, half his savings up the fucking spout.

– And how did he feel about that?

– He was far from fucking happy, obviously. He started demanding I pay him back out of my winnings, but I'd only had a tenner each way. He's making a right scene, shouting and bawling and carrying on. In the end the manager came over and asked us to keep it down or take it outside, like. Well, me laddo just storms out and I'm following him down the street like a pie-can, trying to tell him I'd get him his money back, no problemo. But he wasn't listening. He was straight off marching down the road and he wouldn't listen to a word I was saying ...

■ ■ ■ ■ ■

Gorman leans forward to watch the frogman's head disappear down the hole and then retreats three steps back when the stench hits his nostrils. The guts of London exposed. And that sun blazing away overhead doesn't help either. It doesn't seem to bother Bob Croft, though, the USCCT supervisor; he just stands there chewing on a Gregg's steak bake as he peers down into the murky bowels of E2.

– If he dropped it near the Crown Heights and it got down into the pipe, there's a fair chance it'll stop here, he says. He points up the road. – Bleeding big fatberg up there. About half a ton's worth. You'd need an Exocet missile to get through that fucker.

Gorman feels an involuntary shudder travel down his spine and agitate his stomach. He's seen those fatbergs on the training videos; huge accumulated walls of solidified grease and food and tissue and excrement, the churned result of everyday debris tipped down the domestic sinks and bathtubs and toilets of London. Congealed boulders of waste plugging the arteries of the city.

– Good job we're not doing this on a Sunday, remarks Bob. – All them Ruby Murrays. I tell ya, Graham, if every curry house down Brick Lane flushed its bog at the same time we'd have a fucking fountain of vindaloo on every street corner from here to bleeding Dalston.

It was a line Gorman had heard him spin a thousand times before, but he chuckled along anyway. Christ knows how he could eat, though, stood over that lot. One time Croft had brought up a dead rat on a spade to show him, stomach bloated with sewer gas and shitty water. Biggest rat he'd ever seen, like a small dog it was. No way could Gorman do that job.

Gorman shoots the fetid breeze with Croft until he's satisfied that he's shown enough of his face, then he jumps into the motor and heads back to the station. His finger hovers above the PLAY button but he decides to give himself a rest from the repeated testimony of Mr Carlton Nesta McKenzie. Gorman considers self-doubt to be a weakness and besides, he thinks, he's had quite enough of their mob for one day. He skips through the radio stations, but encounters grinding tedium at every push of the button; a middle-aged Scottish man on Radio 2 chuckling away about his new golf clubs, some dull news feature about global warming on Radio 4, Katy Perry on Capital singing about California Girls for what seemed like the fourteenth time that day.

That's what I need, thinks Gorman; a holiday. He hasn't had a proper break in three years. A Thomas Cook sign whips past his window. He decides to pop in and see if there are any last-minute deals to be had. Take a few brochures home for the wife, have a look through them after dinner. She deserves a break, he reasons. They both do. It would be nice to get away, from London, from teenage savages sticking holes in each other, from the incompetent officers who chase them around their shithole estates.

This fucking job, thinks Gorman.

He goes into the travel shop and selects a few brochures from the shelves. Then he drives back to the station, parks up and sits in the car, flicks through the various deals and destinations.

Welcome to the Caribbean.

He pauses at the Sunburst Deal of the Month: fourteen days at Runaway Bay, an all-inclusive four-star resort and spa situated on the northern coast of Jamaica that offers a tranquil haven for the more discerning sun seeker; one whose hectic lifestyle means they truly appreciate the genuine joy of escaping from it all. That sounds the very fucking ticket, thinks Gorman. Top-quality bars and restaurants, shops laden with designer goods. That's the missus sorted then. An eighteen-hole PGA golf course. That's Gorman sorted. Water sports and scuba diving available daily, he reads. The perfect late deal for those looking for a quick getaway, with prices starting from just £985.

Not bad, thinks Gorman. Could be worse. Could be a lot worse.

There is a photo-spread of a shimmering azure swimming pool surrounded by white umbrellas, then a row of lush green treetops and the ocean and mountains in miniature beyond. Gorman imagines himself slap bang in the middle of it all, his pink bulk stretched out on a sun-lounger, the lilt of music on the breeze, a large, fruit-laden cocktail at his elbow.

Oh yes. That would do him blinding.

The digits on the dashboard tell him its 14:32. Gorman decides to have another quick listen to the boy's interview before he heads back inside. Can't be too careful, he reasons. He tilts the seat back and adjusts the sun visor to keep the glare out of his eyes. The travel brochure slides down his chest and into his lap. He folds down the corner of the page that marks Runaway Bay and tosses it onto the passenger seat. He lets the window down a touch to allow in some air, stifles a yawn and tries to concentrate on words said just twenty-four hours previously.

... So job number one for the next day was to go round to Jack's an get my phone back before the old fool take it down the Cash Converters, innit. But there was no one round there or the next day or the next day either. He finally answered his buzzer about, what ... three or four days later, I think. Something like that. I was expecting the man to be subdued after the previous drama, but he was hopping about with bare excitement, clapping his hands together and giggling away like a big kid. It's the big'un, Carlton, he says, today is the fuckin day! Jack tells me that his man with the horses has given him the biggest tip yet, the once in a lifetime absolute sure-fire winner, no doubt about it. So I thought yeah, all right, fuck it, went down to the cashpoint and got out the maximum allowed, which was £300. More than half my Montego Bay stash. Course I knew it was madness, deep down I knew that. But Jack was strong on this one, believe. Could not lose, he said. Could not lose. Rock solid certain ting, ya get me? Anyway, I ain't never been in no betting shop up until that day an I ain't ever going back in one again guv, trust me.

– You didn't win then?

– I should have known as soon as I stepped in the place that this was no fast-track way to getting rich. Every man in there was old an skanky looking an dressed like a scarecrow, cept for a team of stern-faced Yardie men over in the corner who looked like they were having some little pow-wow of their own, them being the

only ones who didn't have their heads tilted back in front of the ten thousand TVs banked along the wall. No man making his million in this sad little set-up. The place stank of bare desperation; all these old mans stood looking blank-eyed at the screens or else running their pencils up an down their newspapers like they was trying to work out some kind of puzzle, which in fact they was, yeah, the get rich quick puzzle, the one puzzle that puzzles every player in the city, true. I kept my hand tight gripped round my roll in my jacket pocket. I still couldn't believe I had let this old fool talk me into this lame plan. I remember the first time I noticed him looking down the lists of horses in the back pages of the paper an him giving it the big one about how this horse was a dead certainty an how this other horse over here was only fit for the knacker's yard an all that chat. Hey, Jack, I asked him, how come you know so much about betting on horses an you still washing glasses in kitchens? How come you ain't rolling round in some big fancy set of wheels, batting off the pussy an lighting up your smokes with fifty pound notes? How come that ain't happened yet, Jack? You tell me you been playing the horses all your natural life, yet here you still is without a pot to piss in, ya get me? So he starts banging on about all the money he's won over the years and how he pissed it all up the wall, about human nature and how easy it is to mess things up when you think you on a roll, how you can start thinking you is bulletproof an then the next thing you waking up in an alley with empty pockets and a banging head. Human nature, kid, he'd say. Human nature is weak by default. But now all that chat was forgotten. Now he was just full of bare excitement. Look, he says, pointing to the screen, that horse at the top of the list, Crown Majestic, he's the favourite. That's why he's got odds of two to one. You know about gambling, yeah? You bet on horses?

– Not me. I'm too mean.

– Two to one. Two slash one, see? That means if you bet one pound on him and he wins it then you get two pounds back. That is called short odds, he explains, so that means he's the one most likely to win the race. How you get to be the favourite, I ask, how do *they know what the horse gonna do before he do it? Jack said that if the gee-gee has run round the track in a certain way before than he should do it again, just the same. The way I saw it they all dumb animals. How you know the horse ain't thinking nah, man, today I gonna chill, I ain't busting my balls running round no track. I knew it all had the stink of horse-shit about it, an I never thought I'd see the time when I was handing over my hard-earned cash to some lady behind a betting shop counter. But I was in a corner guv, ya get me? Back against the wall an that. An besides, as I kept reminding to myself, it had worked before, yeah? The man had given out good info before, yeah? Paulo an them big fistful of paper, man. I seen it. Rolls and rolls of fifties, man. I wanted a piece of that action, damn right. Every other way of making money had been a dead end. This was it, last throw of the dice, ya get me?*

– So what happened? Fall over and break its leg, did it?

– Our boy Golden Coast was in the four forty-five. We sat down to watch the race before that one. Well, Jack sat down, I was too heated to settle, too nervous, so I just stood there jigging up and down on my heels, my belly starting to churn round like the machines in the launderette next door. We watched the horses being walked round as the names and numbers appeared beneath them. Jack asked me who I fancied. I studied each horse as it trotted round, but I didn't know what I was supposed to be looking for. Except for the colours of the shirts I could not find any true way to tell them apart. They all looked like so powerful, like machines made out of bare muscle. I picked out one called Magic Mountain, which was odds of five slash two. The jockey was wearing a green shirt with a gold X on the back, which I figured could be a lucky sign. Flag of Jamaica, ya get me? Or as near as dammit anyway. That one, I said to Jack. Magic Mountain. That's my boy. The bell rang and they shot out of the cages, all keeping in a tight pack right up to the first curve an then a few of them started to pull away from the rest an I saw Magic Mountain's gold X was among them, third from the front, hooves kicking up the dirt, an before I knew it I was jumping up and

down and hollering. The Yardie men in the corner were all looking round at the rumpus but I didn't care. Magic Mountain, number five horse, put bare daylight between him an the rest of the pack. I kept one eye on the numbers at the bottom of the screen, just like Jack showed me. It was like ... 3 – 7 – 5 ... then ... 3 – 5– 7 ... then it was ... 3 – 5 – 4 ... I was like, COME ON, MAGIC MOUNTAIN! ... 5 – 3 – 4 ... Rah, first place! First place by a million miles! He smashed it guv, totally smashed it! Jack was laughing away at me leaping about and going crazy an this other old timer came up an slapped me on the back and said well done, boy, like it was me who had run round the track. You can pick em, kid, says Jack, you can pick em all right. Jack fetch us two betting slips an says to fill it out for each way, name of the horse and time and place of the race. Damn right, I told him, each and every way. All the way to Montego Bay! I give up the slip an the money to the girl behind the counter. I felt a bit sick when I done that. Three hundred bar, man, rah, my pocket felt very light after that, trust me, though. The girl behind the counter, she didn't seem to feel no way about it, just licked her finger and flicked through the notes, put the slip into the machine, tore the top part off an hand it back over. I kissed it an held it tight. My ticket to better times. Better times an a better place. Montego Bay! Believe! Fourteen to one, said Jack. I didn't think I was gonna be able to watch the action unfold, I was that jumpy and nervous. I had to force my feet to stay rooted to the spot when all they wanted to do was leap over the counter and snatch my money back off the lady. I could feel the sweat starting to trickle down my back. By the time the horses had been slammed in the cages I felt like I was gonna throw up my guts. The room seemed to shrink in on me an the man's voice coming off the TV was all like wah wah wah, like nonsense jabber. Anyway, finally they get off, yeah? I was looking for the red and white checks of the boy on Golden Coast, but I couldn't see him nowhere. Then the pack started to spread out an I saw our boy somewhere in the middle, Golden Coast, number six horse. All I wanted was to see that number pop up on the bottom of the screen an then bang, there it was, yes, number *six, third place. I kept switching my eyes from the pack of horses to the numbers below them, just trying to make that flippin number six move an then rah, second place! An that's where it stayed all round the race an as they all went past the finish line. Second fucking place. It was like my world had just flippin collapsed guv. I felt like I was gonna be sick. Jack, though, he's up on his feet, dancing about like a flippin crazy man, jumping up and down and laughing his head off. He slaps me on the back, all smiles, but then he sees my face and he's like, what? What? You fucking prick, I told him. That was half my flippin money! He was looking all puzzled. What you on about? he says. We won! It fucking lost! I shout at him. All the betting shop is staring at us now. All the old geezers an the people behind the counter an even the Yardie men in the corner are forgetting about their meeting thinking yo, here's some drama unfolding, ya get me. Each way! he says. I told you! Do it each way! Each way? I say, what the fuck is each way? Except I was yelling at the man now, ya get me? Proper losing my temper. He snatches the paper out my hand an stares at it. Oh, I don't believe it, he says. I don't fuckin believe it. You daft get, he says. He starts trying to explain this each way business, but I didn't want to hear it. All I knew was that my money was gone, an I was back to square flippin one, for real. I said to him, don't say nothing to me, man. I'm serious, Jack, I said. Don't say one flippin word. I couldn't believe it guv. That stupid old fool. I won't even lie, I felt like stabbing the man in the flippin face ...*

■ ■ ■ ■ ■

Gorman is asleep, dreaming. In his dream, he is riding a horse in the Grand National. It is a bright sunny day and he is coming last, the rest of the pack streaming away from him, dots of coloured silk getting smaller into the distance. He is riding his horse for all he is worth, stinging its haunches with his whip and digging his heels into its flanks but the beast is labouring badly under his weight. It starts to slow down. The crowd are screaming from the stands, but it's no use; Gorman can feel the horse's legs buckle underneath him. As the horse crumples to the ground and the crowd begins to throw missiles onto the track he sees the last of the pack spin upside down and disappear round the bend as he waits for the baked, hard ground to meet his back.

A sudden rapping of knuckles upon glass.

– Rise and shine!

Voices from somewhere above him.

– Oh, have a look. Someone's dumped a stiff in the car park.

Laughter retreating.

Gorman awakes with a start, pulls himself upright. For a couple of seconds he is befuddled by the incongruity of his surroundings; the steering wheel dug into his belly, the shimmering windows of white light that surround him, the dials and switches of the dashboard swimming into view. The voice of an animated young man threatening to stab someone in the face.

The digital clock reads 14:57.

Oh, for Christ's sake ...

He adjusts the rear-view mirror to reveal two uniformed backs retreating. Woodentop cunts, he seethes. Probably on their way back from an alarm going off in a shoe shop. Fucking muppets. Wouldn't know real police work if it jumped out of a car and shoved a Glock in their mush.

Gorman opens the door and swings out his legs, unfolds himself, bones still stiff with sleep. He stamps his boots on hot concrete to banish the pins and needles that have gathered beneath him. His shirt is clinging to his sides with sweat and there's a dull twinge across his left shoulder blade. He mutters curses under his breath as he rotates his arm in its socket. Give him gyp all night that will.

His mood is lifted when he gets back to the office and there's a message to call Bob Croft. The USCCT Supervisor informs him that they've found a knife. In fact, they've fished out four – two household kitchen knives, a small craft job and a six-inch flick knife.

– That do you will it, Graham?

– Marvellous, Bob.

Gorman hangs up the phone and splits open his special celebration packet of HobNobs; chocolate hazelnut.

■ ■ ■ ■ ■

They pull up outside Conway Court. It is five to three. There is no
sign of Frampton, or his car. Ndekwe kills the engine, leaves the CD
playing.

Halliwell gets out of the car and lights a cigarette. He stands
and smokes, one thumb hooked in the pocket of his jeans, his back to
the car. He makes a slow patrol of the pavement until his cigarette is
finished. He is grinding it underfoot into the grass verge when the
entrance door to the flats opens and a girl emerges, pulling a pram
backwards out of the doorway. Halliwell calls out to her, sets off
walking, but the girl doesn't turn her head to his appeal. Ndekwe
watches him quicken his pace as she swivels the pram around on
its back wheels, pushes it through the shadow of the building and
out onto the street.

– Hold up, love!

Halliwell breaks into a swift trot and gets the heel of his hand
to the door just as it swings back shut, click. Locked. He pulls at the
door, then bangs hard, swears.

The girl looks back over her shoulder, keeps on walking.

Ndekwe sits in the car and watches and listens.

*... I thought, OK, how can I sort this one out? I mean, it was a
complete balls-up from start to finish, and it was all on my account,
let's be truthful. Thing is, I was concerned about the lad at this
point. I'll be straight with yer, I was worried he was gonna do
summat daft and get himself locked up. Oh, I knew he'd been in
bother before. He'd told me all what he used to get up to with his
pals and that. How they used to go out robbing cars and shops and
all that carry-on. Selling drugs. I knew all the kind of caper they*

used to get up to. I reckoned if I didn't come up with summat quick then he'd be straight back down that road ... See, the trouble with me laddo is he can't see any further than the end of his nose. Are you with me? He's not a bad lad, not really. But he gets summat in his head and boom, that's it, full steam ahead. Doesn't think the job through, are yer with me? Like all that Jamaica business. He never stood back and had a proper look at the job, never paused to think it through to its logical conclusion, like. If he had a done, he'd have seen it all coming a mile off ... The thing is, Carlton was trying his best to do summat constructive with his life. You've got to take yer hat off to that, ant yer? Most young lads nowadays don't want to do any proper graft. They don't want to work towards anything; they want it all now, today, instantaneous like. They see summat they like in a shop window and they think they can just reach out and take it. I admired me laddo for getting his head down and grafting, for working towards summat ... but of course I'd bollocksed all that up for him, hadn't I? ...

– Why? You didn't force him to gamble his money away.

– No, but still ... I didn't want to see him get completely snookered ... so I had another one of me bright ideas. Oh aye, they come thick and fast with me. I should be on that programme with all them high-fliers, what do they call it, that Dragons' fucking Den. Hello, Dragons, my name's Jack Shepherdson and my business idea is to get a load of wacky baccy and flog it to the druggies down on Camden Lock. Oh, what a tip-top idea, Mr Shepherdson, here's half a million quid to set you up in your exciting new venture. Do keep us posted on how sales are going, won't you? Toodle pip! Best of British! ...

– And is that what you did?

– Oh aye. Turn me hand to owt, me. So you can put that down on the list as well. First degree murder and possession with intent to supply. There might be a few more additions as well before we're finished. Oh aye, you'll be throwing away the bloody key with me, boyo ...

– *This isn't an episode of* The Wire, *Jack. We don't have first degree murder in England.*

– *Full-blooded murder, then. Deliberate fucking murder. Whatever you wanna call it. Anyway, here's how it come about. I was sat having a smoke with Dale.*

– *Who's Dale?*

– *Dale's the lad who lives in the flat below me. Listen, I'm not a druggie, before you start jumping to conclusions. I just like the odd puff now and again. First had it out in Egypt. Goes nice with a dram, I find. Anyroad, this is a few days after that row I'd had with me laddo. I was telling Dale how I owed my pal a bit of brass and I had to come up with it sharpish, like. Dale says, well why don't you sell a bit of green for me? What, I says, on a commission basis, like? Nah, he says, I'll just lay you a key on at cost and you can pay me back when you've shifted it. I'll take a cut, you make some dough and get some free smoke as well, yeah? ... So he tells me the script, how we'll divvy it all up and that and it all sounds shipshape and dandy to me so I says aye, go on then, full steam ahead. Listen, I didn't have a clue how to weigh it out, or what you flogged it for or any of that lark. I'd just always got twenty quid's worth off Dale when I was flush, and that used to do me for a good few weeks. I didn't know any of the lingo, what a key was or a Henry the Eighth or a farmer's daughter or any of that caper. I told Dale, I told him this was just a mad one-off, and he says aye, no problemo, come back in a couple of days and I'll have it all sorted out ... Sure enough, two days later I'm heading back up to me quarters with a bag full of Jamaican Old Holborn and a set of electronic scales. Dale switched me onto all the weights and prices and it was all systems go ... Then I gave Carlton a ring and told him to get round to mine. He was a bit surly at first, didn't want to fucking know, really. Which I couldn't blame him for, to be fair. Half expected that sort of reaction really. I says to him, I says no, listen, you've got to get round here now, straight away. He wanted to know why, like, but I'm not daft, I knew not to talk about Persian rugs on the phone. Don't talk on the phone, full stop.*

Standard practice. I just told him I had the money he'd lost and so of course then he changed his tune immediately, said aye, that'll do and he was round like a shot ...

– You wanted him to shift this weed for you?

– Well, I just wanted to reassure him, like, let him know he was gonna get his dough back. But when he saw the merchandise he spat his dummy out, saying fuck off, Jack, what do I want with that? He thought I was trying to pay him back in weed. I says no, we can flog all this and you'll get yer money back and a bit more on top, yeah? But he wasn't having any of it. I don't want anything to do with this, he says, I just want my money back. Bollocks to yer then, I says, I'll flog it on me own. And he looks at me and starts laughing his cock off. Jack shotting weed, he says. Jack gonna lick a shot! And he keeps looking at this big bale and then back at me and he's cracking up laughing, giving it all that finger-clicking lark and shaking his head, nearly crying with fucking laughter he was, the cheeky little get ... Right you, yer little twat, I says to him, right, just you fucking watch. I'm gonna turn this bag of stinking green into a big pile of sweet-smelling spondoolicks, I says, and when I do, I says, I'm gonna buy you a first-class ticket to Jamaica. Might even hop on the plane meself! Eh? We'll see who's fucking laughing then! ... Me laddo took a slack handful for his mam and got himself off. I rolled one for meself an'all, stuck a bit of Dean Martin on and started weighing it all up into ounces and half ounces and putting it into freezer bags ... Jesus, it was bloody strong stuff, though. I was getting squiffy just off the fumes coming out of this bag. I had to put the joint out cos I kept forgetting how much I'd weighed and what was going where. After a bit I gave it up as a bad job and went and had a lie down. By hell, it was strong bloody stuff. Too strong for me, anyroad ... I should have known there and then that I weren't cut out for life as a drug pusher ...

– So what did you do?

– Well, I couldn't decide where to start. For the first couple of days I just stayed in and sampled the product, like. By hell, it was

barmy stuff, that supersonic skunk, no two ways about it. I wasn't used to smoking owt that strong. I was used to the other stuff Dale usually got, this home-grown gear. That was all right, a bit milder like ... nowt like this hydroponic shit ... I'd say to meself, go on then, I'll just have a little un, a single skinner with a cup of tea before I go out and before I knew it three or four hours would have whistled by and I'd still be sat in me dressing gown, staring at the bloody telly and covered in biscuit crumbs. It agitated me chest an'all, got that fired up like a bloody furnace again. So after a few days of this I thought aye aye, that's enough research, time to go and do some flogging. I stuck a few half-ounce bags in me jacket and went to the Beatrice. Well, that's where all the druggies knock about, innit, in Camden. I reckoned someone in the boozer would know someone who liked a quality smoke at reasonable rates ... Sure enough, the first person I bump into is this bloke I know's son ... what's his name ... Mark. He had a couple of other blokes in tow with him. The three of them all come and sit down with their drinks. One of em's this scruffy-looking character, hippy type, yer know? Tatty beard and dreadlocks, beads and bits of rags tied into his hair, lumps of bloody metal hanging out of his schnozzle, all that deal. He obviously liked a bit of a laugh and a joke, cos straight away he puts his pint down and looks round the table. Who's got the puff? he says. Then he leans in and sniffs at me like a golden retriever. Is that you? he says. Fuck me, you got a grow in there? Mind you, it did stink to high heaven. That was the biggest problem with that stuff, the bugle that came off it. I'd wrapped it up in tinfoil and then double bagged it into two old carrier bags, but it still gave off a right hum if you got too close. Luckily, we were the only ones in the boozer apart from Dermot behind the bar, and he didn't give a monkey's. I opened a bag under the table for this hippy bloke and he seemed suitably impressed with the goods. He bought an ounce and Mark had half an ounce off us an'all. Turns out this fella worked at that club on the High Street where all the pop groups play, that Koko place. He did all the sound and the lights for em. He asked me if I could get hold of any more

and I said aye, no problemo. So then he asks me how much I could
do a nine bar for. What do you think I am, I says to him, a fucking
sweet shop? No, I says, I haven't got any nine bars. Course, I didn't
have a bloody clue what he was on about, I didn't know what a nine
bar was, did I? He explains what he's after and then he says a price
and I said aye, all right then, champion. He told me to come round
the back door of the club at about six o'clock that night and we'd
iron it all out, like ... for a second I thought, aye aye, he's trying to
set me up here, that was me first thought; that there was some sort
of skulduggery in the offing. But it's that hydroponic shite, it makes
you paranoid. I had to stop smoking it in the end; it was sending me
bloody dingy. I was hearing voices on a night, people talking to me,
whispering me name and that. Put the fear of Christ up me it did.
Only ever had owt like that once before and that was in Spain when I
got cursed by one of them Looky Looky men ... them fellas on holiday,
you know who I mean?

– Look Looky man? Never heard of them, Jack.

– Them African blokes who go round flogging bits of tat on
the beach? One of em put a bastard curse on me. On the beach this
was, in San Antonio. I was sat there trying to read me paper and
they come wandering past, all laden down with their wares, like.
They had these carved elephants, little things made out of wood.
They used to spread all their gear out on the sand, try and get yer
to have a look, get yer to buy summat, like. Anyway, I'm laid out
on me towel, trying to read the Albert Draper, and one of em keeps
shoving this wooden elephant under me nose. I told him no thank
you, not today but he kept persisting, shoving this thing in front of
me paper, going you look, you look. In the end I lost me rag, grabbed
this fucking elephant off him and slung it halfway up the beach. Told
him to go forth and multiply; adios, amigo. Well, he gets his right
doe down then, and he starts pointing to this thing he's got wrapped
round his wrist, this copper bracelet thing, like one of them you'd
wear for rheumatism except this one's got this big blue stone set in
the middle of it, bright blue stone with an eye painted on it in black

*and white. Mister, mister, he's saying, evil eye for you. And he's
pointing to this eye on his wrist and then at me. Aye, all right, I tells
him, marvellous, now fuck off ... Well, I was up all that night shaking
like a dog shitting razor blades. Absolute torment, I aren't kidding
yer. First I was roasting hot then I was like a lump of ice. Aching all
over an'all, like someone had kicked seven bales of shite out of me.
A full night of it I had, pitching about in me bed, half delirious, like.
And the visions, oh Jesus Christ, what a treat they was. Monsters
and bastard demons flitting about in the darkness ... oh aye ... some
of em looming right over me an'all bending down and whispering
right into me lug'ole. Like being trapped in a bloody madhouse it
was, like a waking nightmare, and it carried on all night, an'all. And
all through it there he was, this Looky Looky bastard, stood in the
corner of the room; clear as day he was, pointing at this bloody evil
eye on his wrist and grinning like a loon. All bastard night this went
on. No respite till daybreak, like ...*

– Cursed you, had he?

*– Course, what it was, I'd fell asleep on the beach and got a right
good dose of sunstroke. That's all it was. Laid me up for a couple of
days, though. If it wasn't a curse it certainly felt like a bastard. Mind
you, the next time I was on that beach I made sure I bought summat
off them Looky Looky men. Can't be too careful, can yer? Don't
wanna tempt fate, do yer? ... Anyway, this is what this weed was like,
this supersonic skunk stuff. Like a good dose of sunstroke. And it
stayed with you the day after an'all. Have a decent puff on that and it
took a good few days to leave the system. So I was a bit jittery, a bit
paranoid, to be truthful ... I think that's why I was so quick to stick
that knife in that lad, when I think back. That lad outside the shops.
On any other day that wouldn't have happened. Not in me normal
frame of mind, yer see. Still jumpy from smoking that shite. Worse
than drink, that hydroponic skunk, I'm telling yer. Ten times worse, if
you ask me. I've got meself into some right scrapes through boozing,
over the years, like, but I've never actually ... y'know ... anyroad ... so
yeah, I was a bit wary of this bloke in the boozer, initially, this hippy*

fella and this deal he was ironing out. A lot of money, like. But he was in Mark's company, and Mark was a decent lad so I thought, aye, go on then ... So I had a few jars with em and then I went back home for a wash and a shave, like, and by six o'clock I'm banging on the back door of this Koko gaff. Sure enough this hippy opens up and lets me in. Just the two of us there in this nightclub place. Half an hour later I'm on the bus back home with twelve hundred quid in me sky rocket. All of a sudden I can see why these young kids get into this drug dealing lark. Twelve hundred quid for ten minutes' work? Not to be sniffed at, is it? ...

■ ■ ■ ■ ■

Frampton's car pulls up at twelve minutes past three. The three officers enter Conway Court and climb the stairs to the third floor, to 34b.

There is a long jagged split down the doorframe. Ndekwe gets down on one knee and looks up and down its length. It looks like the door had been kicked off its hinges and taken half the jamb with it. Whoever had hung it back on had bodged it all together with mismatched screws and mastic. No need to have chased the council housing department for the key; a polite knock would probably send the entire lot tumbling inwards.

Ndekwe stands up, inspects the door itself. There is the faintest outline of a footprint just below the letterbox. He takes two paces back and raises his foot. The print on the door is roughly two-thirds the size of his shoe and three or four inches lower.

– Kids, says Halliwell.

Frampton turns the key and they go inside. It is a generously sized flat, sparsely furnished. Frampton goes into the kitchen and starts opening and closing cupboard doors and drawers. Halliwell wanders around the edges of the room and then disappears through a door into a bedroom.

There is a framed poster of Frank Sinatra and a few other

photographs on the wall next to the TV set; a football team in black and white shirts holding up a trophy, a ship tied up in a dock, a solemn-faced boy of around five or six years old stood to attention in front of a pebbledashed wall, a football tucked under his arm. The boy's clothes and the faded colouring of the print suggest the early seventies.

Frampton's voice from the kitchen:

– Pete?

Ndekwe goes through. He can smell something sweet and pungent. Frampton is kneeling down, his head in the cupboard beneath the sink. Ndekwe squats down next to him. There are shreds of green littering the inside of the cupboard and the kitchen floor; a good six or seven grams' worth. Ndekwe scrapes it all together with the blade of his hand, pinches a finger full and sniffs; skunk weed.

There is nothing else of any interest in the kitchen, but they find a set of electronic scales and a bundle of plastic bank bags in a sideboard in the front room, along with a biscuit tin with another small amount of skunk and some loose cigarette papers. Ndekwe takes the Section 18 search authorization document from his pocket and smooths it out on the coffee table as Frampton bells the station for a uniform to come on scene guard until Forensics arrive.

Music starts up from downstairs, the deep bass pulse of dub reggae. The floor beneath their feet vibrates.

Halliwell and Ndekwe go back outside, descend the steps to the next floor down and knock on the door immediately below. The music is unreasonably loud. Ndekwe raps harder, with more urgency. There is some faint movement, a slight dip in volume, and then a man's voice.

– Yeah?

– Dale?

They stand to one side as the security chain is fumbled and snapped into place. An eye appears in the open gap of doorway.

– Who's that?

– Police. Like a quick word, Dale.

– Dale's not here, bruv. Sorry.

The door is clicked shut and the music rises back to its original volume. Halliwell steps forward and thumps again and again with his balled fist, a steady, insistent rhythm upon peeling paintwork.

Angry stomp of footsteps, and the gap in the door opens again, the chain jerked tight.

– Fuck's sake, what? What is it?

Ndekwe holds up his ID.

– Fuck's sake, man.

The chain is released and the door swings open.

It's a typical stoner's gaff; a battered charity shop settee, a couple of deflated bean bags, a coffee table scattered with magazines, torn scraps of Rizla, empty CD cases, plates of half-finished food. A trail of unwashed clothes leads to a darkened bedroom. The smell of stale smoke and fried onions. Daytime television plays silently away to itself in the corner, a panel of middle-aged women laughing at some unheard joke. A single bed sheet hangs at the window and bathes the room in a translucent blue glow.

Dale is an undernourished and ratty-looking young man in his late twenties. He wears a black beanie hat, vest and combat pants. He slides the volume down on his music system and then stands at the furthest end of the room, pulls on his raggedy beard, agitated.

– I ain't got nothing around me, he says.

– Not here for that, says Halliwell. –Not our department.

– What then?

Ndekwe points upwards to the ceiling.

– Jack Shepherdson.

– What about him?

– Do you know where he is?

Dale shakes his head.

– Haven't seen him. Not for about ... a week, I think.

– He's locked up, Halliwell tells him.

– Yeah? What's he done?

Halliwell nods upwards. – Who kicked his door in?

– His door?

– Yeah. You know, that big piece of wood that keeps out all the undesirables.

The young man shakes his head.

– No idea, mate.

– No?

– Straight up. Dale holds his hands palm up towards the ceiling. – Didn't even know he'd been turned over.

Ndekwe studies a poster above the gas fire; a dubstep night at a pub in Hoxton. It promises a 'night of non-stop positive pressure'. A pair of headphones wrapped around a bass bin with twin forks of lightning at either side. Door tax: £5 before 11 p.m.

– Is he in bother, yeah? Dale's voice strives for nonchalance, but he can't hide the keen edge of worry.

– He might be.

– What's he done then?

– Killed someone. Or so he reckons.

– Fuck off! Dale looks between the two policemen. – No seriously, he says.

– No joke, says Halliwell.

– Fuck me, says Dale. He sits down heavily on the sofa and reaches for a packet of tobacco on the table, starts rolling a cigarette. His hands are trembling and it takes him three attempts to light his smoke. He exhales hard and shakes his head, looks up at the standing policemen.

– Who's he killed?

– Some boy over in E8, says Halliwell.

– Jesus.

Ndekwe walks over to the window and pulls the bed sheet to one side. There is a courtyard directly below, a heap of black bin bags stacked against a row of wheelie bins at the far wall. Some of the bin bags are split open, spilling their guts out onto the floor. Ndekwe can see sauce-smeared cans and soiled nappies and what looks like baby clothes and a single red sandal. He can hear children playing somewhere in the near distance, screaming and laughing. He asks his next question without looking round.

– Dale, did you sell Jack a kilo of weed?

– A *kilo*?

Ndekwe can hear the incredulity in the man's reply and he knows that it is genuine. He knows that when he turns around he will see it written also across his face, as real as the washing lines and balconies that hang above the streets and back yards stacked with burst bin bags and the discarded clothes of children.

Ndekwe lets the bed sheet fall back and turns away from the window.

– No further questions.

■ ■ ■ ■ ■

None of the weapons retrieved from the sewer fits the bill. The two household knives have serrated edges and the flick knife is not consistent with the broad entry wound identified by the post mortem. The craft knife had always been the longest of long shots.

Gorman calls the wife from work, asks if she wants him to pick anything up on the way home. He is thinking of a bottle of wine. A nice chilled white. What was that one they'd liked last week? Pinot Griog? It was only Monday, true, but they could still have a drink. Nobody was going to judge him for having a drink, were they? Gorman could certainly fucking do with one.

He calls Ndekwe to break the happy news about the knife, but the DS isn't picking up his calls.

Bollocks to him, thinks Gorman; looks like Mr High Potential might have to actually do some proper police work rather than just driving about listening to fucking CDs. Gorman decides to tell him tomorrow. The knife is a kick in the dick, but it isn't the end of the world. Even if Ndekwe doesn't manage to track down Isaacs and get him to point the finger, Gorman is still confident of getting it all wrapped up before Wednesday. He reckons they've got enough to have him gripping the rail. Pinot Griog, he thinks. Sure it was called that. Australian, anyway; a picture of a tree on the label.

He peers between the blinds at the street below. It's still glorious outside. He and the wife can sit out on the back patio and look through the brochures together. They've got a south-facing garden. Right little sun-trap. Best part of the day, thinks Gorman, these late summer evenings. That little kip earlier has done him the world of good. He feels reasonably relaxed for the end of a Monday. He slips his jacket on, gathers his car keys and turns off his computer.

Home time.

Gorman gets halfway down the corridor before he hears Ndekwe's voice:

– Sir?

Gorman pretends not to hear. He hums a tune under his breath and quickens his feet. But Ndekwe is looming right behind him.

– Sir, quick word?

– Velocity, Gorman offers over his shoulder. – Will that do?

Gorman considers brush-offs and put-downs as essential weapons in the armoury of the modern police inspector. Supervising and coordinating the constant fight against the mayhem of East London was exhausting enough without the petty demands of those who would seek to waste your time and sap your energy with trivial concerns. Gorman is well aware that there is no such thing as a quick word, especially where his new DS is concerned. Ndekwe's previous superintendent had described his star officer as being 'thoughtful and methodical'. This is starting to translate to Gorman as 'painfully fucking slow'. Velocity. He'd seen Gordon Strachan use that one on YouTube, a compilation of quips taken from press conferences and post-match interviews. Ndekwe won't have heard that one cracked before. He won't even know who Gordon Strachan is. Gorman remembers that Sunday when England went out to Germany in the World Cup; every bloke in the station who hadn't managed to book leave was either trying to slope off home or get to a pub with a big screen. Ndekwe had spent the entire afternoon at his desk ploughing through paperwork. Didn't even realize there was a game on until the first long faces had drifted back to the workplace.

Ndekwe catches up with his Detective Inspector.

– I've been listening to Shepherdson's interview, he says.

– He's good, isn't he? Should be on the telly.

– There's something not right, says Ndekwe.

– None of it's right, you doughnut! He's telling porkies!

– Yeah, but it's the way he's telling them.

– It's the way he tells em, repeats Gorman, in a thick Northern Irish accent. Frank Carson. A proper comedian, with proper jokes. Gorman would bet a pound to a shovel of shit that Ndekwe has never heard of Frank Carson either. Probably wouldn't get it, even if he had. Not politically correct enough for him.

– I'm sorry? says Ndekwe.

Gorman sighs, stops abruptly and faces his detective sergeant.

– All right, what is it?

– Shepherdson.

– What about him?

– Well, all this stuff about him selling weed. It's bollocks.

– Have you listened to any of the McKenzie interview yet?

– Not yet, no.

– Well, do yourself a favour, turn laughing boy off and listen to the other fella.

– I will, soon as I've heard Shepherdson's side.

Gorman rolls his eyes theatrically. – Is that all you've done all day? Drive round listening to fairy stories?

– No. I spoke to the newsagent on the estate, I spoke to the guy at the bar where he worked and I spoke to the guy in the flat below his.

– And?

– Well, Shepherdson's flat's been broken into ...

– Yeah, McKenzie's stash got lifted. Look, all of this is in the notes. Gorman flaps a dismissive hand.

– Yeah, but the notes don't tell us why Shepherdson's lying, do they?

– Cos he's a lying old scrote, that's why! Simple!

– Old fella like that? Covering for some kid he hardly knows? Ndekwe shakes his head. – Doesn't make sense.

Gorman has had enough of this. There are heads looking out from office windows, people slowing down in the corridor, bodies hovering around doorways to listen. He nods Ndekwe into an empty office, pulls the door shut behind them.

– Right, he says. – What exactly is your fucking problem?

Ndekwe is taken aback.

– Sir?

– We've got till Wednesday to put a murder case together and you're pissing about with minor details. Why?

– Well, says Ndekwe, I think …

But Gorman silences him with a raised palm. – Shall I tell you what I think, Ndekaway? I think you've been wasting your time. Yeah? I think you're wasting your time, my time and the time and money of the decent British taxpayer. Yeah? We've got another two days at best and you've spent all day driving about listening to confessions that have already been made, information that is freely and easily available to you from the DCs at your disposal. Those interviews happened *yesterday*. Job number one for *today* was to find a witness to confirm at least one of those confessions. Not some bloke in a bar or some other dipstick who wasn't there either – a *proper* witness. Someone who was there when it actually happened. Bam Bam Isaacs. Have you found him?

– No, but first I need to listen to both …

Gorman shakes his head.

– No, what *you* need to do is listen to me. Now, I'm willing to write today off, seeing as how I'm a reasonable man and it's your first day back and all that. But the holiday is finished, yeah? So go home, get your head down and then tomorrow, right, *tomorrow* you're up bright and early and you start looking for Isaacs. You get yourself round every crack den, every baby soldier's hideout and the yard of every silly little tart on the Crown Heights estate. Believe me, if you look hard enough you'll dig him out. These dopey little dogs never stray too far from their own puddles of piss.

– Yeah, but ...

– Don't fucking argue. Get him found, Ndewakay.

– Ndewakay?

Gorman looks at him with belligerent confusion.

– I beg your pardon?

– It's not N*dewa*kay, states Ndekwe. – It's N*dek*we.

Gorman's reptile brain screams danger; the words *institutional racism* appear in his mind's eye in throbbing red neon. He opens his mouth, but nothing comes out, so he clamps it shut again, furiously tries to focus his wits.

UN – DECK – A – WAY.

Shit.

– Forgive me, Detective Sergeant, he says. – A slip of the tongue.

Ndekwe looks at him blankly from behind those small round, glittering glasses. Christian name, thinks Gorman. Soften the potential for offence by the reassuring use of familiarity. We're all on the same team, he thinks. All singing from the same hymn sheet, brothers in blue one and all. Use his Christian name ... no, shit, hang on, that's a fucking minefield as well. What if he's a Muslim? First name. Use his first name.

Gorman alters his body language so it cannot be construed as aggressive or invasive, adjusts the tone of his voice to banish any trace of confrontation and dispenses his words slowly, carefully.

– Peter, he says. – I realize this is your first big job here and you're keen to do this properly and I understand that. I applaud it, in fact, absolutely ... Gorman tails off, feels suddenly vulnerable, like an old dog that has wandered out into the middle of a frozen lake on a winter's day. He can feel the ice beginning to creak beneath him. Tread delicately, Graham, he thinks. Tread very fucking delicately.

He takes a deep breath and continues.

– Look, Peter, we've got a confession and hopefully by tomorrow we'll have a witness. If Isaacs won't talk, charge the pair of them. McKenzie and the old man. Joint enterprise, yeah? It's not that complicated.

He attempts a smile, spreads his hands in appeal.

– Not that complicated? Ndekwe shakes his head. – Sir, with the greatest respect, I've been here nearly three months now and you still don't know my name.

Gorman feels the smile freeze on his face.

– Of course I know your name, he says, through gritted teeth.

– What is it then?

Gorman narrows his eyes, searches Ndekwe's face for any sign of aggression but finds none; just that infuriatingly patient, mildly curious gaze.

– Oh come on, says Gorman. – You're just being obtuse now.

– No, I'm not, says Ndekwe simply. – What's my name?

Gorman feels his fists tighten, his nails digging into his palms. He knows he must extricate himself from the situation before he says something that will plunge him under an avalanche of trouble. He flips through his memory bank for half-remembered training manuals and management courses, but fails to come up with any neat quick-fix slogans to get him out of jail free.

– We'll talk in the morning, he states, with what he hopes is a calm finality.

He gives a curt nod and leaves the room with as much haste as dignity will allow, weaves his way through the officers and civilians who are filling up the corridor outside, bumping into backs and elbows, excusing himself as he goes.

Ndekwe emerges from the doorway and calls after him.

– WHAT IS IT, SIR? WHAT'S MY NAME?

■ ■ ■ ■ ■

Gorman aims his key at his car and springs the central locking with an electronic yelp. His back teeth are grinding together and he can feel the blood pounding in his temples. Mr High Potential, he thinks. Mr Fast Fucking Track Clever Cunt.

Fucking Ndekwe.

N*dek*we, N*dek*we, N*dek*we, N*dek dek dek* . . .

He climbs into his car, digs his phone out of his pocket and calls Frampton.

– Alex? Do us a favour, will you? Get a copy of McKenzie's interview and have a quick listen before you go home. There's a ghetto blaster up in room three. Just check we haven't missed anything ... yeah, well, y'know ... anything his brief might pick up on ... yeah, yeah ... I don't want this going tits up cos of some stupid oversight ... an ounce of tar, Alex, yeah? What? An ounce of tar! Tar! No, it's just a saying ... look, it doesn't matter, right, just give it a quick listen and make sure all the dots join up ... yeah ... good man, Alex. Right, listen, I got to go, I'm driving. Tomorrow, yeah? OK ... yeah ... thank you.

He twists the ignition, guns the engine furiously before crunching into first and wheel-spinning out of the car park.

■ ■ ■ ■ ■

Frampton retrieves a copy of the interview from the Incident Room and locates the machine in room three. He presses the PLAY button, lifts his feet up onto the desk and unfurls the London *Evening Standard*. He checks the evening's TV schedule before flipping to the back page and reading about Chelsea's new £17 million signing from Benfica. Some young Brazilian guy. Frampton seems to remember he had a good World Cup, in the games he saw. Looks like he could be half useful, thinks Frampton, if he settles down and gets used to the weather. All right poncing about in the tropical heat, see how he copes with a pissing wet Tuesday night in November up in Wigan. He checks his watch. Half an hour, he thinks. He'll give it half an hour.

... Spent about a week just locked away in my room playing my tunes an trying to think what I was gonna do, ya get me? It was like all options had been closed off an there was no way to get round it all. After a bit I went and did the rounds, asking for work. I don't mean work as in graft, I mean like work work; legitimate work, ya get me? But it was pointless. I got sore feet from tramping round all the places I could think of, walked all round the town an then back out East, stopping at every bar, café and takeaway I could find, but there was nothing doing guv. Recession, innit. I even went back to that betting shop and offered to sweep up all the torn up tickets, but they weren't having any of that. Then one day I just thought balls to this. I got up, left the flat an went down to the shops. There was no one down there yet so I went an sat on the swings in the park an kept lookout. Sure enough after a bit I seen Bam Bam coming out of one of the houses. I hollered after him and he waited while I ran over. Bam Bam, I said, I need some money, bruv. I ain't got any dough, Kez, he said. No, I need to earn some money, ya get me? He was like, rah, I thought you was a wage earner now. I broke it down for him, how I lost my job at the bar an then half my money on some bad deal. I let him think it was some shady activity type deal. I never said anything about no horse race cos Bam Bam would have just took the bare piss, man. I got the impression he already thought of me as a bit of a dick, ya get me? I didn't want to add any evidence to that verdict or the man would not entertain what I was about to ask of him.

– Which was what?

– So I asked Bam Bam to lay me something on so I could earn some dough, ya get me? He was a bit thingy about it, though. He was like, look Kez, it ain't down to me, yeah? Ain't my call to say where the parcels go. I knew what the man was saying. I had to go an see his superior, innit.

– You mean Aaron Stewart?

– Yeah. So Bam Bam set it up an later that day I goes round the back of the houses an there's this little kid on a bike an he nods me through the doorway into the inner sanctum an there he was, Mr

Knowledge stood there, stern faced, his lieutenants around him an everything. The big boss man. Knowledge is power, innit. Like I say, I knew the man for time but now he had this attitude on him like I was some cat come crawling for a ten quid rock or something. Like he didn't know me at all. But I was in a proper corner, you get me guv? I was boxed in, yeah? I didn't know what else I could do. I knew he was gonna give me some shit before he agreed to any parcel, so I had to stand there listening to him go on with himself about how I was a pussy and this and that and all his little fools sniggering away in the corner. I was prepared to swallow all that, though, in aid of the bigger picture. Then he starts going on about terms and conditions an how things gotta be if I'm coming back on road, but I made it plain to the man, told him I didn't want no full-time position. This is just a one-off ting, I told him, clear some debts up an that's it, Aaron, no more. He didn't like that, being called by his schooldays name an he got really heated, starting pulling himself up to his full height an that, telling me I was in no position to be dictating terms an if we were rolling we were rolling how he say we roll. My way or the highway, innit. Then he starts going on about how I ran from the last job, that ting in Bromley, yeah, an how does he know I ain't still no cowardly motherfucker who gonna run away at the first sign of stress and blah blah flippin blah. He was flexing, but I just had to stand there an take it. After he waved his dick about for a bit he told me he could lay on a key. Weed, I'm talking about. I didn't want to be dealing with no junkies an especially no rock-head cats, cos they are bare hassle, mate. If you shotting crack you gotta put up with people coming back all the time, to an fro, innit. That's how they roll, them rock heads. I seen it before, they get a rock an twenty minutes later they back for another one. Constant hustle, constant headache. My plan was to float about offloading the green to peeps I knew, friends an selected family, innit. It's a pain in the arse, true, but it's gotta be small retail with weed. Ideally, you wanna be breaking it down into stupid little ten-quid bags cos you make more dough like that. But I didn't want to be stood out on no balcony again.

– So you're saying that Aaron Stewart supplied you with drugs?
– Nah, not like proper drugs, just some weed. A key of green
it was, six grand, laid on. That was what we agreed. This meant
I could make one and a half G after payback. I come away from
Knowledge HQ feeling vexed cos of the slating he'd give me, but I
told myself that it was worth it to eat a bit of shit cos of the bigger
picture, innit. I just kept that picture in my head; that strip of beach
with the blue ocean and the mountains in the distance. Montego Bay.
I was nearly there. Rah, I could almost feel that sun on my back ...

■ ■ ■ ■ ■

Ndekwe is sitting stationary in a queue of nose-to-tail traffic, finger-tips drumming the steering wheel. He is starting to very much regret yelling after Gorman like that. There had been no need. In fact, he decides, it was a very dumb thing to do indeed. His first day on his first proper job and he's raising his voice to a senior officer. He briefly entertains the notion that Gorman hadn't heard him. But Gorman had heard him all right. Ndekwe could tell by the way he barged his way down the corridor. Ndekwe only hopes the fact that Gorman didn't come back and collar him meant that the DI was willing to let it slide.

His gaze wanders over to the pedestrians on his left. Beyond the crossing lines of bodies he sees an old man picking through the contents of an overflowing bin, a filthy green sleeping bag draped over one shoulder. He has the flushed red face of the seasoned drinker, half obscured by a matted grey beard that reaches down to his chest. Ndekwe watches him as he roots through the discarded debris of others, pulling apart packages of decaying food and stuffing any salvageable treasure into the pockets of his enormous quilted overcoat. He pulls out a crumpled tin of soft drink, holds it up to his ear like a sea shell, shakes it once, twice, then fastens it to his mouth, tips his head back and drinks. He drains it dry, drops it back into the bin and continues his careful picking through its grimy depths.

The pavement is thronged with rush-hour commuters, but every passing person gives him a wide berth as he shuffles his way around the bin. Ndekwe feels his stomach begin to grumble, realizes he hasn't eaten all day.

The bus in front starts to move forwards, but then lurches to a halt, causing Ndekwe and the concertina of cars behind him to jam on the brakes. The bus doors hiss open and bodies spill out onto the street, flailing arms and raised voices; some kind of altercation. Ndekwe leans across the passenger side to get a better view. A middle-aged man in a suit has hold of two teenage girls by their arms, shepherding them out onto the pavement. The girls, about thirteen or fourteen years old, are trying to pull themselves free, but the man bundles them both through the crowd and shoves them into a shop doorway, stands them to face him, shoulder to shoulder. Pedestrians check their step and walk around them, pointedly ignoring the unfolding drama. One of the girls is wagging her finger in the man's face, her face screwed up with rage. The man is batting her away from him with one hand and holding her friend firmly at arm's length with the other, his fist bunching the sleeve of her jacket.

Ndekwe slips the gearstick into neutral and unclips his seat belt.

But then the man in the suit drops his hands; turns around and heads swiftly towards the bus, ignoring the hail of abuse and angry gestures aimed at his back. He hops on board and the bus slowly rolls forwards again.

Ndekwe fastens his seat belt, puts the car back into gear and follows in its wake.

Maybe Sonia is right, he thinks. Maybe he does need to learn how to switch off.

He turns up the CD and drowns out the impatient peal of horns from the vehicles behind as the traffic gradually gains momentum.

... So I rang Carlton up and told him I had his money, yer know, the money what he lost on the horse ... which, let's be fair, was down to

him, not me. Not my bloody fault the daft little bugger can't fill in
a betting slip at eighteen years of age ... which is a bloody disgrace,
by the way. But like I said, I did feel responsible and I'd rather have
settled up while I had the money than have him hold a grudge. I
could tell from how he was on the phone that he still felt aggrieved
and considered it all my bloody fault. Mebbe it was, mebbe it wasn't.
Six of one, half a bastard dozen of the other ... In any event, I told
him I'd got his money and he said he'd be round later but I said no I'd
better go and give it to him before I spent it in the bookies or some
such tale, and he just laughed and said aye, all right, and he told me
his flat number and whereabouts it was and so off I popped, like ...

    – Do you know the Crown Heights estate?

    – Oh aye, I used to go to a card school on there a few years ago.
This Jamaican fella I used to work with, Harry, him and a few of
his oppos. A good few years back I'm talking now. It was more or
less how I remembered it, mebbe a bit more rundown, like. They
don't exactly splash their money about on these places do they,
the council? Anyroad, I knocked on me laddo's door and his mam
answered. At first I didn't realize it was his mam, even when she
let me in the house and I saw the pair of them together. For a start
he doesn't even call her mam, he calls her Janine. I thought it was
his sister or maybe some bird of his he had knocking about ... Has
Carlton told you about his mam yet?

    – How do you mean?

    – He probably won't have done. I get the impression he's a bit
embarrassed about her. When I first met him, when we were working
in the bar, me and him used to crack on about all sorts, talk about
this that and the other, but he'd never mention his mam. Mentioned
his sister and his aunties and his cousins and his dad, oh Christ,
aye, his dad, always banging on about him. But never once did he
mention his own mother. I thought she might be brown bread or
summat ... or just, y'know, off the scene or whatever. I didn't tipple
that the lass who opened the front door was his mother. Jesus, she
looked rough as arseholes, though. Not old exactly, but she looked

like she'd had a long fucking paper round. She would have probably
been a bonnie lass at one point, but by Christ she'd turned a corner.
You could tell straight off she liked a drink. You could reek the ale
coming off her. Like standing in front of a drayman's horse ... I
told her I was there to see Carlton. She just stood there gawping
at me like I was radio fucking rental. There's music thudding from
somewhere behind her and I can hear Carlton's shouting Jack, come
in, come in ... I follow her through into the front room and there's
a house full, two young lasses with about half a dozen older lads,
Carlton among em, all of em sat watching music videos on the telly.
The lad who I stabbed, that Aaron Stewart, he was there as well. I
didn't really clock him at the time, though. I didn't know any of em.
None of em took a blind bit of notice of me either, all just sat gawping
at the telly, like ...

　　– Is this the first time you met Aaron Stewart?

　　– Yeah, never seen him before. Carlton asks if I've got his money.
I pull me wad out and count off his roll and he clocks all the tens and
twenties and he's suddenly sitting up and taking an interest. Whoa,
Jack, he says, you're smashing it, bruv! You're smashing it! He was
highly delighted was me laddo ... As soon as I hand the dough over
this young lass starts chiming in about how Carlton owes her some
money. This is his sister. Her and Carlton start bickering, really
having a go at each other, calling each other everything from a pig
to a dog. Terrible to hear, brother and sister at each other's throats
like that. Listen, listen, I says, come on, let's not have a row, eh?
Let's have a bit of a do. C'mon, I says, let's have a drink, one of yer
go out and get some tins, and I peel some more notes off and wave
em about between the pair of them and whoosh, the money's plucked
from me fingers and this young lass is straight out the door ... She
comes back with a carry-out and we all have a good drink. Well, me
and Janine did, anyroad. Me laddo hardly drunk owt and neither did
any of the other lads in there. They was all having a puff and that,
y'know, smoking dope, but there weren't much supping going on ...
Well, anyway, I ended up stopping for a good session. The night went

*along and we were all having a natter and what have yer ... then at
some point I realized this young lad sat opposite me was getting on
me case. This is him who I ended up stabbing, this Aaron Stewart,
this Knowledge character. I don't know how long he'd been sat there,
but I suddenly twigged he was trying to be clever. At first I didn't
even realize he was talking to me, I thought he was just ... y'know
... holding court, like. But then I tippled he was having a pop. Can't
recall exactly what he was saying, whether it was just his turn of
phrase or his manner or whatever, but he was definitely trying to
provoke me, like ... I was about to pull him up when I noticed me
laddo's mother had this little pipe in her hand. She's fiddling about
with this plastic bag full of summat or other ... I mean, I knew what
it was, course I did, I'm not bloody simple, but I'd never seen anyone
actually do it before, crack cocaine, like. She loads the pipe up with
these little rocks and just as she was about to light it I saw Carlton
come back into the room and lean over her from behind and take it
out of her hands, lift it off her real gentle, like you'd take a rattle off
a sleeping bain ... Don't, Mum, he said. That's what I heard him say.
Don't, Mum, and he only said it dead quiet, but I heard it above all
the chatter and the music from the telly and this cunt sat opposite
me going on with himself. This fucking Knowledge twat ...*

   – Aaron Stewart?

   *– Aaron Stewart, aye. I wasn't paying him due attention,
obviously, cos then the bastard leans across and pushes me knee,
gives me a right dig he does, and summat in me just snapped and I
stood up and I said all right, son, what's your fucking problem then?
Eh? What's the fuckin Bobby Moore here then, eh?*

   – What did he do?

   *– Well, for one split second he gives me this look like absolute
hatred, like he wants rip me heart clean out of me chest. And then he
realizes everyone's watching so he starts taking the piss, cowering in
his seat, like, going don't kill me, boss, don't kill me, y'know, playing
to the crowd, like. And they're all falling about howling with laughter
saying rah, Knowledge, you going in the boot, man! Man's gonna*

smoke ya! Big bloody joke, aye right. I was fucking fuming, me ...

– You lost your temper?

– Well, aye, but there's not much you can do when everyone's in fits of laughter like that, is there? Plus, I was in someone's house, in their company, like. So I sat back down and said aye, you'll know yer cunt, or some such pleasantry. I'd had a good drink by this point, in case you hadn't guessed. Anyway, that was as far as it went that night with me and him, with this Knowledge, as they called him. He gets off in a bit, after all this, and then the two young lasses left with the rest of the lads and there was just the three of us; me, me laddo and his mam ... I'd already weighed the situation up with his mother. Carlton was the responsible adult of the house. I could tell she was a bit of a dead loss. She got herself in a right old state that night, got completely pissed and then kept sloping off into the kitchen to have a crafty suck on her pipe. You could tell me laddo was embarrassed about his mother making a show of herself like that. He went through a few times and tried to get her to part with the pipe, but she weren't having none of it, snarling and spitting at him whenever he tried to prise it off her. I could hear em both arguing the toss. She got especially arsey at one point, effing and jeffing at him she was. After a bit he gave up trying. We just sat and had a drink and watched the telly while his mam went backwards and forwards from the kitchen with her pipe. It must be bloody good gear that crack cocaine, that's all I can say, to make someone carry on like that ... Anyway, I went round again a few nights after that and flogged a couple of half-ounce bags to Carlton's sister and her mates. Then it became a semi-regular thing, like, I'd pop round and have a few tinnies with Janine or get em all a Chinese or whatever. That Knowledge lad was generally knocking about most nights. We never really exchanged more than a few words after that first time until one night out of the blue he asked me if I could do him a nine bar, on tick, like ...

– Aaron Stewart?

– Aye ...

■ ■ ■ ■ ■

The new Chelsea midfielder apart, there is nothing of any real interest to Frampton in the *Standard*, apart from an article outlining England's chances of winning the bid to stage the 2018 World Cup. There is a picture of Prince William, David Beckham and David Cameron sat around a table. The three men wear matching ties and broad grins for the camera. 'To bring the World Cup to England would be up there as one of the best things I have ever done in my career,' Beckham is quoted as saying. 'With Prince William and the Prime Minister being here, it just shows the strength we have in our country, the passion we have in our country.'

Frampton grins, picks up a pen and circles in a black halo hovering above David Beckham's head.

... I took the parcel round to Jack's. No way was I gonna have it in my own back yard. For one thing, I didn't want my mum to know what I was doing. I knew she'd go sick on me if she thought I was back in that life and I knew she wouldn't believe me that it was just gonna be some one-off ting. So as soon as Bam Bam dropped the parcel off I double-wrapped it all up to stop the stink an I took it round to Jack's in a holdall. I reckoned he owed me, you know? On account of the horse an all that? I reckoned it was the least he could do for me.

– You wanted him to keep the drugs at his flat?

– Yeah. So there I was, late one night, leaning on his buzzer again. I was a bit jumpy cos of all the baby soldiers that were floating round, but I weren't rolling down there with fifty mans or nothing, there was no crew, it was just me on my own an I didn't know any of them an they didn't know me. Still, I didn't want to be caught slipping. I wasn't too wild about being stood on the street for too long. I had to buzz Jack like four or five times before he answered. Anyway, he buzzed me up. He was just sat in his vest with all the racing papers laid out around him. He looked a bit sheepish to see

me again, asked me how I been doing and all that. Then his eyes fell
on the holdall and he asked me what was up. I showed him the green
an he was all no no no, no way, Carlton, you ain't leaving that round
here, all that chat. I reminded the man that if it weren't for him I
wouldn't even be shotting weed, I'd be working like an honest citizen.
Besides, he told me enough stories about his wild and wicked past; I
know he weren't no angel neither. So after a bit of to-ing and fro-ing
I agreed he could have an ounce for himself and he'd get a drink out
of it as well. In any case, I figured the parcel wouldn't be sat there for
too long anyway. I already had a few buyers lined up. I could have
done a nine bar to Melissa's old man easy, but I knew if I did that
he'd want nine bar discount price. And if I went down that road I
wouldn't be making my dough, ya get me? I had to snap into proper
business mode. It had to be single ounces, a ton sixty each, bang
bang bang. It was good weed too. It smelled like good weed anyway.
Jack rolled one up an had himself a little smoke an then he helped me
weigh it all out into ounce bags. Before too long he was chatting all
his tales of the high seas again, laughing an joking just like the old
Jack. So the product was right. I thought it shouldn't be too much of
a stretch. I already had about twenty peeps in mind who I reckoned
would take an oz, big-time burners too. I figured on two or three
weeks of straight hustle an I'd be buying my plane ticket. Best laid
plans though, innit?

   – What went wrong?

   – Well, at first it was easy street. I took ten one-ounce bags from
the holdall an I met Chantelle from the bar one evening on her way
from work an she took a couple of oz. A couple of my cousins took
a bag each an then they came back for a couple more for their little
crews. I told them to keep it all on the DL from their mum, my auntie
Sharon, yeah? Cos if she found out she'd tell my mum straight away,
no messing. I told you, my family is tight, man, yeah? It all went to
shit a few days after that. It was them Bangla boys. I should have
known. I should have been more careful. Them little baby soldiers
hanging round the front doorway of Jack's block. I never paid them

no attention, but they must have smelled that shit on me when I was in and out of there. I remember seeing two of the little pricks right behind me coming down the stairwell one afternoon, but at that point I just thought they lived there, ya get me?

– What happened?

– One afternoon I buzzed up to Jack but there was no answer. I was all heated to get a few more bags, cos there was a party over the other side of our ends the next night and I knew I could get rid of a bit. But I buzzed and buzzed an there was no answer. So I went off to look for the man. I knew it wouldn't take too long – just head for the nearest bookies, innit. Sure enough, that's where I found him, leaned up against the roulette machine, hypnotized by that wall of TVs again. Jack, I said, rah, Jack, come on, man, I got to get my ting. Hang on, he said an we both had to stand there an watch another lame horse race. I didn't even bother asking him which one he had backed, but it obviously weren't no winner cos Jack screwed up his slip an cursed an I followed him out of the bookies. I could tell he was a bit drunk by the way he swayed down the street. He was coughing real bad too; one point he stopped an leaned against a wall, started hawking up a load of green shit onto the pavement. This woman passing by gave us a proper dirty look an I couldn't blame her, man, cos it was just gross, ya get me? I waited till he was finished, standing away from the man, acting like I wasn't nothing to do with him. When we got back to Jack's yard his door was kicked clean off its hinges. I knew straight away what had happened, man. The place was trashed good style. I went straight to the cupboard under the sink but the holdall was gone. I knew that before I even looked. The parcel was gone. Them Bangladeshi boys, innit.

– You think they took the drugs?

– I knew it. Had to be them. I also knew right then that I was fucked. I was squatted down in front of that cupboard just staring at an empty space where the parcel had been, with Jack stomping about in the front room shouting bastards bastards bastards. I felt sick guv, swear down, sick to my flippin stomach ...

■ ■ ■ ■ ■

Ndekwe comes to a stop at the traffic lights on the junction at the bottom of Kingsland Road. He sits and looks idly out of his window. After three months stationed in East London, Ndekwe still feels little or no familiarity with its streets, always more comfortable as soon as he hits the other side of the river.

A present for Sonia, he thinks. He is vaguely aware that it's their anniversary soon. He glances at the date on the dashboard and does a swift mental calculation: next week, in fact. He doesn't want to pull his usual trick and leave it until the last minute. But he has no idea what to get her, not a clue. Three years of marriage. What was the symbolic marker for three? Paper? Tin? Wood?

His gaze wanders over the display in the window of a small florist. Bunches of green and red and white and yellow. Flowers, he thinks. At the very least there has to be flowers. But flowers are a sideshow. They're not the main event. You can't say everything with flowers; there has to be a present as well. He tries to think of what she would really want and then remembers, closes his eyes and shakes his head as if to physically dislodge the thought from his mind.

The lights change down to green and he rolls the car forward.

Greenwich, he thinks. The market at Greenwich; antiques, trinkets, bric-a-brac; quirky bits and pieces. Things for the house. Sonia loves all that kind of stuff, that bohemian vibe. He tries to remember the covers of the magazines she keeps stacked by the bed. A mirror, maybe, or a rug. Maybe something to hang on the wall.

... Y'see I didn't know who he was at that point ...

Ndekwe realizes that Jack is talking away but he hasn't been listening. He turns the volume up and focuses his mind on the words of the old man.

... I thought he was just Melissa's fella, or mebbe one of her mates' fellas. I didn't know he was running the entire bloody estate, did I? He was just a young lad like all the rest of em. Anyway, I sorted him out with his nine bar and didn't see him again for about a week. He finally showed up one night, a Friday night I think it was. I was like hey, come on, son, play the bloody game, where's my money like? Bastard just laughed at me. Sat there on the couch grinning at me like I was some sort of fucking simpleton. Yeah yeah yeah, he goes, yeah yeah, money soon come, he says. This went on for a good few days, like. Every time I was round there I'd say to me laddo, hey, you tell that pal of yours to get his hand in his pocket. He'd just go aye, yeah, I know. But I could tell he was frightened of this Stewart lad. I could tell that by the way Stewart would swan in and out of the flat like he owned the bloody place. Like he was some sort of bastard landlord or summat. I tell yer summat else an'all, I swear I saw Janine larking about with him in the kitchen one night.

– Larking about?

– Aye. Late one night this was. I'd woke up in the armchair busting for a piss and I clocked em both in the kitchen as I was making me way to the bathroom. He had her backed up against the wall, sort of pinned in the corner, like, and I could see she had one hand down his pants. Going ten to the dozen she was. They were both too busy to notice me, but I saw em all right. I don't know if me laddo knew about that carry-on. I said nowt, me ... In hindsight, though, it's obvious the bastard had no intention of paying me. No intention whatsoever. As far as he was concerned I was just a joke, just some silly old sod he'd used and abused. And we're not talking about ten bob, we're talking about over a thousand pounds here, don't forget. It's not like I could just forget about it, chalk it off to experience. Besides, he was taking the piss, let's be right. He was taking me for a cunt, no two ways about the deal ...

Another volley of coughing and barking. Ndekwe unscrews a bottle of water and drinks long and deep, steering one handed as he leaves the East End and gets onto the A12 and dips down towards the Blackwell Tunnel, a luminous square of orange-fringed darkness gradually filling his windscreen. He flicks on the headlights as the car is swallowed up and the daylight shrinks to a dot in his rear-view mirror.

■ ■ ■ ■ ■

A knock on the door of room three. Frampton takes his feet down from the desk and turns down the volume on the CD player as the door opens and Halliwell's head appears.

– What you doing?

– Listening to the McKenzie interview.

– Fuck me, he's not got you at it as well, has he?

– Who?

– Our new DS.

– No, it was Gorman. Wanted me to have another listen.

– Jesus. Fucking Groundhog Day, innit.

– Fucking barmy.

Frampton flicks open the paper again.

– You hear about the knife? Halliwell asks him.

– No. What?

– Come down the pub and I'll tell you all about it. You fancy a livener?

Frampton folds the paper, throws it onto the desk. Stands and scoops up his keys.

– Is the Pope a Nazi?

The two police officers are out the door. The voice of Carlton Nesta McKenzie continues its unheeded testimony to the empty chairs and the cluttered desks, the silent, imploding starbursts on computer screen-savers, the files stuffed and locked with long-forgotten paperwork and the black and red directives scrawled across white boards that are hung on pale green walls fast falling into shadow.

I nearly cut out right there and then, y'know. That was my first thought, I must admit. That's what I should have done, in actual fact; just take the two G I had in my pocket and get down to the travel agent on the double, yeah? But it weren't as simple as that. Cos when I got back home there was Bam Bam and three other boys sat in my front room, blazing up with Melissa and her stupid giggling little mates. They got music banging out of the system and the place flippin stinks, not just weed either, there's that smell like burning tyres. I know that smell for real, no mistaking it. Bam Bam looks up from the sofa and says, Yes, Kez, and his throat is all croaked up and his eyes are even more crazy than usual, skittering about an all glazed over, like glass, yeah? Like two big white marbles rolling around in his ugly little head. And I knew they'd been doing rocks, doing rocks in our home, in my mum's front room, ya get me? I nod to Bam Bam an his boys an then ask Melissa where Mum is, and she's all screwface, like, fuck do I know. I seen the pipe near the ashtray at her feet. You're out of flippin order, Melissa, I tell her, an she's all like who are you, my fucking dad, an her mate starts screeching with laughter. I just go through to the kitchen an put some toast under the grill, but I know I ain't gonna eat nothing cos my stomach's churning round like mental, cos I just could not be in the same room as those fools. Then Bam Bam appears in the doorway an he's like yo, Kez, what's happening? I don't look round an I don't say nothing, just shrug my shoulders. You have to stand guard over the grill in our kitchen else you end up with bare burned toast. He's like, man says payday Wednesday, yeah?

– Who says payday? Isaacs?

– Nah, he means like Knowledge, yeah? So I'm like yeah yeah yeah, but he comes an stands right up behind me: man says come down Wednesday, yeah? I'm like, yeah I heard ya, cuz. But he can sense I'm not a hundred per cent plus he's paranoid on all that rock so he's like a shark when there's blood in the water, ya get me? He's like, yo, problem? I could feel his eyes on the back of my neck. I didn't want to turn round. I couldn't look the man in the face. No, it's all

good, cuz, I said. An he's like, so Wednesday night, yeah? Yeah, yeah I says. I feel a nudge on my shoulder. I glance round. He's got his fist held out. I bump fists but he's that wired it's more like a punch, like he's trying to knock me backwards, ya get me? Wednesday, Kez, he says. Yeah, I flippin hear ya, G. He marches back through to the front room and I take my toast into my bedroom an sit on my bed.

    – Were you scared of him?

    – Bam Bam? Bam Bam ain't right in the flippin head guv. I once saw him empty a boiling kettle over a man.

    – Over his head?

    – Nah, over his thingy ... his private parts, innit. See, thing is, I'd been to school with all these mans an seeing him and Mannix an Bailey an all them mans in my front room brought it slap bang home to me. If I took off with the two grand they'd be back through the door looking for me. An if they couldn't find me they'd do whatever was in their way.

    – What do you mean?

    – You know what I mean guv. They don't care about nothing, they're down for whatever. So I couldn't just ghost, could I? I was the man of the house, you get me? Anyway, after a bit they get off, Bam Bam and his followers an the other girl. I hear the front door shut an then Melissa comes bursting into my room, nearly taking the door off its hinges. She stands over me, jabbing her finger. FUCK DO YOU THINK YOU ARE? DISRESPECTING ME IN FRONT OF MY FRIENDS? FUCKIN BATTY BOY! I sprung up from my bed an grabbed her by the scruff of her neck. She tried to get her nails in my face, but I slapped her hand away, flipped her round an pinned her down to the bed. She's not a big girl, my sister, but she was wired with all the rocks, ya get me? She was snarling and spitting, going berserk, kicking her legs up an trying to twist her head round to bite my hands. It took all my full strength to keep her down there. I ain't never hit a girl in my life, an especially not my sister but I had to give her a couple of backhanders to try an knock the fight out of her, ya get me? I ain't proud of that part. I was brought up to respect

women. I want you to know that. But she was like an animal, yeah? Crack, man, it's the worst. It's the worst thing ever for that flippin paranoia, believe. After a bit she stops struggling, but I don't let her go. That's it now, Melissa, I tell her. That's it, yeah? She's glaring up at me, her eyes bulging with bare fury. She's growling like a dog that's been beaten into a corner. I know if I let her get up she'll come straight at me, so I bundle the duvet around her an roll her off the bed in one double quick move. I was out of the flat and down the stairwell in a flash an I didn't stop running till I got past the shops. I didn't know where to go, so I went back to Jack's. I never told him about the fight with Melissa. He could tell I was heated, though. I didn't say nothing, just helped him clean his flat up. There wasn't too much damage. Them Brick Lane boys hadn't taken nothing but the parcel. To be truthful, there wasn't that much more to take. They'd emptied all the drawers, though, pulled stuff out of the sideboard an scattered it all over the place. Letters an old photos mainly. The door was the main damage. It was hanging off its hinges where they'd kicked it and the lock part had come away from the wall. Jack went to borrow some tools from the guy downstairs and I held the door while he fixed it all back up again. It wasn't perfect, but we made it secure enough until the council got their act together to come and replace it properly. Which would most probably be flippin never. I gotta say, though, I wasn't feeling too concerned about Jack an his busted door at this point, because I had my own problem, my own very big problem, ya get me? Six grand's worth of problem to be precise. I knew there was no sense going out looking to step to these Brick Lane boys. I couldn't march down there on my own cos I'd get cut to pieces, man. Chopped up into little bits, ya get me? An I couldn't go down there with any of my own mans cos I was flying solo, innit. I couldn't tell nobody what had gone down. I was all on my ownsome. Maybe two or three years ago I could have raised a serious crew and sorted it all out proper style. But even if I could find mans to stand with me, that would mean letting them in on the reason for the beef. And I couldn't let word get back to Knowledge *about the parcel. For the first thing he wouldn't have believed me and for the second thing he wouldn't have cared anyway. All he would know is that he ain't getting paid. And you know what that means guv.*

– What?

– Means I'm getting zipped up in a bag, innit.

– You think he'd kill you over a key of weed?

– He'd do it over an eighth. He'd do it over a McDonald's. He was on a mission. I didn't burden Jack with any of this but he knew the missing parcel spelled trouble for me. I didn't blame the man; it was all my flippin fault. It was stupid to keep it at his gaff in the first place. Truth is, I didn't know what I was gonna do. I didn't have a single idea left in my head. After we fixed the door Jack went out an got a bottle of rum. I don't even like rum, but I sat an drank it with him till it got dark outside. I left him crashed out on his sofa an then I went back home. There was nobody there, not Melissa, not my mum, nobody. I didn't know where anybody was an I didn't even care. I fell into bed blind drunk an hoped I never woke up again ...

■ ■ ■ ■ ■

A stiffening south-westerly breeze sends a bank of clouds scudding from the Thames towards the harbour. Ndekwe finds a parking space in the shadow of the *Cutty Sark* and walks towards the market. It is late afternoon, but there are still plenty of people wandering around; families, mainly, parents and grandparents and small children, clutching glossy information booklets and fast-melting ice creams and swollen shopping bags, all looking to wring every last drop of sunshine from the end of the school holidays. The smell of roasting spices from the hot-food stands rouses the juices in his stomach, but Ndekwe presses on to the warehouses. He visits each one in turn, the vendors hemmed in by stacks of chairs, nests of tables, old wardrobes, cocktail cabinets, hat-stands, art deco mirrors, ornate vases and ornaments; the flotsam and jetsam of decades past, dusted down from the back yards and attics of London and beyond, restored, reclaimed and now resold as semi-precious junk, the must-have trophies of the shabby chic lifestyle.

Ndekwe works his way to the last but one warehouse in the row and combs its wares, considering and discarding various items before his eye falls upon something that looks like a wall clock, a wall clock in the shape of a ship's wheel. The centre is a cream and gold disc under thick glass, the width of a dinner plate, its circumference ringed by carefully turned wooden spindles. He studies the face: a depiction of an old-fashioned galleon sits beneath a semi-circle of gradients and numerals; its sails swollen by invisible wind. Italic script marks the outer edging: *Stormy, Rain, Change, Fair, Very Dry.* An ornate black needle points to the right, at rest on *Very Dry.* Beneath all of this, in the same scrolling script, are the words *Widdop & Bingham, 1952.*

– It's a beautiful piece, isn't it?

The woman sitting behind the stall is in her early thirties, purple and red streaked hair tied up in a rag, large silver hooped earrings and a stack of bright plastic bangles from elbow to wrist.

Ndekwe picks it up. It is heavier than he expected.

– Does it work?

– It does, yeah. More reliable than the weather forecast, those things.

– How do they work, exactly?

He examines the back for clues, finds none and turns the glass to catch the light again.

– Erm ... just ... pressure, I think, she says.

– Pressure?

– Yeah, you know ...

Her fingers describe a vague circle in the air, the bangles sliding and clicking together like rainbow-coloured castanets.

– Sort of ... atmospheric ... pressure.

Ndekwe turns the thing around in his hands and then holds it up in front of him by the spindles, twisting it this way and that, as though he were steering a ship through the ocean. He gives it a final close examination and places it carefully back onto the table.

– How much is it?

– To you? Seventy-five.

– I'll give you fifty.

She smiles, shakes her head, no.

– Sixty?

– Sixty-five, she says.

He reaches into his jacket pocket.

Fifteen minutes later he is heading for home with the barometer wrapped in brown paper and cardboard, sitting on the back seat, a darkening sky above him and Jack in the speaker at his knee again:

... Well, it all came to a head one night last week at me laddo's, the Monday or Tuesday night I think it was. This had all been dragging on for about three weeks now, and I'd had me fill of it. So I follows him into the kitchen and we start arguing the toss about this money and he's fucking chuckling away at me again, so I lost me rag and ended up getting a grip of him, didn't I, grabbed hold of him by the scruff of his collar, like. I was only trying to get him to pay proper attention, more frustration than owt really, but he went bloody doolally. He give me a couple of decent digs then he got me by the throat and pinned me up against the wall, and I could feel summat hard jammed up under me chin ... If I could have got me hand inside me jacket pocket I would have stabbed the bastard there and then. In fact, if Carlton hadn't have come into the kitchen at that precise point I think one of us would have been brown bread, no two ways about it. And it would have probably been me, oh aye. Anyroad, Carlton managed to talk this barmy bastard back down to planet earth, stood there at his shoulder and talked to him, reasoned with him, like, told him I was part of the family and all this deal, that he was asking for one last chance for me and all this carry-on. How the fuck he managed to pull it off I do not know, cos this cunt was

cranked up past boiling point, sweating like a bastard, he was. I could feel his breath blasting into me face like a bloody blowtorch. But Carlton kept yapping away to him, dead calm and controlled like, and eventually he lets go of me throat and stands back ... That's when I opened me eyes and saw him tucking this gun into his waistband.

    – He threatened you with a gun?

    – Threatened me with it? Bastard stuck it right under me chin ...

    – You were shook up?

    – Shook up? I was bloody petrified, brother, me blood froze solid in me veins. Oh aye, shook up indeed, have no doubt about that, my friend. Who do you think I am, Gary fucking Cooper? I'm seventy years old, pal. See the thing is, when you get to my age, the spirit is willing but the flesh is weak. My scrapping days are far in the distance behind me. And when someone sticks a gun under your chops then it's time to run up the white flag as far as I'm concerned. I'll be straight with you, like, I thought it was goodnight Vienna. This lad would have done me in, no two ways about it. Wouldn't have thought twice about it. I told yer, these young lads, they're fully fledged killers. Not started shaving, half of em, but they've got no qualms whatsoever about doing folk in. Cold, brother, absolute cold-blooded bastards they are ... Anyway, he clears off, this Knowledge, and me laddo gives me a lecture about how I shouldn't fuck about with people like him and all the rest of it and I remember pulling the knife out in the kitchen and saying how I was going to stab the bastard. Carlton takes it off me and tells me not to be stupid, puts it away in the kitchen drawer. Tells me to leave it there and go and have a drink with his mam, forget all about Knowledge and the money and all the rest of it, chalk it up to experience. The way he was talking there was nowt I could do, this Knowledge fella was untouchable, it would seem ... but when I think back now, about how I did actually kill him, it seems the strangest bloody episode ever. It was almost like it was meant to be, yer know? Like there was no avoiding the deal...

•••••

The station is quieter now, but silence does not settle in Room 3. The voice of Carlton McKenzie does not reach beyond the room and is not disturbed by the footsteps that fall outside, or the crackle of fluorescent lights that are flicked on and hum electric in the surrounding rooms and corridors, or the streetlights outside the building as they blink awake, a string of luminous pearls stretching away from the window into the distance.

And the boy's murmurings do not reach the ears of the young Polish cleaner as she enters the room, plugged as they are by two button-sized earphones that bleed a personalized soundtrack directly into her head, and neither does the light from the flickering LED display catch her eye.

... But I did wake up an it wasn't all just a dream. This was real life guv, ya get me? This was about as flippin real as it gets. I spent the next couple of days at home, just sat round the flat. I didn't want to show my face till I'd worked out what to do. My mum could tell that there was something wrong, but she just thought it was down to me and my sister beefing. Melissa just like completely blanked me, which suited me down to the ground. She was out with her mates all the time anyway, and my mum was at work, so I was just sat round the yard checking the windows every five minutes. I was jumpy, ya get me? I knew there was no way I could get hold of six grand. Not without doing something really dumb, like grabbing a box or something in that line. That's the only way to get money of that amount, go an steam a travel shop or something. Put a bally on and stick a strap in someone's face, yeah? I already told you guv, I ain't about that. I ain't about terrorizing anybody. But what happened next ... changed everything, yeah?

– What happened?

– Well, when Wednesday morning rolled round I was all set to just go an find Bam Bam and tell him the truth. But the fact is,

right, I bottled it. I was scared. I don't mind admitting this to you.
Me an Bam Bam used to be tight, true, but I knew that would not
count for nothing with Knowledge an the rest of his fools. You got to
understand this guv; the man would have smoked me, yeah? No doubt
about it. An even if he had let me live, I'd be his bitch for time. Ya get
me? I would have been working off a debt that could never ever be
paid. Never in a million flippin years, yeah? Ya see what I'm saying?
Anyway, you know it yourself. You know how these mans roll.

■ ■ ■ ■ ■

Ndekwe gets his key into the front door just as the first heavy spots
of rain hit the pavement.

He stands the box that holds the barometer up against the wall
of the hallway and goes through to the kitchen. A strong smell of
chemical lemon; the work surfaces have been cleared and wiped
down and the laminate flooring mopped, recently too; almost
entirely dry now, save for the odd shiny lick. All the pans and large
utensils are hung above the cooker. A fresh load of washing churns in
soapy water behind a porthole of glass. A note on the table propped
up against a vase full of white and yellow flowers: *AT ZUMBA*

Ndekwe pours himself a glass of water from a jug in the fridge,
swallows it in three thirsty gulps and then pours another. Stands
and drinks with the fridge door wide open until it starts to bleep
in protest.

He finishes his drink then he slips his shoes and jacket off in
the hallway and goes upstairs, to the back of the house, to the spare
room. He tries to ignore the half-stripped walls and the few pieces
of furniture pushed back against them, and he tries not to look at
the two wide brushstrokes of blue on the far wall that faces out onto
the back yard; one a deep royal uniform blue, the other as bright
as a cartoon ocean. They had known it would be blue. They had
argued over which shade right up until the point where it no longer
mattered. Both tins were stacked away in the cupboard now, lips

wiped clean, their lids jammed tightly shut, along with the three unopened rolls of wallpaper border, the one with the yellow ducks in racing cars.

Ndekwe reaches under the bed and retrieves the laptop. Then he goes back downstairs, sits himself at the kitchen table, inserts the disc and skips forwards to the place where he last left off.

... Here's the script, right; Stewart buggered off from Carlton's that night and I ended up falling asleep on the couch. Woke up the next day with a blanket chucked over me, like. There was no one else up, only me. I had a swill in the bathroom and made meself a cup of tea and rolled a single skinner from the last bit of this smoke I had on me. That was what tipped the scales, I reckon, smoking that bloody weed, cos I was already jumpy as a long-tailed cat in a room full of rocking chairs. Anyway, before I left the flat I remembered Carlton had stuck me knife away in the kitchen drawer. So, like a fuckin idiot, I goes and retrieves it, don't I? Goes and slides it back into me jacket pocket. That was me downfall, really. If I'd have just left it in the drawer mebbe none of this would have happened. By the time I got down the stairs and was wandering across the estate me heart was going ten to the dozen and I was completely bloody paranoid ... About dinnertime, this was. Middle of the day, like. I thought I'd go and get a paper and some bacca and then head for home, get some proper shut eye. So I went to the newsagent on that row of shops and got me supplies and when I come out there he was, that Stewart lad, him and that little cock-eyed bastard. Both strolling along on the other side of the street. I got me head down and shifted off in the opposite direction, reckoned I hadn't spotted them, like. But it was too late; that Stewart, he'd eyeballed me straight away and he comes marching across the road, like ... he said summat to me, I can't remember what, like, but it was summat derogatory anyroad, some sort of threat. He wasn't after being me pal, that much was clear. I tried to ignore him, I swear to God I tried to keep walking away, but he got hold of me and spun me round by the shoulder, that Aaron

*lad, and that's when I pulled the knife out me jacket ... It was weird,
cos it all seemed to happen in slow motion after that, d'yer know like
it does in a dream? All blurred round the edges. It was almost like I
wasn't there, like it was happening to someone else ...*

The cleaner works her way around the room, wiping, picking up,
putting down, moving aside and rearranging, humming to the
music in her head, oblivious to the continuing testimony in the
corner. Then she plugs the lead from the industrial cleaner into the
wall and buffs the floor of the corridor outside, the words inside the
office obliterated by a high-pitched steady whine.

*... But what happened, right, is that they battered my sister.
Knowledge an Bam Bam an all the rest of those fuckin pigs. They got
her in that boarded up house near the playing fields an they held a
gun to her head an they raped her, yeah? They fuckin raped my sister.
I told you I'd tell you everything, didn't I? I'm telling you it all, yeah?
So this is how it happened. This is why I done the man.*

– Go on ...

*– OK, so on the morning it happened I went round to Jack's an
I stayed there, hiding like a frightened little girl, yeah? I kept telling
myself I was gonna go down there an just tell him straight, but I was
sat in that flat all day just thinking about it, yeah, an I knew deep
down I weren't gonna do no such thing. I started getting all sorts of
mad schemes. But day turns to night an it starts getting dark outside,
an I'm still sat there, yeah? Then they started belling me up, yeah?
Every five minutes my phone is going off, number unknown, number
unknown. But I know full well who it is, yeah? So in the end I turn the
flippin thing off. Jack, he knows there's something wrong, he can see
me getting agitated, but I don't tell him what's what an he don't press
for details. Anyway, I stay in Jack's yard all night. I sleep on his sofa,
yeah? When I turn my phone on the next day there's a message from
my mum. She's saying, Carlton, come home, come home now. I knew
straight away it was bad. Real bad. I could hear it in her voice.*

– *In your mum's voice?*

– *Yeah. When I gets home my mum an my auntie are sat on the sofa with their arms around Melissa. She's got bruises all on her neck and her face an she looks like she's been crying for time. I'm saying what happened an Melissa starts sobbing her heart out, saying don't tell him, Mum, don't tell him. My auntie Sharon gets me in the kitchen an tells me Melissa was coming out the shops when some boys got her to come round to the back of them houses. She said they put a gun to her head an orally raped her. That's the words she used, orally raped. You know what that means, yeah? An then they started belling all their crew up to come down an then they took turns raping her the other way. All the other ways, if you get me. Melissa said she didn't know how many of them there was, but they were getting on their phones an more an more of them kept coming. She said she didn't know who they were, didn't recognize any voices. They had their hoods up an their hands over her eyes, ya get me? Tied her jeans round her head, ya get what I'm saying? But she knew. An I fuckin knew. An I knew why it happened. It was cos they couldn't get me, yeah? They battered my sister cos they couldn't get hold of me.*

– *And this is why you killed Aaron Stewart?*

– *What would you have done guv? You got a sister, yeah? What the fuck would you have done? Be truthful.*

– *This isn't about what I would do, Carlton. It's about what you did.*

– *Yeah, well … I sat with them in the front room for a bit then I said I had to go somewhere. My mum was like, Carlton, don't be doing nothing stupid an I was like nah nah nah … But I knew it had already gone beyond stupid. I said I wouldn't be long. I slipped into the kitchen an took a carving knife out the drawer an put it up my sleeve. Then I went down to the shops an I waited …*

■ ■ ■ ■ ■

– What's this?

Ndekwe looks up, startled. He hits PAUSE. Sonia is stood in the kitchen doorway. He hadn't heard the rattle of the front door or the greeting that she'd sung from the hallway. She holds up the box that holds the barometer, eyebrows raised in enquiry.

– What is this?

– I thought you were at Zumba class.

– It got cancelled. The girl was sick.

– Couldn't they have rung and told you?

– Yeah, they should have done. But what is this, though?

Ndekwe takes off his glasses, rubs his eyes.

– Oh, damn, yeah, he says. – Sorry.

– Sorry? Sorry why?

– It was meant to be a surprise.

Her face splits into a delighted grin.

– Is it a present, yeah? For me?

– Yeah ... well, for us. For our anniversary.

Sonia sits herself down at the table and begins tearing at the paper.

– Don't open it, babe; it's for next week.

– Yeah, but I've found it now.

– Be careful, though, it's old ...

She pulls away the paper and prises open the box. The kitchen light bounces off the glass face of the barometer. The needle has swung across to *Change*.

– Oh! Her eyes widen and the smile freezes on her face. – That's ... nice. What is it?

– It's a barometer. It's a genuine antique.

– Is it? Does it work? She lowers her head and turns her ear to the dial as if to listen.

– It does, he says. – Look ... He points to the needle and then to the rain hitting the french doors at the end of the kitchen. – How cool is that?

– Yeah, she says. – Cool.

– I thought it could mean like, you know ... Whatever the weather ... we'll always be together ... His words evaporate as he reads her face. – You don't like it, do you?

– *Course* I do, she says. – It's wicked! I love it!

– You love it?

– Yeah! It's gorgeous.

– Tell the truth, he says.

– Well ... all right. I don't actually *love* it, she says.

She traces a finger along the arc of numerals and letters and then rubs the glass with the sleeve of her sweatshirt. – But it is nice. Different. Unusual. She bites her lip and looks at him, mock serious.

– No worries, babe, he says. – I'll get you something else.

– Do *you* like it?

He holds it up and looks at it from arm's length. – I do, as it goes, yeah.

– Well, you keep it then, she says. – Get me something else. Deal?

– All right. Deal.

He places it back into its box and Sonia leans over to look at its face and studies the lettering and the ship. She can see her own reflection floating on the surface of the glass.

– I didn't think you liked things like this, she says.

– Like what?

– I dunno ... old things. Antiques.

– I like you, don't I?

She smiles and raises her hand as if to strike him across the head. He cowers as if in terror. She points to the laptop.

– What you watching?

– Listening. It's work.

– Oh, for God's sake ...

She stands up and opens the fridge door, inspects the contents.

– Have you eaten? she asks.

– Not hungry, babe.

She takes eggs and milk and butter from the fridge and places them on the side.

Ndekwe's fingers tap against the side of his laptop.

– Don't mind me, she says.

– You're not supposed to be listening.

– I'm not. Couldn't understand a word he was saying, anyway. Where's he from? Is he Scottish?

– He's from Hull.

– Where's that?

– Yorkshire.

– What's he done? Is he a baddie?

– I don't know yet.

She cracks eggs and pours milk into a bowl, starts beating the mixture with a fork. She glances across at her husband.

– Don't mind me, she repeats.

Her fork sets the yellowy gloop spinning in a furious whirl.

Ndekwe closes the lid of the laptop and rises from his chair.

– I'll listen to the rest of this later, he says. – Throw me another egg in, will you, babe ...

They eat their omelettes and make small talk; the relative benefits of Woolwich arts and crafts market compared to Greenwich, the impending divorce of one of the girls at Sonia's Zumba class, how the sudden rain will be good for the garden. When they have finished their meal and the plates have been washed, Sonia goes through to the sitting room to watch television.

Ndekwe boots the laptop back up, checks the time remaining: two more minutes.

... I'm walking backwards, waving this knife at him saying fuck off, go on, get on yer way, yer cunt, but he's just sneering in me face, says I haven't got the heart or I haven't got the balls or some such thing, and then he claps his hands in front of him, right up under me snout, clapping his hands together like he was a conjurer doing a fucking

*magic trick ... clap ... clap ... and on the third clap I stopped dead
in me tracks and stuck the knife straight into the bastard ... Listen,
I'll be straight with yer, I've fought with knives before. Got into a
scrap with this Portuguese get in Madeira many moons ago, ended
up stabbing him in the arm. That was par for the course for the
Portuguese, though, them and the Spaniards, they all carried bloody
knives, the lot of em. Half the time it's just for show, but if you throw
drink into the equation then you can end up doing someone a proper
injury. But I'd been lucky before, with knives, like. I mean, I'd never
been hurt meself or done an injury to anyone else, not a proper injury
anyroad. Just flesh wounds. Superficial, like. You have to be pretty
unlucky to do someone in by stabbing em, you have to get a main
artery or summat like that. Odds of you getting someone through the
breastplate or the ribs is pretty remote ... but I knew me luck had run
out there and then, though.*

– You knew it was in his heart?

*– Oh aye, soon as I stuck him ... it just spread out across his
chest like a big red flag. He looked down at himself, like, and he tried
to say summat but then he started coughing and retching. He tried
to take a step forward to get a grip of me, but his legs gave way and
he went down like a sack of spuds, dropped to his hands and knees
and started spewing up blood everywhere. And that's when I turned
round and walked off, quick march ... And soon as I heard that
fucking gun go bang, that was me, I was off like fucking ten men.*

– Who fired the gun?

*– Well, it must have been matey boy, that squiffy-eyed cunt.
I didn't exactly hang about to check. I'm presuming it was him
anyroad, cos the other fella was out the game.*

– So you ran?

*– Fucking hell, aye, fast as I could and as far as I could till the
old boiled eggs gave way and I cockled over halfway down that
footpath. I thought I was a goner then, I thought here we fucking go,
fucking OBE for me, you know, one behind the bastard ear ... but no
one came.*

– He didn't come after you? The other lad?

– Did he fuck. Good job an'all, cos I couldn't have done any more running. I just got up and managed to carry on walking until I got out on the main road … and then I just … well, I just walked home … mad as it sounds. I don't remember a great deal about it, to be totally fair. I was in a sort of a daze. I looked down and saw I had this fucking knife still in me hand. In the middle of the bastard street with everybody walking past me. So I got rid of that double quick, like.

– What did you do with it?

– Dropped it down a drain.

– And this is on Hackney Road?

– Aye. And then I just went home. Every step of the way I expected someone to stop me, feel a hand on me shoulder, like. But fuck all happened. I'd just stabbed someone in the chest and the world was carrying on just the same, all the shops were open and people were walking past going to and from work and there were cars driving by and all the rest of it. It was a strange state of affairs, brother. Very bloody odd. Like I said to yer, it was like I was in some kind of dream. I got home and run a bath and then I got into bed. And so … yeah … that was that …

There is another bout of coughing and retching and then the voice of Halliwell saying OK, let's leave it there for the time being. He thanks the old man for his help and notes the time of the interview's termination.

Ndekwe ejects the disc and slides it into the top compartment of the laptop's carry case. Then he makes himself a coffee. He calls through to the sitting room and asks Sonia if she wants a drink.

– No thanks, she replies. – Hey, she says, come and have a look at this. It's that guy you like.

– In a bit, he calls back.

His jacket is hung over the back of one of the chairs. He reaches into the inside pocket and retrieves the CD marked MCKENZIE. He takes it from the plastic wallet and loads it into the laptop.

■ ■ ■ ■ ■

The cleaner comes back into the room and she notices the green lights bouncing up and down on the machine on the corner of the desk. She takes out her earphones and stands and listens for a few seconds, understanding very little of what she hears. Then she unplugs her lead, gathers together her cleaning gear, turns off the lights and leaves the room, shutting the door behind her.

The voice of Carlton McKenzie mutters to the rain bouncing off the windows and the deep-cut shadows on the wall and receives no reply from either:

… I knew I didn't have to go looking for the man. All I had to do was stand outside the shops an word would get to him. So that's what I did. I went and stood outside the launderette an I just waited. I was only there for what, twenty minutes, when the first younger come round the corner on a bike. He skids to a stop when he sees me, spins round an gets off double quick. I can see him pulling his phone out of his jacket an banging in the digits as he pedals off. He gets a safe distance away then stops an holds the phone up to his ear. He's too far away for me to hear what he's saying, but I know who he's talking to, yeah? I know it's on now, yeah? This little kid puts the phone away an sits there on his bike waiting, an I'm waiting as well.

– He called Stewart?

– Course he did. An after about ten or fifteen minutes they come round the corner of the houses opposite, Aaron an Bam Bam. They come marching straight over to where I'm leant against this wall, next to the launderette, an I can see Bam Bam has got his hand under his shirt, reaching down into his waistband, yeah? I straighten up as they get closer. I got my arms behind my back, yeah? Aaron's all screwface an he starts saying something like yes, Kez, but before he can say anything else I slip the knife out from my sleeve, take two steps forward and stick it in the middle of his chest, boom. Bang it in as hard as I can, yeah? Like, fucking allow it, yeah? Then I push

him back into his mate an I turn round and run like fuck. I hear the bullets whizzing past my ears as I run – veep, veep, veep. I was glad it was Bam Bam who had the strap, cos that cross-eyed fool can't shoot for shit. I'm round the corner an racing away, straight down the path an onto the main road. I slowed down running once I was out in the open, cos there's more people around now, ya get me? I kept looking back to see if there was anyone on the street but I didn't see nobody ...

■ ■ ■ ■ ■

Sonia watches TV in the lounge as Ndekwe watches the rain hit the yellow pool of light made by the security sensor lamp in the back yard on the other side of the french doors. It's coming down harder now. He can hear Sonia laughing along with a studio audience.

Ndekwe checks the clock on the wall: 21:28.

He yawns, pinches the bridge of his nose and tries to concentrate on the young man's voice.

... Still, at least she still got to see her father, least he still on the manor. He might be a bit of a prick an that, but at least he still be visible. Up until the other night, right, I ain't seen my dad since I was about five, six years old, ya get me? You should be clear on that from the start guv, yeah? He ain't in my life any more. He ain't nothing to do with me now. I ain't seen the man for time.

After a bit I got sick of hearing Melissa an her mate chatting shit through the wall, so I went through to the front room an watched the telly with my mum. I don't go outside on a night time any more. I just stay in the yard. I ain't been out in the streets since my boy got took, yeah? My boy, Joseph, RIP ...

A bell chimes in Ndekwe's brain.

He pauses the interview, leaps up and goes through to the sitting room. Sonia is curled up on the couch in the semi-gloom, illuminated by the glow of the TV. A quiz show with a panel of comedians.

A man in a bright red shirt is trying to relate an anecdote, but is being interrupted by laughter from the audience and comic interjections from his fellow panel members.

– Sonia, he says.

– Come and watch this with me, she says. – This guy's got jokes.

Ndekwe doesn't look at the screen.

– Sonia, he says. – What was that boy's name?

– What boy? she says. – Come on, come and watch this.

She pats the space on the sofa next to her, but Ndekwe remains standing.

– That boy who got shot in Hackney, he says. – Those friends of your mum's from Sierra Leone. From her church.

She lifts up the remote and lowers the sound from the TV. She wrinkles up her nose, thinks for a second.

– You mean Hannah and Reuben?

– Yeah, Hannah and Reuben, that's it. What was the name of their son?

– Joseph?

Ndekwe cracks his fist into the palm of his hand and the sudden violence of his action makes Sonia jump.

– Peter! What's the matter?

– Have you got their number?

– I've not, but Mum will have it ... why, why do you want their number?

– Is it too late to ring your mum?

– No, she'll be up, but why, what's the problem?

But Ndekwe is already out the door.

– Peter?

– WHERE'S THE PHONE? he yells from the kitchen.

Sonia can hear clattering and banging, things being thrown around.

– YOU SEEN THE PHONE?

She shakes her head and frowns, points the remote, turns the laughter back up.

■ ■ ■ ■ ■

And the rain is really coming down now, a heavy curtain hung from the heavens, its black furls hammering onto the rooftops and the roads and the pavements, bouncing hard and fast and then gathering again in swift-moving rivers that surge along foaming gutters and kerbsides, swirling down the drains and pouring into the underground arteries of the city, once-pure water from above now churned into a fetid undercurrent pulling everything foul and forgotten along in its wake; broken chunks of fat from a thousand kitchens' down-pipes, fast-food fragments, discarded greasy wrappers and the flushed away faeces these things produce, and the water-bloated rats and the condoms swollen with gas, the streaming trails of tissue like dirty clouds of confetti, and tangled in all of this beneath the streets of E2 is a Kitchen Devil carving knife serial no: 7887387, the dried and blackened blood of a young man long since scoured from its silver, dull-edged tail.

... So I went back to Jack's yard. I didn't have nowhere else I could go. I never said nothing. I didn't have no blood on me or anything like that. I just acted natural an never let him know anything had gone down. He went out an did whatever he gets up to an I just chilled in his flat. He comes back around, what, five or six o'clock an makes us both some food. We had beans on toast. Everything just felt weird. An then we were sat eating it in front of the telly when it came on the news. Boy stabbed to death on the Crown Heights estate. Stabbed through the heart, dead.

– How did you feel about that?

– I couldn't believe it guv, swear down. I didn't think for one second the boy would be dead. It said on the news. Died in front of the shops. Jack was chatting away about something or other, but all I could hear was the man's voice on the TV. Stabbed through the heart, he said. I was in bare shock, trust me. A bit later on Jack gets his rum out an has a dram. That's what he calls a drink, yeah? A

dram. Then he tells me he's going away, going back up north. Going back home to see his peoples, yeah? He says I'm welcome to stay in his flat an all that, look after the place while he's gone. I think he was still a bit on edge about the Bengali boys. Think he wanted me to be like his house-sitter or something. I said yeah yeah, sweet as, yeah? But I'd already made my mind up I was getting off. Montego Bay. I had the weed money and my passport an my postcard. I was like fuck it, man, I'm going to Jamaica.

– That was your plan, was it?

– First thought was to get to a travel agent an buy a plane ticket. Then I thought a better plan would be to get on the train from Victoria to Heathrow and buy a ticket there. At the airport, yeah? But then I'm thinking rah, cameras, innit. I was trying to work out whether you'd be looking for me, yeah? How quick you'd get on the case. I knew for a fact that none of Aaron's mans would be talking to no police officer. But I knew my mum would have called the law over what happened to Melissa. I knew that. And once they'd been round my mum's they'd be putting it all together like a two-piece jigsaw. Hardly a case for Sherlock Holmes, innit.

– We never received any call.

– Yeah, well ... I knew I had to get off cos I knew the word would be out on me. So I thought about it all night an early the next morning when Jack got up an was folding his shirts into his bag I says yo, Jack, how you getting up north? He says he reckons he'd be going on the train. So I tells him I'll give him a ride up, yeah? Door-to-door service. He's down with that. So I tell him to be outside his front door in ten an I creep out an find a car parked up behind the supermarket down the road. A Ford Mondeo. So yeah, put that on the sheet as well. Twocking an driving without a licence an no insurance, all that. Put it all down guv; it don't matter to me now.

– And Jack never asked you why you wanted to drive him up north?

– Nah. Well, not at first anyway. He was in a bad way, man. He was coughing his guts up all the time, pure doubled up with it.

I thought it was just from the drink an all the smoking he did. But it did not sound good, trust me. I told him he was better off going to the hospital, but he was like nah, I'm getting off, man. So I gets these wheels an I roll up to Jack's an he's outside with his bag, ready to go. He lays down on the back seat an falls asleep straight away. He stunk of booze still an he slept all the way out of London. I was jumpy as anything, guv. I was sweating, yeah? I kept expecting the flashing blue lights in the rear-view mirror at any minute, ya get me? It seemed to take for ever to get out of the city as well. I didn't even know which way to go. I looked for signs for North London then for the motorway. I was driving around for time, getting more and more heated with this drunken sailor man snoring away behind me. But we got up through Camden an then Hampstead an Finchley ... Golders Green ... Fuck knows where I was going, man, but then I sees the sign for the big shopping centre, Brent Cross, an after that there was the sign heading off: THE NORTH, an I got on the motorway, slammed it straight in the fast lane an put my foot down an looked for the first sign that said Hull. I reckoned I'd be safe up there. I thought you'd never think of coming up that way. It seemed like a good plan at the time. It seemed like the best one I could come up with. I mean, truthfully yeah, whoever heard of anyone running away to flippin Hull?

   – It's not most people's idea of a dream destination.

   – For real. Anyway, after about twenty minutes on the motorway, Jack woke up. I seen his face pop up in the rear-view mirror. Not a pretty sight, believe me. Man looked like he'd just crawled out of a grave, like one of them zombie films. An he's all coughing an spitting out the window an shit. I'm like, flippin heck, Jack, use a handkerchief or a tissue or something, that is rank, man. But he just fires up one of his stinky roll-ups an then it's me who's coughing my flippin head off. Man asks me whose car it is an I tell him it belongs to my cousin, innit. Then he asks why I'm driving him all the way from London to Hull an why don't I just come on the train an I'm like rah, what the flippin heck is this, bruv, twenty

flippin questions? He don't say anything for a bit, but I can tell he's turning it round in his head. I can tell he's not convinced about any of this. I'm figuring at this point that the best thing to do is to tell him as little as possible, yeah? I don't want to make him no accessory after the fact. That's what you call it, innit? Knowledge is guilt an all that. I didn't want to heap any extra trouble on his shoulders, no more than he had already.

– Very thoughtful of you.

– Yeah, well, cos the man was in a bad way an I don't just mean physically, ya get me? He'd always had that raspy smoker's cough, but I'd noticed it was getting worse, all deep an sorta … I dunno … rattling, ya get me? He was spitting up all sorts of shit, like a load of stuff was breaking up inside him an he was trying to get it all out. But it wasn't just that, it was like his mind was starting to come apart as well, ya get me? I noticed he'd started talking to himself. Sorta muttering away to himself like a crazy person. I'd heard him do it in his flat once or twice, when he was staring at the telly or making cups of tea in the kitchen. I thought it was just cos he was old. That's what old people do, innit; chat away to themselves about random nonsense. But as we were going up the motorway in the car I noticed he was doing it almost nonstop, man, like a constant muh muh muh muh muh coming from the back. I could not hear the proper words he was saying, ya get me? Wasn't even sure if they were real words an not just a crazy noise. I was like yo, Jack, what's up, but he'd just say nothing, nothing's up an he'd sort of sit up straight an snap out of it for a bit, mebbe roll another smoke an stick it behind his ear, stare out the window. But then he'd start up again, muh muh muh muh. I could see his lips moving in the rear-view mirror. This was starting to get on my flippin nerves so I put the radio on to drown him out. I punched through the stations an found some dance tune an turned it up. I needed to think; I couldn't concentrate with Jack mumbling away at the back of my head. But then he starts complaining about the flippin music. What the effing hell is this shite? he says. Don't be putting any of this shite on, he says,

I've got a head like a kettle drum, don't need this shite, put something decent on. Put a different station on, put Magic on, he says. So I'm pressing the buttons an trying to find something to shut the man up, but everything that comes on is getting the thumbs down from the back seat, like that's shite, this is shite, can't stand that bastard, on an on an on. Like a bear with a sore head, innit. In the end I push the CD button an it's Kanye West, that tune he had out back in the day, the 'Gold Digger'.. You know the one I mean, yeah?

– Don't recall it.

– Big tune back in the day. Anyway, man leans forward an says that's Ray Charles that an I'm like nah, it's Kanye West innit. Is it fuck, says Jack, that's a Ray Charles song. An he starts singing along, I gotta woman mean as can be, or some such nonsense. I told you before the man could not sing, yeah? He sounds like he's trying to be all American an that, but he just sounds like he's drunk or something, an he's hollering away in my ear an I can smell last night's drink still on him an I'm like rah, Jack, give it a rest, bruv, an after a bit he shuts up. He listens to the tune for a bit an he then he says hey, how come he's allowed to say nigger an I'm not? I'm like, what you saying, man? He's calling someone a nigger, says Jack. If I said that I'd be hung out to dry, he says. He's not calling anyone a nigger, I tell him, he's just talking about a brother, innit. He's not like calling him a name or nothing. Just all part of his flow, all part of the chat, yeah? Oh right, says Jack, so it's all right if a black man calls another black man a nigger, is that it? I don't know what he's trying to get at here, but it seems like it's proper annoying him, ya get me? I try an explain it to him as best I can. It's not like calling someone a nigger, I tell him, like dropping the N-bomb an that, like when someone says it to like hurt someone or hate on someone, ya get me? He's just like saying, yo, my nigga. Ya get me? Like in the hood an that. It's just like the language, innit, the lingo. Do you know what Ray Charles would have said, says Jack, if you'd have called him a nigger? Look, Jack, I tell him, I do not even know who flippin Ray Charles is, OK? All I'm trying to explain to you, if you'd just flippin

listen yeah, is that the man is not calling anyone a ... bad name. Ya get me? So you don't think nigger is a bad name? he says.

– Interesting point ...

– Yeah, but it was like the man was just being stupid on purpose, ya get me? He knew what I was saying, but it was just like he was trying to provoke an argument. If you mean it in a bad way, then yeah, it's a bad word. Like ... if I called you old white trash, I say, that would be hurtful yeah? Not to me it wouldn't, he says, I couldn't give a fuck. Besides, I'm not even white. Rah! What are you then? I says. Black? No I'm pink, aren't I, he says, if we're gonna get all politically correct about it. I'm not white at all, he says. I'm sort of a peachy pinky colour. There isn't any white people. Apart from maybe the Scottish, he says, an he starts chuckling away to himself. I say to him, Jack, you is just trying to wind me up, man. Stop it now. Well, here's what gets me, he says. When I used to come home from sea I'd go and get fitted for a new suit. All the fisher kids would go and get measured up and you'd choose the latest style and colour. One of the colours you could have was nigger brown. That was the name of the style, a nigger brown suit. That was the name of it, he said. I told him I couldn't see what point he was trying to make with all this. The point I'm making, he says, is everyone had a nigger brown suit until the time came when you couldn't say the word nigger. Political correctness. Then you had to say coloured. I'm like, what, coloured? Just say black, I says to him. Black, man. Say it like it is, bro. Yeah, but there isn't any black people either, is there? he says. I mean, he says, you're not black, are yer? You're a half-chat, he says.

– A half-chat? Is that what he said?

– For real. Now that is like an insult, innit, I tell him. That is an insulting word, man. An he's like, oh right, so we're allowed to say nigger but we're not allowed to say half-chat? What the flippin heck is a half-chat? I say. You mean like a half-caste? Yeah, half-caste, he says. Half-chat. Same thing. I tell you what, Jack, I tell him, you can't half chat some shit, for real. An I tell him to shut the fuck up an then we just drive on in silence.

■ ■ ■ ■ ■

Sonia switches off the television and comes through to the kitchen to make a drink. She doesn't speak to her husband nor does he acknowledge her, until the noise of the kettle being filled from the tap and then the clattering of spoons and cupboard doors prompts him to put down his pen and turn off the voice from the laptop.

– Who was that? she says.

– Just work, he says.

– He sounds like a charming young man.

– What do you mean?

– Well, what is that all about, that entire half-chat business?

– You shouldn't be listening, he says.

– Hey, mister, she says, I live here too, just in case you forgot.

– I know, he says. – I'm sorry. But I've got to listen. Not long left now.

– Who is it, though?

– Remember that thing in the paper?

– What thing?

– Boy who got stabbed.

– Oh, that. Yeah, I remember. They got someone, yeah?

– They got two people.

– And this is the guy who did it, yeah?

– Well ... he says he did.

– He's admitted it?

– Yep.

– Cool.

– Yeah, except his mate's trying to claim all the glory for himself.

– Who?

– This other guy. Older guy.

– That Scottish man?

– He's not Scottish.

– Wherever. Sonia unscrews the cap on a large blue jar and

Ndekwe can smell malt and chocolate. – You want a hot drink? she asks him.

– Go on then.

She spoons heaped teaspoons of brown powder into two mugs as the kettle rumbles into life.

– So what's he saying? she asks.

– Who?

– That other guy with the grufty voice, him who's not from Scotland.

– He's saying that he did it.

– The murder?

– Yeah.

– So what's the problem? Just arrest the pair of them, if they both did it.

– Not that simple, is it?

– Why not?

– Cos they're both saying that they acted alone, that the other one wasn't even there when it happened.

– So what does that mean?

She takes the milk from the fridge and sniffs at it before pouring a measure into each mug.

– It means, says Ndekwe, that it's not enough to prove that one of them did it, you've got to prove the other one *didn't* do it. You get me?

Sonia shrugs. – If they both want to be murderers, then let them both be murderers. Lock them both up.

– I'm tempted to agree with you, he says. – But if they both go to court and they both say they acted alone then their lawyers will have a field day.

– How do you mean?

– They could both end up getting off.

– How come?

– Our old friend reasonable doubt.

Sonia stirs the milk around in the bottom of each mug. – Sounds stupid to me, she says.

– Yeah, well, that's just the way it works, says Ndekwe.

– So why have you got to listen to all this tonight?

– We've got to prove one of them didn't do it.

He slides his glasses up his nose with his thumb and forefinger, rubs his eyes.

– This is doing my head in, though, he says.

– It'll be OK, babe. First day back is always a stinker.

– Yeah, but I messed up big time today though.

The kettle clicks off and Sonia makes the drinks, brings the two steaming mugs to the table. She sets one at his elbow and sits down opposite him.

– What happened?

– Had a bit of a set-to with one of the gaffers. Lost my rag a little bit.

– Why?

– Ah, it was nothing, really. He kept mispronouncing my name and it just revved me up. I raised my voice to him. Stupid.

– What, because he got your name wrong?

– I know. It was dumb. I overreacted.

– That's not like you.

– I know.

Sonia looks at her husband then looks at the rain falling outside the french windows. Then she remembers something. – Why were you asking about Hannah and Reuben's boy?

– That guy you just heard? Ndekwe says, nodding to the laptop. – He was Joseph's best friend.

– One of the murderers?

– Yeah. Soon as I saw him this morning I knew I'd seen him before somewhere.

– Where?

– At the funeral.

Sonia considers this and decides she doesn't have any opinion or comment to add. Instead she reaches across the table and wraps her hand around his.

– Listen, she says, I'm gonna have a shower and then I'm gonna get into bed. You coming?

– In a bit. Not long to go now.

She squeezes his hand.

– Don't keep me waiting, Fast Track, she says.

He smiles, squeezes back.

– I won't, he says.

... Got a bit further on an Jack said he needed a piss. The last sign we passed said services twelve miles, so he had to cross his legs for a bit until we turned off at the sign.

– Which services is this?

– I don't know the name. It's a big place with a bridge that stretches all across the motorway. It's got a Burger King, an amusement arcade an a shop with newspapers an drinks an sandwiches. We both went for a piss an I gave Jack some money to buy some food. I told him to get me a BK meal an to get himself whatever he wanted. I didn't wanna hang about in the shop cos of cameras an that. I sat an waited for him an we ate our food in the car. Jack got the newspapers an a big bottle of water. As we pulled away I noticed the petrol light was flashing. The needle was way down in the red, so I swung into the petrol station on the way out an filled the tank up. I filled it right up to the top, about fifty quid's worth. I reckoned that should be enough to get us to Hull. Famous last words though, innit. I paid for the petrol an we got off, but we only got as far as the exit road till the car started stalling. Jack puts his paper down an looks across at me like to say what, what's happening? There was this banging noise coming from underneath the bonnet. Like there's something under there trying to punch its way out. Then there was this massive bang an we lurched to a stop, engine just cut out completely, innit. I was sat there twisting the key but nothing was happening. Cars started blowing their horns an then they're all swinging out to get past us an out onto the motorway. What's happened? says Jack. He leaned across to look at the

dashboard. *Try it again, he says. I turned the key again an nothing happens. He gets out an walks round the back of the car. Then he gets back into the passenger seat. Carlton, he says, did you fill it up with diesel? I filled it all the way up to the top, I tell him. Yeah, he says, but did you fill it with diesel or petrol? Petrol, I tell him, an he's like shaking his head an I'm like what, what? It's a diesel, he says. It's a fuckin diesel car, you fuckin pie-can!*

– You seized the engine.

– *Well flippin seized. We both just sat there for a bit. Cars were slowing down an then swerving round past us out onto the motorway. Fuckin diesel, man; I didn't know what to do. Is he in the AA? says Jack and I'm like, is who in the AA? Your cousin, he says. Is he in the AA? Or one of the other ones? RAC? Green Flag? Which one's he in? I didn't know what to say. I felt sick to my stomach, man. Jack opened the glove compartment, started pulling out CD covers and booklets, pieces of paper, a phone charger and some other bits of crap. He found an owner's manual an started flicking through it. Jack, I say to him, but he's not listening. Have you got your phone on you? he says, you'll have to ring them up. If he's not a member we'll have to pay for someone to come and flush the engine out. He leans across and flicks a switch on the dashboard. Put your hazards on, he says. I'm trying to think what I can tell him when there's a tap on the driver's side window an I nearly jump out of my flippin skin. There's this man standing there. He's got his car parked up behind us an he's doing his Good Samaritan bit, innit. I wound the window down. You all right, mate, he says. Want a hand pushing it over? You're backing traffic up here. Jack got out an I steered the car as him an this man pushed us right over to the side of the exit road. Then him and Jack stand there an start chatting, so I had to snap into action double quick smart, ya get me? Before Jack can give out any info, yeah? I pull the screwdriver from under the seat, stick it up my sleeve an whip my phone out my pocket an press it up to my ear as I get out the car. I grabbed Jack's arm as I walked past, pulling him along with me. Thanks, bro, I say to this man, thanks a lot, we'll head back* up there an call em out. Thank you for your help, I say. Cost you that, mate, this guy says, nodding at the car. Easy mistake to make, though, he says. I just nod and smile an hold my hand up, make out like I'm listening to someone on the phone. Jack falls in beside me an the man gets back into his car and gets off. Jack could see that my phone ain't switched on. Man knows something is up, but he don't know what. He's firing questions at me but I ain't even listening cos I know we ain't got much time. I'm leading him through the car park an I'm on the lookout for a Mondeo. I get one lined up an tell Jack to shut his mouth an stand by the exit an wait for me. For once the man does as he's told. He can tell there's something gone off, yeah? I walk past the car a few times until there's no one in direct sight then I pop the door an I'm in. I get it fired up an swing out of the car park an stop so Jack can jump in. He don't say anything till we're past the other car an out onto the motorway again, jammed in the fast lane an putting bare miles between us an the service station. Then he's like, OK, son, start fuckin talking, yeah? So I told him how I did the man Aaron an that my only hope now is to get out the country before they find me, get to my dad's place in Montego Bay, ya get me? I didn't tell him about what happened to my sister. I thought he didn't need to hear that. I let him think it was just some gang banging shit, ya get me? I told him how I'm planning to fly from one of the places up north, maybe Manchester or somewhere like that. Some place they got an airport. He didn't interrupt me or pass comment, he just listened. An when I finished he didn't say nothing for a bit, then he just said, you stupid effing twat. I told him I was sorry for getting him involved, yeah? Cos not one minute of this was his fault, swear down. Man's had enough to put up with, ya get me? Man thought I was just giving him a lift back home an now all of a sudden he's on the run with a killer. That was not in his original plan, definitely not. I offered to drop him off at the next services, but he tells me to shut the eff up while he thinks of a way round this. We drive along in silence for a bit then Jack says he got a plan. He says we'll carry on to Hull where he needs to sort some business an I could get off.

He says there's a boat that could get me to Rotterdam in Holland an from there I could get a train to Amsterdam an then fly anywhere in the world. I had my passport an the money an I could buy a bag an some fresh clothes, make me look like a legitimate tourist, ya get me? Jack says he reckoned you lot would still be looking round London for me. Reckoned they wouldn't think I'd head up north. Said the docks would be safer than an airport. All I had to do was avoid getting my collar felt between the road and the boat.

– And that was all Jack's idea?

– Well, that is what we come up with between us, yeah.

– So, wasn't Jack shocked or upset at what you told him?

– How do you mean?

– He wasn't at all disturbed by what you'd done?

– I dunno. He asked me if I'd ever killed a man before an I told him straight an I'll tell you, I ain't ever killed anyone before guv. Like I say, I was not involved with any of that gang banging shit, especially not after Joseph.

– Your pal who got shot?

– Here's the thing, right, I still think them bullets were meant for me, ya get me?

– Why do you think that?

– Joseph always liked that jacket of mine. It was a sick jacket, true, a blue an white Rocawear baseball jacket. Two ton worth, yeah? Joseph could never afford anything like that; he was never earning any paper an his people were poor, ya get me? So I let him wear it around. It was too big for him but he didn't care. He thought he looked sick in it, man, proper G. An when the mans on the bike come they thought he was me. That's what I think. That's what I think to this day. There were a million reasons why they could have been looking for me, all of them stupid, but they were reasons all the same. There was not one reason I could think of why anyone would want to hurt Joseph.

– Did you talk about this with Jack?

– Yeah, I told Jack all of this as we were driving along. I told

him about when I went in to see the body, laid out in the coffin. His
people had dressed him in his Sunday best, his church clothes. It
didn't look like Joseph, no way. It looked like a waxwork dummy or
something. I bet you seen loads of dead bodies in your job, yeah?

  – I seen a few, yeah.

  – I ain't never seen one before Joseph. But, anyway, that was
all in the past now so I asked Jack to tell me some more about
Jamaica. I was just focusing on them big blue mountains an that
beach. Them golden sands. I was mapping it all out in my head – get
to Montego Bay, find the Jolly Roger, then save up enough dough to
send for Melissa an my mum. That was the long-term vision, innit.
Short-term plan was to get off the main roads an get to Hull an
dump that red-hot motor. We didn't see no police or nothing on those
back roads. Jack had the map an he was saying get in this lane, get
in that lane, go left, go up here, make a right turn there. I just did
exactly as he said. Man had been all around the world, ya get me?
I ain't even hardly been out of London. I'm serious. Ain't proud of
it, but there it is. Jack, though, he's been everywhere guv, for real.
Or at least he says he has. To hear him go on you'd have thought he
was about two hundred an fifty flippin years old, all the things he's
done and seen. All the places he's been an the people he's met. I said
to him once when were working in the bar, flippin heck, Jack, you're
like that film, innit, that Forrest Gump. *Every event in the history of*
the entire world you were there, bruv, popping up all over the place.
Jack was there for Elvis starting rock n roll in America an then he
was there for the Beatlemania in London an also when England won
the World Cup back in the day. Everywhere, ya get me? Jack was
in America when they shot the president, JFK. He was in Germany
when the Berlin Wall came tumbling down. Rah, I bet if you watched
that old film footage of the first man on the moon stepping out onto
the surface, Jack would be there in the background, hovering about
with his space helmet on and a bottle of rum in his hand.

  – Just an old romancer, eh?

  – Yeah, but the man had been to Jamaica, though, and all

round the Caribbean an that. I could tell that was true by the way he talked about it. He said some of the same kind of things Harry from the Centre used to say when I asked him to tell me about the island; about how the houses were like gingerbread houses an the sea was crystal clear, fish of a thousand different colours darting about between your feet. How the sky would go deep purple on a night an the moon would hang low. How the Rasta man was told to get off the beaches an stay out of the way of the tourists. An you had to be stern faced to people if they talked to you, if they even just asked you the time, man, cos Jamaica was a rough spot an you had to have your head about you, innit. I reckoned it didn't sound much different to the ends in that respect. Anywhere that's poor is gonna be rough, true. But at least in Montego Bay you could feel the sun on your back an live a healthier life, innit, with good an proper food an sunshine an live close to Mother Nature, man, not just pissing down rain an bare concrete everywhere. That's what I thought at the time anyway. That was the dream I was holding onto.

– So you were heading for Hull. Where in Hull, exactly?

– Some guy name of Colin. I had said to him how can you be sure if the man is still at the same address if you ain't spoken to him for time? But Jack just laughed again an said this Colin was like the Olympic torch, never went out. That is the words he used. Rah, Jack was a funny guy when he was on a roll guv. He could come out with bare jokes, trust me.

– What's he say, the Olympic torch?

Sonia is standing in the kitchen doorway in her dressing gown, her hair twisted up in a towel. Ndekwe hasn't noticed her, doesn't know how long she's been there. The heating has clicked off and the room has fallen cold, but Ndekwe hasn't noticed that either.

– Why is he talking about the Olympic torch? she says.

– It's just a joke, says Ndekwe.

He stops the interview and writes something down. Sonia gathers her dressing gown tighter around herself.

– Are you coming to bed?

– Soon, he says.

– I'll wait for you, she says.

– You should go to bed, he tells her.

– How long is there left?

– Not long.

She yawns. – I'll go through there and read my book, she says.

But yeah, I was feeling a bit better about everything at this point. I thought I had a chance to get away. That was what I convinced myself, anyway. It was like just being away from London was enough, a proper head-start. I reasoned that I was probably in more trouble with the rest of them idiots down there, whoever Aaron had been running around for, ya get me. He acted like he was the big face, but I know the pecking order went up much higher than that prick.

– *Names?*

– *I don't know no names. Aaron might have been the big dog round our way, but there's always someone else pulling on the chain, yeah? Always. Anyway, I was more worried about my mum an my sister. I thought about belling up my mum cos I knew she would be worried sick. She would have known by now it was me who did the man, no doubt about it. But then, thinking about it logically, the police must have known that too, yeah? Because my mum would have called the police over my sister, no doubt about that. She would have had them round the yard double quick for real. An then they would have put two an two together, ya get me? You lot up here must have known it was me, yeah? You must have known all the time. I think I knew all this. I ain't stupid guv, an I know you lot ain't stupid either. You knew it was me, yeah?*

– *We didn't know anything, Carlton.*

– *Yeah, but what did you think when you heard about my sister? You must have known then, yeah?*

– *No, we didn't know anything.*

– *What, not even when you knew about my sister?*

– *Your sister never reported any attack.*

– *It happened, though, trust me.*

– *Nobody spoke to us about it.*

– *My mum then, yeah? She must have called you?*

– *No, no one.*

– *All right, all right ... whatever. But you know what, yeah? As we got closer Jack took over the wheel an as we headed for Hull with the sun shining in the sky an the radio playing I thought, rah, we could do this, bruv. We could make a getaway. Hit the road, Jack! Hull ferry, man, direct to Amsterdam! Although I must admit, I was not too happy about him being in that driver's seat. For a start, man had drunk bare drams of rum the night before. For another thing, he drove like an old geezer out for a Sunday drive. But he said it was only fair that he do his share behind the wheel. Besides, we were heading for his patch an he knew the way. We got back on the motorway an he stuck to that inside lane like shit to a shoe, trust me. There was bare traffic overtaking us all the way up the road. I was like rah, Jack, you better up the tempo, bruv, cos you is drawing attention to us chugging along like a tortoise. I turned the radio over to the talking channel to see if there was any more about the thing back down the road. But there was nothing. Just the usual chat about the war an the politicians an the World Cup an all the usual stuff that goes on, day in an day out. Another dead soldier boy is only news for one day, innit. Then it's onto the next one. I kept my mouth shut as we trundled along in the slow lane. Eventually we see the signs for Hull an I start to get excited, man. I ain't never been up there before, but it had started to seem like the flippin promised land to me, yeah? Like it was the gateway to a better place. That's what Jack called it, in fact, the gateway to Europe. King George dock, he said, that ferry take you to Rotterdam, the capital of Holland, yeah, an from there you can go any place in Europe. All connected, innit. Like I said, the plan was to get on the train to Amsterdam airport an then fly direct to Jamaica. I figured there'd be less eyes peeled on the boat, ya get me. Land ahoy, Jack, I yelled, but the man was all*

quiet an subdued now. I could not work him out guv. I thought he'd
be all excited to be back on his home patch after all that time away. I
didn't care, though, I had visions of freedom real strong now. I could
almost feel that Caribbean breeze on my face. I was there. In my
head I was already there.

– Montego Bay ...

– That's the one. I said to Jack, rah, Jack, man, come with me,
yeah? Get yourself over there! Jamaica, man! I told him I'd get him a
job at my dad's bar no problem, or one of the other bars on the Strip.
Bare bars and clubs out there, man. Easier to get work out there than
in Hull or London even. Jack just sort of laughed an said yeah yeah
yeah, but I could tell he wasn't even nearly tempted by the thought.
I could not understand the man. Couldn't believe it when I saw the
sign. Kingston upon Hull, the Pioneering City! Raaas! Kingston!
I saw that as a sign for sure, that was a sign straight from Jah! I
was that excited, bouncing up an down in the passenger seat. Jack,
I says, you never flippin told me you were from Kingston Town,
man! He tells me that the city ain't even called Hull, that Hull is
the name of the river an the real name of the city is Kingston. Why
don't they ever say that? Kingston is a better name than Hull. Hull
sound too much like hell, man. Call it Kingston Town. Kingston upon
Hull! Rah! They should make a big noise about that. They'd get bare
tourists coming over from Jamaica if they told everyone they were
called Kingston.

– Yeah, maybe so. Anyway, tell us about this other guy. Colin,
was it?

– All right, yeah, so we come off the road just past the bridge and
parked up down this side street near some old buildings. Don't ask
me what the street name was cos I don't know. I don't even know
the name of the pub. I think it had a picture of a king or something
on the sign outside. The King's Head, or something like that. I don't
remember, straight up guv. It was an old pub, though, an it looked
like it had just opened its doors for the day. The only person in there
was this little guy behind the bar with a big gold earring. He was

cleaning glasses an he nearly dropped one when Jack walked in. Well eff me, he goes, it's the ghost of effing Christmas past! Now then, Benny, says Jack. This Benny, he leans through a doorway behind the bar an shouts up some stairs: COLIN! COL! LOOK WHO'S HERE! This other guy comes stomping down the stairs an he's like, Jack, you old bastard. He's a real big guy, dressed in jeans an a grubby white vest, big belly an loads of bling on him, bare chains round his neck an rings all over his hands, sovereigns, just like Jack's. He's got bare sailor man tattoos like Jack as well, all up his arms an under his vest. He's straight round the bar an giving Jack a big bear hug. Jack's laughing an slapping him on the back an all that old pals act an then he says Colin, this is Carlton. The man looks me up an down an says oh aye, this is the Yardie man, is it? But he's smiling when he says it, ya know, he don't mean nothing by it. But I'm wondering now what Jack's been saying about me, yeah? How much he's told this geezer about what's been going on.

– And what had he told him?

– I don't know guv. I never asked anything, just kept my mouth shut. This Colin man pours out some drinks an him an Jack start chatting away at the bar. I knew there was something about this man, an the other little guy, that Benny. I went an put some money in the bandit an kept an ear out as they was all chatting. Jack was asking them how business was doing an all that an Colin says shite, Jack, absolute shite. Dead as an effing dodo, he says. Jack says something about how it always used to be a busy pub back in the day an it'd be a real shame if it had to close. End of an era, he was saying. What's the problem then, asks Jack, people just not coming out supping like they used to? Cheap booze in supermarkets, says Colin. Killed it stone dead. That's half the problem. And gay people, says this Benny man. They don't help. An he starts slagging off gay people coming into the bar, saying they were putting off the other customers by shouting an screaming an fighting with each other and rah rah rah. Giving the place a bad name, innit. My ears are pricking up at this, cos I had this Benny man down as a batty boy as soon as

I walked in the place, ya get me? The way he looked an the way he was talking. But here he was slagging off gay people, yeah? I couldn't work out what the score was here. Listen guv, I ain't got nothing against batties or gay people or whatever. Live an let live, innit? As long as they stay away from me, I ain't bothered what they get up to with each other, ya get me?

– Absolutely.

– I ain't prejudiced like that. Anyway, soon after we got there this other guy walks in with a tray of bread rolls, this guy with glasses an a white hat an a long white coat. He gives the tray to Benny, who takes them through the back an says he's going to make everyone some sandwiches, innit. Jack calls me over an me an him an this white hat guy all sit down at a table. Carlton, this is Breadcakes, says Jack, an this other guy gives me a nod.

– Breadcakes?

– That is what he called him. Jack was like, OK, here's the script: Breadcakes goes on the ferry every dinnertime with a delivery. I had to walk on with him, right? Just go straight up the gangplank with him, yeah? Jack reckoned there'd only be one or two people there at that time, and they all know Breadcakes anyway. No one would pay me any attention. All I had to do was just put on a white coat an a hat an carry the tray onto the boat. Act dead natural. Like I'm making a delivery, yeah? Once I was on board, Breadcakes would show me where to hide. This Breadcakes man said I just had to lay down and go to sleep. Get my head down, he said. But don't come out till they've set sail, not for a good hour after that. Jack slips off his watch and passes it over to me. Take that, he says. Boat sails at half five. Wait till seven, then slip out. Maybe half seven. Boat'll be in full swing by then. What you do then is go down to the blue deck an ask for Deirdre behind the bar. Deirdre – you got that? he says. I got it, I say. What's she look like, this Deirdre? I say. Breadcakes an Jack look at each other an Breadcakes laughs. Jack shakes his head. What's up? I say. Nothing, says Jack. Don't worry about it. Just ask for Deirdre. You'll be looked after. Deirdre'll put you in a cabin. Stay

*there till the morning. The ferry takes all night to get to Rotterdam.
It docks in the morning. Do as Deirdre says after that, an you'll get
off fine. Jack reckoned I wouldn't even have to show my passport.
I was starting to feel pure excited. This was like some mad film,
innit. Like some proper* Bourne Identity *shit or something like that.
Breadcakes gets off an says he'll stop by for me tomorrow. Which
should have been today, yeah? What time is it now guv? I should
have been on that boat by now ...*

The interview ends and Ndekwe looks at the clock.

    23:58.

    The rain has stopped and everything outside is dark and still. He
shuts down the laptop and clears away his notes, rinses his empty
cup out at the sink, dries it and puts it back into the cupboard. Then
he goes through to the front room.

    Sonia is curled up on the sofa, fast asleep beneath the red and
green beach blanket they brought back from Portugal. The TV is
playing, the volume turned down to a murmur.

    Ndekwe reaches down and strokes his wife's cheek with his
finger.

    – Come on, babe, he says. – Time for bed.

■ ■ ■ ■ ■

Gorman sips gingerly at his tea, a dull throb in both of his fifty-
eight-year old kidneys, and his office blinds still unopened for fear
of provoking the thunderstorm brewing at the back of his skull. That
second bottle of wine had been a mistake, he reflects, especially on
a school night; a definite lapse of judgement there. He blows across
the surface of the tea; it is too hot to drink and the smell of the milk
is making his stomach heave. He puts the mug back down on his
desk and takes out his handkerchief, mops his damp brow.

    The light on his phone blinks red: Ndekwe.

    Gorman grinds his fist into his eyeballs as if to banish the light, but it is still flickering red when he looks again, and he allows four more flashes before picking up the call and telling his DS to give him five minutes to finish typing up a report, please. He bangs the receiver back in its cradle and swivels round in his chair, scoots himself over to the window and pulls open the blinds. Light floods the office. Gorman swivels back round and propels himself and the chair back to his desk, busies himself with nothing. Four and a half minutes later Ndekwe is tapping on the door with a handful of papers and a sheepish-looking Halliwell in tow.

Gorman feels a start of annoyance; he was fully expecting some reference to yesterday's little set-to in the corridor, but it looks like Ndekwe has seized his moment and put pen to paper. Wonderful, thinks Gorman, this is all we need when we're trying to wrap up a murder; some thin-skinned brother with a written complaint in one hand, a copy of the rule book in the other, and a chip the size of the Post Office Tower on each fucking shoulder. He takes a deep breath and steels himself for the impending avalanche of shit.

But there is no mention of yesterday's name-calling, incorrect or otherwise. Instead, Ndekwe presents a fresh development; the discovery of a couple of stolen cars; a black Ford Mondeo abandoned on the exit lane of a service station on the M1 near Stevenage and another Ford Mondeo, a silver one, parked up in a side street behind a pub in Hull. McKenzie's and Shepherdson's prints are all over both vehicles. Gorman's mood thaws considerably. This is positive news; now they can rearrest both men for the twocks and give themselves a little more breathing space. Excellent news indeed. Gorman straightens himself up, all brisk efficiency and newfound purpose.

– Right, he says. – Let's get the pair of them back in that interview room and rip them both a new one.

He looks at Ndekwe with fresh authority.

– So. Ndekwe. You're up to speed now?

– Just about.

– You listened to that load of old toffee from yesterday?

– Shepherdson? Yeah. And McKenzie.

– And?

– Well, the old man's trying to protect him; that much is obvious. What I can't understand is why.

Gorman leans back and links his fingers across his belly. – Frightened, probably, he observes. – Personally, I think he tells that many lies he can't separate fact from fiction.

– In other words, offers Halliwell, a bullshitter.

– I agree, says Ndekwe. – So it shouldn't be too difficult to prove he wasn't there.

– Exactly, agrees Gorman. – Good. Excellent! He feels the muggy clouds of his hangover begin to dissolve. – So we'll put a line under Shepherdson, then we can cut him loose and concentrate on me laddo.

He claps his hands and rubs them together as if to say that's it, meeting over, let's crack on, chaps. But Ndekwe isn't going anywhere. He flips open his notebook, balances it on his knee.

– Yeah, he says. – McKenzie. Two things bother me there.

Gorman feels his heart sink into the fermenting slush of his beleaguered guts.

– What?

– First thing. If he's got this old geezer willing to take the rap, then why's he so keen to put his own neck in the noose too?

Gorman shrugs. – Who cares?

Ndekwe considers this, then consults his notes again. – Second thing, he says. – The sister. This rape.

– She's adamant it never happened, states Halliwell.

– That doesn't mean it didn't.

– She won't testify, says Gorman flatly, so that's the end of it.

– Well, I'm going to see the mother later this afternoon, says Ndekwe. – I've asked her to make sure the sister is there too.

– I honestly think it's bullshit, says Halliwell.

– Maybe so, Ndekwe concedes. – But I need to hear it for myself.

– Belt and braces? Gorman gives him a sideways look.

– Belt and braces. Ndekwe nods. – But if we say there was no rape, then that begs the question of motive.

– They had beef! Gorman shoots Halliwell a look of barely concealed exasperation.

– Yeah, OK, agrees Ndekwe, but what does that mean, exactly?

– It means whatever these balloon-heads want it to mean! They don't need a real reason to top each other, Gorman says. – Come on, Ndekwe, you know how they roll.

Ndekwe doesn't say anything. He looks at his notebook and then thoughtfully into space. Gorman finds the growing silence uncomfortable. He looks at Halliwell, who is busy studying his fingernails. The Detective Inspector can feel his temples begin to throb. He is about to rise to his feet and dismiss the pair of them when Ndekwe speaks.

– Listen, I need to go and speak to someone before I get back in with McKenzie.

– Who? asks Gorman.

– Hannah and Reuben Musa.

– And they are?

– The parents of Joseph Musa.

– Joseph Musa?

– Shot dead two years ago on the Crown Heights estate.

– I know who he is, Peter, snaps Gorman testily. – It was my case. I interviewed the parents. Why do you want to go and see them?

– McKenzie was Joseph's best mate. That's why I remembered him. We were both at the funeral.

Gorman looks at him quizzically.

– You were at Joseph Musa's funeral?

– I know the family. Well, sort of. They're friends of my in-laws. Churchgoers. I think they'll talk to me.

Gorman shakes his head, mystified.

– About what?

– McKenzie, says Ndekwe.

– Still don't see why.

– Because I listened to McKenzie's interview and he mentions Joseph Musa twice.

– And?

– And it might be worth going and having a chat. At least they'll talk to me. No one else has.

Gorman looks at Halliwell. – What do you think, Tom?

Halliwell makes a gesture of indifference. – Can't hurt, I suppose.

– Look, points out Ndekwe, we're already keeping them for the cars, yeah? What difference does another day make?

Gorman sighs wearily. – All right, he says, but go and draw a line under Shepherdson first. As soon as we prove he wasn't there, his entire thing falls apart and we can get him out the picture.

– Right. Ndekwe nods.

– And we still need to find Isaacs.

Halliwell rises from his chair.

– I'm all over it, he says.

– Thank you, gentlemen, says Gorman.

Ndekwe gathers his things together, gives his DI a curt nod and follows Halliwell out of the door.

Gorman pulls open his drawer, peels two paracetamols from their plastic casing and washes them down with the last mouthful of lukewarm tea. Then he rises from his desk and pulls his blinds shut again.

■ ■ ■ ■ ■

Jack Shepherdson's yellow-tipped fingers flake tobacco into an upturned Rizla that is then twisted, licked and tapped together into a matchstick-thin roll-up. He slips his smoke into the breast pocket of his shirt and leans back in his chair. He looks washed out; the sagging flesh of his face a fish-belly white and his eyes two watery puddles of pale, red-ringed blue, shot through lack of sleep but calm and steady enough; amused, almost, as they regard Ndekwe and Frampton from across the table.

– Where's the other fella? he asks. – The sixties throwback?

– He's not here today, says Ndekwe. – You've got me, I'm afraid.

– And who may you be?

– Detective Sergeant Peter Ndekwe. This is DC Frampton.

– Marvellous. What now?

– Now we continue the interview from yesterday.

The old man nods. – Off you go then, he says.

– Before we start, says Ndekwe, I have to confirm that you're quite sure you don't want a legal representative with you?

– No, you crack on, pal. I'll be seeing enough of them money-grabbing bastards soon enough, I reckon.

– Who?

– Lawyers and all that crowd.

– Not fond of lawyers?

Shepherdson leans across the table. His relaxed, almost jocular manner makes him seem younger than his years, but he looks physically old under the harsh electric light. Ndekwe can see the network of burst capillaries running riot under his skin, the spots of dried spittle gathered in the grey whiskers at the corners of his mouth.

– I'll tell you summat about lawyers, shall I?

– If you must ...

– Good pal of mine, he was a lawyer. And his son-in-law, he became a lawyer an'all. Six years in legal school. This son-in-law, he used to moan like fuck about people asking him for advice all the time. Everywhere he went, as soon as people realized he was a qualified lawyer they were forever telling him all their woes; what shall I do about this, where do I stand on that. You with me?

– Yeah ...

– So he asks his father-in-law. He says, hey, you've been a lawyer for a good few years, what do you do about all these pesky bastards tapping you up for advice? His father-in-law says, I'll tell you what I do; whenever I give anyone any advice, I send em a bill the week after. They never fucking ask twice.

– Clever, remarks Ndekwe dryly. – Like it.

Shepherdson leans in closer. – Yeah, but the best of it is, a week later guess what happened?

– What?

– He gets a fucking bill from his father-in-law! Five hundred fucking quid! Ha! Shepherdson slaps the table, hoots with laughter, rocks back in his chair.

Ndekwe smiles despite himself.

– Very good. OK. Shall we make a start?

– Aye, go on, knock yerself out.

Shepherdson clears his throat noisily, swallows, settles back into his chair, folds his arms. Ndekwe starts the machine recording.

– Tuesday, August the twenty-fourth. Interview with John Henry Shepherdson at Hackney police station, nine forty-five a.m. Officers present; myself, Detective Sergeant Peter Ndekwe, Detective Constable Alex Frampton, and Mr John Henry Shepherdson ... Can you confirm your name for the purpose of the recording, please, Jack?

– John Henry Shepherdson.

– Mr Shepherdson, can you confirm that you have refused the offer of legal representation for the purpose of this interview?

– Correct.

– Thank you. May I remind you that you have been arrested on suspicion of murder and that you do not have to say anything but it may harm your defence if you do not answer in question something you later rely on court, and that anything you do say may be given in evidence.

Shepherdson nods in the affirmative. – Aye aye, captain.

– So, Jack. Where were you on Thursday, August the nineteenth at around one thirty in the afternoon?

– I was outside the shops on the Crown Heights estate, just off Hackney Road.

– What were you doing there?

– I'd stopped at Mr McKenzie's flat the night before and I was on me way home.

– This is Carlton McKenzie of Hyacinth House?

– Correct.

– Were you with anyone else outside the shops or were you there on your own?

– I was on me own. Shepherdson unravels a grubby grey square of cotton from his sleeve, holds it over his mouth and hacks up a gobful of phlegm. He inspects the contents of the handkerchief and stuffs it back up his sleeve. – Excuse me, he says, I aren't being funny or owt, but I've already been through all of this once already. Can't one of your amigos fill you in?

– I want you tell me how you killed Aaron Stewart, says Ndekwe.

– Stabbed him in the chest.

– Where?

– Outside the shops.

– No, I mean whereabouts on his body.

Shepherdson slaps a hand over his heart; once, twice.

– Mr Shepherdson is indicating the left of the upper chest area. You're right-handed, Jack?

– I am, yes.

– And you stabbed him just the once?

– Just the once, yes.

Ndekwe writes in his notebook and reads it back to himself. Shepherdson looks at him, bemused, then raises his eyebrows at Frampton in silent enquiry, but is met with an impassive stare. Ndekwe studies his notes for a few moments then puts down his pen and looks up at Shepherdson.

– Could you describe exactly what happened when you stabbed Aaron Stewart?

Shepherdson looks at the Detective Sergeant as though he is simple. – What happened? Well … he just keeled over, like. Started spewing up blood.

– You only stabbed him the once?

– Just the once, aye. Straight in and out job.

– And then you ran?

– Well, I got off fairly fuckin smartish, aye.

– Quick enough to dodge the bullets. Ndekwe states this as a fact rather than a question.

– Aye, agrees Shepherdson. – Miracle, it was. Like the Lord was looking down on me.

Ndekwe looks at him. Shepherdson meets his gaze equably, his face poker straight. No suggestion of a smile.

– And who had the gun? asks Ndekwe.

– Well, it must have been that little boss-eyed bastard.

– Who's that?

– Bang Bang, or whatever they call him. Fucking Bing Bong. Him with the eyes like football pools.

– Football pools? Frampton looks confused.

– One at home and one away, Shepherdson tells him.

Ndekwe places a mug shot on the table, turns it around to face Shepherdson.

– For the purpose of the recording I am showing Mr Shepherdson a photograph of Samuel Isaacs aka Bam Bam. Is that the person you believed fired the gun at you?

The old man leans in for a closer look.

– Aye, that's him. Fucking happy crack.

– So you both got off and then what?

Shepherdson chuckles, shakes his head. – No, not both of us, just me, he says. He treats Ndekwe to a benevolent, gap-toothed grin. – You'll have to get up a bit earlier in the day to catch me out, brother, he tells him.

Ndekwe smiles in acquiescence. – OK. So what happened after that?

– I just went home. Shepherdson shrugs. – I saw it on the news that night, how he'd supped off, like. Well, I knew there and then I was Donald Ducked. It was only a matter of time before the old knock on the door. So the next day I started making me plans.

– Plans?

– Aye, to get off, like. I made a few phone calls and I packed a case. Then the buzzer went and I thought, aye aye, here we go. I thought it was bound to be your mob, but it was Carlton. He knew the script straight off, did me laddo. It was you, weren't it? he said. It was you who did Knowledge.

– Why did he think that?

– Dunno. Someone must have told him. I didn't say fuck all to him, cos I didn't want him to be one of them ... what d'yer call it? Something after the fact?

– Accessory, prompts Frampton.

– Aye, an accessory after the fact. I told him, keep out of it, I said, just go home, scram, vamoose, and don't come round here no more. Then he sees the case and asks me where I'm going. I told him it was none of his business and if he's got any sense he'll go straight home and not get involved.

– You told him to go home?

– Aye. But he's going on and on at me, so eventually I told him; I told him I was going back up to Hull, like. He asks me how I'm getting up there and I tell him I was gonna get on the train and he starts banging on about cameras and the suchlike. CCTV, yer know? Well, I wouldn't have thought of that aspect of it, I must admit. Me head was a bit scrambled and I weren't thinking right. That bastard skunk weed. Shepherdson taps the side of his head with a gnarled finger. – It leaves you in a permanent fucking haze, that stuff. Like yer brain's full of fog. Terrible stuff. Worse than drink, oh aye. Ten times worse than the drink, in my book.

– Yeah, they should make it illegal, Frampton observes.

Shepherdson looks at him, gives him a solemn nod. – I agree, he says. Then he turns his attention back to Ndekwe. – Anyway, I was at a bit of a dead loss as to what to do at this point. I daren't get a train cos of what me laddo had pointed out, and I didn't have access to a car. And even if I had, it's been years since I've been behind the wheel. So I asked me laddo if he knew anyone who'd lend us a car and he says aye, his cousin's got some wheels. So I had a look at me bankroll and I offered him five hundred quid to drive me up to Hull.

– You paid him to drive you?

Shepherdson nods. – I told him if we got stopped then he could say he was just doing a paid job for me ... legit, like. That it had all been arranged for weeks and he didn't know about the lad getting stabbed or owt like that. We'd just say I'd asked him to drive me up, and in return I was paying for his ticket to Jamaica. That was the script we agreed on. He considers this for a bit then he says, aye, all right then, and he scoots off to get his cousin's car.

– So where were you going to stay in Hull?

– Me old pal, Colin. He's got a pub. The plan was to get on the ferry and then get across to Holland. I reckoned if I got to Amsterdam I could look up a few people and stop with them for a bit while I worked out what to do next. These were old pals I'd sailed with in the past. A few of them had ended up staying out there, subbying, putting up cold stores and what have yer. Colin said he still had a few numbers of some of the lads who he'd worked with. Not the most bulletproof of plans, I suppose. But I was in a state of shock. Didn't have the first clue what to do really. I've never killed anyone before . . .

Ndekwe raises his eyebrows at this, but doesn't comment.

– ... so this was a new one on me, like. Shepherdson coughs into his handkerchief, inspects the contents and folds it back up his sleeve. – I actually did consider handing meself in there and then, he says, believe it or not. Let's face facts; I'm nearly seventy years old. I'm not exactly cut out for a life on the lam, am I? Even Ronnie Biggs threw the towel in when he got to my age. I knew I couldn't just take to the highway and hope for the best. So I had to pull meself together and get meself properly organized. Do you know what, though?

– What? says Ndekwe.

– Deep down, I knew I'd end up in a place like this. He gestures at the walls around them. – In a police station, like. I knew the chances of me getting clean away were slim at best. I thought we'd get stopped on the way up there, or else there'd be a welcoming committee as soon as I stepped foot on the boat. I'm amazed I got as far as I did, to be honest.

– So how did you end up getting arrested?

– Well, we gets on the road, me and me laddo, and off we go, like. I had to tell him to slow down a few times cos he was driving like a bloody lunatic. And he insisted on playing the wireless at ear-splitting volume, so any chance of me getting me head down was clean out the bloody window. So I started asking him about his dad and that.

– His dad? asks Frampton. – Why were you asking about his dad?

– Just curious, I suppose. I knew he had this bar in Jamaica and all the rest of it, but I didn't know the circumstances surrounding it all, how he'd ended up going back out there and all that deal. Mind you, they're notorious for it, aren't they, these Jamaicans, abandoning their families and leaving babies all over the bloody shop … He raises a placatory hand to Ndekwe. – No offence if you're Jamaican, like …

– I'm British, Ndekwe tells him.

– Yeah, I know, but you know what I mean …

– My parents are from Nigeria.

Shepherdson nods as if he'd known this all along. – Well, there you go, you see. Jamaicans are different in my book. Worked with a lot of em over the years, away at sea and on shore an'all. Breed the woman, that's what they'd say. *Breeeed tha wo-maaan.* Shepherdson adopts a comedy Jamaican accent that makes Frampton suppress a small start of laughter and then glance nervously at Ndekwe, who looks completely nonplussed. – Yeah, right, breed the woman, says Shepherdson. – And then bugger off and leave her holding the baby. That's just how they carry on though. Different kids by all different women. That's how they roll, as me laddo would say. So I guessed his old fella had buggered off when he was still a bain. He'd told me they used to live in Brixton, but that's about as far as it went. These young kids now, though ... they're used to living in broken up families, aren't they?

Ndekwe shrugs.

– Well they are, aren't they? Shepherdson insists. – That's the norm in this day and age. I'm not saying it's right or wrong, that's just how people seem to carry on nowadays, whether they're from England or Jamaica or wherever. He makes a sweeping gesture as if to indicate the world outside in its entirety. – Anyway, me and me laddo got on to talking about family trees and all that lark, and he didn't have a clue. I was surprised, actually. For someone so obsessed with getting back to his so-called homeland he didn't know the first bloody thing about the place or his own heritage. Didn't even know he was Scottish, for a start. I asked him if he'd ever traced his Scottish roots and he got all indignant on me. Should have heard him. Scottish, he said, I'm not flippin Scottish!

Shepherdson pulls himself upright in his chair, puts his hands on his hips in mock outrage. – Like I'd accused him of being a bloody kiddy fiddler or summat! Didn't even know McKenzie was a Scots name. That's how daft these young lads are. They get all boastful about which part of town they're from, but they don't have the first idea of how they got there. How can I be Scottish, he says, when me mum is a born Londoner and me dad is from Jamaica? Shepherdson sighs and shakes his head wearily, like a teacher faced with a class of woefully ignorant pupils. – So I tells him all about Cromwell sending the Scottish prisoners of war over in the seventeenth century and how a load more Scots went over from Panama after they made a balls-up of that place. But he never knew about any of this. Didn't have a clue about owt that might have happened before last bloody week.

– OK, that's great, says Ndekwe, but to get back to ...

But Shepherdson is cooking on gas now. He pulls the roll-up

from his breast pocket and points it towards the wall, as though illustrating a tricky equation on a blackboard.

– Glendevon, he says, that's a Scottish place name in Jamaica. Glendevon, Montego Bay ... and there's others an'all, there's a Glasgow and a Dundee in Jamaica. This was all news to me laddo, of course. Never made the connection before. Never knew about the trade links, all the sugar and spices and what have yer that were exported to the ports in Leith and Greenock. There's a Jamaica Street in Glasgow, in Edinburgh and in Aberdeen. He never knew that either.

The bemused look on Frampton's face betrays a similar gap in his knowledge.

– Mind you, continues Shepherdson, I don't think he even knew where bastard Glasgow is. James Campbell; most famous plantation owner on the island. Like the footballer, I told him, that big black fella who played for Spurs, Sol Campbell. Another Jamaican with a Scottish name.

– You been to Jamaica? Frampton asks, genuinely interested. Ndekwe sighs, puts his pen down.

– Loads of times, says Shepherdson, settling back in his chair. – Been all over the world, me. Merchant Navy. Thing is, me laddo's never even left London. Sad, innit. For all his streetwise gangster act, I soon tippled that he was basically bloody clueless as soon as he got outside his own postcode. He didn't have a notion where Hull was. We were about an hour on the motorway and he starts asking me, are we there yet? Like a bain on his way to the seaside, cracking up to get his bucket and spade out. *Are we there yet, Dad?* Shepherdson mimics a high-pitched London whine. – As far as he knew it could have been ten miles away or ten thousand. Completely bloody clueless.

He puts the roll-up between his lips and pats around his pockets for a lighter. – I told him, God help you when you get to Montego Bay. How do you reckon you're gonna carry on there? I says. It's a bloody rough place, I tell him, rougher than Hackney for a start.

He wasn't having this, of course, and he starts telling me about all the stunts him and that gang of his used to pull when they were running about the estate.

– Like what? says Frampton, but his tone is too keen and Shepherdson senses his eagerness.

– Oh just daft things, he says, airily. He finds a lighter deep in his trouser pocket and places it on the table. – Just fighting and carrying on and all that lark. Typical teenager stuff. I don't know how much of it was true and how much was just sheer fantasy on his part. He didn't seem the rough-house type to me. That Knowledge lad, though ... The old man's nose wrinkles up in disgust, as though a foul smell has been released into the room. – The more I heard about him the more I started to think I did that estate a bloody favour. Pure fucking poison that cunt was. If me laddo's tales are to be believed, like. Well, I believed him, anyroad, he says with grim finality. – I know a shithouse when I see one.

– What sort of tales? asks Frampton.

– Just being a complete cunt. Dealing drugs, terrorizing people. Proper drugs I'm on about here, not just a bit of smoke, like. Dealing in fucking misery.

– So you think he deserved to die?

Shepherdson looks at the Detective Constable, takes the roll-up out of his mouth and points it across the table. – Hey, listen, he says. – Don't get me wrong, I'm not trying to justify what I did here. I'm holding me hands up one hundred per cent, no doubt about it. A life is a life, and I've took one and I should pay the price in full, oh aye, don't you worry about that. But I will say this; there'll be a few other lives down there made just that bit less miserable by that Knowledge fella being off the scene.

He inspects the roll-up, taps it twice on the table and drops it back into his pocket, along with the lighter.

– So you drove up to Hull, prompts Ndekwe.

– Aye. I was a bit concerned about the money situation. I had a few bob on me still, the proceeds from selling that weed, like, but half of that was going in me laddo's pocket for doing the driving. I had to pay Colin for the ferry ticket and then keep some in reserve for when I got across the water, for trains and what have yer. Hotels as well, maybe.

– Doesn't leave much left over, Jack, observes Ndekwe.

– Well, yeah, he concedes. – It was starting to dawn on me what a half-arsed bloody plan this was. I was sort of making it up as I went along, I must admit. And I was in no fit state to know what to do for the best, to be entirely truthful. I was jumpy as hell going up that motorway. Every time a jam sandwich appeared behind us I was convinced that was it, the game was bloody up. Two of them popped up in the rear-view mirror at one point, sirens and lights going, the full bells and whistles and I thought, aye aye, here we fucking go. For one horrible second I thought me laddo was going to stick his foot down and make a dash for freedom. I had visions of us being cut out of a heap of twisted bloody metal by the roadside ... Shepherdson shudders. – But they just went flying past, these cop cars. My nerves were in bastard shreds, I don't mind telling yer. Me laddo, he was all right, though, cool as a cucumber he was. Chill, Jack, he kept saying; chill, bruv. Easy for him to say, he hadn't just stuck a bloody knife in someone, had he? Anyroad, I decided to take a quick detour. I was getting too nervy on that motorway. We were getting low on fuel so we stopped at the next services to fill up and get a bit of nose bag.

– Which service station was this?

– No idea. I just saw the sign and told him to pull in. Me laddo went for a piss and I went in the shop and got us a few banjos and what have yer. Then I picked up a newspaper and there it was, headline on one of the inside pages, national bloody press: YOUTH STABBED TO DEATH IN LONDON STREET. Aaron Stewart, eighteen, blah blah blah. That was the first time I knew his proper name. Aaron Stewart.

– And how did that make you feel?

– Feel? I dunno ... The old man pauses and scratches at the

stubble on his neck, gazes over Ndekwe's head into the far corner of the room. – Made it more real, somehow, he says eventually. – Sounds barmy, I know, but that was just how it felt. Like he was a real person with a real name and a mother and father and all the rest of it. I had a quick scan of the article, but it never mentioned about them looking for anybody in particular, no descriptions, like. Just said the murder hunt was underway. Seeing it down in black and white like that, well, it put the fear of Christ in me, I don't mind telling yer. Murder hunt was underway; that's what it said. I could hardly walk straight, I was that shook up. Like me legs had turned to water. I paid for the grub and the paper and got a few tinnies as well. Then I went for a witch's kiss.

– For a what?

– A piss. I'm stood there at the trough when these two traffic cops walk in with their vests and their handcuffs and their radios crackling away. Fuck me, I nearly filled me bags. This big bastard of a copper comes and stands right next to me, whistling away like he didn't have a care in the world. Bastard even smiled and nodded how do at me. Sweet fucking Jesus, I nearly handed meself in there and then. I swear me piss virtually trickled to a halt. Anyroad, I washed me hands and got out quick as I could without actually breaking into a fucking hundred metre dash. As soon as I was out of the khazi I was off like a robber's dog. I went looking for Carlton. He was on one of them space invaders near the entrance. I says to him, hey, never mind blasting fucking aliens, son, we need to vamoose. We need to get off this main motorway, pretty bastard sharp. So we got off at the next slip road. I told him to just drop me off at the nearest station and get himself back home.

– But he didn't, did he? prompts Ndekwe.

– He weren't having none of it. I said I'd get you to Hull, he says, and that's what I'm going to do. I'm a man of my word, he says. See what I mean? That's the type of lad he is.

Ndekwe smiles at the old man. – You think a lot of Carlton, don't you, Jack?

– He's a decent lad. Shepherdson nods. – Don't be taken in by all that tough guy front. He's not the big gangster he makes himself out to be. He knows right from wrong. It's a miracle he's turned out the way he has, really, what with his family situation and everything.

– What do you mean?

– Well, too many of these young lads now grow up without their fathers, don't they? No one about to keep em in check. The mothers can't do everything, can they? Especially if it's a mother like me laddo got dealt, off her bloody biscuit half the time. But even if your mother's on the straight and narrow, there's certain things a woman can't get involved in. D'yer get me? A young fella needs a role model. He needs someone to look up to. Am I right or what?

He appeals to Frampton, who gives him a non-committal shrug in return.

– The only people these kids look up to now, continues Shepherdson, are these drug dealers, with their big cars and their jewellery and all that deal. They see all them nice things and they want them for themselves, pronto like, there and then. Instant gratification. Always looking for the short cut, aren't they? No, he's a decent lad is Carlton. I could tell that anyway, by the way he talked about that pal of his.

– What pal of his? Ndekwe picks his pen up.

– That pal of his who'd died. He told me about him while we were driving up there. Fifteen he was. Shot by some rival mob of young lads. Rival mob of murdering bastards I mean. Fifteen years old. Unbelievable. I could tell him and Carlton had been close by the way he talked about him. He thought a lot of that lad, I could tell.

– What was his name? asks Ndekwe, but Shepherdson isn't listening.

– Shot dead at fucking fifteen year old, he says, genuine anger in his voice. – I'm sorry, but that is a fucking disgrace. And here's the best of it, do you know where he was from, that young lad? Sierra Leone. One of the most violent bloody places on the planet. War torn. Well, anywhere that's covered in diamonds is bound to see a few disagreements breaking out, innit? But that lad had come over here to get away from all that, him and his family. And where does he end up? Right slap bang in the middle of another bastard war. Marvellous, eh?

– What else did Carlton tell you about him?

– Not a great deal. He'd asked me if I'd ever seen a dead body before, that's how he got on about it.

– And have you?

– I've seen a few, like. I saw me uncle Stan laid out when I was a nipper, in me auntie's back room. Never forget it. At first I thought it was a joke, like. He was always a twat for pulling stunts was me uncle Stan. Be right up his alley that, pretending to be brown bread and then jumping up and scaring the living shite out o' yer. But he just laid there. And it looked like he had make-up on. Course, looking back, that's what they used to do.

– Still do, observes Frampton.

– Yeah, but this was like proper thick make-up, Shepherdson tells him. – Like they'd put it on with a yard brush. He was blathered in it, all this white pancake shite and these big daft red lips. Looked like Coco the fucking Clown. Yeah, so there was me uncle Stan, that was me first. Then I saw this bloke get run over once, hit by this car in Dubai. Went somersaulting up in the air, come down like a bag of chopsticks. Bits of him pointing out at all angles. Claret all over the car. The old man grimaces and shakes his head as if to dislodge the image. – Horrible. Obvious he was dead, speed he got hit. They were gathering witnesses, but I took off. I'm not a fan of dead bodies, by and large. Well, nobody is, let's be fair. I don't even like going to cemetery, me. Never seen the point, stood there talking to a lump of stone sticking out the ground. I used to say to my pal, when I'm gone just set fucking fire to me and put me on the allotment. Mind you, I do regret not saying goodbye to a few people. I regret not giving my pal a proper send-off when he let go the rope. Only found out the other week. I hadn't seen him for God knows how long. And we didn't part on the best of terms, which I do regret now. But yer just lose touch, don't yer? And life carries on, regardless ...

– Right, interrupts Ndekwe. – So, you got to Hull and then what?

But, once more, Shepherdson is not listening.

– Used to do the clubs, did Ronnie. He was a bloody good turn in his day an'all, believe you and me. Could take off any singer you care to mention: Shirley Bassey, Sammy Davis, Deano, Frank, the whole gang of em. Was like listening to the records. Jokes an'all. And impressions. Oh, he was marvellous, was Ronnie. Packed em out everywhere, he did. Best showman to have come out of Hull ever, in my opinion. To have come out of anywhere in the north, anyroad. Better than half that shite you hear on the wireless nowadays. Can't believe how woeful music is now. There's no proper songs is there? Plenty of people making a bloody row, but there's no songs. You watch that *Britain's Got Talent* on the telly?

He directs the question at Ndekwe, who pointedly ignores him, and then at Frampton, who looks at him blankly.

– *Britain's Got Shite* more like, scoffs Shepherdson. – Never seen such an average display of bloody dullards in all my born days. About as much charisma as a week old bag of washing. And they all sound exactly the same. Well they do to my ears anyroad. Like a cat caught in a bloody washing machine. Ronnie, though, he was a different class. I'm talking about a proper singer here, a proper entertainer. Better than that bloody Joe Longthorne any day of the week. Ronnie always called Joe Longthorne the man who pinched his career. He was right an'all ... Ronnie knocked Joe into a cocked hat, though. Marvellous singing voice. Sounded a bit like Al Martino, did a few of his numbers, like, 'Spanish Eyes' and 'Here in My Heart'.

Shepherdson closes his eyes, places one hand over his heart and extends the other to an imaginary audience. – *Heeere in maaahhh heeaarrtt, ahm so lone-ah-leee*, he sings, a fractured warbling. He opens his eyes, but instead of an adoring audience in a Las Vegas casino, he's faced with two incredulous police officers. – That was his show-stopper, that was, he tells them, unfazed. – I used to go all over to watch him. I'd sometimes get up and do a few numbers meself. Oh aye, I'm a bit of a chanter on the quiet, me. I can knock a tune out, don't you worry about that.

– So, tell me what happened when you got to Hull, prompts Ndekwe. He glances at his watch. He is getting tired of all this now, the digressions and the anecdotes and the acting up. The old man is faintly amusing up to a point, and there are nuggets of information amid the ramblings, but time is pressing down upon them and Ndekwe has an appointment in Dalston with the Musas.

Shepherdson reaches for his tobacco tin and prises off the lid. He extracts a Rizla and begins to roll another cigarette.

– Yeah, so, anyhow, he says, we gets there about dinnertime. By hell, it never fucking changes, that place. Like the land that time forgot. You can throw up as many new shopping centres and giant fish tanks as you like, but the natives stay exactly the same. Nowt fazes em. We walked into Colin's boozer and there was little Benny stood washing glasses behind the bar. I haven't seen Benny since God knows when, but he just looks up and says now then, Jack, what yer having? Like I'd just strolled in from the night before. He set us up with a couple of liveners and then Big Col comes down from upstairs and he's like, Jack, you old bastard, how yer doing? I could see Carlton was a bit dubious about the company cos Colin is a big exuberant sod. But we all sat down and had a couple of drinks and he soon relaxed, did me laddo. He knew we were among friends.

Shepherdson licks his new smoke together and taps it on the table. – After a bit he was laughing along with all the tales and joining in with the banter. They're good company, Col and Benny. We had a spot of dinner and a couple of games of pool. I thought we'd cracked it then, y'know. That's when I really thought we could pull this caper off. Colin had sorted me ticket out for the boat and he'd managed to track down a couple of the lads in Amsterdam. He said it was all sorted out, a place to stop while I got me bearings and all the rest of it.

– So the plan was for you to get off on the ferry and Carlton to go back down to London, yeah?

– Well, originally, yeah, but that's when Carlton floated the idea about coming on the boat with me.

– He wanted to go with you?

Shepherdson nods. – I think he just wanted to get off to Jamaica. See his old fella and that. I could come to Amsterdam with you, he said, and then I could get off to the airport once you'd got yerself settled.

– He was going to leave his sister and his mum and not say goodbye?

– Well, I says to him, what about yer mam, I says, don't yer want to go back and say ta-ra to her first? He just shrugged. I think he'd sort of given up on his mother. Can't say I blame him. If that was my mother, I'd fucking disown her as well. But I told him, no, you get yerself back down the road and make sure everything's sorted out before you take off. Montego Bay will still be there in a week's time. I knew he wouldn't breathe a word to your lot about owt that had gone on. Anyway, we stopped at Colin's for a bit and then I went to see our John and the bain.

– That's your son?

– Aye, me son and the grandbain. Our Louis, like. I don't get up as much as I'd like, so I was keen to see em before I set sail. Might be the last time, like. That was on me mind, whether or not I'd see em again. Granted, we were never close on account of me taking off when he was little, like.

– You hadn't kept in touch?

– Well, don't forget, all the time he was growing up I was always halfway round the world, either bobbing about in the middle of the ocean or in some foreign port or other ... No, we weren't as close as I'd have liked, but we kept in touch, oh aye ... after his mother died, y'know. Birthdays and Christmases and the like. I was always on the other end of the phone.

– So you didn't tell him anything about what had happened down here?

– Oh, I kept shtum about all this carry-on, obviously. Never let on there was owt up. I'd told our John I was up to see some old pals, which was true, in a manner of speaking.

– I bet they were glad to see you, offers Frampton.

– Oh hell, aye. Shepherdson beams. – Our Louis was made up. Came flying down the path he did, soon as I opened the gate. Grandad, Grandad, he shouted and he jumped right up into me arms. By Christ, he's a beautiful little lad. Head full of golden curls. Takes after his grandad. Big for his age an'all. He's gonna be a prop forward, no doubt about it. Anyway, I'd got him a few bits and bobs, an Action Man and a couple of racing cars and what have yer. He was made up with em. He was larking about with em on the kitchen floor while me and his mam and dad had a brew and a catch-up. Got a good job now, has our John. He's one of the main men at Smith & Nephew's now. One of the gaffers, like. Worked his way up from leaving school. He's always been bright, though. I always said to him that he got the brains of the family. He got his looks off me and his brains off his mother. Aye, one of the top boffins up there, he is. Couldn't tell you what he does exactly, summat to do with chemicals. Goes right over my head, anyroad. She's a good lass an'all, that Rachael. She looks after that house, by Christ she does. Spotless, it is. Immaculate. All double-glazed. Brand-new car in the drive. One of them big widescreen tellies.

Jack spreads his hands far apart like a fisherman describing a catch in his local pub. – They put the racing on for me while they all got ready, cos I was taking em all out for a slap up meal. We went to one them fun pubs, yer know, one of them with the climbing frame for the bains. They're good value, them places. I had a swimmer with jockey's whips and peas. By hell, yer should have seen the size of it, like bloody Moby Dick it was. I'd forgot what proper fish and chips tasted like.

– Better up north, then, is it? Frampton asks, more than a hint of sarcasm in his voice.

– You can't get proper haddock down here, yer know, Shepherdson tells him. – It's all that Vietnamese catfish and what have yer. They try and pass it off as cod but you can't kid a kidder. I know what proper fish should taste like; I've pulled enough of it out the ocean in me time. Anyroad, we had our dinner and then me and the bain larked football on the bit of green next to the pub. Gave his mam and dad five minutes to themselves, like, cos he never stops does our Louis. I wouldn't mind having some of that energy again. Takes me ten minutes to get out me frigging chair nowadays. I went in goal and he ended up winning twenty-two nil. Oh no, hang on, I did score one, but it was disallowed. I wasn't ready, Grandad, he said. Proper got his doe down he did.

– His doe down? Ndekwe frowns, looks at Frampton, who shakes his head, equally mystified.

– Lost his temper, like. You know, threw a wobbler. You know what they're like at that age. Anyway, we had a couple of drinks and then we all went back to our John's and watched a film with the bain. That one where all the toys come to life. By hell, they're advanced now, these cartoons, aren't they? Like watching a proper movie. Looked good on that big telly. And the sound as well! He's got speakers dotted all over the room. Like being at Cecil cinema. Afterwards, I read the bain his bedtime story and kissed him night night. Will you be here in morning, Grandad? he says. We can go an play football in the park. I've got a new England shirt and I'm Wayne Rooney, he says. I says to him, you don't wanna be bothering with football, you wanna be larking rugby! Football's for poofs! All right, Grandad, he says, we can go to shops and you can get me a rugby ball and we'll lark rugby. Well, I was filling up, I don't mind telling yer. Cos I knew that was probably the last time I was ever gonna see him. No probably about it. That was me last time with me grandbain. I kissed him night night again and switched his light off. Stay with me, Grandad, he said. So I stopped there by his bedside while he bobbed off. After that, I went down and we had a bit of a yarn and then I got off.

– And you didn't tell your son about what had happened?

– Christ no, says Shepherdson. – I didn't let on to our John about any of this caper. Never breathed a word. And, in any event, I've surrendered meself to justice, haven't I? I'm putting me hands up and that's the end of it. So there's no need for any of you lot to go hassling any of my family now, is there? He looks pointedly at the two police officers. – They know nowt, none of em. As far as they're concerned I was just up visiting some old amigos and now I'm back down in London. They weren't privy to any of this carry-on. Make sure that goes on record. The old man points to the recording device at the end of the table. – I don't want my family being harassed in any way, shape or form, he says.

– So how did you end up getting arrested? Ndekwe asks him again.

Shepherdson sighs. – Now that was bloody stupid. Me laddo was upstairs when I got back to Colin's. We reckoned it was best to keep out of the road, like, so I made us both a bit of supper and we just parked ourselves down in front of the telly. He was full of it, he was, giving it all the big'un about what he was gonna do when he got to Jamaica. Thing is, between you and me, I always had me doubts, like. I never said owt to the lad, but it all sounded a bit suspect to me, like. A bar in Montego Bay? Sounded a bit pie in the sky, to be truthful. If his old fella was running a bar in Jamaica how come he could never find it on the internet or on one of them maps? I mean, he showed me that postcard, but that message on the back could have been read both ways, are you with me? 'Here is my pub.' That could have meant 'here is the pub that I do all me boozing in', are yer with us?

– That's a fair assumption to make, yes, agrees Ndekwe.

– Ambiguous, in my eyes. But me laddo took it to mean what he wanted it to mean. I never said nowt to him on that score. I knew the meaning *I* took from it. I'm a realist me, oh aye, I've had to be. But I never cracked on to Carlton, never gave him my own personal opinion on the deal. To my reckoning, it didn't matter a jot whether the bar was his dad's or not. The most important thing as far as I was concerned was that me laddo got on his peddler, got out of the environment he was in. If he got away he had a chance of doing summat with his life, whether he was in Amsterdam or Jamaica or Timbuk-fucking-tu. The important thing was to get away. If he stopped round that estate he had no chance whatsoever, are yer with me?

– I'm with you, says Ndekwe.

– Aye, well, as it turned out, I was spot on. His old fella didn't own no bar in Montego Bay. He was a bloody bank robber, that's what he was.

– A bank robber? Ndekwe shoots Frampton a look and then indicates for Shepherdson to continue.

– Here's the script. We were sat there watching the box and that *Crimewatch* came on. They showed this footage of a robbery of a travel shop somewhere in South London. One of them places where you exchange money and what have yer. I wasn't really paying much attention, but I says summat to me laddo and he doesn't answer and I look up and he's staring at the screen like he's seen a bastard ghost. Shepherdson adopts an exaggerated expression of shock, an imaginary fork held in the air, frozen midway to his mouth. – All the colour had drained from his face and his dinner was almost sliding off his knee. That's my dad, he says. That's my dad, there, look. I says, are you sure, like? Are you positive? You haven't seen the man for donkey's years. But he was adamant. That's my dad, he kept saying, and he looked like he was about to burst into tears. His bottom lip was off ten to the dozen.

– He recognized him?

– Aye, they showed a close-up of him, gave a full description. Me laddo knew straight off who it was. Well, that was it; there was no talking to him after that. He starts stomping round the room saying he was gonna go straight back to London and hand himself in. Hand yourself in for what? I says to him, you haven't done owt! All right, he'd robbed that car, I'd sussed that out, but apart from that, hand himself in for what? I'm handing myself in, Jack, he kept saying. You get off, Jack, he said. I'm going back to face the music.

That's when I cottoned on to what his plan was, like.

– What was his plan?

– He was gonna try and get himself locked up for that lad's murder. I couldn't believe it, me. Couldn't believe what he was saying. Shepherdson shakes his head. – Who in their right bloody mind would want to go to jail for summat they hadn't done? And a murder charge an'all. Didn't make sense to me. Utter bloody madness. He's eighteen years old; he's got his entire life in front of him.

– It doesn't make sense to me, either, Ndekwe tells him.

– No, but this is what I reckon, right. Shepherdson leans across the table. – I reckon he was frightened of all them others, that little cross-eyed bastard and all his mates. Like I said, he acts all tough, does Carlton, but I reckon he was terrified of going back to the barrio, are yer with me?

– So you're saying he'd rather go to jail than back to his family? Ndekwe shakes his head firmly. – I don't buy it, Jack.

– No, me neither, agrees Shepherdson, and he looks so comically bewildered that Ndekwe has to suppress a smile. – I says to him, I says, don't talk bloody barmy, just get yourself on that boat and get across the water. Bollocks to Jamaica; get yourself to Amsterdam. Easy to disappear over there, I'll give you a couple of names, I says. Contacts. Work in a bar in Amsterdam, if that's what you want to do, like. You don't have to stay for ever, just lay low for a year or two and then come back when all the fuss dies down. There's kids getting stabbed left right and fucking centre in London. Give it six months and no one will even remember this Knowledge fella, let alone give a flying fuck about him. There'll be another half-dozen like him stacked up in the graveyard. Think about that, I says ... Shepherdson sighs and gives a slow, sad shake of the head. – But he wasn't having none of it, me laddo. He goes stomping downstairs to the bar and starts hitting the bottle. I follows him down and I'm begging and pleading for him to come back upstairs and have a chat, listen to reason, like. But it was no use, he was on one. After a bit I left him alone, cos he was raising his voice and starting to attract attention. So I backed off, went up the other end of the bar and got into a game of pool. Kept an eye on him, though. I reckoned I'd let him sit there and drink himself daft. I was hoping that eventually he'd slope back upstairs and crash out. That things'd look different in the morning and all that lark.

Shepherdson coughs, wipes his mouth with his handkerchief. – But then I clocked that this old queer had parked himself next to him at the bar. That was the only drawback with Colin's place, it did attract a fair few of that type. Part of the reason business was so bad, Colin reckoned. Put ordinary people off. But what can you do, you can't just ban em for no reason, can yer? Get done for political correctness. Anyroad, this character starts cracking onto Carlton and I can see me laddo's getting agitated so I sails over and says, aye aye, come on, petal, leave the lad alone, like. You can see he's not in the mood for company. But he starts being a clever bastard does this queer. Who are you, he says, his fucking dad? Anyway, words are exchanged and I ended up getting a grip of this clever twat. Stood him up by his collar and told him to sling his hook. Well, he tried to stick one on us, didn't he?

Shepherdson lifts himself in his chair, bobs his head forward like he's rising to nod a football into the back of the net. – Tried to put the nut on us. So I had to give him a bastard and that was that, the fucking balloon went up. Carlton's shouting and bawling and Colin's out from behind the bar and I'm trying to get this twat out of the door before it all escalates. Course, it's too late for that, cos all these other bastards are on their feet and they want to fucking know an'all. I thought it was just him on his Jack Jones, this bloke, but he's got a crew with him and they're all getting involved ...

Shepherdson is sat bolt upright now, throwing imaginary jabs and hooks at an invisible mob of attackers.

– Carlton cracks a couple of em and all fucking hell breaks loose. I get this bloke out the door and Carlton's right behind me, followed by this other lot, who start slinging glasses and chairs. I dump this bastard on the deck outside and Carlton starts sticking the boot in, but I'm pulling him away and telling him to get up the road double quick. I manage to march him so far, but then there's about five or six of these other blokes right on our tail, baying for blood. They could have stomped all over us if they'd wanted to, like, but for some reason they just followed us up the road, shouting threats, like. I'm back-pedalling and I've got this pool cue in me hand and I'm swiping it at em like bloody Errol Flynn, trying to keep em at bay.

Shepherdson holds up an imaginary weapon, slashes the air between himself and Ndekwe.

– It was bloody laughable, if truth be told. I wasn't laughing when that bastard police car pulled up, though. As soon as them flashing lights arrived this little crowd turned tail and started walking back to the pub. These two officers step out of the car and make a beeline straight for me, probably cos I'm waving this pool cue about and me laddo's shouting the odds, saying he's gonna fucking kill everyone in sight.

Shepherdson slumps back into his chair, shakes his head ruefully. – There was only one way it was gonna go. I did me best to calm it all down, but next thing I know me and me laddo are cuffed and slung in the back of the car, this officer sat between us. Carlton starts telling this copper how he killed a man in London and all that bollocks and I'm telling him to shut the fuck up and all the rest of it. Anyroad, they take us to Priory Road, sling us in separate cells. After a bit they come and have a chat, and I tell em the score, tell em what we're both doing up there. I knew that was the end of the line, game over. I told em, I said, I'm confessing to murder. That's when they said they were ringing you lot up to come and get us. So I got me head down. Didn't get much kip, though, not on that metal bed. And there was some bastard singing his head off in the next cell. Kept me up all fucking night he did.

– And now here we are, says Ndekwe.

– Yeah, here we all are. And that's it, that's yer lot. Finito. End of. Tot that lot up, put it down in black and white and I'll sign on the dotted line.

– Not as simple as that.

– Yes it is. And I'll tell you summat else as well … The old man leans forward and points a finger across the table. – I've never actually admitted to me laddo about what I'd done. I mean, he knows of course, he's not that bloody green, but I haven't actually come out and said the words. So you can't do him for that, either. You can't do him for being an accessory after the fact or whatever official bloody language you lot use. I know how you bastards operate, don't you worry about that. Well, yer can forget about it, cos the kid's clean as a whistle. Shepherdson thumps himself in the chest. – It was me, he says. – I did it, me on me own, nowt to do with him. It's all on me. So tell me laddo I said ta-ra and tell him to keep out of bother. And tell him not to worry about his dad. None of that matters now. It's not his fault his dad's an arsehole. Tell him he can still go to Jamaica. He could even take his mam, if she gets herself sorted out. He's a good lad, yer know. Don't let him con yer into thinking he had owt to do with any of this. Cos that's what he wants, yer know. He wants to take responsibility. He thinks everything's his fault. Tell him he can hold his head up high when he walks out of here. He's a good lad, is Carlton. Steady as a rock.

– All right, Jack. Ndekwe folds his papers together, replaces the cap on his pen. – I think we'll wrap it up for now.

– So what happens now?

– How do you mean?

– Well, what we looking at, d'yer reckon? Life?

– We're not quite at that stage yet, Ndekwe tells him.

Shepherdson folds his arms. – Don't matter to me, anyroad, he says. – I'll die in jail, I know that. I knew that as soon as I decided to hand meself in. But I've no complaints, brother, none at all. I'm seventy fucking years old. I'm too tired to be running away any more. He sighs theatrically, looks from Ndekwe to Frampton and then back again. – Anyway, he says. – That's us done now, is it?

– For the time being, yes.

Ndekwe switches off the machine. The old man seems to deflate,

199 ••• **SWEAR DOWN**

as if all the air has been sucked out of him. He holds his handkerchief over his mouth as he coughs up something solid from the depths of his chest. Ndekwe waits for the hacking and spitting to subside before gathering his things together and rising from the table. He indicates for Frampton to help Shepherdson to his feet. At the door Ndekwe pauses, spins back round as if suddenly remembering something.

– Jack, that's what I meant to ask you. What colour is Melissa's hair?

Shepherdson wipes his mouth and stuffs the sodden handful of cotton into his pocket.

– Who?

– Melissa.

Jack looks blank, shakes his head.

– Carlton's sister, says Ndekwe.

– Oh aye, yes, sorry. What colour's her what? Her *hair*?

Ndekwe nods. Shepherdson's watery blue eyes search Ndekwe's face for clues, but find nothing.

– Well, it's black, innit, he says.

– OK. Ndekwe nods. – Thank you, Jack.

– Is that it?

– For now, yes.

– Marvellous. Now, next thing, most important ... Shepherdson pulls a roll-up from his shirt pocket and holds it up like an exclamation mark. – Is there anywhere in this building where I can go and have a smoke?

■ ■ ■ ■ ■

There is a yellow post-it note stuck to Ndekwe's computer screen. Halliwell's handwriting. *Call Forensics. Prints ready.*

He does, and Forensics inform him that the fingerprints from 34b Conway Court have been matched to a known CRO, one Samuel Isaacs, seventeen years old, of Jasmine House, Crown Heights estate, Hackney E8.

■ ■ ■ ■ ■

He is everywhere that Ndekwe's eyes come to rest in the room; stood to attention on the wall, shoulders thrown back and proud in his school blazer; beaming from a hearts and flowers frame on the mantelpiece; etched into the oval disc of gold that hangs on the chain around Hannah Musa's neck.

Her boy, Joseph.

My boy, Joseph.

Up until last night Ndekwe had pushed the funeral in Stoke Newington to the back of his mind. The finer details elude him, although he remembers something of the mood of the day, the raw grief that hung in the air. But Ndekwe had been on the Lewisham Murder Investigation Team for a good eighteen months by then, and he'd been wading through days of desperate raw grief for weeks at a time. Senseless death had lost its shocking novelty. He had learned to stand outside of grief, to operate beyond its debilitating reach. The last thing he had wanted was to share the grief of someone he didn't even know.

He'd attended the funeral out of courtesy to Sonia's mum and dad, out of respect for their friends. It was important to Sonia that they kept close links to her parents, especially after she'd married and moved over the river. It was a difficult time back then. Ndekwe was getting in as much OT as he could, and his crazy hours and her parents' increasing infirmity meant that they always had to visit them in Stoke Newington, never the other way round. Isabel and Victor didn't have a car and Victor's legs weren't up for getting on and off buses. So Sunday became the natural day for their visits to the Lanades' – which, naturally, also meant visits to their church. The congregation was important to Sonia's parents – to her mum especially. Before those Sundays, Ndekwe hadn't been to church for years. Not since he had left the parental home at nineteen.

Ndekwe had been introduced to Hannah and Reuben only once previously, one Sunday afternoon after a service. He hadn't realized that the Musas had just landed in London from Sierra Leone. In all honesty, he wasn't paying that much attention; just offered a polite hello, smiled, nodded, shook hands. But if Sonia's mum introduced you to one of her church friends she assumed an instant and immovable bond forged in the glorious light of heaven. Ndekwe would speak to her on the phone and she'd pass on blessings from the congregation, from Abigail or Violet or William or some other half-remembered name and Ndekwe would say, ah yes, OK, thank you, feigning polite acknowledgement. So he hadn't really known anybody else at the boy's funeral. He had recognized a few faces that day, but none he could attach names to; he only really knew Isabel and Victor and a couple of Sonia's aunties.

He'd been on a job at the time; Freddie Bullard, a nineteen-year-old shot in the back of the head as he sat on a swing in a South London playground. It had been in the national papers for a week or so, before Freddie's face had been replaced by that of the Musa boy. In fact, now that he remembers, Ndekwe had been at Bullard's funeral a few days before Joseph's. But that had been out of a completely different sense of duty. It had been a week of sombre church halls and organ music and the sobbing of mothers. Ndekwe had put his feelings in the compartment marked 'not involved', had walled himself off from everything; dead boys in boxes, baby mothers' tears, everything. He was numb to it, the wailing, the questions with no real answers, the senseless sense of waste.

But he still couldn't switch off from work. For the then-DC Ndekwe, Sunday were days for thinking, not rest. And that day he'd been thinking about the Bullard job, standing amid the tears and the singing, Sonia hanging onto his arm, his eyes on the hymn book and Freddie Bullard nagging away at the back of his brain.

So, Ndekwe doesn't remember the finer details of the funeral in Stoke Newington two years ago. But he remembers Carlton McKenzie.

He knew he'd seen him somewhere before, as soon as he peered through the hatch of the holding cell. Not so much the boy's face, but his posture; bolt upright, immobile from the waist up, with those restless hands drumming the top of his thighs, both knees bouncing up and down above a pair of tapping heels. It was the same posture that had caught Ndekwe's attention two years ago; the agitated boy perched on the end of the pew four rows down on the other side of the church, bouncing, tapping, fidgeting. It was as though the impulse for flight was so strong that the boy was in danger of rising from his place in the congregation and levitating to the roof.

And now here are Hannah and Reuben Musa, living not two miles away from the Crown Heights estate, relocated by Hackney Council to a ground-floor flat in Dalston. Hannah pours the tea and Reuben sits by the mantelpiece, silent and brooding in his armchair. He looks much smaller than Ndekwe remembers. Ndekwe recalls Joseph's father as a tall man, carrying himself with an upright dignity on the day of his son's burial. But now he seems to have shrunk. He looks older, too; his hair powdered white at the temples and the light long faded from his eyes. Grief has sped him closer to the grave. Ndekwe has seen that a lot in homes made empty by murdered children, especially those whose parents have a religious faith. It was as if they were waiting for death, marking time before seeing their children again. Ndekwe can see that Reuben Musa has become absent from his own life, retreating into his armchair, watching every second crawl by in living agony. Made stagnant by his sorrow.

Hannah's grieving, in comparison, manifests itself in a tightly wound perpetual motion; all knee touching and cushion plumping, proffering a saucer of biscuits and picking invisible specks of dirt from sofa arms that are already spotless.

– Carlton, she says. – Carlton is a good boy. He is a good friend to Joseph.

The present tense, notes Ndekwe.

– Did Joseph have any other friends? He sips at his tea. The cup is delicate in his big hands, and he worries that he will drop it.

– One or two boys, yes. She nods. – Some Sierra Leone boys

from the school. But Carlton is at our house many time. I like him as a friend for Joseph. He is respectful.

– Did Joseph have any other boys come to the house?

– One or two friends called sometimes. But it was our first year here. We still didn't know many people.

– Do you know Carlton is being questioned in connection with a murder?

– Yes, yes, she says.

But her manner is vague, distracted, and Ndekwe is not convinced that she has properly heard the question.

– You know Carlton is locked up in the police station? You know this?

She shakes her head in the negative.

– I did not know this. But I am not surprised.

– No?

– No. She shakes her head firmly.

– You think Carlton could kill someone?

– I think any person could kill another person. Her fingers reach for the disc of gold that hangs around her neck. – It doesn't take too much, I think.

– Did you know Carlton gave Joseph a jacket?

– Yes. I tell Joseph to give it back. I knew it was given in kindness, but we do not want charity.

– Hannah, can you remember exactly when Carlton gave him the jacket?

She shakes her head, no.

– Was it a long time before the shooting?

– I can't remember. She frowns and looks serious for a second, but then brightens. – But, yes, he love that jacket. Won't give it back. I say to him, Joseph, give that boy his coat back, but he won't do it. He says, I'm only borrowing it, Mum.

– Did Carlton ever give Joseph anything else?

– Anything else? She cocks her head to one side, looks quizzical.

– Was he a generous friend? Did he ever give Joseph money?

– Yes, yes. I know he sometimes gives Joseph money. I found it once and I am angry with Joseph. I tell him, we do not need charity.

– Large amounts?

She looks at Ndekwe keenly.

– Peter, she says. – My son is not a gang member.

– I don't believe he was, Ndekwe tells her.

– Everyone says this. Hannah points to the window, indicating the world outside. – The newspaper says this. That policeman, the one who come to see us, he say Joseph is part of a gang. It is not true. As God is my witness, it is not true, Peter. I know my son.

– Which policeman?

– The fat man with the red hair.

Gorman, thinks Ndekwe. Dear God, imagine these people having to deal with Gorman in their rawest hour of grief. It's a wonder he didn't high five them over the coroner's table.

Ndekwe produces the mug shots of Isaacs and Stewart. He hands them to Hannah.

– Have you ever seen these boys? Either of them?

She unfolds a pair of glasses from a case, perches them on her nose and holds the pictures at arm's length. She nods, yes.

– I have seen the small boy with the crazy eyes, she says. – I remember him at the school. He lives near where we used to live.

– Did he ever come to your house?

– No. I don't think he is a friend to Joseph.

– The other boy?

She looks again, squinting hard.

– He is the boy in the paper.

– You remember him from the estate?

– No. But I think of his mother when I see him in the newspaper. I knew how the pain will take her. My heart cries for her. She places her hand on her chest. – God bless, she murmurs. – God bless.

– Twelve bullets.

Ndekwe turns his head towards the armchair in the corner.

– They fired twelve bullets at my son, says Reuben. – Eight of them from close range.

– I'm sorry? says Ndekwe, then realizes his surprise has made him sound interrogative and overly harsh. He repeats himself, this time in gentle enquiry.

– I'm sorry? Mr Musa?

But Reuben Musa doesn't seem to hear him. He is not addressing the Detective Sergeant; it is as though he is not there.

– Who fires so many bullets at close range? he says. – I will tell you: someone who has lost control. They think they are soldiers, these boys. He shakes his head. – No real soldier would do such a thing.

Eight of them from close range.

A half-formed thought is turning in Ndekwe's mind, a thought that he arrests before it can form on his lips. Instead, he takes a final sip of his tea before setting the cup carefully back down into its saucer on the table.

– Thank you very much for talking to me, he tells them.

– You think Carlton kill this boy? says Hannah. – This boy in the newspaper?

Ndekwe looks at her and then at her husband, sunken deep in his armchair, and then at the photo of their dead son above the fireplace; the picture framed with the crayoned hearts and kisses. But he keeps his thoughts buttoned up at the back of his mind. Ndekwe knows he cannot help these people or bring them any comfort by telling them what he thinks. Not yet, anyway.

– I don't know, Hannah, he says.

They rise from the sofa.

– Give my love to Isabel, says Hannah. – She tells me of you and Sonia. You are doing well, she says. New job, yes? Promotion! She beams at him with genuine pride, as if Ndekwe is her own son and she is basking in the reflected light of his achievement.

– Yes, yes, well ... He bows his head slightly and offers a handshake. – Thank you for your help.

She clutches his hand in both of hers, her grip surprisingly strong.

– Thank you for coming to see us, Peter, she tells him. – And may the Lord smile down and bless you with your own child. Be patient, she says, smiling. – Be patient, be patient. God rewards those who wait on his heavenly grace.

Ndekwe returns her smile through clenched teeth. Isabel, he thinks. Isabel and her wagging tongue and her broad congregation.

Hannah turns to her husband, beckoning him up from his armchair.

– Reuben. Reuben! Peter is leaving now.

– Yes, yes ...

Joseph's father lifts himself awkwardly to his feet and Ndekwe extends a hand. Reuben offers his left, the hand on the wrong side. Ndekwe looks down: the man's right hand is a prosthetic. He hadn't noticed before. The hand is a good imitation, but definitely false; a rubberized palm held half open, the colouring solid, the fingers slightly curled but frozen still, an illusion of life.

Ndekwe drops his right hand and shakes with his left.

– Thank you, Mr Musa, he says.

■ ■ ■ ■ ■

The Incident Room, two hours later. Ndekwe, Gorman and Halliwell are gathered around a desk upon which are spread various reports and records. The sunlight bounces off Ndekwe's glasses every time he raises his head to speak, shining in and out of Gorman's eyes. Gorman has necked four paracetamol, but can feel his headache returning, slowly sneaking up the back of his neck, like a furtive burglar making his way up a drainpipe. He is aware of Ndekwe's dull monotone somewhere above his head, but it sounds as if he's talking through a mouthful of cotton wool.

– All right, all right, hold up a minute, he says, cutting off his

DS in mid-flow. – Let me get this straight. You think Isaacs smoked this Musa boy?

Ndekwe nods solemnly. – I think it's a distinct possibility. Multiple shots from close range, a good proportion of them well off the mark. Just like the bullets fired outside the newsagent's last Thursday.

He points to the photos from the ballistics report; yellow chalk circles on the pavement and walls. – Then look at this, he says, pointing to another photo, a grass surface churned by track marks and raised divots of mud; black and yellow pegs marking the entry points of the bullets. – Same thing, look. Haphazard firing from close range.

– So? We're talking about fucking hoodrats here, not trained marksmen. Gorman sucks on his top lip, but the words have already escaped. What had that course book from that last communications training module said? Swearing is often a sign that a stressful situation is being handled successfully. He repeats the phrase silently to himself then swallows, composes himself, tries again.

– Come on, Peter, he says, half of these idiots can't even hold a firearm the right way round, let alone hit a moving target. What's your point?

– The bullets were both from a Browning 9mm, explains Ndekwe. – Both instances. You'd expect a wide spray of bullets from a MAC or an Uzi, but if you unload a clip from a semi-automatic pistol at close range you'd expect most of the bullets to hit. Or at least land somewhere near to each other.

– Unless you can't shoot for shit, observes Halliwell.

– Or unless you're seriously visually impaired, says Ndekwe. He forks his fingers and points them towards his eyes.

Gorman thinks that this is bullshit. He looks to Halliwell for support, but the Detective Constable has adopted a studious expression intended to convey deep analytical thought, but which instead makes him look as though he is gazing vacantly into an abyss. – What's your point? Gorman asks Ndekwe.

– If Samuel Isaacs, aka the cock-eyed cavalier, did kill Joseph Musa then McKenzie would have known about it.

– Peter ... Gorman massages his temples with his fingertips. – Do you seriously expect me to dig up a two-year-old murder?

– No, that would be utterly pointless. Unless we had fresh evidence.

– Which we don't.

– No, agrees Ndekwe. – But what if McKenzie gives up Isaacs?

Gorman can't quite believe what he is hearing. He leans his elbows on the desk and holds his head in his hands, closes his eyes for a second or two and sees a clean white beach fringed by a calm blue ocean. He breathes deeply; once, twice. He can smell cocoa butter and hear the gentle chatter of imaginary parrots in the imaginary trees above him.

He blinks his eyes back open and lifts his head, but there is no Jamaican beach, no tranquil retreat, no escape hatch to paradise; just the busy hum of the room and the heat shimmering through the windows and Ndekwe staring at him with those earnest glittering eyes of glass.

– Look, he tells him. – Pull Isaacs, nick him for the burglary at Shepherdson's flat, see what else he says. Do not accuse him of murder. He points a finger at Ndekwe. – Repeat: do not accuse him of murder. OK?

Ndekwe looks genuinely insulted.

– Gaffer, please! he says. – Give me some credit.

– Just get Isaacs to put McKenzie at the murder scene, Gorman instructs him. – Forget Joseph Musa, just concentrate on the job we're on with, yeah?

Gorman watches his officers leave and then checks his watch. 12:02.

Time for lunch.

■ ■ ■ ■ ■

They almost drive straight past him. They are heading down Mare Street back towards the Crown Heights estate and there he is, sat in a McDonald's window, sucking on a milkshake and tapping away on his phone.

– Fuck me, says Halliwell. – Have a look.

– What?

Halliwell twists around in his seat, tries to peer out of the back window as they roll past. – That's Isaacs.

– You sure?

– Positive.

Ndekwe swings the car over to the next available parking space. Halliwell gets on the radio and requests the armed back-up unit.

They sit and they wait. Ndekwe unclips his seat belt and adjusts the rear-view mirror until he can see the window where Isaacs is framed. He has his phone to his ear now, leant back in his chair, swilling his shake around in the cup.

– What's the ETA? asks Ndekwe.

– Soon as.

– When, though?

– Soon as they can. Five minutes. Ten, max.

Ndekwe looks at the clock on the dashboard and then checks it against his wristwatch.

– Get onto them again, he says.

Halliwell sighs, but does so.

Ndekwe glances at the wing mirror. A crawling line of vehicles backed up the length of Mare Street. He checks the rear-view again. Isaacs has finished his call and is back to tapping out text messages. He holds his phone up in front of him, surveys the screen and then slips it into his tracksuit pocket.

Ndekwe thumps the steering wheel.

– Fuck it, let's do this.

– Pete, the place is fucking rammed with kids!

– He won't be carrying on the street, he's not that stupid. Ndekwe reaches for the door handle.

– Pete, protests Halliwell, but Ndekwe is out of the car and striding through the traffic, heading for the golden arches on the other side of the road. Halliwell curses, unlocks his door and springs out of the car, jogs after his Detective Sergeant.

■ ■ ■ ■ ■

The place is indeed rammed with chattering teenagers and families with small kids. Isaacs doesn't notice the two police officers until they have slid into his booth, Halliwell alongside him and Ndekwe looming opposite.

– Hello, Samuel, says Ndekwe.

Isaacs stiffens up in his seat. His eyes look even more disturbing in real life; one eyeball swivels wildly around in its socket like a drunken spotlight, the other jammed in a permanent squint inwards, as though it was a ball bearing and his nose a magnet. Only the tilt of his head gives any indication as to where he is attempting to direct his gaze.

– I'm DS Ndekwe. You know DC Halliwell?

– Old pals, aren't we, Bam Bam?

Isaacs doesn't reply, just bows his head and sucks noisily at his milkshake.

– What's up? Cat got your tongue?

Isaacs drags up an enormous belch, wipes pink from his mouth. The sudden rudeness of the noise makes the kids at the next table hoot with delighted laughter; two little boys and a girl, around six or seven years old. Their mother tut-tuts them into a sniggering silence. Ndekwe senses that her scolding is borne as much from caution as disapproval. She steals a glance at the three men and their obvious tension, averts her eyes and nudges her offspring, bids them to be quiet, to eat their fries. The children sit stock still, hands clamped over their mouths, eyes dancing with mirth.

– Listen, Samuel, says Halliwell. – You're in a bit of bother, mate.

– I ain't your fucking mate, says Isaacs.

– That's probably just as well, says Ndekwe, because we're arresting you.

– Arresting me for what?

– Burglary.

Isaacs tilts his head back to one side and regards the Detective Sergeant.

– You for real? he says, sneering.

– We've got your prints all over the gaff, Halliwell informs him, and a size eight Air Jordan on the front door.

Ndekwe shifts in his seat, peers under the table.

– Just like those bad boys you got on there. What size are you, Samuel?

– Suck my cock, says Isaacs.

More giggles from the table next to them. Ndekwe glances across at the children, at their mother swiftly clearing their table, dropping greasy food wrappers into brown bags, crowding half-empty drink cartons onto trays.

– Come on, kids, she says. – Come on now.

They gather together their toys and trays and rubbish and take their leave. Ndekwe waits until they are out of earshot and then informs Isaacs that he is being arrested on suspicion of a dwelling burglary and that he does not have to say anything but it may harm his defence if he does not answer in question something he later relies on in court, and that anything he does say may be given in evidence.

Ndekwe's phone buzzes in his pocket. He takes it out and looks at it: Gorman. He decides not to answer. Outside, he sees the twirling blue lights of the CO19 armed response unit pulling up on the opposite side of the road. Isaacs follows his line of vision and sees this too. He grins a slow mirthless grin, drains the last of his milkshake, rattling the thick liquid up the straw. He picks his shades up off the table and folds them around his head. Then he stands up and pulls at the waistband of his tracksuit bottoms, makes an elaborate show of checking his watch.

– Make it fucking rapid, yeah?

■ ■ ■ ■ ■

Back at the station, Bam Bam's mood is further darkened by the news that his usual brief is in court and cannot pull out at such short notice and so the office is sending down a junior in his place; one Catherine-Jane Connelly, a slight young woman in her mid-twenties in a dark suit and scraped-back hair, whose poker-faced demeanour fails to hide her obvious nerves. She arrives at the station and introduces herself to Ndekwe and then Isaacs, who looks her up and down with undisguised contempt before opting to ignore her completely.

The interview room: Isaacs and his brief on one side of the table, Ndekwe and Halliwell on the other, the machine recording between them. Isaacs slouches in his chair, arms folded, an attempt at studied nonchalance betrayed only by the almost tangible waves of resentment that radiate from him.

Ndekwe slides over the mug shot of Jack.

– I am showing Mr Isaacs a photograph of John Henry Shepherdson. Do you know this man, Samuel?

– Nope, he says, without looking.

– You sure?

– Yup.

– Mr Shepherdson is the resident of 34b Conway Court. The flat that you broke into.

– You don't have to answer that, Connelly tells Isaacs.

An indifferent silence from the other side of the table, a practised silence borne of many hours spent in interview rooms much like this one in police stations across London. Isaacs yawns and stretches. He looks at his watch. His brief makes notes and then puts her pen down.

– Are you denying breaking into Mr Shepherdson's flat? asks Halliwell.

– I ain't saying shit.

– Do you know where Mr Shepherdson is right now?

– Nup.

– He's locked up. He reckons he killed your mate.

Isaacs doesn't bat an eyelid. – I ain't got any mates, he says.

The solicitor clears her throat. – I'm sorry, she says, but as far as I'm aware this has nothing to do with why we are here. Can we stick to the matter in hand, please?

She turns to Isaacs. – Samuel, you don't have to answer any questions that do not directly relate to the offence you are being charged with.

Isaacs shrugs, slides a hand down into his pants and rummages around his crotch.

Ndekwe offers another photo across the table.

– I am showing Mr Isaacs a photograph of Aaron Stewart. You knew Aaron, didn't you, Samuel? He was your mate, yeah?

Another shrug from Isaacs.

– No?

Stony bored silence.

– Come on, Samuel, you must have known him. You were arrested together, several times. Ndekwe flicks open a file, picks out the PNC record and starts reading aloud. – Possession with intent to supply, Section 5 public order, suspicion of attempted robbery ...

Isaacs looks at him askance, curious despite himself. – Attempted robbery? Attempted robbery of what?

– Global Travel, Bromley High Street, reads Ndekwe.

– When was that?

– The fifth of April, 2008.

Isaacs sucks on his teeth. – That thing, he says. – That was fuckin bullshit. There was about ten or twelve mans got lifted for that, an they all busted case. So fuck you and your attempted robbery.

– So you did know Aaron Stewart, prompts Halliwell.

– Knew the man from around. Isaacs shrugs.

– And you knew he'd been stabbed to death on the Crown Heights estate last Thursday, states Ndekwe.

– Right, that's enough, says Connelly, who has been listening with growing irritation. – Detective Sergeant, if you do not desist from this line of questioning I am removing my client from the interview immediately.

Ndekwe holds up his hands.

– OK, fine. OK, he says. He studies the papers in front of him for a few moments and regards Isaacs again, who is grinning openly at him.

– You do still live on the Crown Heights estate, yeah? 14 Jasmine House? That is your given address?

– That's my granny's place.

– Right ...

Ndekwe places McKenzie's face next to Stewart's and Shepherdson's.

– I am showing Mr Isaacs a photo of Carlton McKenzie. Do you know who that is, Samuel?

– Nup.

– Have another look. Take a really close look.

Isaacs sighs, picks up the photo and makes an elaborate show of taking a really close look, his left eyeball turning somersaults. He tosses the photo back onto the table.

– Nup.

Ndekwe taps the photo with his pen.

– Carlton McKenzie. You don't know him?

– Nah.

Ndekwe flicks through another file, consults another piece of paper.

– You were arrested together in ... 2006 and again in ... 2007.

– For what?

– Section 5 public order.

Isaacs glances at his brief. – This is just bullshit, he says.

She nods in firm agreement. – It is, Samuel, she says, and unless the Detective Sergeant gets back on track we'll be leaving this interview very shortly. She flashes a look at Halliwell, who regards her impassively.

– Do you know Melissa? Ndekwe tosses the question in casually, almost as an afterthought. He writes something down in his notes as he waits for the answer.

Isaacs shifts slightly in his chair.

– Nup.

Ndekwe looks up. – You do know who I mean, though, yeah?

Isaacs bites at his thumbnail and spits something from between his teeth onto the floor. – I don't know nobody or nothing, he says.

– The charge, please, Detective Sergeant, says Connelly.

Ndekwe leans forwards. – All right, here's the thing, he says. – We're holding Carlton McKenzie and Jack Shepherdson on suspicion of the murder of Aaron Stewart. Believe that? They both reckon they killed your mate. Not together, though; they both say they acted alone. What do you make of that? Bit of a coincidence, don't you think?

– *Detective Sergeant.* There is ice in Connelly's voice now, but Ndekwe is ignoring her completely, his gaze locked on Isaacs' skittering eyeballs.

– Why would an old guy like Shepherdson stab a man like Aaron Stewart?

Connelly slaps the table with the palm of her hand, making Halliwell jump and Isaacs grin even wider.

– *Detective Sergeant! I am removing my client from this interview with immediate effect.*

She stands up, almost shaking with rage and adrenaline. She begins to gather together her papers.

Ndekwe continues to ignore her. – What do you reckon, Bam Bam? he asks, raising his voice a notch. – An argument? A deal gone wrong?

Isaacs tilts his head around the room, says nothing.

– This is an outrage, seethes Connelly.

Ndekwe stands up and plants both hands on the table, leans across. He's now talking to the solicitor, but he's looking straight at Isaacs.

– Well, I think he does know Carlton McKenzie. And I think he knew Aaron Stewart and I think he was there when Aaron Stewart was killed. Weren't you, Bam Bam?

Isaacs sits up and leans forward to meet him.

– Samuel to you. He smiles. – You fuckin choc-ice. Now get me out this shithole, yeah? I got places I need to be.

•••••

Ndekwe is giving Samuel Isaacs a lift home. Isaacs does not want a lift from Ndekwe, does not want to be seen in his car, but he is in a proper hurry and the lift he demanded from Catherine Jane Connelly was not forthcoming owing to her having to fly off to another appointment. So it is with great reluctance on Samuel Isaacs' part that he and the Detective Sergeant are now driving slowly through the postcodes, Isaacs sunk low on the back seat, passenger side, the peak of his cap pulled down over his face, eyes hidden behind sunglasses.

– Shame about Knowledge, says Ndekwe. – But I suppose it's good news for you in a way, yeah?

No answer.

– Instant promotion eh, Bam Bam? Numero uno, yeah?

Isaacs yawns loudly, without covering his mouth.

– Bam Bam, says Ndekwe. – The names people give each other, eh? Bam Bam. What sort of name's that?

– It was my little brother, says Isaacs. – He couldn't say Sam Sam.

– Oh really? I thought it was after the baby in the *Flintstones*. You remember that?

Non-committal grunt from the back.

– No? Fred and Barney? Cartoon family of cave people? Yabada-badoo, all that bollocks?

Isaacs shakes his head. – You're a fuckin sad case, you, mate.

– Nah, but I tell you what, though, says Ndekwe. – It suddenly hit me this morning why they call you Bam Bam. When I went to see Joseph's mum and dad.

He keeps his eyes on the road, but Ndekwe can feel the prickle of tension behind him.

– Cos you can't shoot for shit, can you, Bam Bam? he says. – You and your eyeballs, yeah? You just let go the full clip and hope one of them hits, yeah?

Ndekwe makes a gun with his fingers and sweeps it from side to side, sprays imaginary bullets along the width of the windscreen.

– BAM BAM! BAM BAM! BAM BAM BAM!

– Bullshit, spits Isaacs.

– Well, I'll tell you what, says Ndekwe, I'll ask Kez, yeah? I'm going to be talking to him later on. He must remember how you got your name. Says he's known you for time.

– Yeah, well, he's full of shit as well.

– Yeah, but he's got a cool name so you're probably just jealous. Kez: that's a pretty cool name, yeah? Better than fucking Bam Bam. Ndekwe laughs out loud. – Sounds like something a little girl would call her pet doggy. He adopts a simpering baby voice. – Bam Bam! Here, Bam Bam! Good doggy!

– You're chatting pure shit, mate. Isaacs is trying to keep his voice level, but Ndekwe can tell he is rapidly losing his cool.

– Joseph didn't get no street name, did he, though? Why was that, Bam Bam? Cos he weren't part of your gang? Is that why?

– Is that why what? Isaacs asks.

– Is that why you shot him?

– Look, snarls Isaacs. – Just take me to where I need to be, yeah? I don't have to listen to this bollocks.

– Yeah, no problem, Bam Bam. You'll have to direct me, though. I'm a south-side boy myself. Ya get me? Deep, deep south. Still don't know my way round this manor.

Isaacs pulls himself up and stares at the streets slipping by outside.

– You going the wrong way, innit, he says. – You wanna be back that way.

– You what, mate, says Ndekwe. – Straight ahead?

They arrive at the top of Dalston Lane and Ndekwe swings a left onto the Lower Clapton Road. Hits a clear stretch of road and puts his foot down.

– Nah, back, man, protests Isaacs. – Turn back ...

Ndekwe flicks on the radio. Katy Perry singing about a teenage dream. He cranks up the volume and carries on down the road, deaf to the mounting protests from the back seat. He turns the car right at Stamford Hill, past the Seven Sisters tube and onwards, into Tottenham towards N17.

– What the fuck is this? yells Isaacs. – Where the fuck you going? Turn back!

– You what, mate? What you say? Turn it up, yeah?

The music swells and fills the car and the windows vibrate with the bass. Katy Perry sings about getting drunk on the beach, about being young for ever, about running away and never looking back.

– STOP THE FUCKIN CAR! shouts Isaacs.

Ndekwe takes a sudden left and then a right and then another left and then they are on the edge of a large council estate. Ndekwe knows this place and so does Isaacs. Broadwater Farm. Ndekwe keeps driving until he zips past a row of shops with a group of youths gathered around two parked cars on the corner. He slams on the brakes and Isaacs is thrown forwards and then backwards into his seat as Ndekwe reverses at high speed before a wheel-spinning turn brings them screeching to a halt outside the shops.

The youths turn to look at the squeal of brakes and pounding music. One or two of the younger ones scoot off, but most of the others slide down from the car bonnets and straighten up, staring hard from beneath hoods and caps.

Ndekwe kills the ignition, but leaves the radio blaring. He gets out of the car and strides round to the rear passenger side, pulls open the door.

– Come on, Bam Bam, he says. – Out you get, mate.

Isaacs shoots a startled look up the road. The youths on the corner have fanned out and are walking slowly towards the car.

– Fuck this, man, he says. – Take me home.

– Nah, you can walk from here, yeah?

Isaacs tries to slam the door back shut, but Ndekwe reaches in and catches hold of his flailing arm.

– GET THE FUCK OFF ME, GET OFF ME YOU FUCKING PIG ...

Ndekwe drags Isaacs out of the car. No sooner has he hit the concrete than Isaacs scrambles up onto his feet and he's away, sprinting hard up the street.

Ndekwe watches him disappear past the shops and around the corner then turns to face the first of the approaching youths. The tallest among them steps forward, a rake-thin boy with dead insect eyes beneath a red bandana. He takes in Ndekwe, the car with the open door and the music banging out into the street.

– Wha g'wan?

Ndekwe smiles and salutes his eyes against the glare of the sun.

– All right, mate, he says. – Can you tell me the way back to Hackney?

■ ■ ■ ■ ■

– Carlton, says Gorman, this is Detective Sergeant Peter Ndekwe. He's got a few more questions he wants to ask you.

McKenzie extends his hand across the table to Ndekwe, who, after a beat's hesitation, shakes it, bemused. There are capital letters inked in a Gothic script down the inside of the boy's forearm and Ndekwe tilts his head slightly to read them: LOYALTY ABOVE ALL LAWS.

– You believe that, yeah?

– What?

Ndekwe indicates the tattoo. McKenzie pulls out of the handshake, folds both of his arms across his stomach.

– Had that for time, he says.

– Marked for life now, remarks Gorman.

– Nah, you can get em lasered off.

– Expensive, though.

– I ain't bothered about it. McKenzie unfolds his arms and drops his hands into his lap. – I'll just wear sleeves, innit, he says.

Ndekwe reminds everyone present of the time, date, their full names and reaffirms McKenzie's eschewal of legal representation. That done, he sets the recording machine in motion, the red LED lights leaping in time with his words.

– We found the cars, Carlton. The Mondeos.

The boy nods. – I hope it ain't too messed up, he says, that one at the services. That's a new engine that, if you put the wrong juice in.

– Well, let's just hope he's insured, shall we, says Gorman, but McKenzie doesn't seem to pick up on the sarcasm. He nods in accordance with the Detective Inspector:

– Yeah, he says, insurance should cover it.

– You'll be charged with two counts of twocking, Ndekwe tells him.

– All right ...

– OK. Well, that's that. Now tell me about Aaron Stewart.

McKenzie rolls his eyes. – I already told him yesterday, he says, indicating Gorman.

– Yeah, says Ndekwe, but you haven't told me.

– So I got to tell it all again?

– Not all of it, no. Just the important bits. Like, how did you kill Aaron Stewart?

– Stabbed him.

– How?

The boy eyes him cautiously. – How do you mean how?

– Did you stab him once, twice, three or four times, what?

– Just the once.

– Whereabouts?

– Just ... there ... McKenzie leans across and points at Ndekwe's heart.

– Mr McKenzie is indicating the left-hand side of the chest ... Ndekwe sits upright, squares his shoulders and leans forward so McKenzie's finger is almost touching his shirt. – So you stabbed him in the heart, yeah?

– Near enough I s'pose ...

– How hard?

– Hard enough.

McKenzie withdraws his finger. He drops his hand back into his lap and then slides it onto his knee, clamps down hard to stop his leg from bouncing beneath the table.

– It stuck right in him, yeah? says Ndekwe. – All the way in?

– Yeah.

– And what then?

– I just ran.

– Straight away?

– Damn right.

– And you left the knife in him?

A bemused frown from across the table. McKenzie rubs a hand across his face. Uncertainty. Ndekwe feels Gorman stir in the seat beside him, sensing blood.

– You left the knife stuck in him, repeats Ndekwe. He looks over his glasses at McKenzie then back down through his glasses at his notes.

– Nah ... McKenzie shakes his head, slowly; but he sounds far from certain.

– So what did you do with the knife, Carlton?

– Erm ... The boy bites his lip, as if trying to remember; casts his eyes around the room, as if looking for the answer, but there is nothing to look at; just drab olive walls and a window too high to afford any view. He shakes his head. – I just ... just threw it away, innit, he says.

– You pulled it out of him after you stabbed him, clarifies

Gorman. – Is that what you're saying?

McKenzie nods. – That's it, yeah.

– That's not what you said before, is it?

McKenzie looks perplexed. – What did I say before?

– You said ... Ndekwe consults his notes. – This is what you said, Carlton. 'I slip the knife out from my sleeve, take two steps forward and stick it in the middle of his chest, boom, bang it in as hard as I can, yeah? Like, fucking allow it, yeah? Then I push him back into his mate an I turn round and run like fuck ...' He looks up from reading. – That's what you told DI Gorman on Sunday, yeah?

McKenzie shrugs. – If that's what I said then that's what I said.

– That is exactly what you said, Carlton. Ndekwe taps the papers with his pen. – I've got it written down here.

– OK ... well, whatever, yeah.

– But now you're saying you pulled the knife out of Aaron Stewart's chest after you stabbed him.

The boy shrugs. – I must have done, yeah.

– Where did you put the knife?

– Threw it down a drain.

– You're absolutely certain of that?

– Yeah yeah yeah, like that ... McKenzie mimes an invisible slam-dunk to the floor. – I remember it now; a drain at the side of the road, yeah.

– Whereabouts?

– Hackney Road.

– All right. Ndekwe puts his pen down. – So ... why did you stab Aaron?

– Cos of what he did. McKenzie looks at Ndekwe and holds his gaze. There is nothing in the boy's eyes but cold black fury.

– Because of what he did to your sister, yeah? says Ndekwe.

– Yeah.

– What you *claim* he did, clarifies Gorman. McKenzie ignores him, keeps his eyes on Ndekwe.

– It's the truth guv, he says.

– What about the others? asks Ndekwe.

– What others?

– Well, it wasn't just him, was it? You said that it was Aaron Stewart and Samuel Isaacs and a few other boys who had attacked your sister.

– Yeah, that's it.

– So why didn't you go after all the others as well?

– They weren't there; it was just Aaron and Bam Bam.

– So why didn't you go back afterwards and get all the others?

– I don't know. McKenzie squirms in his seat. – I should have done, he says. – I should have done that ...

Ndekwe writes something down in his notes. He reads it back to himself, nodding. Gorman sighs, looks pointedly at his watch. McKenzie looks from one officer to the other.

– So what now, then? he asks. His fingers appear at the edge of the table and begin their quiet drumming.

– What do you mean 'what now then'? sneers Gorman.

– When you gonna bring them other mans in?

– What other men?

– Bam Bam an Daffy an Maddix an Bailey an all them others.

Gorman shakes his head dismissively. – You might as well forget about this rape thing, son.

– What you mean, forget it?

– Well, for a start, says Gorman, your sister totally denies it. She says it never happened.

– Ask my mum then, innit.

– Your mother says she's completely changed her story. Your sister said she was attacked and then said she wasn't. Didn't even call the police.

– That's cos she's scared.

– Or lying.

– Carlton, says Ndekwe, I arrested Isaacs yesterday.

McKenzie sits bolt upright. – Yeah? You charged him, yeah?

– Are you hard of hearing, son? Gorman leans across the table.
– Your sister hasn't reported any offence. As far as we're concerned,
there was no rape. It didn't happen.

– It happened guv, believe.

– Only according to you, scoffs Gorman.

The boy shoots him a look of pure contempt. – Listen, it fucking
happened, all right?

– Oi! Language!

– This is fucked up, man! McKenzie jumps to his feet, sends his
chair clattering over backwards and heads for the door.

– SIT DOWN! roars Gorman. The boy stops dead, fists balled by
his sides, but he doesn't turn around.

– All right, Carlton, says Ndekwe. – Let's all calm down now,
yeah?

He rises slowly from his seat and walks around the table, sets
the chair back upright.

– Come on, he says. – Come on, Carlton. Sit back down.

– Yeah, Carlton, says Gorman. – Sit down and chill out, yeah?

McKenzie plants himself back in the chair and wraps his arms
around himself, starts rocking gently backwards and forwards.

– OK, listen to me, Carlton, says Ndekwe. – Yesterday, right, I
arrested Samuel Isaacs for breaking and entering.

No comment from McKenzie.

– He broke into Jack's flat. It was Isaacs who took the weed.

No indication that McKenzie is even listening. He stares into
space and does not reply.

– Did you hear what I said?

– Yeah, yeah, yeah ...

– Why do you think he would do that?

McKenzie shrugs.

Gorman props himself up on his knuckles and looms across the
table. – Oi! he snarls. – Have you gone deaf, son? Detective Sergeant
Ndekwe is asking you a question.

McKenzie pointedly ignores Gorman, gives his begrudging

attention to the other man. Ndekwe softens his eyes and speaks calmly.

– Why would Isaacs take the weed, Carlton? You said it was him and Stewart who gave you it to sell, yeah?

– Yeah ...

– So why would he break into Jack's flat and steal it?

– Probably cos he was ... he was trying to ... what's the word? *Provoke* me, innit.

– Provoke you? Why?

– So he could start some drama an that.

– Why?

– I don't know why.

– No idea?

– That's just the way he is, innit.

– All right. Ndekwe writes something down and then lays down his pen. – Let's talk about Jack, he says.

McKenzie shrugs. – What about him?

– He insists it was him who killed Aaron Stewart. Not you.

– He's full of shit guv. McKenzie inspects his fingernails, puts one into his mouth and chews.

– Why would he say that though?

A non-committal silence.

– Threaten him, did you? says Gorman.

McKenzie takes his fingers from his mouth, aims his reply at Ndekwe; – I didn't threaten anyone, he says. – I ain't about that.

– So why's Jack claiming to have murdered Aaron Stewart?

– I don't know.

– Why is he trying to protect you, Carlton?

– I don't know.

Gorman heaves a sigh, hauls himself to his feet.

– Right, he says. – I'll leave you to it. And I suggest that *you* – he points at McKenzie – start cooperating.

He claps a paternal hand on Ndekwe's shoulder, tips him a conspiratorial wink and leaves the interview.

– For the benefit of the recording, DI Gorman has now left the interview room.

Ndekwe waits until the footsteps have receded along the corridor outside before he speaks again.

– He thinks a lot of you, you know. Jack, I mean.

McKenzie bridles at the suggestion. – What you saying?

– Not trying to say anything, Carlton; just an observation. He thinks you're a decent young man.

McKenzie says nothing.

– No opinion on that?

– Listen ... I think Jack carrying a lot of guilt, man.

– How do you mean? Guilt about what?

– Because ... like ... his boy an that.

– What do you mean?

– Cos, like, when we were up there with his man an that ... in that pub ... that day we got lifted, yeah?

– Up in Hull?

– Yeah, yeah. I knew something was wrong then.

– In what way?

McKenzie looks to the door. – Is he coming back?

– He won't be, no.

McKenzie pulls his chair closer to the table. Ndekwe checks the red lights of the recording from the corner of his eye as the boy leans in and begins to speak.

– I'm sat there listening to them chatting an it gradually comes clear that this Benny and Colin are a pair of batties together. The mans in the pub, yeah? They fussing and quarrelling with each other like an old married couple, ya get me? Then a bit later Jack says he has to go an sort something out, this bit of business. Says Colin's gonna lend him his car. He tells me to wait at the pub with Benny and Colin, but I'm like, nah, I wanna go with you, Jack. I didn't know these people an I ain't being funny or nothing but I did not feel entirely comfortable in that situation, ya get me? McKenzie waits for Ndekwe's nod before continuing. – Well, at first, man did not want me along with him, I could tell. But I was insisting, yeah? I didn't want to look rude or ungrateful, but I did not know these mans and I wanted to stick with Jack, an not hang about in a strange place with a pair of flippin fags, ya get me?

Ndekwe nods, indicates for McKenzie to continue.

– Well, finally Jack agreed I could go with him, yeah, but I could tell he weren't too happy about the situation. We went back out to the car but halfway there the man nearly fell over with a coughing fit. He was bent double in the street, gasping for breath. He got his inhaler out an started sucking on it, but it was like the life was being squeezed out of him, ya get me? I was in a bare panic guv. I thought the man was gonna collapse there on the pavement. I lowered him down to the kerb and sat there with him while he got himself back together. His breath was all ragged and there was strings of spit hanging out of his mouth. He spat all over the pavement a few times an I asked if he was all right an he was like, aye, I'm shipshape. We got to the car, but Jack's hands were shaking that much he couldn't get the key in the door. I told him I'd drive, an took the keys out of his hand. He was shaking like mad. I helped him in the passenger side an got behind the wheel. I wasn't convinced about this mission, whatever it was. The man did not look in any fit shape to be going anywhere. He was sat with his head pressed up against the side window. He was deathly white guv, white as a sheet an he was sweating like a pig as well. Flippin heck, Jack, you sure you all right? I says. I'm fuckin marvellous, he says. I could tell the stubborn old fool weren't gonna be talked out of this thing, so I started up the car and told him to tell me the way to wherever we were headed.

– And he didn't tell you where you were going?

– Nah, but I had a bad feeling about it from that point onwards. I could tell Jack was freaking out at the thought of this thing, whatever it was he was out to do. I used to get the same way back in the day if we were going out on road. I used to get all tight breathed and panicky, just like that. But I used to keep it all inside, ya get me? Swallow the fear, innit. I could tell Jack was the same way. But the man was on a mission. Wherever we were going, I could tell it was important to him. An if it was gonna get wild, I wanted to be there, ya get me? Man had done a lot for me, yeah? Whatever was gonna happen, I wanted to be right there in his corner, true ... So, he tells me to turn the car round an drive back down the road. We keep going for a little while then there's this shopping place off to one side, a place with all big shops like a JD Sports an a Boots an all that. We swing in there an Jack says to park up outside the Toys R Us. He tells me to wait in the car an he goes in there. Man comes out ten minutes later with this big Transformer robot.

– A robot? Ndekwe looks quizzical.

– Yeah, like Optimus Prime, innit. Like a doll, a figure, ya get me? He opens the boot an sticks this Transformer in an gets back in the car. He's wheezing an gasping again. He gets his inhaler out an starts sucking. I ask him where we're going an he says we're going to John's ...

– His son's?

– Yeah, that's it. He tell you all this, yeah?

– He mentioned him, that's all.

– What's he say?

– Nothing, he just ... Carry on, please, Carlton.

McKenzie looks warily at the police officer, but continues. – All right, so he gives the directions an we drive down past the bit where all the sailing ships are an past the docks. That's where you'll be getting the ferry from, says Jack. Then he tells me to turn off the main road an onto this estate. We're driving around for time, down one street an then another. It's like the man is having problems remembering this place. He asks me to slow down an he digs this piece of paper out of his pocket. He's checking all the street names. Don't you remember where he lives? I ask him an he says he's never been before. I ask him when was the last time he saw him an he says the fourth of February nineteen seventy-three, boom, exact, just like that. That's like a flippin lifetime ago, innit. That's like, what ... McKenzie does the calculation in his head. – ... thirty-seven years ago, man! Rah! I'm about to say something else when Jack says, here we are, look, go down here. I turn down this street an Jack says to slow right down. He's looking for the number of the house. We go round a bend an then he says, OK, park up anywhere here. There's this guy washing a car on the other side of the street. He's got the hosepipe coming out of his front door an he's running the jet of water over the roof, chasing all the suds down into the gutter. Jack tells me to stay in the car an he gets the robot from the boot an walks across to this guy washing his car.

– This is his son?

– Yeah, his son John, who he ain't seen for thirty-seven years. I sit an watch it all go down from the car. I keep my hat pulled down low an try to look like I ain't gawping, but I'm keeping an eye on tings, ya get me? Jack is stood a little way off the man. I can see he's doing all the talking. Man's not even looking at Jack, just hosing his car down. But I knew he was on edge, it was plain as day. Body language, innit. You can tell ten million miles away when a man gonna make a move. An I was already halfway out the car when the man threw his hosepipe to the floor an started pushing Jack back into the road. I'm straight over there, like whoa whoa whoa, easy now, bruv, easy now, he's an old man, ya get me? The man takes a step back as I come to him. I weren't gonna do anything guv, swear down, I was just gonna get between them at most, ya get me? Stop it escalating, innit, cos there was pure hate in this man's eyes. I was worried he was gonna start swinging for real, ya get me? Jack's like, I said stay in the car, didn't I? His son looks me up and down, big sneer twisting his face. Disgust, ya get me? He was disgusted. Who's this then? he says. This your latest bit of stuff?

– Bit of what? Stuff? Ndekwe starts to smile despite himself, but then he notes the deadly serious look on McKenzie's face and he sets his own expression in accordance.

– Man nearly went down then. Man nearly got put on his arse, trust me. Instead I just puts my hands up an tells him his dad has come a long way to see him, yeah? Man's come through a lot to offer the pipe of peace, yeah? He just fucked off and left, says this man, this John. Can't just turn up here and walk back into our lives like nothing's happened, he says. The hosepipe is pumping bare water out across the grass verge an into the gutter and there's a big puddle creeping round our feet. Jack's saying, son, son, I had to go, son and he's trying to reach out a hand, but the man starts raising his voice an saying how he knew this was a bad idea an for us to both fuck off back to wherever we come from. I'm trying to be the peacemaker in all this, saying, listen, bruv, give him a chance, give the man a chance, yeah? We're going back an forth like that when I notice Jack staring towards the house. This little kid has come wandering out the front door an he's stood there looking at us all.

McKenzie sits up straight and stares past Ndekwe, as though entranced by some unseen vision in the distance.

– He's about five or six years old. Cute little guy in a Batman T-shirt an this mop of curly hair. He almost looks like a girl with all them curls. But he's a lad all right. He's got a toy gun in his hand, one of them space laser things. Dad, he says. Go back inside, Louis, says John, an Jack is like, Louis, Louis, an he drops down to one knee an holds the Transformer out to the boy ...

McKenzie shifts his chair back from the table, turns it sideways on and holds out his hand. He beckons to an invisible child. – Louis, he's saying, Louis; it's me, Grandad. The lad just looks at him. Then he points this toy gun at Jack: POW POW POW!

McKenzie makes a gun with his fingers and jerks it up and down three times. – The boy just turns and scoots back into the house. Jack puts the Transformer on the pavement and stands back up. He's coughing that hard it's bringing tears. He wipes his mouth and his eyes an then turns to this John. Will you give it to him for us? he asks. Man says nothing, don't even look at him, just picks the hosepipe back up and keeps moving the water over his car. John, says Jack, but John's like, just fuck off, will you? So Jack turns and heads back to the car.

McKenzie pulls his chair back round to face the table. – Flippin heck guv. I was heated, yeah? I was angry, ya get me?

– Why?

– What? McKenzie looks confused.

– Why were you angry? prompts Ndekwe.

– Cos ... cos that's *raw*, man! Know what I'm saying? I tell the son, that's fucking *well* raw, bruv. What the fuck's it got to do with you? he says. But he don't say it aggressive, just sort of hurt and ... what's the word ... *defensive*, ya get me? I can tell that the man is hurting. My dad left me as well, I tell him. Shit happens, yeah? He looks at me an I can see the pain in his eyes guv, the bare pain. He says, Did your dad leave your mam for another man? I didn't know what to say to that. Man can't help the way he is, I say. And I can't help the way I feel, he says. Man puts his hosepipe down an turns an walks back into the house. After a few seconds the water stops. I'm waiting for man to come back outside, but he don't show. Jack sounds the horn from the car. He's waving at me to come back. The pool of water is creeping up around Optimus Prime, so I pick him up an take him to the doorstep. I leave him there an then I go back to the car. Jack's sucking on his inhaler like he's trying to suck the breath back into himself. He looks flippin awful, like he's about to pass out. I don't say anything to him. I fire the motor up an drive away.

– You didn't know Jack was gay?

– Nah. Jack tells me the script that night back at Colin and Benny's. How he got married when he was in his early twenties and him an his wifey had John soon after. Wonder we managed to make a bain, says Jack, what with me away at sea all the time an half pissed when I came home. Wonder any bains got born on Hessle Road, he says. Bain means baby, yeah? Anyway, he tried to settle down an that, but all the time deep down he knew he was ... y'know ...

– What did you think about that? About Jack being gay?

– That's what Jack asked me, if I thought any different of him. I said no, I still thought he was a bare prick. Ha! I think he liked that one. I ain't even gonna lie though guv, I don't care nothing about where Jack sticks his dick. But I don't agree with him having kids, yeah? I'm against that. He shouldn't have got married if he's a batty, yeah? And especially not to bring a baby child into the world. Ain't fair on anyone, innit. He reckons it was different back then, growing up where he did and all that. Hard to be your true self, everyone got to be a big macho man, ya get me? Maybe that was true back then, yeah, but it's true now, innit? If you ain't stern faced you get rolled over, ya get me? You grow up somewhere like that you gotta stand tall, you gotta act like a man. Same thing now guv. Same thing now. There ain't no progress in that department, trust me ...

He trails off and stares at the wall at the far end of the room.

– Listen, says Ndekwe. – Carlton, I've got to ask you this.

– What?

– Was there ever anything between you and Jack?

McKenzie makes a face as if he is about to vomit.

– Aw, please ...

– I have to ask, Carlton.

– I ain't a queer.

– But you care for him, right?

– Nah, I don't flippin *care* for him. Rah! Fuck's sake, man! McKenzie folds his arms and sits back in his chair, sucks his teeth in disgust.

– I don't mean in that way, Carlton. I mean ... he was a sort of father figure, yeah?

McKenzie laughs a short, mirthless laugh. – You reckon? Well, listen to this: I saw my real dad on that day as well, yeah? Believe that?

– You saw your dad in Hull?

– I saw him on the TV. We were sat upstairs in Colin's pub, watching the TV and eating our dinner. First off, my ears pricked up when the man said Atlantic Road, Brixton. Then they showed the CCTV footage They showed them coming through the door and all the ruckus, the two of them fighting with the security guard and his bally getting pulled off his face an that. They didn't show the bit where the guard got blasted in the leg, but they freeze-framed the pictures of the mans running out of there and they made them bigger, like a close-up, ya get me. And it was him. It was my dad. His face filling the flippin TV screen. I knew it was him, clear as day. The man even said about the security guard mentioning about his teeth, the two front teeth, he said, which was wrong, cos it's all his teeth, yeah? He got the full set, all gold, yeah? But even without that I knew it was him. I knew him straight away. Roger Barrington McKenzie. Jack looked up from his beans on toast and he was like, yo, what's up with you, you seen a ghost? I told him. I said, Jack, that's my dad. McKenzie points across the room, then looks at Ndekwe. – I was flippin gutted guv. I said to Jack, I said that's it, I'm handing myself in, bruv. He was all like nah nah nah, we come this far, we can't give up now. I said to him, what's all this flippin we business? *He* weren't on the run ... he ain't gotta be looking over *his* shoulder, ya get me? It was just me, bruv. And I ain't got anywhere to run to any more. There ain't no bar in Jamaica. There ain't no Montego Bay for me. There ain't no future. It's all fucked up, yeah? Ain't no point in anything any more.

A silence hangs heavy in the room. The red LED lights sink and disappear and only leap back into life when Ndekwe speaks. – So what then?

McKenzie blinks, looks at the Detective Sergeant as if he had forgotten he was there.

– So then ... then I went downstairs and started drinking, yeah? Benny was like, rah, what you doing down here, man, get yourself back up them stairs yeah, but I told him true. I said, Benny, man, it's all fucked, there ain't no point, just give me a flippin drink, man. Jack comes down and starts yapping at my shoulder, giving it the big one saying I got all my life in front of me and all that chat, but I knew it was over, yeah? I knew it was the end of the flippin road. I told him to get back upstairs but he wouldn't go. He said he wasn't gonna leave me, yeah? He told Benny not to give me any more drinks but I was like, fuck off, Jack. I'm a grown flippin man, I can do what I like, yeah? So he just shrugs and goes up the other end and starts playing pool, but I can tell he's keeping tabs on me, keeps glancing over and nodding at Benny but Benny's shrugging his shoulders, like, yo, he's your problem, not mine.

– You were upset?

The boy shakes his head. – I was flippin angry guv. I was ready to go pop, I can see that now. And when that batty man come an sit next to me there was only one way it was gonna go, you get me?

– Who, Jack?

– Nah, this other man. Just some man who was in there. He starts giving it all the chat, saying how he's never seen me in there before and all that, an where am I from an do I want a drink. I told him, I give the boy fair warning. I says, yo, get the fuck out my face, man, I ain't in no mood, but he persists, yeah? He's like ooh touchy an being all that faggy way. He was like a proper fag, man. Not like Jack. He was like simpering an batting his eyelashes at me like a flippin girl, man. What's wrong with *you*? he keeps saying. What's put you in a mood an then he says, come on give me a smile, you miserable sod, an he reaches out an touches my cheek an that's when I switched an I banged him out; just stood up an took him to flippin school, showed him who was wearing the effing trousers, innit.

– You hit him?

McKenzie nods. – They had to drag me off the man. Benny and Colin an a few others. Jack's straight over shouting whoa whoa whoa, but I've lost the flippin plot by then, threatening to smash up any mans who come near me, yeah? This batty is curled up in a ball on the floor, screaming his head off, yeah? There's all his boys standing up an it's gonna go right off, so I get the fuck outta there guv, kicking over tables and chairs an that. I get away up the road outside, storming off, head on fire, just flippin raging and I'm crying as well, bare tears streaming down my face, just flippin anger and rage an flippin frustration, yeah?

He stops and wipes his mouth with the back of his hand, looks at Ndekwe, who indicates for him to continue.

– I can hear voices behind me, an it's all these mans spilling out the pub an I see some of them have got pool cues and beer glasses in their hands and there's Jack bringing up the rear shouting, all right pack it in, that's enough. I don't know who he was shouting at, them or me, but I just stopped dead and turned around and said, come on then, I'll smash the fucking lot of ya, one at a time or all at flippin once, come on then, you set of fucking fag motherfuckers. I'm stood there screaming at these mans an they get right up close an start swiping at me with these pool sticks an throwing glasses an they're bouncing off me an smashing on the road. They're all pointing and snarling an that, but none of them got the heart to step up and do the job proper. Jack's trying to drag me away but I ain't having none of it now, I was ready to go to war guv, believe. An that's when the police car passed on the other side of the road an slows down an does a U-turn. Jack's like, yo, run, Carlton, leg it, man. I'll tell them I did it, he says. I'll tell them it was me. You get yourself off, Carlton, he says.

– So why didn't you?

– Cos I knew it was over, yeah? I told him to get back to the pub, but he insisted on staying. The police roll up an these two officers get out the car. I just stand there with my hands out waiting for the cuffs, shouting yo, it's me, come on, lock me up guv. These other mans are melting back up the road an Jack's arguing the point with one of the officers. The other cop comes to have a word with me but Jack's getting in his face an trying to put his hands on him, which was a big mistake obviously, cos in the end the copper cuffs us both and bangs us in the back of the car an takes us to the cop shop. I tells them in the car, yo, it's me. I'm a murderer, man, yeah? I killed the boy on the news. It was me. An Jack starts saying, don't believe him, it was me, I did it. I'm the murderer. We're both shouting at each other in the back of this car: I'm a murderer! No, I'm the murderer! An the officers are yelling at us to shut the fuck up. It was funny guv, trust me. They got us back to the police station an they didn't know what to do with us, we were both shouting an arguing with each other. So they stuck us in separate cells an the next thing I know is they telling me they've rung for you lot to come up and get us, take us back to London an that. It was funny, though. Jack shouting that he was a murderer, I mean. I AM A MURDERER, he was yelling, top of his flippin voice. LOCK ME UP! I AM A MURDERER! I KILLED A MAN!

McKenzie smiles properly for the first time that afternoon.

– Rah! Like anyone gonna believe *that*, yeah?

■ ■ ■ ■ ■

The lift doesn't work. Ndekwe climbs five flights of stairs before he finds the right landing. He stands and leans against the balustrade and gets his breath back before he knocks on the door.

The woman is small and youthful looking, with tired brown eyes and dark blond hair scraped back from a sharply pretty face. She looks Ndekwe up and down. He shows his ID.

– Janine McKenzie?

She nods, lets him in wordlessly, shows him through to the front room.

The flat is bright and clean and smells of flowers, although there are none to be seen anywhere. A teenage girl sits painting her fingernails on the sofa, feet tucked up beneath her. She looks older than fourteen, her pale, caramel-coloured features made crudely adult by a thick mask of make-up. Ndekwe thinks he can see the faint suggestion of bruising beneath the foundation on her neck, but it could just be the way the shadow falls across her face. She's rocking gently backwards and forwards, the hiss and splash of tiny drums and cymbals in her ears, wires emerging from her blond hair extensions and trailing down to her lap, which cradles a purple MP3 player. She does not look at Ndekwe or acknowledge his greeting; instead she divides her attention between her fingernails and the pop videos that play soundlessly on the TV in the corner.

Janine sits on the sofa beside her daughter, bids Ndekwe to set himself in the armchair opposite. She taps a cigarette out of a packet, offers the packet across.

– Ah, not for me, thanks, he says.

– Thank God for that, she says. – I only got four left. She lights up and reaches for the ashtray. – I was supposed to be stopping on my fortieth, she says. – Not much chance of that now.

She touches the girl's knee.

– Melissa?

The girl does not respond. Janine picks up the remote and turns off the TV.

– Oi! I was watching that!

Melissa tuts and tugs out the earpieces, still fizzing with music, lets them fall into her lap. She balances the nail-varnish bottle on the arm of the sofa and then extends both of her hands in front of her, palms down, waggling her fingers as though she were casting a spell.

– This is Detective Sergeant Ndekwe, Janine tells her. She nudges her knee again, points across to Ndekwe.

The girl doesn't look at him. – Is it? she says. She raises her hands to her mouth, blows across each freshly painted finger.

– How are you, Melissa? asks Ndekwe.

– All right. She shrugs.

Ndekwe takes a photograph from his inside pocket and hands it across to Janine. She looks at it.

– This the fella the other officer was talking about? she asks.

– Yes. Jack Shepherdson. You ever seen him before?

– Never. Janine offers the photograph back to Ndekwe, but he indicates for her to pass it along to her daughter.

– Melissa, says Janine, you ever seen this man anywhere?

– Nup.

– You ain't even looked at it. Look at it properly.

Melissa sighs, makes an elaborate show of looking at it properly then shakes her head, no. – Ain't never seen him, she says.

Janine hands the photo back to Ndekwe. – When can I see my boy?

– Soon, I hope.

– Are you gonna charge him?

– It looks like it, Janine, yes.

– With what?

– Murder.

She winces at the simple brutality of the word, shakes her head. Ndekwe can see the tears begin to shine her eyes. She takes a deep pull on her cigarette and exhales hard; the smoke caught swirling in a broad stripe of sunlight, a blue-grey veil hung across the room between them.

– Did you know Aaron Stewart? Ndekwe aims the question at both of them, but Janine answers.

– Yeah, course I did. Everyone knew him.

– Samuel Isaacs?

Janine's lip curls up in disgust. She leans forward and points the lit end of her cigarette at Ndekwe.

– Do you know what they did, she says snarling, those pieces of *shit*? Do you know what they *did* to my girl? She stabs out her cigarette in the ashtray and swivels round to her daughter, takes hold of her wrist and pulls at the sleeve of her tracksuit top. – Show him the bruises on your arm, she says. – Show him!

– *Mum!* yells Melissa. She snatches her hand away, rolls her cuff back down. – Mum, *shut up!* she says. – Just *shut up*, all right?

– Your brother is going to *jail*, Melissa! Janine takes hold of her daughter's shoulders, tries to pull her around to face her. – He's going to be locked up for a very very long time. Don't you understand that?

– IT *AIN'T – MY – FAULT!* Melissa hurls each word straight into the beseeching face of her mother and then pulls herself free of her hands, hitches herself further away up the sofa. – Just leave me the fuck *alone*, yeah?

Ndekwe edges forwards in his seat, lowers his voice.

– Melissa, he says. – Melissa, listen to me: nobody is saying it's your fault. But if those boys have hurt you, we can arrest them and lock them up and we can make sure they never bother you or your mum ever again. But I can't do that unless you tell me the truth. You have to tell me what really happened. Do you understand?

– Nothing *happened* though, she says.

– That's not what your mum's saying. It's not what Carlton's saying.

– Carlton didn't say nothing, she says.

– Why? Cos he wouldn't talk to the police?

She screws up her face and doesn't answer.

– You think the police are the enemy? asks Ndekwe.

– I don't give a fuck about the police.

– *Melissa!* says Janine. She looks at Ndekwe. – I've tried to tell her, she says.

– Yeah, well, says Melissa. – It don't matter what anyone else says, it's what *I* say that matters, yeah? And I ain't saying *nothing*.

She picks up the remote control and points it at the TV. The room is filled with a bumping grinding beat. Dirt Digital; a gang of surly young men in hoods and gold jewellery are sitting in a darkened warehouse, surrounded by bottles of champagne and gyrating girls.

– Melissa, says Ndekwe, the court might give Carlton a lighter sentence if we can prove that he was provoked in some way, yeah? It's called aggravating or mitigating factors.

She doesn't reply or give any indication she's heard. Just watches the video, head nodding with the beat, mouthing the words.

Ndekwe looks at Janine, appeals to her with a wordless gesture.

– Melissa, urges her mother, listen to what the officer is telling you. He's trying to help us.

No response. She is glued to the TV screen.

Ndekwe produces an MP3 player from his pocket, switches

it on and starts scrolling down through the tracks. The girl's eyes swivel over to him. It's the first time she's so much as glanced in his direction since he came into the room.

– What's that? she says.

– It's your brother. Want to have a listen?

She shrugs.

Ndekwe looks at Janine. – Do you want to listen?

– What is it?

– Carlton's interview.

She nods cautiously.

He finds the track and presses PLAY, holds the machine up in front of him. Janine leans forward and, despite herself, so does Melissa.

– Turn that TV off, says Janine. – Lissa, turn it off. She takes the remote off her daughter and hits the mute button.

Carlton's voice in the tiny speaker.

. . . What happened, right, is that they battered my sister. Knowledge an Bam Bam an all the rest of those fuckin pigs. They got her in that boarded up house near the playing fields an they held a gun to her head an they raped her, yeah? They fuckin raped my sister. I told you I'd tell you everything, didn't I? I'm telling you it all, yeah?

Melissa is shaking her head. – Bollocks, she says. – Fucking bollocks!

– Hang on one second, says Janine. – I don't think this ... But then she stops herself, tilts her head to listen.

. . . There's a message from my mum. She's saying, Carlton, come home, come home now. I knew straight away it was bad. Real bad. I could hear it in her voice. When I gets home my mum an my auntie are sat on the sofa with their arms around Melissa. She's got bruises all on her neck and her face an she looks like she's been crying for time. I'm saying what happened what happened an Melissa starts

sobbing her heart out, saying don't tell him don't tell him. My auntie Sharon gets me in the kitchen an tells me Melissa was coming out the shops when some boys got her to come round to the back of them houses. She said they put a gun to her head an orally raped her. That's the words she used, orally raped. You know what that means guv, yeah? An then they started belling all their crew up to come down an then they took turns raping her the other way. All the other ways, if you get me. Melissa said she didn't know how many of them there was, but they were getting on their phones an more an more of them kept coming. She said she didn't know who they were, didn't recognize any voices. They had their hoods up an their hands over her eyes, ya get me? Tied her jeans round her head; ya get what I'm saying?

Ndekwe presses STOP.

Janine stares at the machine in dumbfounded horror. Then she looks at Melissa and sees the tears sliding down her daughter's face.

– Lissa, she says. – Oh Lissa, babe ... She pulls her daughter to her, gathers her into her arms, but the girl pushes her away and leaps to her feet.

– I don't have to listen to no more of this *bullshit*!

She snatches up her nail varnish and stomps out of the room, slamming the door behind her, and then another door somewhere down the hallway slams too, followed by the muffled pounding of music. Janine yells after her, but there is no reply. She glares at Ndekwe.

– That was a bit much, weren't it?

– I'm sorry, he says. – I thought she might cooperate if she heard Carlton's voice.

– I'll go and talk to her in a minute, says Janine, and then bursts into sudden tears, hiding her face behind her hands as she sobs.

Ndekwe waits for her to compose herself. Eventually the noise subsides and she lowers her hands.

– Are you all right?

Janine nods. – Yes, yes. She pulls a handful of tissue from a box on the coffee table and blows her nose, wipes her eyes. She reaches for her cigarettes, lights up another. She stands up and goes over to the windows, tilts two of them open and waves the smoke outside before sitting back down.

– What about her father? offers Ndekwe. – Will she listen to him?

She shakes her head. – I've not told him.

– Why not?

– Cos he'd go after them. He'd do something stupid.

– Well, we can go after them, Janine, and we can get them in court. Bam Bam and all the rest of them. But we need Melissa to testify.

Janine doesn't say anything, just sits and smokes and stares out of the window at the flats opposite; a young woman ironing in her front room while watching TV; a middle-aged man sat on his balcony reading a newspaper; two young boys hanging over the next balcony along, pointing to something below them. One of them shouts down a name and there are other young voices raised in reply.

– Tell me about the morning it happened, says Ndekwe.

– Just like he said on your recording. I was here with my sister. She'd popped round for a cuppa. I sent Melissa out for some milk. She was gone about an hour. I thought she'd forgotten about it, just gone off somewhere. Then she came back. She looked like she'd seen a ghost. I was like, Oi, you, where's that bloody milk? Then I saw her top was all ripped round the neck. I saw the bruises on her neck.

Janine draws a deep breath; composes herself and carries on.

– At first I thought she'd just been in a fight. But then she kept saying, they took it in turns, they took it in turns. Who did? I said. Who took it in turns? She wouldn't answer me. Then she collapsed into tears. She was hysterical. I'd never seen her like that before. That's when I rung Carlton.

– And he came straight away?

– Yeah.

– And what did Carlton say to her?

– He didn't say anything. He just sat with her on the sofa, holding her hand. She told him what had happened. Just him. Wouldn't look at me or Sharon. He sat and held her hand for a bit while she calmed down and then he went out, said he had to go somewhere.

– Did he say where?

– No. But it was obvious he was gonna go look for them.

– Did you know he had a knife?

She shakes her head slowly, no.

Silence in the room.

Voices raised outside.

Music from down the hall.

Then she says: – How long will he get?

– I don't know, Janine.

– You must have an idea, though? She looks at him imploringly.

– Depends on the judge, Ndekwe tells her. – Anything from fifteen upwards.

She flinches. – Oh Christ, she says. – Oh, for fuck's sake. Fresh tears wobble and spill.

– But if the court knew what the motive was ... I mean, from what I can gather it's out of character. I know Carlton's been in trouble before, but it was never for violence, was it?

She shakes her head firmly. – No, just stupid things, really. Running about with them *arseholes*.

– Who?

– Aaron and Bam Bam and all that lot.

– How well did you know them?

– I've known them all since they were kids, she says. – That Isaacs boy, he's always been trouble. Ever since he was little. Janine swallows hard and her face and neck tighten as she composes herself. – But Carlton ... no ... he'd not been in any bother at all recently. Not for a long time.

The music from down the hallway stops. They both turn their heads and listen. They hear the thump of footsteps and then the slam of the front door.

– Why won't she press charges? asks Ndekwe.

– I tried to make her. I wanted to phone the police straight away.

– So why didn't you?

– She made me promise not to. She said they'd firebomb the flat.

– Who? Stewart and Isaacs?

She nods, rubs at her eyes. – Now she says it didn't happen. Says she just got into a fight.

Ndekwe allows his gaze to wander around the room. It feels warm and homely in here; the clothes folded into a neat pile on the table next to the ironing board, the shelving unit full of CDs and DVDs, the family photographs on the wall. This is a happy home, thinks Ndekwe. Was a happy home. There is a stack of birthday cards next to an empty vase on the shelf near his chair. He lifts off the top one: *Forty and Fabulous!* – a cartoon drawing of a glamorous girl about town with hat and handbag and rock-star shades.

– That was from Carlton, Janine tells him. She puts a hand up to her ear, touches the gold hoop at her lobe. – He gave me these earrings, she says.

Ndekwe opens the card and reads the message inside: *Mum, you never get old! You are simply the best! Happy Birthday, love from Carlton xxx.* He closes the card and replaces it on the shelf.

– Did you know that Carlton was planning to go to Jamaica? he asks her.

– Him and his mate used to talk about it. She shrugs. – I didn't think they was really serious, though.

– His mate? Joseph Musa?

Her face splits into a smile. – Yeah. He was a lovely boy. I think that was a wake-up call for Carlton, actually, what happened to Joseph.

– How do you mean?

– He just stopped going out after that. It was like he realized where it was leading, the road he was going down.

– What road?

– Hanging about on the estate with all them arseholes.

– Carlton said he was going to work in his dad's bar.

– Did he? She sounds genuinely surprised.

– Said his dad sent him a postcard from Jamaica.

She frowns. – News to me, she says.

– Did you know your husband was still in London?

She shakes her head. – Not until the other night, no.

– He's wanted for armed robbery.

– Yeah, I heard he was on the telly. Don't surprise me. Not my problem any more.

– You've never kept in touch?

She laughs bitterly. – No.

– Why do you think Carlton never told you about this bar in Jamaica?

She shrugs, taps her cigarette into the ashtray. – No idea. She takes a drag, exhales, thinks. – Probably wanted to spare my feelings, she says. – Carlton knew my opinion on that wanker.

– When was the last time you saw him?

– Wish I had a pound for every time I been asked that, she says. – I'd have enough for a bloody penthouse in Ibiza.

– Or Montego Bay even. Ndekwe attempts a smile, which is not reciprocated. Janine just stares out of the window at the balconies opposite. She looks younger than forty, but old beyond her years, too.

– We can arrange protection, Ndekwe tells her.

She doesn't reply; just sits and smokes and stares.

■ ■ ■ ■ ■

Ndekwe drives home through early evening traffic. He thinks about Carlton McKenzie, wonders whether he really believed that his father was waiting for him in a bar on Hip Strip in Montego Bay. He thinks about Jack Shepherdson's son, and wonders if he ever knew where his father was. Then he thinks about his own dad. Thinks about what it must be like to not know where your father lived or how he lived; or, worse, to not even care. He looks at the time: it is 17:24, and he knows that on a Tuesday at twenty-four minutes past five Cecil Ndekwe will be making his final foot patrol along the ground floor of the Elephant and Castle shopping centre, checking on the shops and their workers before heading for the staff room at five thirty on the dot, carefully hanging up his hat and taking the bus home, where Christina Ndekwe, his wife of thirty-five years, will be making them both dinner. He will sit in his armchair and read the *Evening Standard* and then listen to the BBC World Service or watch television until ten p.m. when he will have a small glass of rum before retiring to his bed. Ndekwe remembers summer evenings standing on the armchair in the front room, peering out of the window, waiting to see his dad, waving madly as soon as he saw that dark blue uniform turn the corner at the top of the street. He remembers thinking that his dad must be a very important man indeed to have a job where he wore a uniform with a badge on the breast pocket and shiny silver buttons on the cuffs.

He turns the radio on, but the presenter's artificial bonhomie is banal and tedious and after a few minutes he switches it off. It feels somehow strange to drive around and not hear Jack Shepherdson's voice. It occurs to him that he's heard more from Jack Shepherdson in the last two days than Jack's own son has in the last thirty-seven years. How must it feel, he wonders, to never talk to your father? To let birthdays and holidays and Christmases go by and never write his name in a card or know where to send it; to never hear his voice, but to know he was out there in the world somewhere, walking and talking and working and laughing, living a life surrounded by people whom you did not know and who did not know you? To have a parent who was, to all intents and purposes, dead, but to know they were still alive.

Ndekwe closes his window. Today doesn't feel as warm as this time yesterday. Last night's rain seems to have drained some of the heat out of the day. September soon, thinks Ndekwe. Autumn, with its darkening days and colder nights.

He remembers the barometer in the boot. He drives to Greenwich, parks up near the harbour and walks down to the market and the warehouses. There are fewer people around than yesterday. Most of the places are either closed or in the process of packing up.

He finds the warehouse, but the girl with the rainbow bangles isn't there; her place behind the table is now occupied by a skinny middle-aged man with grey hair slicked back into a ponytail. He is writing something down in a book. He glances up at Ndekwe's footsteps.

– Closing in five minutes, chief, he says.

Ndekwe places the barometer down on the table.

– I need to return this. Bought it yesterday.

The man gives it a cursory glance, continues to write.

– What's wrong with it?

– Nothing. It was a gift for the wife, but she doesn't want it.

– Got a receipt?

Ndekwe automatically reaches for his pocket, but he already knows he doesn't have a receipt.

– She didn't give me one, he says.

– Who didn't?

– The girl who was here yesterday.

The man shakes his head. – No receipt no return, I'm afraid.

Ndekwe stares at the thin strands of grey pulled tight across the top of his sun-pinkened skull, willing the man to look up and acknowledge him, but he does not.

– But this is your place, yeah? says Ndekwe.

– It is, mate, yes.

– Then you must recognize this as belonging to you, surely?

Ndekwe pulls apart the packaging to reveal the thick glass

casing, the italic scripture, the ancient sailing ship blown along by invisible wind.

The man glances, shakes his head, continues to write.

– Can't do anything without a receipt, chief.

Ndekwe leans both hands on the table and lowers his face in search of the man's eyes.

– How can I give you a flippin receipt if I wasn't given one in the first place?

– Can't do anything without a receipt, the man repeats.

Ndekwe prepares to launch into a spirited appeal in favour of fair-trading and the importance of customer care. But then another thought leaps into his head, and he finds himself turning and walking away.

– Oi, says the man. – Don't be leaving this here!

– Keep it, Ndekwe calls back over his shoulder.

He walks out of the cool gloom of the warehouse and into the lengthening shadows of the afternoon. By the time he's hit the brightness of the main street outside Ndekwe has broken into a trot. He checks his watch: just after six. Sonia won't be home for a good hour yet, an hour and a half, possibly. He has time.

A voice is raised from the shadows behind him.

– COME BACK WITH THE RECEIPT, YEAH?

Ndekwe ignores the voice and heads for his car, hopes the traffic isn't too bad heading back through the tunnel.

■ ■ ■ ■ ■

Ndekwe is at the kitchen table going through his notes when he hears Sonia call for him to come upstairs. He calls back in the affirmative, but he is deep into his work and almost immediately forgets. She calls again, twice, before he hears her coming down the stairs. He curses quietly and begins to gather together his papers. She pads into the kitchen barefoot, in her pyjamas.

– Peter, she says. – Are you coming up?

– I am, babe, yes, just let me clear this up ...

– I've spiked, she says.

He looks at her vacantly.

– My temperature, she says. – It was up this morning and it's stayed up.

Realization dawns. – Ah, yeah, he says. – Right ... OK, I'll just tidy this away and I'll be ...

– Now, she says, and she takes his hand, pulling him up from the chair. – Just leave that, come now.

He follows her up the stairs and tries to clear his mind, to concentrate on the more immediate job in hand. He watches her buttocks move beneath thin cotton, follows her into the dimly lit bedroom, watches as she unbuttons her top and slips off her pyjama bottoms as he himself undresses, trying to hold in his head the curve of her breasts and the flat of her stomach as she slips beneath the covers, trying not to think instead of silent shopkeepers or boys bleeding to death in gutters or a scowling, swivel-eyed youth pumping bullets into a brick wall. He slides into bed and climbs on top of her, kisses her neck and shoulder and chest as she reaches down and finds him, pulling and stroking until he becomes firm, then she opens her legs and tries to guide him inside, but she is too dry and he is not hard enough.

– Hold on, she says.

She pushes him up and off her, leans across and slides open the bedside drawer, takes out a tube and squeezes it into her hand, works it inside herself.

– OK, she says. – OK, try now ...

Ten minutes later they're lying separate beneath smoothed-down sheets, a screaming volume of silence between them, and the edges of the room beginning to fade into the oncoming evening. Ndekwe listens to her breathing, tries to ascertain whether she is falling into the beginnings of sleep or whether the steady sigh means something else entirely. He considers slipping out of bed and creeping downstairs to collect his papers together off the kitchen table, but just as he considers it safe to move, her hand finds his, and she wraps her fingers around his, squeezes tight, once, twice.

Tomorrow, he thinks. I'll sort everything out tomorrow.

– Pete?

He resolves to remain silent, tries to relax his body into some semblance of sleep, but Sonia's hand is squeezing his hand again, harder this time.

– You awake, Pete?

– Yeah, he says.

Silence and falling gloom.

Then: – Pete?

– What?

– Do you still want a baby? Her voice is tiny in the dark besides him.

– Course I do, he says. – *Course* I do.

She rolls onto her side to face him, but he keeps his eyes on the shadows on the ceiling above. He can feel her wet eyelashes on the side of his face and her warm breath on his neck.

– Are you sure, she whispers. – Don't say it if you're not ...

– Course I am ... He cradles her chin in his hand and wipes the wetness away from the corners of her eyes with his thumb.

– Is it cos of your job?

– Is what cos of my job?

– What you've said before about ... y'know ... bringing kids into the world. Into this type of world.

– No, it's not that ...

She squeezes his hand again, harder. – *Promise* me, she whispers. – *Promise* me that you want this child.

– I promise, babe, he murmurs, and he strokes her hair, tenderly kisses her forehead. She responds by pulling herself into him, sliding her hand down across his chest and down his leg, running her fingernails gently up and down the inside of his thigh. He feels his penis twitch and she senses the movement, cups his scrotum in her hand.

Buuuzzzzzzzzz.

Ndekwe's mobile; muffled, buried somewhere among his clothes that are strewn on the floor. He turns his head to check the clock on the bedside table. It's too dim to see the hands, but he guesses it is around half past nine, quarter to ten.

Buuuuuzzzzzzzzz.

– Don't answer it, babe, she says.

– Uh uh, he agrees.

It stops. And then almost immediately starts again.

– It might be my mum, he says.

– She'd call the house, she says.

Buuuzzzzzzzzz.

– Oh, for God's sake.

He gets out of bed and scrabbles about on the floor until he locates his phone, tangled up in his trouser pocket.

It's flashing: GORMAN.

– Sir?

Gorman speaks, quickly, urgently, and Ndekwe listens without comment except to say, OK, I see, yes, yes, no problem, see you there. He kills the call and starts to gather together his clothes.

– What's wrong? asks Sonia. – Peter, what's wrong?

– It's Jack, he says. – *Fuck's sake* ... He hops around the room, trying to work his foot into a trouser leg turned inside out.

– What's with the language? Who's Jack?

– Where's that other sock ... *Damn!*

Sonia sits up in bed, the covers gathered around her neck, watches her husband getting dressed in the half-light.

– Peter, where you going?

He pulls on his shirt, buttons it up with hurrying fingers.

– The hospital, he says. – St Bart's.

■ ■ ■ ■ ■

There are five other beds on the ward, all of them occupied by men of advanced years. Most of them are asleep or drifting in and out of fitful sleep. Apart from the uniformed officer sat at the door to the ward, Ndekwe is the only visitor. He exchanges a greeting with the uniform and sits and waits at Jack's bedside. The duty nurse has assured him that the doctor will be along in a few minutes.

According to Gorman, Shepherdson had pressed the buzzer in his cell and complained to the Desk Sergeant that he felt dizzy, had asked to be let outside for some fresh air, but had only got halfway down the corridor before his legs turned to jelly and he crumpled into a gasping heap. Gorman had been roused from his bottle of wine and summoned immediately, his initial irritation giving way to worry and then outright panic when he saw Shepherdson lying unconscious on the ward. Ndekwe guesses that Gorman's concern is more for himself and his blotless copybook than the prisoner collapsed in custody on his watch. After a brief and heated confab in the visitors' waiting room, Gorman departed for home, issuing Ndekwe with strict instructions to call him if there were any developments.

The old man is unconscious, a respiratory mask fastened across his face, three white tubes feeding into a bedside machine that marks each manufactured exhalation with a sonorous pulse. An IV line stretches between the cannula embedded into the back of his hand and the plastic bag of translucent liquid hanging by the bed. He looks old, much older than his seventy years; the sprouting liver spots on his sagging neck, the shining pink curve of his skull visible beneath the greying curls dampened down by sweat. There is a line of dried saliva running from each corner of his mouth and down beneath his chin, chalky white rivulets engraved on his slackened face. He looks like an oversized ventriloquist's dummy laid silently to rest in his box. Ndekwe has to stop himself from pulling a tissue from the box on the bedside table and wiping the saliva tracks away.

He watches the shallow rise and fall of Jack's chest beneath the pale blue hospital gown, each rasping breath behind the plastic mask marked with the bleep of the bedside machine. The hospital;

where life is delivered and then preserved at all costs until it finally slips away. Ndekwe hates hospitals; he and Sonia seem to have spent much of the past three years in their antiseptic rooms and harshly lit corridors, waiting on test results and listening to the measured advice of experts, holding hands and steeling themselves for another crushing disappointment.

The last miscarriage had nearly finished them both off. The second in two years. Portugal was supposed to have been a reprieve from the endless rounds of prodding and questioning, the religiously observed routines of temperature control and marking off of calendar dates, the timed bouts of desperate and mechanical coupling that only served to erode rather than add to their increasingly fragile unity. But Portugal had provided no real respite; indeed, the unspoken tension between them had only seemed to congeal, like blood from a wound left to fester under the glare of the sun.

– Detective Sergeant?

The duty nurse has returned with the doctor, a serious-looking woman with a clipboard and an armful of files and a name badge that announces her as Dr A. L. Kumar. Ndekwe rises to his feet and extends a hand; he towers over her and her hand feels like a child's in his.

– How is he? he asks.

– He's in the advanced stages of pulmonary tuberculosis.

– That sounds serious.

– It would have been a lot less serious if he had been taking his medication. Her tone is professionally neutral, but Ndekwe senses more than a hint of exasperation. – I understand Mr Shepherdson has been in police custody for – she looks at her notes – three days?

– Well ... since Sunday night.

– And he has not been given his medication?

– He didn't have any medication, as far as I know.

– As far as you know ...

She flicks through the notes on the clipboard at her chest

and then beckons him to follow her off the ward and out into the corridor. He follows her into a small office and she closes the door behind them. She remains standing and does not ask him to sit.

– Mr Shepherdson was admitted here six weeks ago and given a chest CT scan, she informs him. – We found evidence of myco-bacterium tuberculosis in both lungs. He was placed on a course of Isoniazid. Has he been taking this medication?

– I ... we were not aware that he was on any medication.

She purses her lips. – You were not aware that he was ill?

– Well, no, not really, he ...

– You did not notice that his breathing was laboured? That he was coughing up large amounts of sputum?

– He's a heavy smoker.

She frowns. – Was there any excessive sweating?

– He was being questioned in police custody. He was ... Ndekwe lets the words trail off into nothingness. He feels foolish and exposed before this woman's cold exactitude and cannot think of anything to say except: – Will he live?

– We are conducting some tests to ascertain whether the bacteria in his lungs have become active. If they have, and if they have spread to his spine or his brain or any other internal organs, then the risk of fatality could be increased.

– So he could die?

She shrugs. – At his age and in his condition, yes, he could die.

– What can we do?

Her eyes widen behind the lens of her glasses and Ndekwe can tell it is only her innate professionalism that is stopping her questioning the inclusive plurality that his question has suggested. She speaks slowly and deliberately.

– As I have stated, we are undertaking tests to try and ascertain the status of the bacteria and the extent to which they may have spread. That is all I can tell you at the present.

– There's nothing I can do?

– I suggest you contact Mr Shepherdson's next of kin.

She sits down behind her desk and clicks her computer screen into life, starts typing. Ndekwe feels as though he has been dismissed. He also feels sick to the pit of his stomach.

– He's going to die, isn't he?

– Until we get the results of the test I am not in a position to say.

– Yes, but in your professional opinion, I mean.

– As I have stated, we must wait for the results of the tests. Until then all we can do is try and keep him stable.

– But you must have some idea. What are the odds?

She looks up from her computer. Ndekwe can see that she is starting to lose her patience. – Detective Sergeant, she says, I am a doctor, not a bookmaker. I do not give out odds.

Ndekwe thanks Dr Kumar and returns to Jack's bedside. The old man seems to have aged yet further. He has suddenly become very old indeed, a sucked out husk bereft of spark and swagger and vitality; every imperfection of his ageing countenance laid cruelly bare under the stark electric lights; the broken veins spread around his nose and across the cheeks, the paper-thin tissue of his eyelids and the hanging jowls of his neck. Ndekwe imagines he can see the skin yellowing under his gaze. He watches the steady pulse of the respirator and the rise and fall of the old man's chest.

– Jack, he says. – Wake up, Jack.

He puts his face down next to Jack's.

– I know you were there, Jack, he whispers. – I know you were there.

The rasp of shallow breathing and the bleep of machinery.

Ndekwe goes and stands near the window and watches the car headlights on the main road below. He tries to remember what forms of ID were recorded on Jack's arrest sheet. The old man had arrived at Hackney police station with a bag containing only a few clothes, some money and a passport.

In the event of an emergency ...

Ndekwe finds the duty nurse and thanks her before leaving the hospital. He sits in his car and calls the station and gets the Desk

Sergeant to send an officer to dig out Shepherdson's passport, asks him to call him straight back as soon as he's got the information.

Ndekwe sits and watches the building, the lights burning in the windows and the steady flow of people through its doors. He wonders how many lives will be prolonged between those walls tonight, how many will slip away. He has read somewhere that most deaths and births occur at around three in the morning. He wonders if there is any truth in that and decides there is not. Why would life be given and taken away according to some kind of cosmic timetable? That doesn't make sense, he thinks, makes no sense whatsoever. He checks his watch: not yet midnight.

His mobile goes off and the Desk Sergeant at the station informs him that the name given on Jack Shepherdson's passport to be contacted in a case of emergency is Ronnie Dakota. There is an address in Plumstead and a phone number. Ndekwe notes both of these down.

The number is answered on the fifth ring, a teenage girl's voice. Ndekwe asks to speak to Ronald Dakota. The girl asks him to repeat the name and then to hang on one minute, please. Ndekwe can hear a television and muted words in the background and then there is an older man's voice on the end of the line.

– Yes, says the man. – Yes, who is this?

Ndekwe introduces himself and repeats his enquiry.

– Ronald Dakota, says the man. – *Ronnie Dakota?* Ndekwe can almost hear the man's cognitive wheels turning down the phone line. He's about to prompt him when the man speaks. – Oh yeah, you mean Ronnie Lodge. Oh Christ, he hasn't lived here for ... what ... over twenty-five years, mate.

■ ■ ■ ■ ■

Ndekwe holds the square of paper between thumb and forefinger, offers it across the table, close enough for McKenzie to read the small black type.

– Know what this is?

– No.

– It's a receipt.

McKenzie looks puzzled.

– It's a receipt from Mr Akhtar's shop. You know Mr Akhtar, yeah?

McKenzie shakes his head.

– Yes you do, Ndekwe tells him. – He owns the newsagent's. Where you stabbed Aaron Stewart, remember?

Ndekwe places the paper on the table, directly beneath McKenzie's nose.

– This is a till receipt from last Thursday, he tells him. – Thursday the nineteenth of August, sale made at one thirty-two p.m., for goods purchased to the total value of four pounds and ninety-two pence. Now, check this: there's three items on here, one for a pound, one for three pounds fifty-four and another item that costs thirty-eight pence. Ndekwe indicates each amount in descending order. – Now, he says. – What could those three things be? What do those prices represent? Can you guess? Took me ages to work it out. But you should be able to tell me straight off, cos you were there. Weren't you, Carlton?

McKenzie doesn't say anything, but Ndekwe sees his eyes widen in realization.

– Well, I'll tell you anyway, shall I? A copy of the *Racing Post* is a pound, yeah? A half-ounce packet of Old Holborn tobacco is three pounds fifty-four. And a small pack of blue Rizla is thirty-eight pence. Now, who do you know would make a purchase like that?

The youth says nothing.

– Carlton, do you know what joint enterprise is?

– No.

– Let me break it down for you, yeah? Joint enterprise is when two or more people embark on a project with a common purpose that results in the commission of a crime. Do you understand that?

– Nope.

– Yes you do, you know full well you do. You're not a stupid boy, Carlton. You and Jack both claim to have killed Aaron Stewart ...

– I killed him, states McKenzie. – Me. He points to himself and pushes the receipt back across the table.

– ... and do you know what, continues Ndekwe, you're both absolutely right. In the eyes of the law, you both killed that boy. Doesn't matter who held the knife. Whoever stabbed the boy, the other man didn't stop it. In the eyes of the law, that means you're both responsible.

– Man wasn't even there.

– I think he was.

– He weren't guv, swear down.

– How do you explain this then? Ndekwe taps the receipt.

No answer.

– Come on, Carlton, explain this receipt to me. Tobacco, *Racing Post*, cigarette papers. Started betting on horses and smoking roll-ups, have you?

– No ...

– He was there with you, wasn't he, Carlton? Jack was there with you when you stabbed Stewart.

– No.

– Shall I tell you where he is now?

No response from the boy. He hitches his chair back and folds his arms, looks at the wall, the floor, the door, anywhere but the police officer staring intently at him from across the table.

– He's in the hospital, Carlton. He collapsed last night and now he's in the hospital.

McKenzie shakes his head. – I ain't having it, mate, he says.

– I went to see him. He's got a drip in his hand. He's hooked up to a machine that's keeping him breathing.

The boy's leg begins to bounce up and down like a piston. Ndekwe can see tears begin to glisten in his eyes.

– Carlton?

McKenzie lifts the bottom of his T-shirt and wipes his face. – Is he gonna be all right? he asks casually, as though enquiring about the weather, or the latest football results. But he cannot hide the panic in his voice.

– I hope so, says Ndekwe. – Because when he wakes up I'm gonna nick him. I'm gonna nick him and I'm gonna nick you.

McKenzie looks at Ndekwe – All right, listen, he says. He shifts his chair close into the table and looks Ndekwe directly in the eye. – Jack was there, yeah? But he weren't actually there ...

– What? He was there but he weren't there? Ndekwe screws up his face scornfully. – What's that supposed to mean?

– I mean, he was there, like in the shop and that. But he never came out. He stayed in the shop guv.

– Bollocks.

– Swear down, he never came out ... He was frightened, yeah?

– What do you mean he was frightened?

– He was in the shop when they rolled up: Aaron and Bam Bam. He must have heard all the shouting, but he stayed in the shop. McKenzie looks intently at Ndekwe, searches his face for some sign of agreement. – So he weren't no joint enterprise or anything like that, yeah?

– Right, hold on. Jack went down to the shops with you?

– Yeah, yeah, yeah ...

– He knew about what happened to your sister?

– Yeah. He heard me on the phone to my mum in his flat an he came back with me.

– He came back to your mum's place?

– Yeah, but he didn't come in. I was running an he was struggling to keep up an that, yeah? He couldn't get up the stairs. He was leaning against the entrance, coughing an that. I told him to wait for me down there. An when I come out he could see I was angry, yeah?

– And you told him what had happened?

– Yeah. He could tell it was about to go down, yeah? He knew.

– He knew you had the knife?

– I didn't have it on show or nothing ... but he knew it was ... Listen, man tried to stop me, yeah? Man was walking behind me all the time, yeah? Trying to get me to stop. He kept saying we should call the police, yeah? Let the police deal with it, he said. But I wasn't listening to that. I wanted that prick. I would have killed him with my own bare hands.

The boy curls up his fists. – But I couldn't find the prick. I went and battered on his door and Bam Bam's too. Went round to that place they got, that house, yeah? But they weren't there. They were nowhere to be found.

– Go on.

– Jack persuaded me to go back to his flat. We stopped at the shops. He wanted his ting, his smoke, yeah? I was stood waiting outside when they rolled up. Knowledge an Bam Bam. An then ... the rest of it was just like I said. I stabbed that fucker an Bam Bam got his piece out an started blasting an I was out of there guv. I ran back to Jack's.

– And what about Jack?

– He said later that he just waited in the shop till everything had gone quiet ... Then he stepped out an saw Knowledge on the floor. Said he pulled the knife out of him an dropped it down a drain. Got off back to his place. We stayed there all day an night, waiting for the knock. But no knock came. Couldn't believe it. Then we saw it on the news that night. How he was dead an that. So the next day we decided to get off.

– And that's how it happened?

– That's it. That's all of it ... Listen, though, it weren't no joint thing, right? He tried to stop me, yeah?

– OK, Carlton, but you should be aware that ...

But the boy cuts him off with a raised palm. – No guv, he says. – You be aware of this; it was me who killed him, yeah? It weren't no joint enterprise or any of that. It was me, all of it.

He holds Ndekwe's eyes intently, willing him to agree.

– Right, says Ndekwe. He puts the cap back on his pen and

shuffles his papers together. – Well ... OK, let's stop it there for now. We should be winding this up later today. We'll get you charged and get you a lawyer and get everything rolling.

McKenzie shakes his head firmly. – I don't want no lawyer, he states.

– Well, you'll be given one anyway. Everything needs to be sorted out and it's got to be done through the proper channels.

– Yeah ... OK, but listen, yeah? McKenzie swallows hard and wipes his mouth. – I got something else.

– What?

– My boy.

– Joseph?

McKenzie nods.

– What about Joseph?

– It was Knowledge that made me do it.

McKenzie bites his lip and looks away. His eyes are brimming wet again.

– Made you do what? Ndekwe tilts his head to try and meet the boy's eyes. – Carlton?

– I saw it coming a mile off, says McKenzie, but there weren't nothing I could do to stop it or get out of the way either.

– Stop what? Carlton, stop what?

McKenzie stares fixedly at the table as he speaks, his voice flattened and dead.

– He started asking me questions about Joseph. Thing is, when he first came on the manor Aaron never even took any notice of him. He was a kid to him, yeah? Two years younger. Soon as he knew I was chilling with him some nights, though, that was it, he got all curious, wanted to know who he was, where he was from, all that. That was the thing with Aaron, you weren't allowed to have any other friends and acquaintances, ya get me? If you were rolling with him it had to be all his way, just his hand-selected boys, no outsiders. You got to keep your game tight, G. Game gotta be tight. That was all he ever he used to say. Keep it tight, Kez. Paranoid guv, that's what it is with these mans.

He glances up to check that Ndekwe is still listening. Ndekwe nods, urges him on. McKenzie picks the receipt up and begins to turn it around in his fingers.

– And when he started asking about Joseph my flippin heart sunk cos I knew it was either gonna be: yo, Kez, get that boy to do this thing or that thing, or it was gonna be the other way; who the fuck is that prick an what he want? Joseph's face weren't ever gonna fit. I knew that. He weren't into no hustle. I told you before, that was why I was chilling with him at that time. I was getting tired of all that struggle. But Aaron wanted to know what me and Joseph got up to, what we talked about, all of that. I knew what he was thinking, and I told him straight. I said, look, you think I'm flippin dumb, fam? Think I'm chatting my head off to some little kid? That's what he thought Joseph was, yeah, just some little pussy ... just cos he was always happy an laughing all the time an didn't wanna be no player, ya get me? Joseph didn't care about having a big pile of paper or having the latest kicks on his feet or any of that. He was just a carefree boy who wanted to do normal things. Football and Xbox, innit. He liked school, all of that. He was just normal, ya get me? But Aaron didn't trust that. He's thinking that I'm slipping, yeah? That I'm chatting business to Joseph.

– And were you? Ndekwe reaches across and gently takes the receipt out of the boy's fingers, slides it back into his pocket.

McKenzie shakes his head firmly. – Swear down guv. I never told Joseph nothing about what I did on road. But after that thing in ... where was it, Bromley? Yeah, that travel place ... After that I'd had it with Aaron and Bam Bam an all that other lot. Aaron broke that girl's jaw, the girl in the shop. It wasn't just that, though ... Aaron was off the hook well before that guv, well before that, trust me. I know you got a book on the man, but you ain't got anywhere near the full story, believe. He was doing things that made me feel sick.

– Like what?

– Like Joseph.

McKenzie falls into silence, staring at the table top. Ndekwe is about to prompt him when he starts to speak again.

– It was me an Bam Bam who did it. But fucking Knowledge was the cause of it. See, thing is, I don't care that the man's dead or his mother's crying over him or his baby mother's crying over him or anything like that. I ain't even gonna lie, I did everyone a favour guv. Trust me. I probably saved you another ten future murders further along the way, yeah? Aaron was causing beefs left right and centre, all over the area and beyond. He wanted to be the big thing, innit. Anyone who disagreed got dealt with. The man was building his empire, no doubt.

– So how did it come about?

McKenzie swallows hard, takes a deep breath.

– OK, so him and Bam Bam come round the flat one day an he just sit there an says that chatty boy gotta go, Kez. I know straight away what he saying. An the way Bam Bam was all agitated as well, I just knew they been plotting about this together. I think Bam Bam wanted to go and do it there and then, the sick little fucker. They'd both been doing bare rocks all morning, I could tell. I argued with him till I was flippin blue in the face, but he just kept saying, it's gotta be done, Kez, just gotta be done. This is how he was, yeah; it was all about him being the big dog with the big bark an everyone else falling into line. I didn't wanna work under them conditions, believe me. This was half the reason I'd stopped running about with these idiots. But I knew there was no way this could be avoided.

– So let me get this right. Stewart told you to shoot Joseph?

McKenzie nods and then wipes his eyes on his T-shirt again, rubs his hands on his jeans. – I rode the bike, though. Bam Bam had the strap. Bam Bam was yelling in my ear, close, get closer. But I just span the bike around him. I didn't even look at him. He had my jacket on. I couldn't even stand to look. I just gave it full throttle, yeah, so I couldn't hear him shouting and crying. I just kept going round and round, I dunno, three, four times. Bam Bam emptied his ting an he shouts go, go an then I just twisted it back and we got off. An ever since then it was bare needle between me an Aaron. So when I went and asked him for that weed he was laughing guv. Laughing. Had me back on his bit of string, yeah? Dangling me about like a puppet.

He inhales, exhales, composes himself and raises his head to face Ndekwe. – Yeah, so I rode the motorbike and Bam Bam fired the gun. They made me do it. They said I'd told Joseph all this stuff but I ain't even gonna lie, I never told him nothing. I kept him away from all that. Tried to anyways, innit.

Ndekwe looks at the boy. Neither of them says anything. The red lights of the recording machine fall flat.

Then Ndekwe speaks. – OK, Carlton. You go back downstairs and get your head down. This'll all be over very soon.

Ndekwe gets up, goes to the door and taps on the window. He indicates for the officer stood outside to escort McKenzie back to the holding cell before returning to his seat and beginning to write.

McKenzie stands up as the officer enters. He looks earnestly at Ndekwe, who is engrossed in his writing.

– What about Jack? he says.

– What about him? Ndekwe doesn't look up.

– Is he going to be all right?

– I don't know. I'm going to go to the hospital later on today and see if they've got the results of the tests.

– What tests? Tests for what?

– They've had to do some tests ... Ndekwe shrugs, continues to write. – I'll know more this afternoon.

– Let me know, yeah?

– I will Carlton, yes.

– Promise, yeah?

Ndekwe looks up from his paperwork – I said I will, didn't I?

The boy nods. – All right, he says. – Sweet. He turns to the escorting officer and indicates that he is ready to leave.

Ndekwe waits until they have gone and then puts down his pen, calls Halliwell on his mobile.

– Tom? Ndekwe. Listen, Tom, McKenzie's just coughed to Joseph Musa ... Joseph Musa. Yeah, I know ... Look, just find Samuel Isaacs ... Yeah ... Yeah, I know, Tom. Just get the little fucker and bring him back here, yeah?

■ ■ ■ ■ ■

WEL-COME TO MAH WOOORLD ...

Heads swivel to Ndekwe's desk at the sudden burst of music; the slick pseudo-American voice, the tumbling drum intro and the swelling strings of an artificial orchestra. For a few brief seconds the Incident Room is filled with blaring, incongruous noise, until Ndekwe finds the speaker icon with his cursor arrow and adjusts the volume down to a less intrusive level. The heads turn back to their own screens; resume their own keyboard tapping and telephone conversations.

The opening words of the song are repeated in flashing letters across the top of the web page: *Ronnie Dakota – Welcome to My World!*

A photo below this; a middle-aged man in a tuxedo, bow tie left untied and draped casually around his neck, his arms spread wide in greeting. He wears a broad twinkling smile and a deep mahogany tan, his hair quiffed up into a shiny jet-black pompadour. The blurb beneath the photo tells Ndekwe that Ronnie Dakota is one of the capital's premier singing stars, a top-class entertainer who can light up any room with his own individual brand of showbiz magic. Book Ronnie Dakota for your special occasion, it says, and turn a night out into a memory. There are quotes from the proprietors of various clubs and hotels, all bearing testament to Ronnie's prowess as a versatile song and dance man. A rare and shining talent, says one. The atmosphere was electric, claims another.

– Didn't think this was your cup of tea, Pete.

Ndekwe glances up. Frampton has wandered across from the other side of the room and hovers at his shoulder, studying the

screen with bemusement. He lowers his head to listen to the music.
– Sounds like that Vic Reeves, he remarks. – That pub singer ...
Hurdy hoody hooooo ... Frampton joins in with a few exaggeratedly
tuneless bars, but stops when Ndekwe doesn't acknowledge him. –
Who is it? he asks.

– I don't know, says Ndekwe. – He's on Shepherdson's passport
as his emergency contact. He mentioned a Ronnie in the interview;
I can only presume this must be him. Ndekwe studies the face on
the screen. The man looks to be in his late fifties, early sixties. Could
be an old photo, though. He checks the small text at the bottom of
the web page: Copyright Ronnie Dakota, 2001. There's a contact
number, but no email. The entire feel and design of the page look
dated, reminiscent of the earliest efforts of the dot-com boom, when
websites were little more than glorified contact sheets. Ndekwe
copies the number from the screen.

– You went to see him last night, yeah? asks Frampton. – How
is he?

– Unconscious, when I saw him.

Frampton considers this. – You seen Gorman this morning?

– He's upstairs with the Super. I'm expecting the call any
minute.

Frampton does not comment; instead he takes this as his cue to
wander back to his desk and immerse himself in some paperwork.
If the shit was about to hit the fan then Frampton intended to avoid
any collateral damage by keeping his head as low as possible.

Ndekwe picks up the phone and dials.

– *The number you have dialled has not been recognized. Please
check and dial again. The number you have dialled has not been recognized. Please check and ...*

Ndekwe checks the number and dials again, but is answered
with the same automated denial.

He sits and taps his teeth with his pen, thinking. Then he pulls
the piece of paper from his pocket, the one with the Plumstead
number.

– Hello?

It is the same man's voice from the previous night. Ndekwe reintroduces himself and explains his reason for calling back.

– Well, like I told you last night, the man says, we bought the house off him years ago, about ... this would be ... ooh, be about eighty-two or three, I reckon.

– Do you know where he moved to?

– Yeah, I do, as it happens. They took over a boozer in Greenwich. Can't remember the name, though.

– They?

– Yeah, him and his pal. Only met him the once.

– Northerner?

– I think he was; yeah, now you come to mention it. But we're talking, what, nearly thirty years ago. He'll be an old fella now, I would reckon.

– This pub, was it the Queen Mary?

– No idea. Might have been. Like I say, early eighties this was.

– Thank you, says Ndekwe. – You've been very helpful.

– S'all right. What's it all about, anyway?

– Oh, it's nothing to worry about. Just an ongoing thing I have to clear up. Nothing important.

– All right, says the man. – Best of luck.

As soon as Ndekwe puts the phone back in its cradle it rings. The red light indicates that the call is coming from the desk of Chief Superintendent Walker.

– Sir?

– Pop up will you please, Peter?

– On my way.

Ndekwe stands and scribbles something on a post-it note, peels it off and hands it to one of the civilian support staff at the end desk.

– Ursula, will you do me a favour, please? Will you check this name on every available database? Any info at all would be great.

She smiles at him. – No problem, she says.

■ ■ ■ ■ ■

The Super commends Ndekwe on his successful delivery of the right result, noting in particular his new Detective Sergeant's thorough approach and dogged application in unravelling what he understands has been a particularly problematic case. Joint enterprise is often a tricky charge to pin down, he notes, and one which can very often result in a great deal of wasted time for all. Many a guilty man has walked free because of the muddy waters stirred up by the question of joint enterprise. And sterling work on wrapping up the Musa case, adds Walker. A most welcome bonus, he observes. Gorman nods grave acquiescence, but contributes very little else to the meeting, does not broach the thorny subject of Ndekwe charging into McDonald's and confronting Bam Bam Isaacs without armed back-up, which Ndekwe had been half expecting. The meeting ends somewhat abruptly with a congratulatory handshake from Chief Superintendent Walker and an instruction for Ndekwe to tidy up the few remaining loose ends and deliver Carlton McKenzie and Samuel Isaacs to the courts within the next twenty-four hours. The message was delivered with a warm handshake and a tight-lipped smile, but its meaning was obvious: charge McKenzie, let the old man go.

A call from the station to St Bart's hospital confirmed that Jack Shepherdson was now fully awake and sat up in bed, frail, still, but perfectly able to receive visitors. Ndekwe is instructed to attend his bedside, relieve the uniformed officer of his guard duties and inform the old man of his official release from custody.

Dr Kumar is on her lunch when Ndekwe arrives at the hospital. He sits in the office at the far end of the corridor from the ward and waits for her return. A young male nurse is studying a newspaper crossword as he eats his packed lunch at the desk; sandwich in one hand, pen in the other. He prints out a word in the margins, counts the letters silently, scribbles it out, sighs and shakes his head. He looks up at Ndekwe.

– You any good at these?

– Sometimes. You stuck?

– Nine down: Fiendish sailor crosses the street protesting.

– How many letters?

– Thirteen. Sixth letter is 'S'.

Ndekwe leans across to look; the nurse turns the paper around to afford him the correct view. He tosses the pen onto the desk.

– You have a go, he says. – It's getting right on my wick.

Ndekwe scrutinizes the black and white grid as the nurse finishes off the contents of his lunchbox. Most of the letters have been altered and amended several times, rendering the answers illegible.

– Fiendish sailor ... crosses the street ... protesting, repeats Ndekwe. He frowns. – How about 'pirate'? That's a fiendish sailor.

– Yeah, I thought that, says the nurse, polishing an apple on his sleeve. – Not enough letters, though.

– It's not, no, but if you add ...

– Detective Sergeant.

Dr Kumar enters the office with an armful of paperwork, which she dumps on the desk before opening a filing cabinet and riffling through its contents. Ndekwe rises to his feet, but she doesn't look round or acknowledge him.

– Dr Kumar, he says.

– You're here to see Mr Shepherdson. She states this as a matter of fact.

– How is he?

– He's awake.

– Have the results of the tests come through?

– Not yet.

– Can I see him?

– Yes, but I don't want him upset or agitated.

She selects a file from the drawer and flicks through its contents.

– I'm here to discharge him from custody, says Ndekwe. – I just need him to sign some papers and then that's us finished.

Dr Kumar nods, absorbed in her reading. Ndekwe understands that he is being pointedly ignored. As a police officer, he is accustomed to surly silences, but such treatment seems inappropriate in this setting. Hospitals are supposed to be places where help is dispensed to those who need it, he thinks. He looks at the nurse, but he's got his head back in his crossword.

– I'll pop back after I've seen him, says Ndekwe, and he leaves the office without waiting for a reply. On his way down the corridor he spots the uniform who has been assigned to bed guard step out of the lift ten paces in front of him. Ndekwe calls out, and the officer stops, turns around and nods in recognition.

– Sarge.

– Where the fuck you been?

The officer frowns. – Just been outside for a smoke. Why, what's the ...

But Ndekwe has already shouldered past him and is striding quickly through the doors and onto the ward.

Lunch is being served. Ndekwe can smell boiled mince and vegetables. He passes sleeping bodies beneath sheets and propped up patients picking at platefuls of steaming food until he comes to Jack's bed, second from the end of the row.

It's empty.

Ndekwe checks the bedside cabinet and drawers: empty.

– He's gone, mate, remarks the man in the next bed.

– Gone? Gone where?

– Dunno.

– When did he go?

– Bout twenty minutes ago.

– Did he say where he was going?

– Never said a word. Just got dressed and buggered off.

The man smiles helpfully and shovels mashed potato into his mouth. He seems to be enjoying Ndekwe's mounting concern. A welcome slice of drama in his otherwise dull and sterile day.

– I reckon he's gone for a decent nosh-up, he remarks. – Food in here's a bleeding disgrace. He holds a forkful of greying mince and carrots up for Ndekwe's inspection. – Look at that, he says. – I wouldn't give that to a dog.

But Ndekwe has gone, striding quickly back up the ward, stepping around slow-shuffling men in dressing gowns and nurses pushing serving trolleys full of food, breaking into a trot and then a run as he pushes his way out through the double doors.

■ ■ ■ ■ ■

– He's *what*?

– Gone. Done a runner.

– I thought he was meant to be at death's door.

– Well ... he's gone.

– Oh, for fuck's sake ... Gorman plants his elbows on his desk and cradles his head in his hands, rubs his temples. He can feel the rapid onset of a migraine.

– He's not at his flat, Ndekwe tells him. – No sign of him going back there, either. Neighbours haven't seen him.

– Well, where's he gone then?

– No idea. Frampton's out there now, looking for him.

– And they just let him walk out? At the hospital?

– No one saw him go. None of the staff anyway.

– The stupid old bastard ... Gorman's hand strays to the back of his head, his fingers repeatedly smoothing the strands of hair across his bald patch.

– The doctor reckons he could fade fast if he doesn't take his medication.

– Well, that's his lookout ... Gorman starts to rearrange his desk; tidies away pens and pencils, knocks a pile of paperwork into a neat, straight-edged stack.

– How do you mean?

– Nothing to do with us, says Gorman.

– He was in our care.

– *Was*, Peter, corrects Gorman. – *Was* in our care.

– Yeah, says Ndekwe, but ...

– Listen, snaps Gorman. – Bollocks to him, yeah? If he wants to ignore medical advice, that's up to him. Gorman gathers a pile of biscuit crumbs together with the blade of his hand and sweeps them off his desk and into the bin. – He's a grown adult, he says. – He can make his own decisions.

– Sir, I don't think ...

– Let it *go*, Peter. Gorman doesn't meet Ndekwe's eye, but his tone is officious and unmistakably final. – We've got our result, he says. – Just let it go. He heaves himself to his feet and wipes his hands and trousers free of crumbs and then plants himself back down again, links his fingers across his belly and regards his Detective Sergeant with a careful, deadpan indifference.

Ndekwe knows that he is talking to a man who has made up his mind. He decides to steer the conversation into less troubled waters.

– Any sign of Isaacs? he asks.

– Not yet, says Gorman. – But he'll turn up. Halliwell's all over it.

He picks up his phone and dials a number, places the receiver to his ear. He nods towards the door for Ndekwe to take his leave.

When he returns to his desk Ndekwe finds a note folded over and stood in an upright triangle at his keyboard.

Ronald Joseph Lodge, born 05.12.44, Kingston upon Hull ... Died 23.07.10, Lambeth, London. No previous convictions, no criminal record. Hope this helps – Ursula.

■ ■ ■ ■ ■

The anonymous call is logged into the CAD room of Hackney police station at 20:06. The Force Incident Manager gives the instruction to deploy Alpha One for an investigative assessment. Sixteen minutes later, a van containing a team of firearms officers carrying Heckler & Koch MP5s, G36 Carbines and drawn Glock 9mm pistols rolls up at the rear of the boarded up houses that fringe the playing field opposite the row of shops at the edge of the Crown Heights estate. Squad cars block both ends of the surrounding streets and the emerging officers urge people to clear the area and return to their homes. Shoppers emerging from the newsagent's and chemist are shepherded back inside. Other residents in the high rises above come out onto their balconies to watch the unfolding action, roused by the swivelling blue lights and the barking of the megaphone. An ambulance crawls to a halt at the top of the street, fifty feet or so from the Armed Response Unit.

Six armed officers jump out of the van, three of them assuming positions at the front door of the house; another three adopting a similar stance to the rear. Telescopic sights are trained on the windows on all sides of the property. The officers stand and wait, weapons drawn. At the radio command in their earpieces they batter their way into the house, announcing their presence with splintered wood and yells, booted feet thundering up the stairs.

A faint metallic odour greets the officers coming through the back door. The kitchen lino is slick underfoot and the first officer slips, his arm grabbed and caught by his colleague, who prevents him from going over.

There is a young man laid on his side on the floor, a broken marionette in a pool of glistening crimson, one side of his face burst open like a ragged brown and pink flower, the other side frozen in a still-furious scowl; the one remaining eyeball rolled back in its socket, locked in a lifeless gaze towards the ceiling. His jeans are soaked black at the crotch and there is a strong smell of piss and shit. The cupboard door beneath the sink is open and a black bin bag spills its contents out onto the soiled floor: dozens and dozens of clear plastic baggies crammed with tiny yellowy-white rocks, some of them burst open and scattered amid the pools of blackening blood.

There is more blood and flecks of congealed grey matter splashed up against the window and across the sink and unit tops.

A uniform appears in the kitchen doorway.

– All clear at the front. Nothing upstairs.

He looks at the body on the floor.

– Deceased male in the kitchen, he says. – Looks like he's took one to the back of the head. All clear. Repeat, all clear. Request paramedics.

He unfastens his helmet and takes it off, wipes his face and neck with the back of his sleeve. His hair is plastered down wet and he is panting hard, the adrenaline still pounding around his bloodstream.

One of the officers at the back door, the one who nearly slipped, is leant against the sink, his breath coming in ragged gulps.

– You all right, Mike?

He looks up and nods weakly, his face drained of all colour. This is his first call out with the CO19.

– You sure?

He nods again, then turns and pushes his way past the other uniforms, stumbles outside and sinks to his knees in the garden, puking the contents of his stomach into the bed of weeds that fringes the collapsing garden fence.

■ ■ ■ ■ ■

It is late evening in London, the sun beginning its slow descent over the steel and concrete edifices that cluster around the river, the people in the shops and the bars and the buildings and the streets crawling like insects below the cooling ball of fire that hangs above and gives life to all: the two Detective Constables sat in the busy Shoreditch beer garden arguing about football over pint glasses of cold lager; the fat ginger-haired Detective Inspector deliberating over bottles of wine in his local Budgens; the irate Italian man shouting at the girl gathering up the glasses in a bar down Liverpool

Street; the middle-aged African man in Dalston sat staring blankly at a TV screen from his armchair as his wife busies herself in the kitchen; the girl with the rainbow-coloured bangles holding up a ship's wheel-shaped barometer to a potential customer in the cooling shade of a Greenwich warehouse; the mother taking the hair extensions from her daughter's head as they sit together on the sofa watching television; the young man cooped up and sweating in the back of the G4S van as it heads towards Pentonville, his travelling companions kicking and screaming and pounding on the thin partition walls around him; the old man wheezing into a handkerchief as he passes a plastic carrier bag wrapped around cold metal to an Irishman under a pub table in Camden; the young woman in her bathroom in Woolwich gazing anxiously at an emerging blue line on the plastic stick in her hand.

And the car that disappears into the glowing orange-trimmed darkness of the Blackwell Tunnel, silent save for the voice recorded that afternoon and now playing through the speaker at the driver's knee.

What'll I get for this? It's gonna be life, yeah? Yeah, yeah yeah, I know that. I'm gonna get slammed, innit. Man was gonna shoot me, though, so I could plead self-defence, yeah? Man was going for his piece, yeah? Still, I gotta be realistic, I know that. But life don't mean like actual life nowadays, do it? It mean, what ... fifteen years? For stabbing someone up I get fifteen years, yeah? Minimum tariff, innit? So I'll be what, thirty-two when I come out, yeah? Even earlier for good behaviour maybe. I know how to behave myself guv. I'm from a good family, I told you that before. An anyway maybe the UK be completely different in fifteen years' time, yeah? What about that? Maybe they cleaned everything up, got rid of the ends, make everything safe for everyone, yeah? Cos remember this, everything coming to London now, yeah? Like the Olympics an that, you see what I'm saying? Man don't have to go out to the world no more, the world coming to the UK, ya get me? And after the Olympics they

*gonna have the World Cup here, innit? We putting a bid in, yeah?
They gotta clean everything up for that. World coming to look at
us, yeah? Focus be on us. Fifteen years, man. 2025! Rah! I reckon
that will be a good time, a very good time to be a man. To be a fully
grown man, ya get me? And everyone saying that global warming a
bad thing, but think about this – beaches in London, yeah? Beaches
on the Thames! Tourism! See what I'm saying? It's all good, man,
it's all good. Yeah, I'm gonna get a trade inside. Gonna use my time
productively, ya get me? Gonna read bare books. Chance to regroup,
innit? Retrain, yeah? This country needs plumbers, innit. I read that
somewhere. We need bare tradesman. Send me to Brixton guv. I
know I gotta go to the local nick first, but send me to Brixton after
that, yeah? I know some mans in there. I know a man in there got
bare qualifications, certificates for this an that. Get a trade in there.
Come out to a proper future. Brixton, that's the place. Maybe even
see my dad in there, yeah? Tell that fucker what I think of him for
real, yeah? Anyway, listen, I got to say right now, I don't regret
doing what I did. Yeah? Knowledge, I'm talking about. I got no guilt
over him. An I'm glad that other prick is dead, too. I'm glad for the
both of them, trust me. I only wish I'd done the rest of the crew as
well. You can put that down on my official statement, yeah? Put that
down guv. This is recording still, yeah? Put down that I wish I'd
have got a strap an blasted every one of them evil motherfuckers in
the face. I'm getting slammed anyway, yeah? Put that down on my
statement: Mr McKenzie says he wishes he'd have wiped out every
one of them cowardly rapist pricks. I might be a bad man but I'm not
evil, like them mans. I'm holding my hands up to everything, ya get
me? To Joseph an everything. Tell his mum I'm sorry as well. Tell
her there was nothing I could do. Tell her for me, yeah? All right,
that's it. That's everything. So you got to let the old man drift in the
wind now. He was no accessory to anything. He was just trying to
help me. But the actual thing itself was all down to me, every last bit
of it, yeah? No one here to say what actually happened now. No one
can say for certain now except me, innit. I'm the only one left. OK,*

that's it. I'll make my phone call now. I know the script. You owe me at least one phone call, yeah? I wanna call my mum, tell her what's happening. An turn that flippin machine off now, guv. I ain't got nothing more to say.

THANK YOU

Luke Brown, Alan Mahar and everyone at Tindal Street Press for backing the book.

Jon Elek and AP Watt for their continued support.

Mike Thomas, Victoria Thomas and Sharon Fielding QPM for their patient guidance under repeated questioning.

Dave Lee for the pictures.

Jenn Ashworth for the reading and writing.

Niall and Debs for the special tea for me tonight I'm having.

Ron and Lynne for teaching me right from wrong.

Ruth, Josie and Sonny for everything else.

Huge respect is extended to Clive Hopwood, Pauline Bennett and all the Writers in Residence that form the Writers In Prison Network for their grace under pressure.

And massive thanks to all the men who came to the writing workshops at HMP Wolds, Everthorpe and Full Sutton.

Stay Free.